Where There's
A Will

BOOK YOUR PLACE ON OUR WEBSITE AND MAKE THE READING CONNECTION!

We've created a customized website just for our very special readers, where you can get the inside scoop on everything that's going on with Zebra, Pinnacle and Kensington books.

When you come online, you'll have the exciting opportunity to:

- View covers of upcoming books
- Read sample chapters
- Learn about our future publishing schedule (listed by publication month *and author*)
- Find out when your favorite authors will be visiting a city near you
- Search for and order backlist books from our online catalog
- Check out author bios and background information
- Send e-mail to your favorite authors
- Meet the Kensington staff online
- Join us in weekly chats with authors, readers and other guests
- Get writing guidelines
- AND MUCH MORE!

Visit our website at
http://www.kensingtonbooks.com

Where There's A Will

**Margie Walker
Shirley Hailstock
Bridget Anderson
Shelby Lewis**

**with
Donna Hill**

Dafina
Books

KENSINGTON PUBLISHING CORP.
http://www.kensingtonbooks.com

DAFINA BOOKS are published by

Kensington Publishing Corp.
850 Third Avenue
New York, NY 10022

All Kensington titles, imprints and distributed lines are
available at special quantity discounts for bulk purchases for
sales promotion, premiums, fund-raising, educational or in-
stitutional use.

Special book excerpts or customized printings can also be
created to fit specific needs. For details, write or phone the
office of the Kensington Special Sales Manager: Kensington
Publishing Corp., 850 Third Avenue, New York, NY 10022.
Attn. Special Sales Department. Phone: 1-800-221-2647.

Dafina Books and the Dafina logo Reg. U.S. Pat. & TM Off.

First Kensington Trade Paperback Printing: June 2004
First Mass Market Paperback Printing: October 2005
10 9 8 7 6 5 4 3 2 1

Printed in the United States of America

CONTENTS

Prologue

*P*urvis Wayan leaned back in his creaking leather chair, took a puff from his cherry-flavored pipe and blew an aromatic scent into the air of his cramped office.

"Well . . . it's done, Henry old boy," he said aloud. He looked down at the last will and testament of his departed friend Henry Chambers that rested on his scarred desk. "The last thing I get to do for you, old buddy. Yessir." He sniffed loudly.

Purvis and Henry grew up in the tiny town of Liberty, Georgia, closer than most brothers. They fished together down at the old creek on Saturday mornings then tried to see who could out lie who with the biggest fish story. It was usually Henry, Purvis recalled. They played hooky together, double-dated, and he was the best man at Henry's marriage to Hazel— God rest her soul. Henry went into law enforcement—the only black officer on the force. Purvis opened his own law office.

But ten years on the force and being subjected to the inherent prejudice and lack of opportunity, Henry took all that his manly pride could stand. He resigned and opened

Chambers Investigations, the only black private investigation agency from there to Savannah.

Humph, that Henry took special pride in being "the only one." "I wanna take things into my own hands, Purvis," he'd said in that heavy voice of his the day he hung out his shingle. That was Henry: needing to be in control, on top of things, turning over every rock. Unanswered questions were the only things that could get Henry to cussing for days. Henry wouldn't rest if he couldn't put the pieces together. Purvis was sure gonna miss Henry. That he was. He wiped his damp eyes.

Purvis scratched absently at the gray stubble forming on his narrow chin, wondering what was in those sealed envelopes he'd given to Henry's four daughters after the reading of the will. He'd watched those girls sprout up from nothing more than potato buds—following Henry around on his cases every time he would let them—into beautiful, independent women, too independent for the likes of Liberty, Georgia. They'd grown up and moved away, building their lives in the big cities.

But they were back now: Taylor, Maxine, Samantha, and Morgan, even if it was on such a sad occasion. How long they'd stay was anybody's guess. But if he knew his old friend Henry, whatever he had up his sleeve and in those envelopes would have those girls jumping through hoops in no time.

Purvis sighed. Yessir, he was sure gonna miss Henry. He pushed himself up from the chair and ambled over to the narrow window. "I sure do wonder what was in those envelopes . . . and the one he left for me as well."

CURTAINS

Margie Walker

Chapter 1

Maxine ran a steady, even pace along the footpath that twisted in and out of the forest on her early morning jog.

Sweat streamed down her face. She wiped it from her eyes, but was largely resigned to endure the salty droplets, for sweating was an inherent part of physical exercise. When one jogged, especially in the heat, one perspired.

Maxine understood that correlation. The scowl on her face intimated what she didn't understand—her sisters' refusal to close Chambers Investigation. Since the reading of the will, their determination to maintain the private investigation firm their father founded ten years ago intensified, which in part, explained her presence in Liberty, Georgia. Otherwise, she wouldn't have set foot in this town again.

They called her last night, Wednesday, to announce their decision, or rather, their heartfelt feelings about the matter. Although they had been as excited as if struck by serendipity, none of the three could give her one solid, logical reason for keeping the firm open. They, nor she, even knew the financial condition of Chambers Investigation.

She promised them an accounting by the end of the week,

at which time she hoped to have completed computerizing his records. However, they dismissed the profitability of the business as a consideration outright. Simply, they believed it was the right thing to do. Heritage and pride were not counted in a business year-end profit-loss statement!

They weren't thinking straight, she argued silently. They were caught up in the thrill of fulfilling their father's dying wish that they solve three cases he couldn't before he died. All of the sisters had one, except her.

She was glad to have been excluded, she told the silent cynic. Unconsciously, she shook her head in denial that she was jealous that he'd left only the books for her to do.

Exhaustion began to take its toll on Maxine. Drawing her concentration more on breathing than thinking relaxed the frown on her face.

She considered that maybe she had started her run too late, for it was at least eight o'clock, and already felt like Liberty's noontime feverish temperature, which was known to cause heat strokes. If she were a candy bar, her caramel-brown skin would be melted by now.

Amusing herself, she thought about the aerobics instructor she loved to hate for forcing the evening class she attended in Houston to "make it hurt." While she would never attempt a marathon, she prayed she had enough strength to make the return trip—totaling roughly six miles, instead of her normal four—back to the house.

It was quiet and peaceful on the trail. There was nothing but forest: dogwood, pine, and maple of all sizes and ages, some thousands of years old. Slithers of the mid-summer, hot sun penetrated right through their density. But Maxine refused to allow the elements of heat and miles to beat her. The need to finish her run at a jogger's pace spoke to her determined nature. Some would call it stubborn.

Arms pumping and knees lifting, breathing in through her nose and out through her mouth, Maxine calculated she was about half a mile from the house. She could see the swing adjacent to the pond her father had built near the back of their place, a big white colonial with a wraparound porch in the middle of five acres. The magnolias on the west side of the house provided a scented course home.

A noise flitted at her senses seconds before a tree limb fell in her path. She merely hopped over it, figuring a bird had landed on a weak limb.

A splatter of dirt flew up from the ground where her foot next landed, causing Maxine to revise her first opinion. Her steps faltered. Sweat merged with the curious frown on her face.

Though the next sound was as slight as a ping, she discerned it distinctly: it was clearly a gunshot, and it was fired in her direction.

Maxine took off. Fear added an extra beat to the rhythm of her heart and a sprinter's burst of speed to her legs. She knew she wouldn't be able to spot anything through the dense forest and didn't stop to look.

Another shot whizzed over her shoulder, accelerating her pace. Pulse pounding, feet barely touching the ground, her five-six, one hundred twenty-five-pound slender frame ducked and dodged branches whipping at her from all sides as she raced for safety.

Maxine didn't stop again until she was in the kitchen, leaning against the breakfast table, huffing and puffing, trying to catch her breath.

Her breathing returned to normal, and she wondered what the hell had happened.

Chapter 2

Frozen, taut with attention, wide eyes scanning the signs of disaster and gluttonously feeding on the silence, Maxine stood just inside the first room of the Chambers Investigation office.

The only sound she heard was the wild beat of her heart as it pounded like a kettledrum solo in her bosom. Her arms tightened around the box she had lugged up two flights of stairs because the ancient elevator was on the blink, and took the first step in retreat.

As the quiet lingered, her pulse slid slowly toward normalcy, and questions replaced her fear. The scene before her made her wonder if there was a connection to her jogging incident when she felt certain someone had fired at her.

Who did this? she wondered, staring in dismay at the chaos.

Chambers Investigation was a two-room office. It was not a daunting challenge to clean in the way of housekeeping, which she had done yesterday. She had even considered slapping a new coat of paint on the dull gray walls.

Not a shred of her hard work remained.

Every drawer of the twin, steel-gray file cabinets in the

far corner of the room was open and empty; the files of cases littered the hardwood floor that she had buffed and polished with a rental machine. Torn and tossed manila folders lay scattered atop the mess, which had been deliberately and liberally drowned under coffee grounds, granulated sugar, and powdered cream.

A decision regarding the paint job was forced on her now, for swirls of red spray paint zigzagged every surface.

"Wow! What happened here?"

Maxine's pulse flew to the ceiling as she turned sharply at the sound of a male voice.

"Sorry. Didn't mean to scare you."

While her pulse came down upon seeing a familiar face, Maxine's fury at being startled didn't. "Then why didn't you knock?"

She felt the energy emanating from him that spelled COP, his face serious, dedicated. Her intruder was Lucious Kimble. Sergeant Lucious Kimble of LPD, the Liberty Police Department. He was a sharp dresser, his color coordination impeccable, his sports coat, cotton shirt, and slacks ensemble tailored to fit his lean, sinewy build. They'd met when she and her sisters buried their father a month ago.

"I thought you heard me."

Maxine didn't fall for his guileless smile for a second, although it did accent the cute dimples on his brown face with its prominent features. She muttered an expletive under her breath as she turned her attention to the destruction. "Since you're here, why don't you do your job." It wasn't a question; her throaty, velvet voice rang with reproach.

"And that is?"

"You can't possibly believe this office has always looked like this," she replied indignantly. "Somebody broke in and just went . . ." She paused to search for the right word. "Berserk. It looks like a tornado passed through here."

"It certainly does."

Maxine scowled at him, and then realized he was pulling

her leg. His eruditical, dark brown eyes were aware, roaming the room, although he didn't move a muscle: over six feet by two inches, and a slim one hundred eighty pounds at least. He stood tall and straight like a Georgia pine. But if she had to guess based on his accent, which was nonexistent, he wasn't a native of Georgia, for he spoke in a neutral way, without inflections, in a deep-timbered voice.

"What do you think about the decorations?" she asked.

"Not much," he replied. Then he moved, strolled to the door of the inner office and looked in. "We haven't had a rash of break-ins in this area that I know of."

"Oh, so you just happened to be in the area?" she retorted with sass in her tone.

"This looks personal," he said, giving her his dreamy chocolate eyes. "You just got back into town Tuesday night, and you went straight to the house. The only other place you've been is here. Have you had a run-in with somebody already?"

Maxine wanted to stomp her foot. Or better yet, stomp his. It was then she realized she was still holding the box; it contained receipts and papers that belonged at the office, instead of at home where her father kept them. Her laptop was inside the box, too.

As if clairvoyant, Lucious walked over and took the box from her. He looked around for a good place to put it, and she did, too. Finding none, he set it on the floor at her feet.

That was as good a place as any. Maxine wondered where to start first, as she absently ran her hand over her oval head, fingers through her dark, shoulder-length bob.

"No, I guess not." Lucious answered his own question, as he dug in his pockets, and then pulled out a tissue, which he used to pick the phone up off the floor. He listened for a dial tone. "It's still working." Holding the phone, he dialed a number. "This is Kimble. Get someone over to the Chambers Investigation office to dust for prints. Yeah, the place has been trashed. Okay." Replacing the receiver, he set the phone on the desk. "I don't suspect that whoever did this left any prints, but an officer is coming over, so don't touch anything until he does."

"Oh great," she muttered, annoyed by another setback. "Wait," she exclaimed. "How do you know how long I've been in town? Have you been following me?"

"You need to get a stronger lock for this door," he said, looking up from inspecting the doorknob. "No, I wouldn't say that."

She narrowed her smoky brown, almond-shaped eyes at him, demanding, "What would you say, then?"

"I'd say you better watch your back," he replied.

Being a Chambers didn't earn her any brownie points. Even as the townspeople revered her father, they didn't like it when he showed them that Liberty wasn't the crime-free, small town it promoted itself to be. Some called it meddling. Maybe they feared that's what she had come to do.

"Is that a threat?" she asked incensed, instead of afraid.

"No, ma'am . . . a warning," he replied, reaching inside his coat pocket. He withdrew a white card and extended it to her. "Here are all my numbers if you need to reach me."

Maxine eyed the proffered card with ambivalence. Finally, she took the card, muttering, "For all the good it'll do me."

"It'll do you good to be careful."

Maxine rolled her shoulders, then leaned over backwards, stretching the kinks from her tired body, sore from all the bending and stooping. She was in her father's inner office, putting a paper clip on a stack of papers representing notes for one of the cases on which he had worked.

Some of the files could be thrown away, she mused. They were so old the manila folders were the color of vanilla extract. But she didn't want to toss them haphazardly.

Her eyes scanned the room where the least damage had

been done as she recalled that the officer who came to dust for prints all but told her not to hold her breath for a capture. She had covered the slashes to the leather seat with masking tape and replaced a roller that she assumed had fallen off during the vandal's tirade.

Maxine returned to the front room, where she had cleared one side for the files she had been able to reassemble. New manila folders and labels would have to be bought, she reminded herself, setting the papers atop a similar neat stack.

Whoever ransacked the place sure made her work harder as case notes had gotten separated from their proper folders. Such was the batch of papers and folders that covered the teacher's desk her father had used for making coffee. She felt her attempt at forbearance fading. Unless she worked through the night, it was apparent she wasn't going to finish cleaning up today. It was nearly three now.

Maxine filled her delicate cheeks with air, and then released it through her full, lightly colored ginger lips. She couldn't believe she gave up her summer vacation for this, she thought resentfully. She and a few people from her cooking class on South American cuisine had planned a two-week trip to Belize. She had had to cancel, of course, because she couldn't postpone family business until November, when she had another week of vacation coming.

Now that her father was gone and her sisters lived elsewhere, she silently vowed that this was her last time in Liberty.

Her stomach growled, demanding attention. It was thinking about South American cooking, which she certainly wouldn't find in this town.

Maxine also accepted that she wouldn't get much more accomplished without sustenance.

Chapter 3

A taste for a greasy hamburger and fries took Maxine to Arlene's, a popular soul food restaurant with take-out. She would have loved a leisurely lunch break but with so much still to do, she couldn't afford the time. She didn't dare miss the locksmith who promised to come before closing: the only one in town, he did not suffer from lack of business and waited on no one.

Arlene's used to be a one-shack building of tin and wood where orders were placed and picked up from the window. Patrons used to stand about where she stood now, braving the elements while waiting for their orders. It was now enclosed and attached to a new addition with double-wide doors that led into the dining area. Visible through the opening were about eight card-playing tables with seating for four at each on an antique painted, cement floor. Framed posters depicting aspects of African-Americana culture hung from the paneled walls. Arlene's wasn't fancy in looks, menu, or price, but as she placed her order with the man behind the window, she trusted that the food retained its home-cooked taste people loved.

"Ms. Chambers . . ."

From the designated Take-Out area, Maxine looked through the passageway to see Dr. Charles White waving at her from the dining section. Having placed her order, she walked to his table, where he was having lunch with another doctor, as defined by his whites, and a stylish-looking woman, professionally dressed in a blue suit.

"I didn't know you were back in town," he said, half-rising as Maxine neared the table.

"Dr. White," Maxine replied, accepting his proffered hand. "I just got in yesterday."

Dr. White was on the staff at Liberty General Hospital; a cardiac specialist, he had attended her father. He was a teddy bear of a man: big, but not fat, average height, with a compact build. Kind eyes peered from his round, mahogany bean face.

Dr. White took his seat. "Do you know Dr. Owen Hofsteader and Ms. Barbara Goldman? . . . Dr. Hofsteader is chief of staff . . ."

"Dr. Hofsteader, Maxine Chambers," Maxine introduced herself, shaking the chief of staff's hand. His face bronzed by the sun, he was tall and reed-thin, with hawklike features. In his mid-forties, he was a nervous type; his hands were clammy.

"I heard a lot about you from your father," Dr. Hofsteader said, then discomfort consumed him as he didn't know what else to say.

"And Barbara here . . ."

"Barbara Goldman." A small, buxom blonde, her hair twisted on her head, and with a string of white pearls around her long elegant neck, extended her hand to Maxine. "I understand you and I have something in common," she said, with a powerful, lightly accented Southern-belle voice.

"Oh? What's that?" she asked, thinking Liberty hadn't changed all that much. The grapevine was as effective as ever, even though the population had grown considerably since she was a child.

"You're here to rectify the books for your father's investigation firm, and I'm trying to bring the hospital's accounting department into the millennium," Barbara replied with amusement in her voice.

Maxine joined the threesome in laughter on their insiders' joke about the hospital. "I hope you'll have an easier time than I've had so far."

"Oh? Is something wrong?" Dr. White asked.

"Oh, no," Maxine assured him, reminding herself to watch what she said around these people. "I only meant that my father's bookkeeping is probably as old as the hospital's." She didn't consider that a secret to take to the grave.

"Does that mean you've decided to keep the firm going?" Dr. Hofsteader asked conversationally. "I understand it's the only one . . . I mean," he said, swallowing his embarrassment. "Well, you know what I mean."

"Yes, I know," Maxine let him off the hook with a kind smile. Chambers Investigation was the only African-American–owned firm from here to Savannah.

"Well, are you going to stick around?"

Barbara Goldman wouldn't let the matter drop; she was as curious as her gray-green cat's eyes suggested, Maxine thought, pegging her as a gossip. "My sisters and I are keeping our options open." She wondered what the grapevine would make of that non sequitur.

"Hey, maybe we can get together sometime," Dr. White suggested cheerfully in the sudden quiet. "The city's art festival is this weekend. I understand the gallery tour is going to be great this year."

Maxine wasn't sure how to interpret the invitation from him. Her baby sister Samantha scoped the 411 on Dr. White last month and declared him unfit as a social contender: he was a divorced father of three, meaning his salary was eaten up by alimony and child support.

In a tone that promised serious consideration, Maxine lied, "I'll see."

"Order ready for Maxine," the man behind the register in Take-Out called.

"That's me," Maxine said. "It was nice meeting you," she said to Dr. Hofsteader and Barbara Goldman. To Dr. White she said, "It was good seeing you again."

"Good luck with your father's books," Barbara wished her.

"The same to you," Maxine replied, walking off to collect her greasy burger and fries.

Maxine was pleased by what she had accomplished as she planned to leave Chambers Investigation at seven that evening.

It wasn't perfect, and that paint job was waiting, but she'd put just about everything back into place. Tomorrow she would get started on what she had come to do in the first place, she thought firmly. As for the rest of the cleanup, she'd work around it.

She debated leaving the box she had lugged in this morning. She liked to keep home and work separate, but something told her to take the box home. Besides, she remembered she had left her laptop in the box. Maybe she could get some of her intended work done tonight.

The hallway was cast in low lighting. Deserted.

Maxine drew a deep breath. When she worked late at the bank, the path from her office to the elevator was bathed in light. No shadows. And where there were dark spaces, a security guard escorted her to her car.

She locked the door of Chambers Investigation, listened for the bolt to click into place on the new lock before she was satisfied. With the box under one arm, the keys held like a weapon in her right hand, she embarked on the journey to the elevator . . . at least it was working again . . . turning up the hallway and then making a left turn at the opening.

The elevator car arrived. It was empty, and Maxine got on and pressed the button for the first floor.

As the car descended, she took her first breath since she locked the office door.

From the deserted lobby, she pushed past the glass doors back first.

Downtown Liberty wore a contemporary facelift, while retaining its Georgian architectural style. It was only half alive as the sun started to set in the blue sky, but she was pleased to see a few people on the tree-lined sidewalks and cars on the clean, wide boulevard as she headed for her car. It was in the parking lot, a long, narrow strip of flattened gravel sandwiched between the older of two, six-story Liberty Professional Buildings. They had to be the drabbest on the block.

She had parked her car, a navy Camry, right under the light post; she spotted it from roughly ten feet away. The tension in her body began to melt away; even with the box, her steps grew buoyant . . . until she saw the flat tire at the back of her car.

"Dang," she muttered in frustration. She looked around and seeing no one, wondered sarcastically where had all the people she saw moments ago disappeared to?

Resigned, she set the box on the ground and opened the trunk to withdraw the spare tire and tools to change the flat. Kneeling to place the jack behind the tire well, she noticed the front tire was flat as well.

"Damn," she swore, standing to her full height in slow motion. Her irritation mounting, she paced the side of her car, gripping the jack and wrench in her hands and calculating the probability of two flat tires on the same side. As the car was parked head-in first, she walked around the back of the car to the other side.

"Shit." Maxine caught herself before tossing the tools to the ground in total disgust.

Chapter 4

"I'll follow you home."

The tow truck driver didn't arrive alone. Minutes after Maxine called on her cell phone, rescue arrived. More than she bargained for.

The owner of the tow truck was Mike, his name emblazoned on the red truck in fancy white lettering. Lucious Kimble dressed in his cop's attitude and casual attire, pulled up seconds later.

"Thank you, but that's all right," Maxine declined politely.

It was obvious Mike knew his job; he was quick and efficient. Maxine wished he could go a little faster.

"Ms. Chambers," he started, his voice tight with frustration.

Maxine walked off, following Mike to the last flat on the back right-hand side of the car, and Lucious Kimble trailed after her. She felt like a participant in an unchoreographed dance number, with a partner she didn't want.

With an arm across her middle, and her other hand under her chin, Maxine tried her damnedest to ignore him. She was trying to remember if any of her sisters had run into problems not associated with the cases they handled. No doubt they pissed off somebody, but why would that person come after her? Maybe someone wanted Chambers Investigation closed, and she wasn't moving fast enough. God knows she'd gotten enough questions about it today.

Lucious drew a calming breath and started again, this time with patience in his voice. "Ms. Chambers, this is the second incident . . ."

"Third," Maxine said absently. She threw her hands up in the air, peeved with herself that she'd forgotten all about the incident on the trail this morning.

Finding the office trashed robbed her of the memory of the gunshots fired this morning. She had subsequently convinced herself that a kid who didn't know the first thing about safety had gotten hold of his parents' unguarded weapon.

"Third?" Lucious echoed. "You care to enlighten me?"

Now, she wasn't so sure, Maxine mulled. Three incidents in a day hardly seemed coincidental. "I think someone took shots at me this morning while I was jogging."

"You think?" he asked sarcastically.

"I just forgot about it, okay?" she said excitedly, still wondering if the incidents were related.

"That does it," Lucious said firmly. "Mike, you done?" he asked.

"What does it?" Maxine asked. She didn't like his tone, nor did she appreciate his meddlesome behavior.

Mike stood, holding a tire in one hand, the jack and wrench in the other. "Done."

"Where are your car keys?" Lucious asked her.

"Right here in my hand," Maxine said as she dangled them in his face, then snatched them back. She dared him to try and take them from her.

"You got everything? . . . What about this?" he asked, giving Maxine no time to answer as he picked up the box and set it in the trunk.

"Y'all have a good evening," Mike said, walking off to his truck.

"Wait? What do I owe you?"

"I'll just add it to the C.I. tab, Ms. Chambers," he replied without stopping. "We can keep the same arrangement I had with your dad."

Even though she had only gotten a superficial look at her father's books, she didn't remember seeing any notations about MIKE'S.

"Get in."

Maxine bristled at the command. *If she wasn't eager to get home,* she thought defiantly, grumbling under her breath. His time to act was this morning when his job was evident; it was not his job to boss her around; she was not his responsibility.

"Don't forget your seat belt," he said, walking to the white, unmarked police car parked next to hers. "I'll be right behind you."

Maxine started her engine and gunned it.

"And no speeding," he yelled over the roof of his car before he got in.

"You're not my daddy," Maxine sassed safely in her car, under the roar of the air conditioning. She backed up, then sped off the lot.

Over an hour later, Maxine walked into her kitchen to see Lucious sitting at the breakfast table, eating last night's leftovers. He'd also found the homemade lemonade in the refrigerator. She stared at him, surprised by his audacity.

"You told me to make myself at home." he said.

Maxine shook her head. A smile curled on her mouth. "Did you leave anything for me?" She had showered and changed into a pair of walking shorts and a T-shirt, featuring the Tasmanian devil. She felt a hundred percent better and realized she was glad for company.

"Yeah, plate's in the microwave. Already warmed."

Maxine poured herself a glass of lemonade from the refrigerator before she got her plate and joined him at the table.

"This is good," he said. He washed down a mouthful with a swallow of lemonade.

Maxine chortled. "You must be hungry."

"No, really. This is better than Arlene's. Believe me, I know," he assured her before taking his next bite.

Cooking was her hobby. She could prepare dishes whose names she could barely pronounce, but last night she had had a taste for fried chicken, black-eyed peas, and rice, with cabbage and cornbread. She guessed it was something about being home that inspired a down-home meal.

Maxine swallowed the food in her mouth before asking, "What are you doing here? I mean, why did you come to Liberty? It doesn't seem to fit you."

"Crime is everywhere," Lucious replied around the food in his mouth. "Even in Liberty."

"How well I know," Maxine said with a chuckle. "But you know what I mean."

Lucious shrugged. "Thought I'd give small-town living a try."

Maxine doubted it was as simple as that. "Did you know my father?" she asked, changing subjects.

"As well as anyone knows anyone."

"Are you always so evasive?"

"Are you always so straightforward?"

Maxine opened her mouth to answer yes. But it was hasty and too easy, and she was not an impetuous person. Now, forced to reflect on her previous ungracious behavior, she wondered why she and Lucious seemed to have gotten off on the wrong foot. "Sometimes," she replied at last.

Lucious drank another swallow of lemonade and kept his hand on the glass, even though he'd set it on the table. Uncannily quiet, his expression thoughtful, he said, "Your father was a decent man. He helped a lot of people . . . even me. It was because of him that I decided to come back after college. I respected him . . . a lot. He'll be missed."

With that declaration, he released the glass to fork another bite of food into his mouth. Maxine felt a surge of pride for what he'd said about her father.

Still, she had mixed feelings about the firm. On one hand, she was proud of her father's bold step toward independence. It was what he preached to her and her sisters. "Liberty is not just the name of the town," he used to say.

"There seems to be quite a bit of interest in the future of Chambers Investigation," she said with the hesitancy of probing. "I'm not sure if that's good or bad."

She hadn't been all that excited about her father's job when he was a police officer. The feeling didn't change when he left the force to open Chambers Investigation.

"Well," Lucious said around the food in his mouth, "you have to figure that for as many people who your father helped, there are just as many whose apple carts he turned upside down."

As a child, Maxine recalled, she had been afraid to voice her fear of losing him, afraid it might come true if she said it aloud. He had been their only parent for so long, since 1973, when their mother died.

Even though she had been better able to handle his announcement to open a P.I. firm, she was amazed to realize her childhood fear remained.

"Who for instance?" she asked.

"Charles White for one," Lucious replied.

Maxine bristled slightly, for his response implied that she'd been followed again, but she cooled her temper as his eyes brightened with a teasing look.

"Charles White is a good catch for a woman with little or no prospects for a mate."

Maxine's mouth twisted and her eyebrows rose dubiously in a you've-got-to-be-kidding look. "Are you trying to tell me that Dr. Charles White is a lady's man?"

"He used to be a married one," Lucious replied. "His wife . . . ex-wife hired your father."

"My daddy worked on philandering cases like that?"

Maxine said, stunned. She couldn't picture her father sneaking around to catch a husband in the act of cheating on his wife.

"He had bills to pay, too. It was easy money. The doctor wasn't too discreet."

Maxine knew it was not wise to discount anyone at this point, but she couldn't picture Charles White vandalizing the office, or hiding in the bushes to take potshots at her. Maybe she was prejudiced against him because of what Samantha had told her. "Would he hold a grudge?" she wondered out loud.

"It's been a couple of years. If he did," Lucious said, "I imagine he would have gotten over it by now."

"Do you know if my dad was working, or ever worked a case that could lead to retaliation?" She was disheartened to realize she didn't know the answer. It revealed how little concern she'd shown about his life.

"Is that what you believe the vandalism is all about?"

"Don't you?"

They held each other's gaze a long time. Or so it seemed to Maxine. She felt as if Lucious was not only weighing his reply, but also making a determination about her.

"I don't know," he said at last. "You've barely touched your food. "You're the accountant of the sisters, right?"

The sudden shift of subjects didn't escape Maxine's notice. Nevertheless, she felt relieved, as if released from some pent-up emotion she couldn't discern.

Lucious assumed he was correct about her profession, adding, "Henry talked about your wizardry with numbers all the time."

Maxine smiled softly. "I'm not an accountant."

"Oh?" he paused. "I was so sure that's what he said."

"He probably did," Maxine replied. "My undergraduate degree is in mathematics. When an offer to further my education came with a job opportunity, I went to grad school for banking.

"I supervise a division that handles commercial loans," she

answered before he could ask, and then watched him mull her profession with a hint of amusement on her face. She found people had two extreme views of banking, either limited to the teller at the window, or to the rigid, penny-pinching executive who lunched and martinied the day away. She was neither, and even though her title of vice president was fancy, she was one of fifteen vice presidents. Still, she enjoyed her work and was handsomely rewarded for it.

"I imagine a lot of money passes through your hands," he said, brushing his together, wiggling his eyebrows, inveigling amusement.

Maxine chuckled. "A lot of paper, but not the spending kind."

"So you work at a bank in a big city," he said conversationally. "I imagine you like living in Houston well enough."

She bobbed her head musingly. "Houston's slow and hot."

"A lot like home," he said, guessing correctly.

"Yeah," she agreed. The familiarities were like numbers, which comforted her. The rules were easy enough to follow if you knew the formula. The hardest was to learn which formula to apply in her dealings with people. She had.

"But Houston is ten times bigger than Liberty. Did you fall into the big-city living easy?" he asked.

"It grew on me," Maxine replied. She had a Taurean temperament and didn't particularly care for the bustle of the city. But office life provided the conventional security she seemed to need. "I went to school there. All of the adjustments seem so long ago." She believed she handled them well.

She also believed her sisters were just as satisfied with their career choices, which made it difficult to discern why they were willing to give them up. That was the only way to keep the firm open.

"I got the impression from your dad," Lucious said, breaking into her thoughts, "that of all of the sisters, you would be the one to come home first."

Chapter 5

The early birds had caught their worms and left before the sun put its hot stamp on the day the next morning.

Maxine took a sip of her lukewarm coffee, careful to control the sway of the swing on the front porch. She stared out absently, seeing nothing of the morning's beauty.

It was nearly ten, and already the heat was oppressive, which partially explained her shoeless attire in a white tank top and purple running shorts.

She had believed she was going to have a hard time getting to sleep last night after the day she had had. Instead, guilt kept her awake, accomplishing the same results. She slept straight through the alarm set for six. By the time she woke up, the alarm had shut itself off and the numbers on the clock were flipping to 8:46.

Oddly, she felt rested, albeit disquiet. The tangential thoughts that volleyed in her head through the night were still wrestling with her feelings, seeking closure . . . absolution . . . a meaningful peace.

What Lucious had said about the impression he'd gotten from her father reawakened her guilt, a cord of dreadful regrets. It started when her father died a month ago. She had believed she'd let it go.

Henry Chambers was a big man, muscular, and six feet tall. Unfortunately, the picture of power and health she had of him all her life was destroyed by the frail, helpless man befallen by a worn-out heart that occupied her memory now.

Maxine swallowed the lump in her throat. She frowned while taking a sip of her cold coffee.

Taylor, her second oldest sister, encouraged her to stop beating herself up over it. "Be grateful for the time you did have," she had told her.

Maxine stopped the swing to put the cup on the floor, folded her legs Indian-style, then dropped her head back to rest on the top of the swing.

The movement triggered a slight veer of her thoughts, and she sat upright abruptly. She had discovered a curious item that she planned to follow up on today. While going through her father's box to separate business receipts, she had found an empty folder. It caught her interest because of the numbers—seven, ten, and one—written on the flap.

Maxine sighed, resettled comfortably, and tried to clear her thoughts. She might need a nap before the day was over, she chuckled softly.

When she finally did get to sleep around four this morning, it was Lucious she dreamed about. Thinking of him caused her to take stock of herself.

And to question and wonder whether she was really as satisfied with her life as she claimed to be.

"Damn you, Lucious Kimble."

He made her remember things she should forget. In the eleven years since she graduated from college with her bachelor's degree in mathematics, she could count the number of times she had come home to visit her father on one hand. And none of those had been in the last three years, not including his funeral and the reading of his will.

Likewise, it was Lucious's fault that she was thinking of

things she never stopped her busy life to entertain till now . . . a man in her life, a family all her own.

She tsked, with her head swaying from side to side. Busy Maxine, that's who she'd been. Busy getting her education, busy getting her career off the ground, busy getting her life in order.

In all that busyness to make her father proud and show him that all the efforts, money, and time he had invested in her were not wasted, she'd forgotten family.

She wondered if her sisters felt the same, if that was why they wanted to keep Chambers Investigation open.

Maxine heard, then saw, a light blue sports car pulling into the gravel driveway. She sat up, her feet on the floor, trying to identify her morning visitor. The car was a Dodge Viper, an expensive toy, and it had been treated with loving kindness: tires shining, fancy hubcaps gleaming.

The door opened, and Lucious unfolded his long body to step out. A prickle of sensation skipped across Maxine's bosom as he sauntered to the porch. He wore a yellow pocket T-shirt, belted and tucked into a pair of khaki shorts. His long bow legs were bare, his feet in sandals.

"Mornin'," he said, climbing the steps onto the porch.

"Good morning," she replied. "You must be off today."

"I'm not the only one," he replied, standing inches from her. "I went by the office, expecting to see you. Are you all right?"

"Were you worried?"

"I tried to call. The phone's been disconnected."

Maxine was amused and pleased by his concern. "No one is here often enough to justify keeping it on," she explained. "It didn't make sense to pay a bill we didn't have to. We have each other's cell phone numbers."

"I don't," he replied. He dropped onto the swing next to her, causing it to sway. "Why didn't you go in this morning?"

"There you go again," she said warningly. "I told you last night I can take care of myself."

Lucious glowered at her. "Can't you just humor me while you're in town?" he retorted with irritation in his tone. "It won't be for that much longer."

"No, I guess not," Maxine said, with somber musing. She felt as if she were lying to him. The truth was she didn't know what her sisters were going to do. She had yet to decide herself.

"Now, will you answer the question? Why didn't you go in?"

"I overslept," she replied. He looked at her suspiciously. "That's it, I swear. Since I have to meet with Mr. Lofton at the bank at three, I decided to wait until later before I headed to the office."

"What do you say we take a look at that trail? See if we can find anything."

Maxine hadn't forgotten; it was simply an unpleasantry she didn't want to deal with just yet. Besides, it was the kind of thing her father would have done. And as much as Henry tried to influence her to take an active role in his profession, she wasn't interested and had no desire to be an investigator.

"Even if we find anything . . ."

Lucious cut her off. "Will you stop arguing and just go put on some shoes? I have everything we need in the car."

If turnabout was fair play, then it was only fair that she caught Lucious staring at her legs as he'd caught her eyeballing his.

Maxine decided then that if the opportunity presented itself, she was going to bed this man before her week's trip was over.

They were on the forested trail, with Maxine leading the way. She looked over her shoulder occasionally to gauge distance and make sure she maintained a line of sight to the house.

She believed they were nearing the spot and slowed. She felt Lucious stop behind her.

He'd brought his tools of the trade, and she hoped, some tricks, too, for she doubted they would find a slug that could lead to a weapon and possibly an owner. Additionally, she believed the shots fired at her had come from a distance, meaning there would be no gunpowder, only a bullet entrance wound on a tree. *If* they were lucky enough to find it.

"Do you remember what it sounded like?" Lucious asked.

Her father introduced her and her sisters to firearms and proper usage and safety before they were big enough to hold a gun without a two-handed grip. "The sound of violence" was one of his favorite phrases when he investigated a shooting as a police officer. She remembered that bullets varied from .22 to .60 caliber; hence, the larger the caliber, the greater the extent of the damage.

So if her shooter of yesterday used a rifle instead of a handgun, they might find a slug that wasn't too terribly damaged. Remembering that gave Maxine new hope.

She stilled, trying to recapture what she had heard. Moving branches. Twigs cracking under her feet. Her harsh breathing.

She walked a few steps forward, her eyes on the ground.

She stopped and turned, facing Lucious. He was about four feet away. Her eyes narrowed in remembering; it didn't help. "I just remember a bang, bang," she said, disappointed. "Three shots in total."

"All right, all right," he said in a mollifying tone to keep her frustration from rising.

Recognizing the snarled branch buried within the earth, Maxine kneeled for a closer inspection and found the tree limb that had fallen into her path. The bullet had come over her left shoulder, she recalled, looking up, meaning it could have embedded in a tree to her right. She stood slowly, searching her options of trees. She examined two possible trees before she struck gold with the third, finding telltale damage to the bark. "Bingo."

Lucious looked over her shoulder, then kindly took over her spot at the tree. "Is there a chain saw at the house?"

"A chain saw? What do you need a chain saw for?"

"I could dig this slug out," he replied, "but I run the risk of causing marks that would destroy the ballistic value. With a chain saw," he said, demonstrating with his hands on the tree, "I could just remove this portion."

Her shoulders slumped with her sinking hopes. "I don't know if there's one at the house."

"All right, I'll work around it," he said, pulling out his roll of yellow tape. Placing twelve-inch long strips in an X on the tree, he asked, "What's on your agenda today?"

Maxine knew he was just making conversation, for he was deeply involved in his procedure. "I have an appointment with Daddy's banker," she replied. "I hope he doesn't give me any grief because the county has yet to send a copy of the death certificate."

"They shouldn't," he replied. He stuck a redheaded tack into the center of the tape, then pulled out his ball of string. "Take a funeral program just in case, though. You never know."

"That's a good idea," she said, watching him tie a knot on the head of the tack. Letting out string from the ball, he backed away from the tree carefully.

"What are you doing now?" Maxine asked, following the string like a kitten.

"I'm trying to determine the triangulation," he replied, looking behind him before he stepped backwards.

Maxine didn't remember her father performing this procedure. Of course, he never took her or her sisters with him if gunplay was involved. Especially her. As it turned out, she could cite the safety rules backwards and forwards, but she had been a poor shot. She was never comfortable with the feel of a gun in her hand.

"I'm going to have to come back out after awhile and get that slug," Lucious said, from roughly twenty feet away. "Do you have a problem with my being here in your absence?"

"Oh," Maxine said disappointed. "I would like to be here when you do that."

"It'll probably be around one-thirty or two before I get back. As soon as I get that bark out, I'll just turn it over to Bob in the ballistics lab when I go to work. Hopefully, he'll be able to tell us whether the gun is registered or not."

"Can . . . I mean, may I come along? I haven't been in a police lab in ages."

Lucious backed right out of her sight. "Don't you have something else to do?"

With amusement in her tone, she said, "Why Sergeant Kimble," loud enough to cover the distance, "if that didn't sound like you've had enough of my company . . ."

"No, no, that's not it," he said hastily, and reappeared just as quickly. "I just meant . . . well, last night you said that you got tired of your father dragging you around on his cases. I just thought perhaps. . . . Sure. You're welcome to come."

Maxine nodded absently. He ducked from sight again, and she let the forced smile on her face go.

Was that the impression she had given her father when she had complained about the lessons and lectures on investigation procedures and what not? Was that why she had ultimately been relegated to keeping his books?

While she had found police work uninteresting, being in his company, having his attention, was what she clamored for most.

Apparently, she thought somberly, her complaining negated what she thought he already knew. She simply loved being with him.

"Got it," he called some distance away. "I know what kind of gun was used."

Chapter 6

"I'm going to stick my neck out and say our shooter was inexperienced."

"Lucky for me," Maxine chortled snidely, taking a bite out of her sandwich.

She and Lucious were sitting at the kitchen table, having a lunch of chicken breast sandwiches with lettuce, tomato, and onions, and steak-size fries minutes before noon.

"You're right," Lucious agreed. He bit into his sandwich, and then set it on the saucer to pick up the plastic bag containing three rust-colored shell casings.

As luck had it, upon first returning to the house Lucious located a chain saw among the junk in the garage. He returned to the trail to take a slice out of the tree, while she rummaged the refrigerator and found something to cook.

"Do you recall *The Rifleman* show?" he asked, still holding the plastic bag.

"I've seen the promotion for the black-and-white reruns," she replied, "but I never watched it."

"Well, if you want to see the kind of rifle that most likely fired these bullets, that's the show," he said. "The Winchester is not your everyday, bad-guy kind of weapon anymore, but it's a beauty."

Maxine flashed him a wry look, thinking, *Cars and guns for men, makeup for women.* "If you say so."

"But you have to know how to make the adjustments when you use it," he said, replacing the plastic bag for his sandwich. "Our shooter was about fifty yards away—that's half the length of a football field."

"What's your point? That the distance affected the accuracy?"

"It shouldn't have. Now, if he was about two hundred yards away, then he would have had some major calculations to make."

"Aim, fire, shoot," Maxine said. "You're making a big deal out of my poor marksman."

Lucious shook his head from side to side. "It doesn't always work that way. Bullets don't maintain a straight line forever. Sometimes they rise above the line of sight or drop below it, depending on the wind, rain, or rising heat waves."

"So you're saying the shooter didn't factor in the heat, in this case, and that's why he, or she, missed?"

"That, and it's also likely, he didn't have a telescope."

"Okay," Maxine said, with a point to make. She swallowed the food in her mouth before continuing. "Who would own such a classic . . . beauty?"

Before Lucious could reply, his beeper went off. He looked down at his waist where it was hooked in his belt. "It's the station," he said. "May I use your phone?"

"I'm sure we sent that death certificate out over two weeks ago."

Maxine felt her day was quickly descending toward nonproductiveness. She should have gotten an earlier start, she chided herself.

"If you did, I didn't receive it," she replied to the rotund, fifty-something, black woman standing behind the counter.

Her nemesis, she described kindly, was a dark-skinned, overweight woman with a round face. Despite her obesity, her appearance was impeccable; her attitude wasn't. She had revealed a beautiful smile when Maxine initially arrived a few minutes ago. Maxine hadn't seen it since.

"What is it, Gloria? Maybe I can help."

Maxine nearly sighed with relief at seeing Barbara Goldman step out from an office behind the counter in the hospital's administration suite.

"Oh hi, Maxine," Barbara said, recognizing her.

"Barbara, I'm so glad to see you."

"What's the problem?"

Barbara addressed both Maxine and Gloria, but Gloria answered first.

"The death certificate for Henry Chambers. According to my records, it was mailed two weeks ago."

Before Maxine could repeat herself, Barbara said, "That means you have a copy of it. Why don't you just make another one for Ms. Chambers?"

Maxine caught Barbara's firm-eyed look accompanying the question that wasn't, in the command, couched as a request. The sight of them was incongruent—comical, even: Barbara, standing all of about five-two at one hundred fifteen pounds, confronting Gloria's five-five, one hundred sixty-pound welterweight stature. Gloria didn't say a word, but nodded slightly and turned to vanish behind a door across the one Barbara had come from.

"It'll only take a minute," Barbara said, smiling. Her toasty-warm personality returned as she leaned on the counter.

"Thanks, Barbara, I appreciate this," Maxine said. Leaving the house minutes after Lucious did, she went to the office and nearly got into it with the building supervisor over repainting the Chambers Investigation offices. The little weasel, she recalled, whipped out the lease her father had signed. If her sisters insisted on keeping the firm open, she was going to insist on moving from the present location. That was her first run-in of the day, she thought, disgruntled.

"The bank won't give me access to my father's deposit box without that death certificate," she explained to Barbara, making conversation.

With the certificate, maybe she could find the answer to a question she had unearthed in her father's box last night. She was hoping something there would explain the numbers seven, ten, and one that he'd written on an empty, yellowed folder.

"First Liberty?" Barbara said, casually smoothing her hair. "They're strictly by the book. I had to stop banking with them. How's your bookkeeping coming?"

"Very slow," Maxine replied.

"If you need any help, just give me a call," Barbara suggested.

"That's nice of you to offer. Thanks. But I can handle it really. The problem is getting to it. I just finished putting the office back in order."

Barbara frowned puzzled. "Back in order? That doesn't sound like the Henry Chambers I know."

"Somebody broke in and trashed the place," Maxine explained.

Barbara clasped her cheeks, exclaiming, "Oh, my goodness. Was anything stolen?"

"No, just vandalized," Maxine replied. "I wish whoever did it would have thrown away some of that stuff. Daddy kept files dating back to when he first opened the firm."

"Wow," Barbara said. "That was what . . . eight, nine years ago?"

"Ten."

"Hey, look," Barbara said, "after work this evening, I'm going over to the Cove. Why don't you join me for a drink or two around 5 o'clock? I have to attend the board meeting at 7:30, and if I go home, I might not make it back."

"The Cove?"

"Yeah, it's the jazz bar in the Marriott. I'm sorry. I forgot you haven't been here long."

There was only one Marriott in town, which should be easy to find, Maxine thought. She would no doubt need a drink by then, if the day she was having was any indication.

"I'll be there," Maxine said decisively. Just then she noticed Gloria returning.

"Here it is," Gloria said, passing an envelope across the counter to Maxine.

"Thank you, Gloria," Maxine said sweetly.

"You're welcome," Gloria replied grudgingly.

If Barbara had not been present, Maxine thought amused as she walked off, ain't no telling what Gloria would have told her.

Maxine stood at the cavelike opening of the Cove, forty-five minutes later than the time she agreed to meet Barbara for drinks. The band was into a jazzy version of "Rock Steady." The music was tight and energetic, but the vocalist was no Aretha Franklin.

The lights were dim, yet it was bright enough to make out the semicircular design, with a circular bar in the center of the club. At least a dozen patrons were seated in eggplant-purple leather seats around ash wood tables. The standard burning candle in a bottle occupied each table.

She spotted her party. More than the one person she expected, in fact. Barbara was sitting next to Dr. Charles White at a table not far from the band. They were the only mixed couple in the place.

Maxine was more than mildly surprised. She never thought she'd see the day, remembering a time when it was forbidden—not as long ago as some would like to believe—regardless how platonic the relationship was. Even though this was the new millennium and Georgia was known as a progressive state, they still lived in Liberty. *Defying social custom at their ages,* she snickered.

Forty wasn't old, she reminded herself, which she guessed was the neighborhood of Barbara's age, even though Barbara had an aura of youth about her. Charles looked a little older, forty-five or so.

Maxine proceeded to the table, chiding herself laughingly for her own brand of prejudice. It was then that it really hit her: Charles and Barbara were having an affair! She had a feeling she was the only one who just realized it.

"I'd about given up on you." Barbara spoke loud enough to be heard over the band.

"Glad you could join us," Charles said, standing to hold out a chair for her.

"Thanks," Maxine said, sitting at the table where a platter of finger foods sat in the middle. "You know how it is. Just when you think you're done, something else crops up."

"No more vandals, I hope," Barbara said.

"No, no, nothing like that," Maxine replied, thinking about her transactions at the bank. The safety deposit contained just what had been stated in the will—their mother's rings, coins dating back to the 1900s, and U.S. Treasury Bonds—but no reference to those three numbers. "Not a problem, just an annoyance. I've taken care of it."

Under a bed of fading music, the drummer announced a short break for the group. Trying to get the attention of the waitress, Maxine recalled the arithmetic done in her head on those numbers, getting eighteen when added, seventy after multiplying, while divided by three yielded a mean of six. The subtraction options could take her into the next year. She was ready to concede the numbers didn't relate to anything.

A waitress appeared to take her order of a white zinfandel. The noise died considerably, and the din of conversation took over.

"Please, have some of these," Charles invited, biting into

a buffalo wing. "Barbara told me what happened," he said, chewing. "I must say, I'm still surprised by the level of crime that occurs here, even though I know better."

"I just wish I knew why," Maxine said.

"What did the police have to say?"

"Besides take a report, there's not much they could say or do."

"You're mighty generous," Barbara said. "I'd be scream-ing bloody murder."

Maxine chuckled. "I did. I'm over it now." The waitress returned with her drink, and she took a sip. "Enough about my troubles. How are things going with you two?"

If she committed a faux pas, it was too late to correct it. She picked up a stuffed pepper—she realized too late—and bit into it. She tried to be cool as she chewed.

"I think they imported those from Texas," Barbara said, trying to keep from laughing as she signaled the waitress back to their table. "Water. Room temperature, no ice," she instructed.

She didn't have a man 'cause her daddy had showed her the qualities of a man. She wasn't willing to lower her stan-dards or put up with some fool's bullshit!

"You're drunk, Maxine Chambers," Maxine said loudly to no one but herself. She wasn't sure how many drinks she had had, but more than her normal two glass limit, for sure. Hell, she practically closed the bar, staying until the last set and walking out with the drummer.

"What was his name?"

Maxine blew out her cheeks: it was hot inside the car. She took her eyes off the road for a second to look at the clock on the dashboard: it was 2:37.

"That's A.M., girlfriend," she chided herself loudly.

Maxine knew she really had to concentrate on driving and gripped the wheel with both hands.

She was feeling no pain.

Damn! She hoped she didn't say something tonight—no, last night—which she would regret. She was a little fuzzy in the head, but knew she couldn't blame her loose tongue on the alcohol for telling about the office being wrecked. Only she and Lucious knew she had been shot at, or that the bullet he dug out of the tree would identify the weapon.

Barbara and Charles were gone by the time she finished that third drink, she recalled, but she had to start keeping her secrets better. Until she knew what she was facing and who was involved.

She turned the air to full blast; she was getting too comfortable. She almost missed the exit off the highway to her street.

She turned on the radio and found a station that played music she could tolerate. The unmistakable guitar of Jimi Hendricks blasted from the car speakers. Though more in keeping with Morgan, her older sister's generation, she'd heard it enough to know some of the lyrics.

Off-key and out-of-tune, she sang with Jimi, "There's a red house over yonder . . ." When the words escaped her memory, she simply hummed along, anticipating the bridge, "Wait a minute, something's wrong; this key . . ."

With terrible suddenness, the car jerked forward without the help of her foot on the gas pedal. Maxine cried out. The jarring impact sobered her instantly and completely.

Her heart was thudding in her bosom as she glanced in her rearview mirror. All she could see were bright headlights, blinding in their intensity. Instinctively, she gripped the steering wheel tightly with both hands, struggling not to panic.

Her car was struck again from the rear. It lurched forward, and she didn't know what to do. She hit her brakes, and the jolt from behind was greater.

As the violence intensified so did her internal reactions. Her fear turned into terror and her heartbeat accelerated. She started to panic.

Panicking would get her killed if she didn't get it under control, she thought, trying to get her bearings. The lights on the road were far and few between. She couldn't remember the distance from where she was to the first house.

She did remember there was a bridge crossing coming up somewhere.

How many people had run off the road and into the bridge, she wondered and recalled excitedly.

What should she do? She didn't know what to do.

Damn, the alcohol she consumed was making her stupid!

Chapter 7

It must have been a Jimi Hendricks special, but she was in no purple haze any longer. Massaging the bump on her forehead, Maxine had enough wherewithal to know that she was in trouble. Even though she was safe now, the deliberate attempt on her life increased her apprehensions.

She was sitting in the passenger seat of Lucious's car. The radio was on, and it was obvious he had been listening to the same radio station.

A pair of Liberty's finest had been nearby, she recalled. Close enough to see her car weaving across the road at a high rate of speed. Not close enough to know that she had been driving for her life.

The vehicle behind her must have pulled off on a side street. She didn't know where it went, only that it wasn't there when the sirens and lights from the black-and-white began, followed by a bullhorn-amplified voice instructing her to pull over.

By then, however, she was going so fast she lost control of her car and drove into the ditch, an eight-foot gutter of red dirt. The good news was the ditch was dry; the bad news was the front of her car suffered extensive damage.

The driver door opened, and Lucious slid into the seat. "How many drinks did you have?"

"I don't know, Lucious," she said, somber and embarrassed. "Too many, for sure. But . . ."

"You're right about that," he said, cutting her off. "The good thing is that you were obviously struck from behind. Mike's gonna take your car in, and he'll . . ."

"But how am I . . ." she started in protest, but the look on his face silenced her. He was pissed, maybe even angry or mad. "Yes, Lucious," she said obediently, "whatever you say."

Lucious's foreboding manner felt like a tangible obstruction. Maxine sat as still as silence while he tended the small cut on her forehead, the only visible evidence that she'd been in a car accident.

It was quiet throughout the house, especially in the kitchen, where she was sitting in a chair at the table. While there shouldn't have been any, tension danced in the room. It was like a smoke you couldn't put your hands on, but knew it was there nevertheless.

He had driven her home a little more than thirty minutes ago. She had to shower immediately, wash the perspiration of fear from her body. Now she was dressed for bed in her father's old, checkered cotton robe over her short pajamas.

The harder Maxine tried to breathe normally, the more irregular she breathed. Irritation joined her gratitude for his first-aid care. But it wasn't her foremost desire. He was stoic and all business; while she wanted to be held, hear sweet murmurs from his lips, feel his mouth on her flesh.

Something about seeing her life flash before her eyes affected her practical nature, Maxine thought, for the impulse to do something she might regret was heavy in her heart, creating excitement in her loins.

Yeah, she knew what she'd thought on the trail with him,

she rejoined to the cynic in her head. But that was just talk to hear herself think.

Now, she found herself wishing.

But she repressed the wild urge, clasping her hands together tightly and restraining them primly in her lap.

"I'm fairly certain you don't have a concussion," Lucious said, stepping back to inspect his handy work. He tightened the cap on the bottle of alcohol and set it on the table.

Maxine tried to be flippant, giving him a cheek-to-cheek profile. Her jaw ached with the forced smile on her face. "Make sure there won't be a scar."

"Think you'll be all right alone here by yourself?"

Maxine felt it before she could do anything about it. The smile dropped from her expression like an anchor into water as her eyes widened with fear. She heard, and knew for certain he must have, too, for her heart beat alarmingly loud in her bosom. Her mouth was open, as well, but she didn't know what she was going to say.

A tender dimension of sensitivity came over Lucious's expression, and the next thing Maxine knew she was gently locked against his chest, his arms around her waist. What followed happened so fast—the touches of comfort, then of warmth, parted lips seeking, searching, desperate contact that promised sweet release. She was dizzy with passion.

Chapter 8

Maxine was pleasantly sore the next morning. She lifted her face to the warm water spraying down on her from the showerhead, smiling unconsciously.

She thought about what her sisters would say if she told them a man had slept in her bed last night.

Her baby sister, Samantha, would no doubt demand clarification. "Was that a shut-eye sleep, or the kind where sleeping didn't have anything to do with what you did in bed?"

Morgan, the oldest and naturally the most prudent of them, wouldn't say a word. Her pinched-mouth look of disgust would express her feelings about the matter.

Taylor, the attorney, would crudely cut to the chase. "Did you make him use a rubber?"

Maxine laughed, amused with her thoughts as she began lathering her body with soap. "Yes, I did," she replied to the imaginary question.

Well, was it worth it?

It was her own internal question, and Maxine shuddered with delight in remembrance. "Most definitely," she said softly with emphasis into the water.

The publicly elusive Lucious Kimble, with secrets he

wouldn't or couldn't share, was as effusive as hell, like fire and brimstone in bed, she recalled with a shiver.

Let's not get carried away, she admonished herself. *It was great sex, good for the body.*

It also cleared her head. With last night's incident on the edge of her memory, she knew what she had to do now. No more wondering or debating coincidence. Even without a ballistics report, she had to discover the identity of a cowardly marksman. She had to figure out what she'd gotten into, why, and find the individual who wanted her dead.

"Knock, knock, knock," Lucious said from the other side of the bathroom door as he knuckle-rapped it. "Breakfast's ready."

The din of silver clicking against glass, rather than conversation from the two people sitting at the breakfast table, slowly chipped at the sense of well-being Maxine had felt moments ago.

She and Lucious sat across the table from each other, eating the wonderful breakfast he prepared: the scrambled eggs light and fluffy, the toast nice and crisp, the cantaloupe diced for easy bites. She couldn't give him credit for the milk they drank, but she had complimented him on everything else.

Her every attempt at conversation had been met by a monosyllabic reply from him. Brooding, a storm cloud showed in the lines over the bridge of his nose, threatening to erupt.

It was obvious that Lucious had something to say, Maxine thought, chewing. As long as it wasn't an apology for last night, she wished like hell he would get it out of his system.

Unable to stand it anymore, she set her fork on her plate and leveled her eyes on him. He took a viscous bite of toast before looking up, noticing her peeved expression. His jaw slowed as he chewed, eyeing her with a wary look on his face.

"What?" he said, swallowing hard.

"You're the one with the 'what,' " she retorted. "Why don't you just spit it out?"

Lucious sat upright in his seat, his hands under the table in his lap. He stared at her intensely for several long seconds before he spoke.

"Don't you want to know if I'm involved, or even married?"

Caught off-guard by his question, Maxine blinked rapidly. It was the last thing she expected from him. She was sure she'd made no promises she didn't intend to keep, even in the sweet agony of passion. He couldn't have expected a commitment from her after one night of sex. *Or, did he?* she wondered.

"The horse is out of the barn," she said, picking up her fork to resume eating.

"So that's how it is, huh?"

Maxine stared headlong at Lucious. He was serious, and kind of cute, wearing last night's clothes. "I don't know you well enough to guess at your interpretation of that," she replied hesitantly. "Maybe you better tell me what you want."

"It was good between us."

If she were honest with herself, Maxine thought, she rather liked his old-fashioned, proprietorial attitude. "Begging for compliments on your performance?" she asked, a barely visible smile stealing across her face.

"Damnit, Maxine," he said, tossing the napkin from his lap and onto the table angrily. "Why you got to be like that?"

Schooling emotion from her expression, Maxine put her fork down and folded her arms on the table. She had remained uncommitted, albeit not uninvolved on purpose. She hadn't thought about what she wanted in her man. While Lucious came close on the surface, being gainfully employed was not enough. There was simply no time to explore a relationship with him. She was leaving town in less than a week.

The cell phone, muffled by its concealment in her handbag on the counter, rang. Maxine sighed relieved as she got up to get it.

"Hello? . . . Oh, hi, Barbara." She leaned against the counter. "Oh, I forgot all about it. But I won't be able to make it to the festival. Something unexpected came up that I need to deal with." She was going to the office today, having remembered her father used to have a safe. *It might reveal something useful,* she thought doubtfully. "Around five this evening? I think I'll be free by then," she replied. "Bring somebody?" She looked at Lucious, who stood up to put his empty plate in the dishwasher. She didn't know if asking Lucious to be her date for Barbara's party was a good idea. "I'll see," she said noncommittally before ending the call. "See you later."

Maxine suffered an inexplicable wave of loneliness after Lucious left. A temporary truce, the breakfast discussion was put on hold as he promised to return and escort her to Barbara's party that evening.

Even though the house seemed even more quiet than usual in his absence, she couldn't allow herself to be overwhelmed by the tension he had injected into the morning: she had things to do, and people to see.

It was nearly ten o'clock by the time she walked from her bedroom near the front of the house to her daddy's home office in the back. Comfortably dressed in a gold blousy shirt cuffed at the elbows, soft jeans, and Polo tennis shoes with matching gold socks, she carried a colorful straw handbag that was big enough to contain her laptop. But her computer was not what she intended to put in it.

She flipped on the wall light switch, brightening the cubbyhole space. It used to be her mother's sewing room, but she could barely remember that time. The only evidence was the tiny, silver-framed, black-and-white photo of her mother atop the chipped davenport her dad used as his desk.

Maxine inserted the key into the lock in the center of the desk and opened the drawer. She could barely believe it was her hand that reached inside and withdrew the holstered 9 mm Beretta.

Her hands shook as she thought about what she was doing.

Her life was on the line, she reminded herself, unconsciously squeezing the handle of the black semi-automatic. Some crazed individual had forced this action upon her: she didn't intend to be an unprotected, sitting duck again. Only provocation would determine whether she would be able to fire at anybody.

Maxine drew a deep breath, hardened her body, and checked the clip. Finding it empty, she retrieved the box of shells.

Determination etched on her face, she sat in the chair and began loading the fifteen-round magazine, one bullet at a time.

There was no comparison to what she'd been through the past several days, she reflected. Her life in Houston was uneventful, normal.

She and her sisters had been raised to be independent, secure in themselves and what they were about. Since she'd been in Liberty, she no longer felt the certainty about her life, who she was, or what she wanted.

There were drawbacks, for sure—the scary and life-threatening incidents notwithstanding, she clearly recalled. But not all of it had been bad.

Lucious accounted for part of the change she felt.

She stopped a moment, wondering what he would say about her "packing," she thought.

She picked up her previous line of thoughts facilely. She had never gone to bed with a man as quickly as she had with Lucious. But he was only a small part of her internal metamorphosis.

Maxine smiled unconsciously.

In just a matter of days, she seemed to have fallen into a comfortable routine. It was rather enjoyable going to the office on her terms, calling the shots without a handbook of guidelines filled with procedures. There wasn't the orderliness she adhered to on her job, or even her social life, in Houston.

She didn't really know this Maxine she had become, she thought, slipping the clip in place. But she didn't dislike her, either.

As Maxine had hoped, the offices of Chambers Investigation were immaculate, the walls painted light blue, the shade she requested. As she expected, the safety box her father had kept in the bottom drawer on the left of his desk was empty.

Disappointed, Maxine blew out her cheeks. She knew it was useless contacting the lawyer who drew up their father's will. He had given them everything their father left him to give.

She dragged her handbag from under the desk and withdrew her father's old green ledger and began to rifle through the pages.

Although she tried convincing herself otherwise, she was sure those numbers held significant meaning. To which case, she didn't know, but she knew her father: he was never a doodler in deed or thought.

She didn't know what she was looking for exactly: she'd been through this book before and nothing had stood out as unusual. This time, however, she keenly scrutinized dates . . . particularly those dated in July, October, and January, the months matching the numbers, seven, ten, and one.

The task consumed less than an hour, for the cases he worked starting from last year through this January neither started nor were resolved during those months. It was impossible for him to have done anything this June, she recalled, a ripple of sadness coursing through her.

Maxine knew he would not want her sitting here feeling sad and sorry for herself. Until she figured out what to do next, she sat back in the swivel chair, reviewing his ledger.

Her father was a meticulous note taker, a holdover from his days as a policeman. But it was not unusual that more information was not included, for there were times where client confidentiality was of utmost concern; hence, particulars about a case were deliberately omitted.

Thumbing through the ledger, she paid attention to the penciled reminders he made to himself in his own unique code. *Check M for H,* read one notation. *Car* was written by itself on another page. She turned back, hoping for a date reference, and found it: *3/16/00, Atlanta.*

Maxine shifted, hunching over the book she had placed on the desk in front of her. She flipped forward a page, looking for a phone number or a name.

Finding none, she closed the book. Her eyes squinted in deep thought as she tapped the book's hard cover with her forefinger incessantly, absently. The timing, she recalled, coincided with a hefty deposit into the firm's account.

Was privacy not an issue? she wondered, mulling the implication of the importance of such a case. She couldn't even be sure that the case originated in Atlanta.

How did she find out? she asked herself, absently drumming her fingers on the book.

"You got to give a little to get a little."

That was one of her father's favorite sayings. Even before he became a private investigator, the adage served him well as a police officer. There's no reason it couldn't work for her.

The only problem, however, Maxine sighed, was finding who, among the many people her father associated with, he had befriended and trusted enough with his secrets. Purvis counted in that small number, she knew, but her father's long-time friend was out of town.

Chapter 9

"How many people did she invite?"

"She said a few close friends," Maxine replied. "About twelve or so."

She and Lucious were heading to Barbara's for the party. It didn't mean she had overlooked or forgotten that the violence was escalating, moving closer to home, from the impersonal office to her. Which she considered very personal. But sitting at home, stewing about it served no purpose. Besides, on the heels of what she'd consider a less-than-productive-day, she needed the respite the party promised. Maybe she would learn something useful.

Barbara lived in the exclusive Maple Hill neighborhood that reminded Maxine of River Oaks in Houston. Grand homes, spacious yards, and not a black-and-white police car in sight.

The wealthy didn't have to leave their enclave for anything, she thought, for if it couldn't be delivered, it could be bought from the myriad of stores, shops, and boutiques in the neighborhood mall.

"Maybe I need to move back to Liberty and give Barbara a run for her job," she said in jest, admiring the view of the haves from the passenger seat of Lucious's car.

"If that's the only reason," Lucious said, "then you'd better marry a rich husband first."

Maxine smiled at the tinge of amusement in his voice. Even though they forestalled finishing their breakfast conversation, she was content with the tacit truce between them. It was almost friendly.

"I didn't know Barbara was ever married," Maxine said, thinking friendship was one of the things she wanted in her relationship. Before she decided to settle down with a man to build a future, they had to first be friends.

Casting a sidelong glance at Lucious, she felt he concealed secrets, maybe demons. She couldn't say whether he would ever part with them enough to let her, or any woman, into his life.

"That was before she moved here," Lucious said. He added as an aside, "At least, that's according to the grapevine. I only know she moved to town with money."

"I'm still amazed by the power of gossip in this place," Maxine said with a chuckle.

Lucious quipped, "Gossip provides leads when there's nothing else."

Maxine's eyes brightened as surprise lit her face. "My daddy used to say that."

"I know," Lucious replied.

He deftly parallel parked between a Lexus and a Porsche on the street before a mansion-size, multileveled home with a green slated roof and a row of boxwoods out front. Over a dozen pane windows fronted the handmade brick structure, a meticulous and elegant combination of contemporary taste and an appreciation for a bygone era.

The home was in keeping with its owner, Maxine thought, accepting Lucious's hand as they headed for the circular driveway leading to the house.

"I would hate to be the maid," Maxine said.

"I hear she doesn't have a maid," Lucious replied. "Probably doesn't trust anybody touching her things."

Maxine muttered inaudibly. She didn't get that impression about Barbara, but she conceded Lucious knew more about Liberty and its residents than she did. She was tempted to ask him if he knew whether her father had a confidante among them. Embarrassed by her lack of knowledge, she kept her counsel of questions.

When no one answered the doorbell, Lucious turned the knob. Finding it unlocked, they walked in the high-ceiling foyer. Starting with a green marble floor, upscale, expensive, and tasteful described the furnishings they passed. The path took them to the back of the home where the "just a few close friends" numbered well over twenty people.

Chuckling, Lucious said for her ears only, "I don't know what I'd do if I had these many friends."

Maxine noticed he was smiling a real smile—bright and infectious—and she couldn't help thinking he should do it more often. "I'll have to agree with you on that one."

"That must be a first," he said, with no hostility in his voice. "I'll have to make a record of it."

"Oh, get out of here," she chided, hitting him on the arm playfully. "Have you spotted Barbara yet?"

They both looked over the crowd: some were in the kidney-shaped pool, cooling off, several were getting drinks from the manned bar, while others were in line at the buffet tables. Barbara was in that group.

"There she is," Lucious said, pointing. "While you let our hostess know that we've arrived, I'm heading for the bar. Would you care for something to drink?"

"A beer if they're serving it," Maxine said, the expression on her face matching her dubious tone. "Wine, if not," she added.

Lucious nodded and walked off. Maxine noticed Barbara had moved away from the group, now talking to Dr. Owen Hofsteader and a frizzy redhead who looked as skinny as a beanpole in a pink shorts ensemble. As she made her way to them, Barbara looked in her direction.

"Hi," her hostess said gaily in greeting. "I'm so glad you could make it." They shook hands. "You remember Owen."

"Dr. Hofsteader," Maxine said. "It's good seeing you again."

"Same here," he replied, accepting her proffered hand. "And it's Owen."

"And this is Sylvia Hunter," Barbara said, introducing the other woman.

"Hi, it's a plea . . ." Maxine said, her hand extended. She cut the polite greeting short, rebuked by the sudden stillness and hard cast of the woman's green eyes.

Finally, as if shoved into politeness, Sylvia said weakly, her mouth barely moving, "Hi."

"Did you come alone?" Barbara asked.

"No," Maxine replied. "I brought Lucious Kimble."

"Kimble? Kimble?" Owen said, trying to put a face to the name. "Oh yeah, the police officer. I hope it's pleasure and not business," he added laughingly.

Maxine wondered if he meant anything by the remark, or if it was just a bad joke. She forced a look of mirth on her face, nevertheless, feeling no need to clarify.

"This must be him now," Barbara said.

Her eyes having ferreted him out, approval beamed in their depths, Maxine noticed. She wondered where Charles White was.

Was that jealously in her heart? she questioned, her gaze mimicking the others to see Lucious heading their way with a tall glass of beer in each hand. His muscled, supple body in a light blue shirt, khaki shorts, and sandals, moved with the grace of a big cat. He was clearly the most handsome man at this gathering, Maxine thought. She wasn't so sure anymore that a relationship with him wouldn't be worth exploring.

"Good show, Maxine," Barbara said, her voice lowered suggestively. "He's a cutie."

Cutie indeed, Maxine thought, trying to contain her smile. "Yes, he is," she said, pleased.

"Hello, everybody," Lucious said, nearing them.

"Sergeant Kimble," Barbara said, "How nice of you to join us. Welcome to my home."

"Charles bought it for me."

"It's a beautiful painting," Maxine replied. She wasn't lying, but she was surprised. She and Barbara were looking at a clearly ethnic painting by an African-American artist on the wall above a husky oak table in the hostess's study.

Barbara had drawn her away from the party ostensibly to see her new possession, but Maxine suspected her hostess needed a moment to recoup in order to last another couple of hours. It was after eight, and none of the guests seemed ready to leave. She and Lucious were, however. Except for the name, Henry Chambers, few of those attending the party even knew her father.

"I do hope Charles will be able to make it," Barbara said, her tone wistful as she looked at the delicate gold watch on her wrist.

"Where is he tonight, by the way?" Maxine asked. In truth, she hadn't missed him.

"Something came up with one of his kids," Barbara replied. "His oldest son, Charles, Jr. That boy is nothing but trouble."

Maybe that accounted for Owen's remark about Lucious's presence, Maxine thought. But she didn't want to give Barbara the impression that she was interested in her boyfriend's son and changed the subject. "Is Sylvia a friend of yours?"

It had been so obvious that Sylvia made a point of moving elsewhere whenever she or Lucious was near, as if they had the plague. She didn't understand how Owen tolerated her dragging him around as she had.

"Yeah," Barbara said with amusement in her voice. "She's kind of quirky, but she's okay once you get to know her."

That wasn't likely to happen, Maxine thought.

"She's a Wellington," Barbara added, mimicking a smug, haughty demeanor. "You may not remember her grandmother.

Martha Wellington. She used to be the director of the city library."

Maxine shrugged her ignorance. "I don't recall."

"Old man Wellington was an investor of some sorts, had a lot of patents that made millions. The family was big in local politics. Sylvia has to be worth two or three million."

She should spend some of it to get her hair styled and on a new wardrobe of clothes, Maxine thought. Tactfully, she kept her opinion to herself and muttered an unimpressed, "Hmm." The name didn't mean anything to her, and quite frankly, she was sorry she ever raised the question about Sylvia.

"If she and Owen tie the knot, that will add another million or two to their lives," Barbara went on garrulously.

Maxine smiled wordlessly. It was quite possible that Barbara was being overly friendly to make up for the rude behavior of her friend, Sylvia. She considered telling her it wasn't necessary; she'd dealt with people like Sylvia and knew their numbers were unlimited.

"Are you all done with your father's book?"

"At last," Maxine replied with a gentle chuckle, a relieved sigh.

"So what are you going to do now? Return to Houston?"

"Not for another week," Maxine replied. She might have to leave her car because she doubted it would be ready. "I'll drive to Savannah Saturday and fly out Sunday."

"Oh, I guess we won't get a chance to have a Texas barbecue before you go," Barbara said with disappointment.

"That would be nice," Maxine said, as if seriously entertaining the idea. She recalled that one of Barbara's guests had brought the subject up when they learned she was visiting from Houston. "I don't know enough people in town," she said at last, deciding against it.

"Well, you met everybody here," Barbara said. "And certainly Lucious knows some people."

"Let me think about it."

"Hey, Barb," a male voice called.

"Well, the break is over," Barbara said laughingly. "Shall we rejoin the party?"

"Do you know anything about Dr. White's son?"

"I presume you're referring to Junior," Lucious replied. "Yeah, I know him. Unfortunately, so does the entire police department. His parents' divorce left a bitter taste in his mouth, and he takes his anger out in destructive ways. Why do you ask?"

They were riding home with Lucious behind the wheel. The stars high in the sky kept the night from being pitch black, and the air conditioner held the heat at bay.

"His name came up in a conversation," Maxine replied. She didn't mind pursuing the topic of the doctor's son with Lucious, who would understand her interest. "He's the reason Dr. White didn't show up for the party until late. Was he troubled before the divorce?" she asked.

"If he was," Lucious replied, "it didn't come to the attention of the police. He's a regular now. Dr. White will eventually get tired of the expense of having to bail him out."

With her head leaned back against the rest, Maxine tried to get an image of him in her mind. In looking for a motive, his was the first name she had heard that could possibly answer who most likely held a grudge against Chambers Investigation; hence, her. "How old is he?"

"Mm, fifteen, sixteen."

Pondering this information, Maxine thought it wasn't far-fetched for an angry teenager to rationalize away his father's fault for the breakup of his family. In his convoluted thinking, he would place the blame on someone else.

"Do you think he's capable of violence to the point of murder?"

Lucious mulled his answer before he replied. "We all are, under the right conditions," he said thoughtfully. "I'll check into it, see if he can account for his whereabouts."

"Thanks."

"Don't mention it."

Lucious fiddled with the radio dial and found the station that played a mix of oldies and contemporary music Maxine had picked up the night of her accident. A finger-snapping tune filled the car, with its funky bass beat thumping against the speakers.

"I'm not ready to call it a night yet," Lucious said. "How about you?"

"I'm game if you are."

"All right, let's go sweat."

Monday came all too quickly. The peace and quiet that existed Saturday and Sunday ended. Lucious was gone, and Maxine was alone.

She felt a sense of déjà vu, recalling the last time Lucious left her bed. After the euphoric remembrance of passions spent, she felt assailed by a forlornness she never experienced in Houston after spending a night with a lover.

They had danced like college students at a juke joint with a live DJ Saturday night, and slept in Sunday morning. She kept waiting for the proverbial other shoe to drop, but Sunday passed in relative quiet, her internal stirrings quelled in Lucious's passionate arms.

Maxine sighed as she started her father's old gray Chevy Impala. She longed for yesterday as she backed out of the garage, mindful of her plan to talk to people her father had befriended and trusted. Since she didn't know any such people, she would have to settle for the next best thing. Someone trustworthy who knew her father. Mike topped her short list. While there, she could also check on her car, then head for the office to contact her insurance company.

Maxine drove off to implement her plan.

Chapter 10

MIKE'S was more than a tow truck service. Maxine saw it was also a car repair garage when she pulled into the graveled parking lot in the front of tin stalls attached to a small building. Her car was in one of the stalls, but unlike the cars occupying the other two, no greasy mechanic was working on it.

It was not a good sign, Maxine thought, as she parked and got out. She shielded her eyes from the sun, trying to spot Mike among the men. She didn't see him, so she walked to the first stall. The mechanic was under the car, and she kneeled to ask, "Where can I find Mike?"

"Probably inside where it's cool."

Any dummy should know that, his tone suggested.

"Thank you," Maxine said, heading for the door inside the stall that led to a small, but air-conditioned room. Car products and items occupied every visible space on the wood-paneled walls. There was an old cash register set up on the corner of the counter, which broke up the room and led to a back office.

"Mike," she called out.

"Yeah, I'm back here, what you want?"

Maxine followed the voice to the back room, where Mike was sitting in his cramped office behind his junky desk. He was bent over cash register receipts and an old-time calculator.

"I hate to bother you, Mike," Maxine said.

"Oh, Miss Chambers," Mike said, suddenly flustered. He sprang from his seat and knocked over a soda can, then tried to catch it before the contents spilled over his papers.

"That's about how my day's been going," Maxine said, masking her amusement. She waited for Mike's reaction, and when he laughed, she joined him.

"You know, sometimes I think I need to hire somebody to do the books, but I'm determined not to be beaten by the numbers," he said. "You know what I mean?"

"I think I do," Maxine replied. It was the same reason she hadn't tried to call her sisters a second time and ask for help.

"Please have a seat," he said, scrambling around the desk to clear off the chair that was loaded with car mechanics' books.

"I could come back at a better time," she said, sitting in the chair. "I saw my car. How long do you think it's going to take to get it road-ready?"

"At least a week," he replied, returning to sit behind his desk. "I'll have that estimate ready for you later this afternoon."

"No problem," she lied. She hated the idea of returning to Houston and leaving her car. "I'm using dad's old clunker," she said, amused. "The radio doesn't work, but the air conditioner seems to be in good order. Considering how hot it's been, that's a better-than-even trade."

Mike said laughingly, "That old clunker is in great shape. I put a new engine in it earlier this year, and the tires are not even four months old."

"Well, that's good to know," Maxine said. "I have another question for you."

"Shoot."

"I looked through my dad's ledger, and I couldn't find a bill from you or any kind of receipt. Obviously, you did some work on his car." With her straw handbag in her lap, she draped her arms over it and crossed her legs at the thighs. "Last week when I had those flats, you told me that we could keep the same arrangements you had with my dad. Do you mind telling me about those arrangements?"

Just the sudden change of the atmosphere caused Maxine to squirm uncomfortably. Seconds of dead silence and tension parched the room. Mike's healthy, outdoorsman pallor paled and shadows of pain lit his azure eyes. She almost dreaded the answer her question would yield, but she had to know.

Mike shrugged his muscular shoulders wedged in a red T-shirt. "I guess it's not a big secret since it happened so long ago. I tend to forget about it sometimes. Well, I try to anyway," he said with a self-depreciating chuckle. "I guess you can't never forget nothing like that."

Grateful that Mike hadn't thrown her out of his office, Maxine breathed. "Nothing like what?" she asked, now more than ever eager to know.

"Being locked up for a crime you didn't commit, facing a death penalty."

"Ohhh," oozed from Maxine's throat as soft as an inaudible breath. Surprise slightly altered the look on her face.

"If it wasn't for your daddy, I could'a been a dead man . . . a ghost looking for justice."

Intrigued, she listened quietly as Mike told his story. It was peppered with words like *hellion* and *po' white trash* that accorded him no respect from the locals, and easy pickings for the murders.

The town was in a state of panic and fear over the rapes and brutal murders of three women. The first two victims were hookers, but the pressure for Sheriff Bob Jenkins to find this sick killer "got hot real quick," Mike said, "when they found Martha Wellington. The maid found the body. She had been raped and murdered in her home."

Maxine's demeanor changed from stoical to animated at the mention of the name, and surprise slipped through her neutral expression. "Wow!" she whispered. Martha Wellington was Sylvia's grandmother, she recalled, thinking Barbara didn't tell her about the fatal assault.

"Did the police ever find the real killer?"

Sitting in the car with the air conditioner running, Maxine considered having a radio installed in her father's old car. But it wasn't the thought dominating her muse now.

Still, it was why she hadn't learned the murdered victim was Dr. Owen Hofsteader until she got to the office after leaving Mike's.

It had been the talk of the town earlier today. She guessed by now it had only grown more intense as the hours passed. It was now almost four. She was just across the street from the hospital, waiting for Gloria to get off from work.

The area used to be mostly warehouses, which had been transformed into space for artists, cafés, specialty shops, and restaurants. The hospital, a six-story, red brick building, was in the center of it all. Despite the hour, traffic was barely existent.

Maxine had been in a metered parking space for about ten minutes, thinking back to her interview with Mike.

Even though Mike's story had a happy ending, it was obvious he would never forget it. Still, his tale was one of a thirty-year-old crime. Her father was a rookie cop, the only African American on the force at the time. She was three years old.

Most of the players were already dead, including the real murderer-rapist. The culprit was a police officer, by the name of Lester Clark. Her father caught him while he was attempting to break into another woman's house. She would have been his fourth victim had Officer Henry Chambers not noticed the police car parked where it shouldn't have been.

Mike was ultimately released, but his bitter memories lingered.

Maxine could clearly see the anguish on his face when he said, "Your father was the only one who believed I was innocent. That may not seem like much, but when you don't have anybody on your side . . . Well, it was everything to me. I'll never forget him for it."

She caused a man to revisit his pain for no reason at all, Maxine thought disheartened. She didn't like the feeling of being a bully. Unfortunately, she wasn't left any alternative.

She didn't know if Gloria would talk to her or not; she didn't know what she could learn from it, but Gloria was born here for certain, according to Mike. While she didn't believe her father had befriended Gloria, she'd gotten mixed signals about Barbara, who possessed the knowledge of a local, but who wasn't.

Besides, she didn't know too many other people.

Just then, Gloria walked out the front doors with a group of women. From the side mirror, she spied Gloria walking to the opposite end of the street and crossing to the other side. Only one woman remained with her.

She shifted the car into drive, looked both ways on the two-way street, then executed a bat turn. Her big sister would have been proud of her, she thought, driving to the end of the block where she stopped for the light.

To her left, she saw Gloria sitting with her companion at the bus stop.

The light turned green, she made a left turn, then circled in a parking lot, back onto the street. The light was red when she reached it, but drew no attention from Gloria until she turned onto the street fronting the bus stop, where she braked.

"Need a ride?" she called out to Gloria.

Gloria and her companion exchanged wary looks with each other, then trained their belligerent gazes on her. She didn't want to know what kind of person they thought she was.

"It's me, Gloria. Maxine Chambers. I need to talk to you."

Gloria sat in silent thought for a moment. "Can you drop my friend off, too?" she asked after a while.

"Sure."

"Come on, girl, it's a free ride," Gloria said, rising to walk to the car.

"Ain't nothing free."

Maxine heard the women grumbling between themselves. Gloria reached the car and pulled the door open. She turned back to her friend. "You coming, or what?"

"You go 'head," the other woman told her. "I'll read about them finding your big dead body in a ditch somewhere."

Gloria flashed a look of disbelief at her friend, and another one to Maxine that said something altogether different.

If she had to interpret that look, Maxine thought it said, *If this little old heifer try something, I'll kick her ass.*

Gloria harrumphed and got in the car, and the passenger seat moaned under the strain of her weight. "I live across the tracks, in the Tree Lane Apartments."

That wasn't far from her father's house, but still three bus transfers away, Maxine thought, nodding, as she pulled out into the traffic.

"What you want to talk to me about?"

The fact that she had gotten into the car suggested to Maxine that Gloria had a few words for her, as well. "I'd like to apologize if I got you in trouble with Ms. Goldman."

Gloria tsked. "Shoots, girl, I ain't worried 'bout Barbara Goldman. I was running that office long before she got here, and I'll be here when she leaves. People like her don't stay no place long. Besides, she didn't even come to work today."

"Because of Dr. Hofsteader?" Maxine asked.

"Yeah," Gloria replied. "Probably go babysit that old

skinny heifer, Sylvia. I don't know what Dr. Hofsteader saw in her. He was a decent enough man."

"You know Sylvia?"

"I know she's rude, and that's the nicest thing I can say about her."

Maxine nodded, but she didn't want to tell Gloria that she shared her perception of the woman. Still, she was wondering how best to approach Gloria. Some people only answered the question you asked them: she wondered what was the right question to get a useful answer.

"Now, what you want to talk to me about?" Gloria asked, cutting her a sidelong glance.

Maxine smiled to herself, thinking one approached Gloria straight ahead. "My father's death certificate."

"I already told you," Gloria said, her tone miffed. "If it didn't go out, it ain't my fault. As soon as the paperwork was signed by the chief of staff, that's Dr. Owen Hofsteader"—she paused a second—"it used to be. Anyway, I filed a copy and put the other copy in the mail to your daddy's house. I knew y'all would need it in order to finalize his business and stuff."

"Was it possible that someone could have taken it?"

Gloria thought about her answer before she replied. "Yeah, I guess so. It was on the counter in the outgoing mail tray. But who would want to do that?"

That was a good question, Maxine thought. And one she hoped to find out. "Did Dr. White ever bring his son to the hospital?"

"Naw." Gloria stretched the negative reply out. "From what I hear, the boy can't stand his old man. The dirty dog. Why is it that every time a black man makes a little money, he got to run and get himself a white woman?"

Maxine merely shrugged her shoulders. "Where does the family live?"

"Over in Piney Groves," Gloria replied.

"Piney Groves?" Maxine repeated curiously. "Where is that?"

"That's the new subdivision on the east side of where your house is," Gloria replied. "It's a nice area."

"Oh, really?" Maxine replied, intrigued. *If* Charles, Jr., was her man, and *if* revenge was his motive, then he certainly had opportunity.

It was a long ride, but Gloria's highly opinionated commentaries made it interesting. Still, Maxine knew she had to be careful about what she accepted as truth.

She could believe that as popular as her father had been with everybody, there were still some who believed he'd forgotten his place. From Gloria's perspective on the changes the city had experienced, growth and progress were not luxurious for everyone—only those with money.

"Girlfriend, nothing's changed here," Gloria said, disgust and sadness in her voice.

On a lark, Maxine asked, "Gloria, are you familiar with the story about the police officer who committed a series of rapes and murders in the seventies?"

"Girl, that was the biggest thing in town," Gloria said excitedly. "All the black folks thought they were go hang that boy. Well, Mike ain't no boy no more, but they treated him like he was one of us, you know?" she posed rhetorically, her eyes cut a sidelong glance of camaraderie. "In their eyes, he wasn't much better," she added as an aside. "The good white folks were all riled up, like a feeding frenzy of piranha," she added with a rasp of disgust. "When the real killer was caught, you talk about hush-hush. They got dry as a well."

Chapter 11

"You look awful," Maxine said, examining Lucious from her front door. He was in his non-uniform uniform: gray slacks, white shirt, and had his .45 holstered under his green blazer. Exhaustion showed in the slump of his shoulders and his eyes, red-rimmed, consumed by lack of sleep.

Lucious stared at her from head to toe—her hair tied up at the back of her head, the green halter top, and raggedy cut-offs. Maxine had to tell her traitorous body vibrating under the intensity of his gaze that she didn't dress for him. He called last night to say he couldn't get away, but he would try to see her this morning. She really hadn't expected him to show up because of Dr. Hofsteader's murder.

"You look great as usual," Lucious replied at last, a weak attempt at a smile on his face. It was replaced by a deadpan expression. "But I'm too tired to be tempted."

"Is that supposed to be funny?" she quipped sarcastically. But she was smiling, a brazen gleam in her eyes. His remark had the disconcerting ring of a husband of many years. Yet, his presence at nine in the morning felt familiar, comfortable even. She had a feeling that with the right move on her part, she could make a liar out of him. But she had enough confusion in her head right now.

"Come in," she said, standing aside, allowing him to enter.

He held out a white bag to her. "I brought breakfast."

Heading for the kitchen with Lucious behind her, Maxine peeked inside the bag. "Bagels and cream cheese. Now, this is tempting," she said. "I've probably put on ten pounds since I've been here."

"If that's true, which I doubt," he said, as they reached the kitchen, "they've fallen nicely."

Maxine ignored his flattering remarks. *Behave!* she admonished her libido.

She set the bag on the counter so she could place her straw handbag on the floor and gather the notes she'd spread across the table. "Orange juice in the box," she said. "Why don't you pour two glasses?" She didn't want him standing around idle, gawking at her; she already felt a tepid heat curling up her spine.

Lucious removed his jacket and hung it over the back of a chair, then placed his gun atop the refrigerator in its holster. "What's all this?" he asked, spreading his hand over the table to encompass her notes.

"Stuff."

"In other words, none of my business?"

Maxine looked up to see that devastatingly intense gaze of his trained on her. "No," she said, sighing deeply. "I just thought that since your hands were already full with a murder investigation, you would prefer a little respite from my problem."

Lucious nodded as if satisfied with her answer. "The case has got me going already," he said wearily, passing a hand over his head.

She felt the same way, Maxine thought. When she arrived home last night, feeling defeated by her lack of progress, she filled the time writing everything she remembered from her interviews with Mike and Gloria. After a good night's sleep, she hoped things would fall magically into place this morning. It hadn't happened so far.

"I don't want to talk about it right now," Lucious said, ending his muse. "Tell me what you got so far," he said, crossing the room to the cabinets for glasses.

"It seems like a whole lot of nothing," Maxine replied with frustration. "My initial goal was to interview the people who knew my father. Mike was on my short list. Then I decided to interview Gloria because of something Mike said."

"Gloria?" Lucious replied, getting the carton of orange juice from the refrigerator. Setting the glasses on the counter, he filled them with juice.

"She works in the administration office at the hospital," Maxine replied, taking the bagels from the bag to set on a plate.

Lucious downed one of the glasses of juice as she relayed how she initially met Gloria. He refilled it and set both glasses on the table. "What did Mike say that led you back to Gloria?"

"Well, it was nothing except the fact that Gloria was a local," she said, lathering cream cheese on the bagels. "With the grapevine being as it is, I was hoping she could tell me something that might provide a clue as to who might have held a grudge against my father."

"Did she?"

"If she did, it went by me," Maxine said. "All I got was a vague group of unknowns who thought my father forgot he was black."

Lucious muttered unintelligibly with a wry twist of his lips. "Got any coffee?"

"I'll put a pot on if you want some." She placed the plate of bagels in the microwave, set the timer, then got coffee started.

Lucious was leaning with his back against the counter, a thoughtful muse on his face. "When did your father get ill? I mean, had he suffered from heart problems before . . . before you and your sisters arrived?"

Maxine was at the sink, filling the pot with water. "I don't know for sure," she said. "I know his last case was two months before he was hospitalized. If he was sick before then,"—which was a distinct possibility, she thought—"he never let on and he never said a word to us. Why do you ask?"

"Just curious."

While Lucious busied himself setting the table for coffee, Maxine found herself thinking about teenagers and grudges and misplaced blame that spelled Charles White, Jr. Even though his name lingered in her thoughts like a vulture waiting for an animal to die, she was concerned about all those "ifs" that pointed to him as her prime suspect.

Still, she couldn't be deterred no matter how uncomfortable it made her feel, she reminded herself. Particularly since she didn't have anything else to go on.

Maxine blew out her cheeks. "Do you have any idea what the numbers seven, ten, and one could mean?" she asked.

A pensive look shadowed Lucious's expression, his forehead a ridge of lines, his eyes narrowed. "Let me see them."

Maxine stooped to look inside her straw bag. As she pulled out a sheet of paper and stood, the bag slumped over on the floor and the gun slid out.

Their eyes met. Maxine's held an "oh-oh" look, her breath suspended in her bosom. While her father may have had a permit to carry a gun, she didn't. Lucious lifted a brow, then wordlessly took the sheet of paper from her hand. He looked at the numbers while she breathed a sigh of relief and discreetly returned the gun and uprighted her bag.

The microwave bell rang, signaling the bagels were ready. Maxine set the plate of warm bagels on the table. The coffee began to percolate.

"It's a code," he said.

"Duh," Maxine said sarcastically, her hands on her hips.

Lucious laughed. "I don't know what these numbers mean. I presume you got them from your father's notes," he said, his voice and demeanor taking on a serious tone. "They're too small for a combination lock. Did you try the post office?"

"I haven't," she replied. Maybe she shouldn't have assumed the attorney had given her and her sisters everything.

The paper rustled in his strong grip as he asked, "And you sure these are right?"

"If you mean did I copy them correctly, yes," Maxine said confidently. "They were in his handwriting on a manila folder. I threw the folder away because there was nothing in it."

"I see," he replied thoughtfully, again, looking at the numbers. "Let's assume they're his code, and since he was a cop, let's break the numbers down."

"I've done everything to those numbers, from arithmetic to assigning dates to them," she said. "And they don't match anything I've been able to find in terms of cases he worked on particular dates."

"Okay," he said, pulling a fountain pen from his shirt pocket. He leaned over the table, writing as he spoke. "Instead of seven, ten, and one, look at them as seven, one, zero, and one."

Maxine looked at the numbers he'd written. "You've only added another unknown."

"Where's your phone?"

"Huh?"

"All these 'duhs' and 'huhs' from you this morning make me think you need some more rest," he said chuckling.

"Ha-ha," she said humorlessly as she bent to get her phone from her bag. She handed him the phone. While he dialed a number, Maxine filled two cups with coffee, then sat at the table.

"Hey, Mark, it's me, Kimble. I need you to check the files for a number for me. One, zero, one, seven. . . . Yeah, I know that's an old one. Call me back at this number when you pull it up," he said, giving Maxine's number. "Thanks, buddy." Ending the call, he flipped the phone closed and placed it on the table as he sat.

"What was that, some kind of police file number you gave him?" she asked, talking around the food in her mouth.

Lucious took a bite from a bagel. "Uh-huh," he said. "The number you have represents its age. Your dad would have used it." Licking cream cheese off his hand, he added, "Since LPD has spent a little money updating its files, including putting the old cases on computer, Mark should get back to me in a few minutes.

"As you can imagine," he said, taking another bite, "I wasn't able to get around to interviewing that White boy."

Maxine swallowed the food in her mouth before she spoke, then washed it down with a sip of juice. "How bad is this case? What happened to Dr. Hofsteader? One of the reports I heard on the radio said his throat was slashed."

Lucious shook his head in disbelief. "The news people are almost as bad as the gossips in this town. He was stabbed to death. It was made to look like he came home and interrupted a burglar."

"But you don't believe that's what happened?"

"There are no signs of a break-in," Lucious replied. "And that information," he added, his gaze leveled on her, "stays in this room." He drank a couple of swallows of coffee. "I suspect he knew his killer, let him, or her," he said, a head nod indicating deference to her, "in the house. Nothing was stolen, but a knife, which we believe is the murder weapon, is missing from his kitchen."

Jokingly, she asked, "Think Sylvia Hunter got pissed at him and killed him in the heat of passion?"

"It was certainly my first guess," Lucious said, chewing.

He drank more coffee and sat silent, still, thoughtful. Maxine was trying to picture Sylvia committing murder. It wasn't hard, Sylvia's size notwithstanding. But she had to consider that her perception of the snobbish woman tainted her judgment.

"You said Gloria was sure she put your father's death certificate in the basket of outgoing mail?"

With food in her mouth, Maxine nodded, muttering an affirmative reply. She swallowed. "Why? Is that important to Dr. Hofsteader's case?"

Lucious set his cup on the table. "We found a copy of the death certificate at Dr. Hofsteader's. He apparently had been reading it. We found it on the magazine rack he has in his bathroom."

The phone rang, and Lucious grabbed it, answering on the first ring.

Shock was like a living thing in Maxine. She felt it in the emotion expressed on her face, in the icy grip wrapped around her heart.

She heard Lucious mumbling a bunch of "Uh-huhs" into the phone, but she couldn't even ask him what he was "uh-huhing" to. She felt paralyzed even though she sat trembling, disturbed by her thoughts.

How was she going to tell her sisters that their father may have been murdered? Hell, she was having a hard time accepting it herself. Still, it cleared something Gloria said: "Some people think he forgot his place."

The breath Maxine had been unconsciously holding rushed from her in a gasping shudder that shook her body. She knew she was jumping to conclusions, but couldn't help it for the ugly scenarios running through her mind.

What was her father's death certificate doing in Dr. Hofsteader's possession?

Only one conclusion came to Maxine. Even though Dr. Hofsteader had signed off on the certificate that listed her father's death as natural, stemming from a heart attack, he had a change of mind. Something about it raised his suspicions, she thought somberly.

She recalled not really subscribing to Gloria's opinion regarding how some people felt about her father. She chalked it up to jealousy, for he made his own place and refused to be labeled. She remembered when he was the most respected and most popular man in town. His enemies were the criminal elements who disrespected the law. She had been certain about that, and he affirmed it with his actions.

Now she had to consider lawbreakers weren't the only enemies, that once off the police force, the bigots had gotten bold. Hanging her father from a tree would have been too obvious. A heart attack accomplished the same results.

"Maxine . . ."

It took Maxine a moment to come out of her disorientation and focus on Lucious. Concern marred his expression, and he took her hands in his. The iceberg she'd become began to thaw with his touch.

"What will it take to have my father's body exhumed?" she asked, recalling that because he died in the hospital an autopsy was not a state requirement.

Lucious looked at her with a deep scrutiny. "Maybe you had better back up and tell me what you're thinking."

He had spoken softly, but his voice had a hard edge to it. And Maxine knew. "I'm sure you've thought the same thing." She retrieved her hands and folded them in her lap.

"You need conclusive proof, not circumstantial evidence, that his death wasn't natural," he replied. "And I promise you right now, if it's there, I'll find it."

He got to his feet, taking both coffee cups with him. He poured them down the sink, then refilled the cups and returned to the table. Steam rose from their tops, and Maxine wrapped her hands around her cup.

"That was Mark on the phone," he said, taking a careful

sip of the hot coffee. "The numbers correlated with an old case. Closed. It was solved by your father."

"What was the case?"

"A police officer gone bad."

Maxine frowned. "Three women were raped and murdered. Mike was suspected and jailed. The town folks were ready to string him up. The last victim was Sylvia Hunter's grandmother, Martha Wellington. The name is not familiar to me."

"Unless you were going to the library when you were two or three years old, you wouldn't remember her," Lucious said. "The name Wellington died when she did. Sylvia's mother was already a Hunter by then."

Her gaze suddenly brightened. "What if Dr. Hofsteader knew something about the old murder that made him want to sever his relationship with Sylvia?" she said eagerly.

"That's another leap over the same horse." His unimpressed tone deflated the balloon of her excitement. "That case and this one are probably not related at all." Maxine bristled. "Don't knot up on me. Hear me out first.

"The bad cop had a sister. She was a teenager at the time; name's Sarah. I'm going to interview her, if she's still in town. I don't believe there's a connection to the Hofsteader case. Still, I'm going to pursue it like any other murder investigation and let the chips fall where they may.

"Meanwhile, I want you to look through your father's things again, see if he was working on something before he got ill."

"There's an indication that he was working on something that originated out of Atlanta." Recalling the coded notes he'd written in his ledger, she dug inside her straw bag for it. She withdrew the ledger and opened it on the table. "This date is all he wrote down," she said, pointing. "It correlates with the time he made a hefty deposit."

"Okay," Lucious said thoughtfully. He reached inside his

coat pocket and pulled out a worn reporter's notebook. "I'll get a copy of the Chambers Investigation phone records for that time," he said, writing in the book.

That done, he put his notebook in his jacket, his pen in his shirt, then sat back in his chair and stared at her.

Maxine wondered what was on his mind now when his expression altered slightly. The look didn't exactly spell trouble, but it caused a nervous fluttering in her stomach. She opened her mouth to taunt him about being too tired—a defense mechanism to her own feminine rising—but the teasing light in his eyes was different, not sexual. She clamped her mouth shut and waited.

"You've really gotten into this, haven't you." It was a statement, not a question, issued with a wee bit of a smile curling around the edges of his firm lips.

"Well," Maxine started hesitantly. She wasn't prepared for those feelings, either, she thought. She felt hard-pressed to remember why she hated Liberty so.

"Don't deny it," he reproached her with laughter in his voice. He took her hand in his, just a light touch with his fingers. "Face it, lady-love," he said. "It's in your blood."

Maxine shivered inwardly. "I don't know about all of that," she said, feeling the heat rise in her face.

Lucious enjoyed a healthy laugh. "I see contrariness is in your nature, too. No problem," he added, getting to his feet. He held her hand fully in his. "Since I probably can't convince you to stay close to home, I guess I better do something else."

His gentle tug brought Maxine to her feet. "Something else like what?" she asked, eyeing him coyly.

"Make sure you know how to use that gun."

Chapter 12

Don't jump to conclusions. And don't do anything rash. The cool air breezed over her flesh like goose bumps. Maxine sighed as if it was a manna from heaven: it was certainly a relief from Liberty's heat.

With Lucious's warning echoing in her mind, she strolled the corridor in the Dogwood Mall behind a group of five teenagers: two girls and three boys. She didn't fear his latter warning in the mall, but it was too late for the former. Charles White, Jr., her primary interest, was one of the five teens: he remained indicted in her thoughts.

She rationalized it was not farfetched to suspect Charles White, Jr. Firing at her with an old gun, trashing the office, and trying to run her off the road all had the earmarking of a teenager's retribution. Her father had provided the ammunition his mother needed to take his father to the cleaners for cheating on her. It left him without a father, but as her father was dead, she was the next best thing.

The mall wasn't crowded, but even if it were, Maxine didn't think it would be hard tracking them. They were boisterous and playful, their behavior as typical as their expensive designer attire. They joshed and joked with each other, in no obvious hurry. Their leisurely frolicking forced her to stop occasionally and pretend interest in a window item.

Trailing discreetly as they continued on, she wondered about their ultimate destination. She felt as if she had been following people for most of the day. First she followed Lucious to the police department, where he allowed her to read the report of the thirty-year-old case, involving the crooked cop, Lester Clark. She couldn't get a copy, so she'd taken notes in a much more legible penmanship than her father's.

It was strange seeing her father's handwriting, she recalled, looking at a long, pencil-slim burgundy suit in an executive shop for women as the kids stopped to inspect cell phones at a booth set up in the center of the mall corridor. But not as strange as Lucious finding his death certificate in Dr. Hofsteader's home.

She decided to keep it to herself before contacting her sisters . . . at least until she knew for sure whether their father's cause of death was natural or not.

Before leaving the police station, she'd placed a call to Gloria at the hospital because of something she'd read in the report. The fallen police officer had stolen more than lives, she recalled reading. Jewelry, trinkets, and even expensive silverware had been taken either from their bodies or their homes. Except for some jewelry and art pieces from China that used to belong to Martha Wellington, most of the items had been recovered from the officer's home, which he shared with his retarded sister, Sarah Clark. The report identified her as thirteen years old and mentally retarded, and ended there.

Maxine felt there was more to be said. Either it had been left out on purpose or pulled from the official report because Sarah Clark was a minor. If her feelings panned out, she guessed the most logical place to look was the hospital. It was why she had put in a call to Gloria.

Liberty didn't have a mental institution back then, she recalled. Students that had been so-labeled when she attended school were lumped in an outside classroom away from the so-called "normal" or "regular" students. None of the black students was sent to Mercy Asylum in Savannah for help. Sarah Clark wasn't black, but submitting her to Mercy had to be preceded by a recommendation from the hospital.

Maybe Gloria would find something useful, Maxine thought, watching as the group ducked into an electronic store. Standing on the other side of the glass window, she got a full frontal view of the youngster. While he favored Tommy clothes from head to toe, she didn't see trouble spelled in his expression, nor his manner. He was a rather handsome boy, with long, elegant eyelashes and inquisitive dark eyes. He stood about five-seven and looked as if he would grow to be taller than his father. He was dark like his father, and seeing the way he flirted with one of the girls, she suspected he had a roving eye like his father as well.

Ever since she started following his movements almost an hour ago, the more she wondered whether his acting out was a plea for attention from his father.

She'd purchased a Liberty map for directions to Piney Groves, the town's only African-American, middle-class subdivision. The neighborhood was clean and enticing, mostly two-story homes, with some pools, but all with well-tended yards and the proverbial police patrol, she recalled. As it was so hot out, there were few people on Blossom Street. She was working on her fake survey pitch—the approach she planned to take to get inside the Whites' home—when a red Mustang pulled into the driveway.

The youngster ran out, with his mother yelling after him—"Don't you dare leave this house, Charles, Jr.!" He jumped in the car, and the driver, another teenage boy, backed out full speed and drove off. She followed them as they picked up the girls, then the other young man their age.

The kids moved on, and Maxine no longer had to wonder

where they were headed. She heard even before she saw the nerve-wracking video games in an arcade. It was filled to capacity with kids of all ages. She watched her quarry buy tokens as his friends were doing, then he disappeared into the back of the arcade.

Worrying her bottom lip, Maxine thought and rejected approaches. A survey of any sort was out of the question; she doubted she could pull him away from his game. The arcade was like a drug to teenagers. She knew from her friends with children that they were absolutely witless in front of a video game: it was going to keep Charles hooked for a long time.

The tiny peel of her cell phone interrupted her thoughts. Maxine reached inside her straw bag to get it. "Hello," she said softly, walking to the other side of the corridor.

"It's me, Gloria. Have I got some juicy stuff for you. Why don't you meet me at Cafe Express? How long will it take you to get there?"

"They were hillbillies!"

From that statement, which sounded more like a guilty sentence on Gloria's tongue, Maxine concluded that Lester and Sarah Clark were not native Georgians. Thinking all bigots weren't white, she knew the Clarks could have come anywhere from Alabama, West Virginia, or Kentucky.

Sipping lemonade from tall frosty glasses, they were sitting at a corner table in a glass-encased back room, awaiting their orders.

Cafe Express was a trendy restaurant specializing in coffee and sandwiches. Maxine didn't think it was a good idea meeting here, but Gloria insisted it was safe, as the hospital administrators were attending Dr. Hofsteader's funeral.

"I couldn't find a picture, but according to Dr. Pryce, that's who did the evaluation, she was malnourished and underweight. She was a tiny little thing . . . didn't weigh no more than eighty-five pounds. That's entirely too small for somebody sixteen years old," Gloria added, appalled as if personally affected.

There was hope for Gloria after all, Maxine thought. "I thought she was thirteen," she said, more for clarification than challenge, recalling the police report her father filed.

Gloria was positive about what she'd read. "That's how old she looked," she said with emphasis. "She moved to Liberty with her brother from West Virginia when he started working for the police department. That was a year before the killings started."

Maxine stared out the window absently at the parking lot, which was surrounded by an eight-foot wooden fence. She could tell Gloria was excited about the task she'd given her; however, she didn't see how the information was of use.

The waiter, a dark-haired college student in a short-sleeve white shirt, with a green bow-tie and blue slacks, returned with their orders. He set a huge sandwich of several meats on rye before Gloria, and a simple turkey on wheat in front of her.

"Is there anything else I can get you ladies?" he inquired.

"No, thank you," Gloria replied. She was already cutting her sandwich in half before the waiter left.

She might as well enjoy her lunch, Maxine thought, resigned. "What about her parents or other relatives?" she asked conversationally before taking a bite from her sandwich.

Gloria shrugged. "Dr. Pryce couldn't get her to talk about them," she said around the food in her mouth. "All she talked about was Lester . . . when she wasn't doped up."

"Why was she drugged?" Maxine wondered.

"She went berserk when she found out that her brother was dead. It was the only way they could control her. She spent two weeks in the hospital before they carted her off to Mercy in Savannah."

"I can't believe that nobody picked up that something

was wrong with her," Maxine said. "It's not like you can hide retardation."

Gloria stopped chewing and looked at her curiously. "Who said she was a retard?"

Maxine paused, with food in her mouth. She was certain that was in the police report. Swallowing her food, she asked, "Wasn't she?"

"Not according to Dr. Pryce," Gloria replied. "She was disturbed, but that was because she had been having sex with her brother. I forgot what they called that, but . . ."

"Incest," Maxine said, halting the flow of Gloria's next words. She considered that maybe someone did notice something awry about Sarah Clark, but misinterpreted the signs as retardation.

"Yeah," Gloria said animatedly. "Didn't you get it, all that talk about her going crazy when he died. She was in love with her brother. Dr. Pryce wrote that she threatened everybody's life after your father shot him. There was no reasoning with her about anything. All she wanted was Lester."

Maxine didn't know what to say after that as she resumed eating. After all, she and Gloria were now indulging in pure, ancient gossip, she thought.

"We didn't have no social services for children thirty years ago," Gloria added between bites. "They sent her to Mercy to get her head straight. They didn't have nowhere else to send her."

"That makes her forty-six now," Maxine said after a quick calculation. "She's conceivably still alive. Does anybody know?" she asked. It was too much of a stretch to think that the woman would seek revenge after all this time.

"I don't know the answer to that," Gloria replied, taking a sip of her drink. "But I do know that she had been pregnant."

"What happened to the child?"

"I didn't say she was pregnant at the time," Gloria said. "She had been pregnant before. Dr. Pryce believed that the child was her brother's, but she wouldn't talk about it."

"Then how did he know she had been pregnant before?"

"They did a physical examination."

There was no mention in the police record that an infant had been unearthed on the property. *After thirty years and a closed case, they weren't likely to go looking now,* Maxine thought. "Where did they live?"

Chalk it up to morbid curiosity, Maxine thought upon finding herself where she wouldn't be caught dead in the dark of night. Nearing four in the afternoon, it was very much daytime as the high sun beamed with scorching intensity.

Still, with beads of perspiration popping out across her forehead and on her arms, Maxine felt on haunted grounds. Unconsciously her hand tightened around the handle of the gun in the big, right side pocket of her baggy pants.

Weeds had overtaken most of the dirt street. She had driven on grass to park ten feet from the dilapidated shack, overgrown with vines crawling up the sides and choking the entrance. Wood that was gray from age boarded two window openings. Maxine guessed that had been done by the police after Lester Clark had been killed and Sarah taken away.

She couldn't explain her presence, except a need that she had to see for herself how the Clarks lived—more like husband and wife, instead of brother and sister.

Traipsing passable grounds on the left side of the house where more vines clung and possible entrances or exits were boarded up, she wondered what happened to the child, the one Sarah allegedly gave birth to.

Was it possible that Sarah's child was still alive?

The child would be thirty years old now, but she didn't have a clue whether it was male or female.

Bushes of tangled weeds and snarled tree limbs blocked her from going all the way to the back of the house, so she retraced her steps to the front yard.

Coming here was just a stupid whim, Maxine chided herself, disgruntled. The thirty-year-old case was closed. More than likely there was no child. She had to concur with Gloria's theory that the remains of an infant were buried somewhere on this property.

All utterly useless information!

The sound of an approaching vehicle stopped Maxine in her tracks. With her pulse hopscotching all over the place, her brain urged her to run. Her head whipped around left to right, eyes wide like that of a doe, looking for a place to hide. Unless she climbed a tree, there were no hiding places.

Breathe, Maxine! she silently exhorted herself, trying to get her pulse under control. She drew a deep breath and headed for her car, walking stiffly, hurriedly, while working on the story she would tell if caught. She knew the "if" was wishful thinking; she was not going to make it.

A big truck with a flatbed on which a bulldozer rode pulled up alongside her car and parked at an angle. By the time the door had opened and the driver had gotten out and walked toward her, Maxine had her story straight.

With a cigar clamped between his teeth and brown hair stuffed under a baseball cap, he reminded her of a redneck character in a Jeff Foxworthy joke. He wore a short-sleeve plaid shirt tucked into well-worn jeans and spit-polished black cowboy boots.

"You from the Realtor's?" he asked, the cigar still in his mouth.

"Uh, no," Maxine replied. "I stopped by to see this place. I've been looking for property in a secluded area like this."

"Ain't we all?" His rhetorical question cut her off. "This one been sold, so you out of luck."

"Just as well," she said, feigning a touch of disappointment. "I'm sure it would cost a mint to fix up. Who bought it?"

The sound of a pickup truck approaching seized the man's attention. He gave Maxine his back as a white pickup truck parked alongside his. There were four men riding in the back, and two more stepped from the truck's cab

Maxine wondered if the man would ever answer her question.

"You ain't from 'round here, are you?" he asked, over his shoulder.

Chapter 13

Maxine wasn't ready to go home, call it quits for the day. She left the abandoned shack in search of "the" black community, the one she remembered as a girl growing up in Liberty . . . where Old Man Stevenson's store was the place to shop, especially for moon cookies; a hangout in the recreation room at Liberty Park, with its rickety swings, broken seesaws, and the only public pool exclusively used by African-Americans; the house where Mrs. Bobbit baked the best doughnuts in the world from her kitchen and drove around in her son's truck, selling them and lunch meat sandwiches to anybody and everybody for $1.75.

All the places were gone with the exception of Arlene's. The nightclub Lucious had taken her to, had opened in recent years.

It was named Hannibal, after the famous African general. That's where she finally ended up at 7:30 P.M., before the place got crowded. Still, a dozen or so patrons were well into their second rounds when she found an empty table in the back. The DJ, separated by an enclosed, raised space, spun contemporary jazz and rhythm & blues. She didn't have to yell to place her order for beer, in the can, with a glass. "Please."

The club was located in a strip mall with a hair and nail salon on one side and a doctor's office and police storefront on the other.

Her drink came as she ordered, and Maxine took a long swallow before she settled back in the chair. She was tempted to slip her shoes off under the table, but instead put her purse on the floor, hooking the strap to her knee, ever aware she was "packing."

She had forgotten all about the gun when that construction crew leader caught her on the old Clark place, she chided herself laughingly. He was a "good 'ol boy," guarding the secrets of his clients like a hawk. He never did tell her who had bought the property. She decided to ask Lucious. That was, if she could ever catch up with him.

She hadn't heard from him all day. She called the station and was told he wasn't in, but was given no other details. She decided not to leave a message, for fear he'd drop whatever he was doing and come running to her rescue.

It would have been a futile trip, she thought. Although she could think of one thing he could do to rescue her from her boredom, she amused herself.

Sighing, she drank another sip of her beer, then sat up with her elbows on the table. Since he hadn't been called to investigate a shooting today, she thought chuckling, he must have figured she was all right.

Her gaze scanned the club. Maxine had to admit she was a little impressed. Murals of Hannibal adorned the walls; even with the dim lighting, his conquests and his elephants crossing the Alps were visible. Everything else was regulation club décor: small round tables complete with candles burning in cheap vases.

She clubbed infrequently in Houston, preferring small parties and get-togethers with friends and close associates. She enjoyed a busy life, both professionally and socially, and didn't like spending her down time in smoke-filled bars with strangers.

The tempo, the style, and the volume of the music changed. It picked up, contained choruses to dance by. Before she took her next sip of beer, couples were on the dance floor. Sitting with her back pressed against the chair, she concentrated . . . to block out the music from her head, the useless muses from her mind.

Who knew she was coming to town?

"Nobody," she muttered in the glass as she drank.

Well, nobody she knew, Maxine amended, setting the glass on the table. It dawned on her that someone out for revenge wouldn't have been waiting until she came to town; he, or she, couldn't have known that. Besides, if revenge was the motive, then that individual would have sought her out, even if it meant tracking her to Houston.

The pondering led her to one conclusion: her presence posed a threat to somebody with something to lose. It had taken her return to Liberty to scare someone enough to want her out of the way . . . permanently.

"Can I get you another beer?"

"Thanks, no," Maxine replied, reaching for her bag. "Just let me get the tab, please."

"That'll be three dollars."

Maxine rolled her eyes at the price of a beer as she withdrew her billfold from the bag. She gave the waitress a five-dollar bill. "Don't worry about the change."

"Thank you," the waitress said as she left to take another order.

Maxine sipped the rest of her beer. Her hand still on the handle of the glass, she felt as if one matter was solved. Confident she was on the right track at last, she thought about her next strategy: Mike. She trusted him, she thought. More importantly, he would know who the newcomers to town were.

However, she was still wondering whether Dr. Hofsteader's murder had anything to do with her. She hoped she wasn't raising a ghost with her concern. Even Lucious didn't know why he had a copy of her father's death certificate.

Her father could have been suffering chest pains for years and not said a word, nor done anything about it. She couldn't recall him ever being sick, and knowing him, he found even a headache an abomination, an insult he wouldn't acknowledge.

But there was nothing suspicious about natural cause, she thought, blowing out her cheeks.

While plausible that her father's death had been manufactured, there was another possibility that didn't have a thing to do with him at all. *It could be nothing more than the hospital's chief of staff reviewing documents,* she rationalized.

Or, she thought, her hand over her mouth with amazement on her face, *he was reviewing the work performed by doctors he was responsible for. Namely, one doctor: Charles White, Sr.*

Her father had been no less talented and competent than any other police officer; still, she knew he had to be twice and even three times as good as anybody else. Dr. White, regardless of his education and training, was still an African-American; hence, his work was subject to constant review.

Could Hofsteader's possession of her father's death certificate be as simple as the chief of staff double-checking the work of his black cardiologist?

"Wanna dance?"

It was that time, Maxine thought, her eyes scaling up a long, dark arm. "No, thank you," she said to the gold-toothed man. Slipping her handbag onto her shoulder as she stood, she explained because it was prudent to do so, "I'm calling it an evening."

"Oh, got to get home to the old man, huh?"

"Yeah," Maxine replied. She didn't even bother to correct him as she started for the exit.

"Tell Lucious Larry said hi."

Maxine didn't stop walking as she shook her head amused. "I will," she promised.

That night was a repeat of a previous one for Maxine. Instead of sleeping in peaceful, dreamless oblivion, she tossed and turned her way into a fitful sleep.

She dreamed of dead babies crying. A miniature skeleton chased her around the old shack where Lester Clark had lived with his sister as his wife. Bunches of them appeared. They kept popping up everywhere she went . . . springing at her from the top of the file cabinets in her father's office, skipping on the freeway behind her car, jumping out from behind the bushes on the trail.

They weren't talking or giving her clues. They were just crying. It was a dirgeful wail, like that of an old woman in grief, not the pitiful whine of a baby. Little bitty skeletons all over the place.

With her nightmare melding seamlessly into wakefulness, Maxine sat up in bed. She toyed with the idea of getting up for a glass of milk. Maybe a beer would be better.

"Don't make a sound."

That was a surefire way of ensuring the opposite, Maxine processed quickly, her mouth open to scream. Before it left her throat, a hand clamped over her mouth. She froze instinctively—at least on the outside—for her innards were involved in a fervid war dance, with her heart beating a tom-tom in her bosom.

"We're not going to harm you," the voice promised.

We, Maxine keyed in on. She quieted and her senses picked up the truth of the spokesman's words, noting the hand over her mouth was a soft one. Albeit big, it was untouched by hard work. Her chest stopped quivering, and the hand was removed.

"You won't get hurt."

"Then what the hell are you doing in my house?" Maxine flinched inwardly, hearing her mouth talking shit. While she was scared, a point proven by the fact that her heart was still pounding out a furious beat, she didn't feel in fear of her life. It was then that she realized the last voice she'd heard was different from the first. It was a tenor, and it had a nervous edge to it.

"I just came to tell you it ain't me."

Same voice, but more forceful than before, she noted. It was pitch black in her room; no shadows anywhere. She distinguished the rhythm of two . . . three different breathing patterns. There was movement at her side from where the hand had come. The individual stepped away from the bed.

"You got to call off your dog."

Dog? Maxine frowned, befuddled. She knew she was wide awake. Maybe this was some new language with its own secret code that teenagers spoke these days.

Aw, she breathed knowingly. The base word was teenager, and she realized who—at least one of them—was in her room. "Please accept my apologies, Charles White, Jr.," she said unapologetically. There was outrage in her voice: she wanted to get up and take a belt to his butt. Instead, prudence ruled. Slowly, imperceptibly, she slid her hand under her pillow . . . her fingers inching toward the gun.

"I wouldn't do nothing to you." It was almost a plea. "Your ol' man was good to me. I know he did what he had to do."

By "ol' man," Maxine inferred he was talking about her father. It was also clear that Lucious had gotten around to interviewing the young Mr. White.

"Why couldn't you come to me in the light of day?" she asked.

"Why didn't you come to me?" he shoved the words back in her face. "You were at my house. You followed me and my friends to the mall. You couldn't ask me nothing?" There was anger, outrage in his voice.

"You seemed busy the last time I saw you." Maxine knew her reply was weak, but she didn't want to get into a lecture about discretion in investigatory work.

"That's all I come to say. Call off L.K. I can't get in no more trouble."

Processing L.K. to mean Lucious Kimble, she asked, "And why is that?" her voice lifted in sarcasm.

"My dad's gonna get me a car if I stay out of trouble the rest of the summer."

"I see," Maxine replied. Maybe she should try bribery.

"Well . . . good night."

Maxine heard the footsteps as they shuffled from the room. As she got up to get that beer, she heard car doors slam, then the engine start. Before she made it to the kitchen, that red Mustang was gone.

Chapter 14

Maxine decided not to tell Lucious about her midnight visit from Charles, Jr., only her change of heart about him as a suspect. It looked as if she wouldn't get to do that anytime soon.

"I'm back."

"Back from where?" Maxine replied into her cell phone. She was sitting at the desk in her father's old office at Chambers Investigation, with her notes opened next to her laptop. The laptop's screen was opened on the homepage of the Liberty Appraisal District. Inactive, the screensaver of floating fish appeared, with the sound of gurgling water.

"I'll tell you all about it later," Lucious replied. "Where are you?"

"At the office," she replied, propping the phone between her ear and shoulder so that she could talk and type at the same time.

"What are you doing at the office?"

"I needed to go online and look up some information," she replied, pressing a button on the computer. While talking, the screen she wanted returned, and she scrolled down the site. "In order to do that, I had to come to the office because there's no line at the house." She stopped to ask, "Were you able to get the phone records?"

"I'll tell you later," he stated firmly.

Maxine frowned with a look of annoyance on her face, wondering what was going on: why couldn't he just tell her *yes* or *no?* He broke into her peeved musing. "When are you going to be done?"

"I plan to leave here shortly," she replied, thinking this shouldn't take long as she clicked on the word RECORDS. "I've got a couple of errands to run, but they can wait. I can meet you someplace; just tell me where."

"I've got something else to do first," he said.

Pausing pensively as the screen rolled to the next page on the site, Maxine could tell Lucious knew she was anxious to hear his news. She felt as if she had not been doing much else except guessing lately, and none of her guesses had been accurate. The screen showed REAL PROPERTY and BUSINESS & MINERAL PROPERTY, from which she had four search methods to choose from. She clicked on the last choice, ADDRESS.

"Then I guess I'll proceed with my original plans," she said, watching another page come up from her previous effort. It showed a form.

"What would that be?"

Typing in the address from her notes onto the page online, Maxine replied, "I've decided to do that barbecue tomorrow night, so I'm going to the store to get a few things." Clicking SEARCH, she decided not to tell him that Mike's was her first stop after she left the office: she could keep secrets, too. "I called Barbara this morning before I left the house. She promised to invite a few people. Why don't you invite some, too? But don't invite Larry," she added hastily. The brother had too much gold in his mouth for her, she recalled.

"Where did you see Larry?"

Maxine started to tell the truth, but changed her mind. "I'll tell you later."

"Oh, so it's like that, huh?"

"That line is so tired," she chided him, amused. "Where's the best place to shop for fresh meat?"

"Right here."

Maxine shuddered visibly as a smile broke out across her face. She rearranged her posture lazily in the chair, the on-line site temporarily abandoned. "Well, come on over and let me baste you up with a dash of paprika, and rub some lemon juice all over you, and stuff you with some fresh garlic," she said, her voice enticingly low and soft.

"Ooo," he said chuckling. "Sounds like fun. Don't start without me, okay. I'll meet you at the house . . . say about six."

Maxine promptly returned to her previous position. The man just had no romance in his heart, she thought. But it wasn't exactly his heart she wanted right now, was it? "Why so long?" she asked, her eyes scanning the summary of her search results.

"If I get away sooner, I'll be there sooner. Take care."

"Yeah," Maxine replied absently, her eyes riveted on the screen. The dial tone buzzing in her ear, she ended the call, closed the phone, and set it on the desk. Her eyes never left the screen that revealed not only a legal description of the property, but the appraised value of $100,000. The land alone was worth $85,000, but it was the owner's name that surprised her: Sylvia Hunter.

It was another beautiful, albeit, super-hot day. Not even noon, and Maxine's clothes were sticking to her skin. She was fighting lethargy, as well as the extra weight of the gun in her straw bag. She wished she'd left it in the car as she leaned against the car Mike was working on at his shop.

"She's from here, but she's only been back for a couple of months," Mike replied. "Well, maybe a little longer than that," he amended, lifting his head from under the hood of the car with a dipstick in his hand.

Having discovered the oil level was low, Mike walked to the back wall that was stocked with car supplies and pulled down a red plastic bottle and a funnel. When he returned to the car, he said, "I don't think she's going to stay long, though."

"What makes you think that?"

"I hear she's selling off some property," Mike replied, sticking the funnel in the fill tube. Twisting the top off the bottle, he added, "She brought in an old truck the other day that she wants me to try and sell." He poured the oil in the funnel. "The bumper's got to be fixed first," he said, wiping his hands on a rag he pulled from his back pocket.

"Do you know who's buying her property?"

"I hear Dr. White is in the running for that old Clark place. But that just may be talk," Mike said, with a shrug.

"What about Barbara Goldman?" Maxine asked.

Mike nearly cut her off with his reply. "She's not from here."

He was not the first person to tell her that, and she couldn't seem to get it through her thick skull. "How long has she been in town?"

"Hmmm," Mike pondered, absently fiddling with the rag. "About the same time as Ms. Sylvia. Maybe after she came, but not long in between."

"Thanks, Mike," Maxine said on a long sigh. "I appreciate it."

"Well, I don't know how much help I was," he said with his customary self-effacing manner.

She didn't either, Maxine thought, adjusting her straw bag on her shoulder. She was still pondering whether Sylvia's ownership of the old Clark place was relevant.

"Your car should be ready by next Tuesday," he said.

"I'll be back in Houston by then," Maxine said. She had made reservations before she spoke to Barbara this morning to fly out of Savannah Saturday night, she recalled. She had to remember to ask Lucious to drive her to the airport.

"When you call to let me know for sure it's ready, I'll decide then whether to have it flown to Houston, or figure how to make another trip back here next weekend."

She was sitting on his bare back, reveling in his complete vulnerability to her. Like putty in her hands. Hands warm and tender and loving as they slowly slid up and down his back, slippery from the cool raspberry oil.

She could see the tension rippling his body as he tried to maintain his cool. She could almost feel his muscles bunch up, then relax when she massaged every inch of his back . . . and down. She didn't intend to leave a speck of his flesh untouched.

Just the thought of it fired every nerve in Maxine's body, filling her with anticipatory excitement. Standing at the counter in her kitchen, mixing dry ingredients to baste the meats for the barbecue, she shivered.

Nearly dumping too much salt, she chided herself. "Better pay attention to what you're doing and stop daydreaming," she said, moving to stand over the sink, littered with slabs of ribs, strings of smoked hot sausages, four fryers, and a roast.

She swayed absently to the beat of Al Green singing "Love and Happiness" from the miniature Bose radio that Sam had bought their father last Christmas. She hoped the music didn't change by the time Lucious arrived.

Leaving Mike's, she went to the grocery store to make the necessary purchases for the barbecue. Before heading for home, she made a last-minute side trip to the bath and beauty shop, where she bought all kinds of scented bath beads and oils. As a matter of fact, she thought, she had enough for this weekend and the next. Just in case she had to come back to Liberty, she told herself.

She had time for just one more trip when Lucious phoned to say he was going to be later than expected, she recalled, thinking of the other little thing she'd purchased. She could hardly wait to see his expression when she modeled it for him, she thought, pouring her liquid mix over the meat. A wave of warmth shivered along her pulse as she began to rub the seasonings into each piece. There was a knock on the kitchen door, and her adrenaline level shot up like a flash.

Maxine looked from her hands to the door. "Just a minute," she called, turning the faucet head away from the meat to rinse her hands under the running water. She grabbed a nearby dishtowel and headed for the door, wiping her hands.

"Barbara . . ." Maxine said, startled, opening the door. "I didn't hear you drive up," she said, wondering why she'd come to the back door. She had assumed it was Lucious.

"I was in the neighborhood," Barbara replied. "May I come in?"

"Oh, sure," Maxine replied, stepping aside.

Barbara walked in, and Maxine closed the door. "I remember you said you always let your meat sit overnight, and I wanted to see what you put in it."

"That's what I'm doing now," Maxine replied. "Can I get you a beer?"

"If you're having one," Barbara replied. She sat at the kitchen table and looked around as Maxine headed for the refrigerator.

"Now what are you doing in this neighborhood?" Maxine asked. She pulled the top from the lid, then tossed it in the trash and handed the can to Barbara. "Glass?"

"No, thanks," Barbara replied. She took a sip of beer.

"Just checking out property for sale," Barbara replied. "My tax man is telling me that I better collect some debts; otherwise, I'll end up giving Uncle Sam everything."

"And we can't have that now, can we?" Maxine replied, with just enough annoyance in her voice to let her feelings be known. It was obvious Barbara was looking to become an absentee landlord to some poor African-American family: that's who lived on this side of town.

Barbara must have gotten the message, for she began fiddling with the pearls around her neck. "I hear you and your sisters have decided to keep Chambers Investigation open," she said.

Returning to her work at the sink, Maxine chuckled. "Who told you that?"

"It's all over town."

"As usual," Maxine said, "I'm the last one to know. I haven't spoken to my sisters since I faxed them a report on the company's finances."

"Is it true?"

"No decision has been made with regards to the company," Maxine replied, her back to Barbara, her hands again messy with oil and seasonings as she rubbed the meat. She wondered why she suddenly felt uncomfortable, why she was looking at the set of knives in the wooden block at the opposite end of the counter, calculating how long it would take her to reach them.

"That's too bad."

"What?" Maxine asked quizzically before she turned to look at Barbara. Her attention fine-tuned on the gun, pointed her way, in Barbara's hand. She stood there as though fastened to a wall, her heart thumping against her rib cage, staring transfixed at the gun.

"Too bad you came back here, too bad you didn't take care of y'alls business when your sisters were here with you, too bad you wouldn't leave well enough alone," Barbara said as calmly as if rattling off a grocery list.

"I wasn't sure at first," Barbara continued. "I was going to leave it alone when it was quite evident that nature was going to take care of Henry for me. Then I learned about the cases he left y'all to finish up for him."

All pretense of her gentle nature vanished; hatred warped her face.

"I didn't have a case!" Maxine wanted to slap herself. The first breath she'd taken since seeing that gun, and what does she say? Her brain was definitely not in it, she thought, desperately trying to get her fear under control. *Panic will get you killed,* she remembered her father saying.

"It doesn't matter. When you came, Owen remembered. He started doing some checking," Barbara said, gritting her teeth with disgust. Her eyes were orbs of gray-green granite. "Your father recognized me in the hospital. At first, I didn't think he did; I couldn't see how. I don't look at all like I did when I left here thirty years ago." Her expression metamorphosed quickly to that of a guileless woman with an aura of youth and touch of class. "I can thank my late husband and Dr. Roger Blake, the cosmetic surgeon who made me the beautiful, desirable woman I am today."

Maxine had to agree that the description of a scrawny little kid that Gloria had described as Sarah Clark didn't come close to looking like the woman standing in her kitchen with a gun, not a Winchester rifle. She disagreed with one thing, however; Barbara Goldman/Sarah Clark was insane. Her father was right on that count, after all. "Where are they? Dead, too?"

"I'm afraid so," Barbara said softly, without regret.

"Nobody knew who you were," Maxine said rationally. Barbara flashed a look of disbelief. "Owen, maybe," she conceded. More than likely, she thought, when her father recognized Barbara, he asked the doctor to do some checking for him. "You were safe. Nobody had a clue." Except Henry Chambers, she thought proudly, and there was little he could do from his hospital bed.

"Owen contacted Mercy," Barbara replied. "They told him they had to let one of their doctors go because he became involved with one of the patients. After that, it was just a matter of time."

Guessing, Maxine said, "You were the patient and the doctor they fired was your first husband?"

"Yeah, you know men," Barbara said. "Give 'em a little pussy, and they lose their minds," she laughed gaily.

"Yeah," Maxine concurred with a nod as she slid sideways.

"I'm not stupid, so don't be dumb," Barbara warned her, her violence bubbling to the surface again. She held the gun a little tighter, a little straighter at Maxine.

"What I don't understand is how you found out that Owen was doing some checking," Maxine said, stalling. She didn't care who found out what right now: she was buying time toward freedom.

"I had my ways," Barbara said. She lifted her left hand to check the watch on her delicate wrist. "It's almost time to go."

"What are you planning?" Maxine asked, her heart picking up speed in her bosom.

There was a knock on the back door. That had to be Lucious, Maxine thought, relief coursing through her. But only for a second, for she realized that he would be putting himself in as much danger as she was if he walked through that door. The thought of him shot and killed caused the blood to slide through her veins like cold needles. Why didn't she give that man a little more lovin'? Why didn't she take all he offered?

But Barbara didn't look concerned at all about being discovered and caught, she noticed, frowning curiously.

"Stand over there," Barbara commanded her away from the sink with a wave of the gun.

Maxine obeyed, while Barbara backed her way to the door. Her eyes and the gun remained on Maxine as she reached behind her to unlock the door and twist the knob.

She had found a villain in everybody except Barbara Goldman, Maxine was thinking. Dr. White would have been next, but she was waiting to hear what Lucious had to report first. Lord, if he walked through the door, she promised never to try her hand at investigation work again. Give her the bank any old day.

The door opened and Sylvia Hunter walked in, wearing a

yellow jumpsuit, dressed in cheer. Maxine blinked doubly confused.

Barbara was all business. "Got the car?" she asked Sylvia.

"In place at the end of the trail," Sylvia replied in a Valley Girl voice. "Hi, Maxine," she said, wiggling her fingers in a wave.

Maxine realized she must have looked like a retard, standing there with her mouth open, perplexed as hell.

"I needed a little help with you, sister girl," Barbara said as if that were a compliment, with amusement in her face.

"What did you touch?" Sylvia asked, making herself at home in the kitchen.

"That can of beer. Pour it out and we'll take it with us. Oh, don't forget to grab a bottle of seasoning or something."

"For what?" Maxine blurted out. She couldn't help herself.

Looking over the seasonings on the counter, Sylvia replied, "So it'll look like you ran out of something and left to go to the grocery store."

"Do you know that her brother killed your grandmother?" Maxine asked, with outrage in her voice.

"She was a mean old bitch," Sylvia replied, selecting a bottle of ground cinnamon. "I didn't like her no way." She emptied the can of beer down the drain. "That might be good on the meat," she said, pocketing the can. "Where are the car keys?"

Using the gun as a pointer, Barbara said, "There they are on the floor by the chair."

Sylvia picked up the straw bag and handed it to Maxine. "I'm not sticking my hands in this junkie thing," she said with disdain. "Get your keys out of there."

Maxine nearly gasped gratitude. *Please, Lord!* she begged silently, *Don't fail me now*. Her hands were shaking as she reached inside her bag and pulled out her set of keys. It didn't take a genius to see that they had thought of everything. Well, almost; they couldn't have known about the gun. She applauded their planning nevertheless.

Sylvia snatched the keys from her, then sassily walked to the back door. She kissed Barbara on the cheek. "Good luck," she said, before slipping out into the night.

Barbara's gaze swept the room. "That's it. Let's go."

Maxine followed the direction of the pointed gun. With every step, she felt her breathing become more shallow, her muscles growing rigid, her heart beating more eager for life as she walked out the back door. She prayed it wasn't a march to her death, gripping the handles of her bag as she walked out the kitchen door.

Barbara followed close behind.

Chapter 15

"Your father stole the only thing I ever truly loved in this world. Can you imagine how I felt . . . a sixteen-year-old girl left alone in this world? I didn't have nobody after Lester was gone . . ."

Maxine knew she would never understand Barbara's pining over the love she lost in the incestuous relationship with her murdering brother. The fact that she was now intimately involved with Sylvia revealed just how emotionally damaged she was. There was no reasoning with her: Barbara would never admit that she was sick in the head.

"Lester took care of me. I knew he took other women, but it was me he loved. Me. Nobody else. He was the best. Even better than your Lucious."

Maxine wanted to ask about Charles White, but Sylvia's presence answered that, for it was apparent Barbara was using him to cover her relationship with Sylvia. An African-American man was more acceptable than another woman, especially in Liberty. Besides, Maxine reminded herself, she had to find an opportunity to escape while keeping her feet under her on the dark trail. The penlight Barbara forced her to carry was so small she could barely see in front of her.

"Those doctors at Mercy kept telling me it wasn't normal. Moral," she rasped snidely. "Moral, my ass. At first I wouldn't listen to them. I wouldn't speak to them at all that first year. Then when I did, I was too stupid to realize that if I just went along that I'd be able to get out of that place."

"Duh," Maxine silently chided Barbara, and then nearly tripped. Reacting too soon she caught herself, instead of falling. *Serve you right,* her big sister would have scolded. Now, she'd have to wait for another chance to stumble.

"But I figured it out soon enough. And when I did, I couldn't believe it took me so long," Barbara laughed. "All I had to do was flash my womanly wiles. I had plenty of practice with Lester. I didn't think he would mind. That's probably what held me back in the first place," Barbara rambled on.

Where was that snarled branch that curled in and out of the ground? Maxine asked herself. She remembered tripping over it the first day she ran this trail. But they were not far along enough; they had just passed the pond.

"I started with an orderly, but that was too easy," Barbara said with a tsk. "I tried an intern, but he wouldn't fall for it. He was too . . . ethical." She accented the word mockingly. "Then came the man I ultimately married. It took six months before all that talk about normal and ethical and moral flew right out the window," she said, laughing, amused. "He declared me healthy enough, and Mercy let me go, then he joined me. Of course by that time they'd fired him because some old prude nurse told about our affair. But we didn't have anything to worry about because they weren't going to say anything and ruin the institution's chances of getting its state funding. After that it was a piece of cake. Until you came back and Owen started digging into people's business.

"Sylvia didn't like him no way. He was a bore. An absolute utter bore. I hated the time she had to spend with him."

Maxine tripped and let herself fall to the ground.

"You clumsy bitch!" Barbara screamed. "Get up."

As Maxine slowly got to her feet, making sure they were planted apart, she grabbed the top of her straw bag, and swung it upwards with all her strength into Barbara's face.

Everything after that happened just like in the movies: Barbara dropped her gun and fell over backwards. Maxine pounced on her. Barbara was stronger than she looked; for every fist she took, she gave back. The women were on the ground, wrestling and rolling over branches, each going for superiority over the other. Barbara grabbed a branch and swung it, missing Maxine's head. It broke on her shoulder, but the pain enraged Maxine more, gave her that extra strength she needed.

And that was all it took.

Chapter 16

With the door of the refrigerator open, Maxine shoved the large roasting pan filled with meat inside. The barbecue was definitely on for tomorrow, she thought, closing the door. She didn't care that her guests would be members of the Liberty Police Department.

The cavalry arrived late, as usual. *If you want it done right, do it yourself,* she recalled her father saying many times. The town would be in shock by morning, when it learned two of its fine, outstanding citizens were locked behind bars.

"What I didn't tell you about the certificate we found in Hofsteader's bathroom was that he'd written a phone number on it," Lucious said.

Leaning with her back on the refrigerator door and arms folded across her bosom, Maxine looked at Lucious headlong. A sense of tingling delight began to flow through her. He was sitting at the table, still wearing the excited energy those in law enforcement felt at the successful end of a case. Her father had been like that, she recalled fondly.

"The area code was a no-brainer, but I was surprised to find out who it was," he continued.

Maxine didn't want to hear all this now. She had the answers she needed. Even from his hospital bed, knowing his end was near, her father was doing what he most loved, investigating. She was comforted by the thought and now, just wanted to cuddle and be held. "Who was it?" she asked, taking a seat next to Lucious at the table.

"It was the number to Mercy in Savannah," he said with eureka. "I spoke with Dr. Banfield, the new administrator."

"I'm all ears," Maxine replied. She wasn't the only one who experienced an unpleasant adventure. She learned of Lucious's escapade while she showered, washing away residual anxieties, lathering in soap and confidence of her safety. On his way to her house, later than he had promised to arrive, he spotted her father's car, driven by a woman other than she. He chased Sylvia down, and in enraged fear, she taunted him for being too late to save her life. Sylvia was only half-wrong, she thought, gravitating to the pull of his masculinity.

"That's who I spoke with," Lucious was saying. "He informed me that Dr. Hofsteader had already called him. He was looking into the situation when I called. Now, I'm afraid I have to make a little assumption to explain what I think happened."

"I'm still listening," she said, a wistful sigh in her throat, wishing he would hurry. This time was just a little different from the last time she nearly lost her life, Maxine thought, pleased with herself. Again wearing barely nothing—the other little something she purchased—under her father's robe, fear compounded her emotions then. This time, lust was all alone in her body.

"Stop that," he said, capturing her wayward hands, which were absently stroking his forearm.

"There's something about death that makes me want to keep close contact with warm flesh and blood." With the warmth of his touch shooting through her body, she rather liked his quiet, deep nature, she thought, no longer threatened by his secrets: she knew how to get them out of him, and tingled with delight.

"Banish the thought, 'cause you're not dead," he said, leaning over to give her a quick kiss on the mouth. Sitting back, he resumed, stating, "Your father may have recognized Barbara Goldman when he was in the hospital."

Maxine started to tell him that Barbara had already filled in the holes he was still grappling with in his story. He would find out tomorrow when she gave an official report to the police. Other things occupied her mind tonight; now, watching his eyes, the way they glazed dreamily when he was excited. He was almost where she intended to have him eventually, thinking about the raspberry oil. She could almost smell it on his body.

"Even though she had had cosmetic surgery, your father must have seen something familiar in her. I'm guessing he said as much to Dr. Hofsteader. He wouldn't trust Dr. White because he wasn't from here. I don't know why Hofsteader just didn't go to the police, but I suspected he wanted to be sure and not run the risk of ruining someone's reputation if he were wrong. Anyway . . ."

"Dr. Banfield suggested we look for a lesbian couple, or a prostitute who served male and female clients," Lucious said, explaining what typically happened to a child exposed to an incestuous relationship. "Well, when I got back here . . ."

"Lucious . . . ," Maxine said, cutting him off. "Do you want to be my friend?"

He frowned that familiar bewildered look of his, his brows drawn together in an agonized expression. "I thought I was," he replied.

"Now that we have that out of the way," she said primly, thinking she had another reason to return to Liberty as she leaned over to grab the front of his shirt. He made two, now. "Then shut up and kiss me."

"Oh," he said startled, but not displeased. "It's like that, huh?"

Maxine bobbed her head up and down. With a smile on her face and eyes riveted on his mouth, she said, "Yeah, that's how it is."

•—◆—•

Whoever said that Liberty, Georgia, was a place where nothing happened was sorely mistaken, Purvis thought as he stared out of his office window. Below, the town looked quiet and peaceful, ready for a Polaroid. But Henry knew better and Maxine found out the hard way. Girl nearly got herself killed in the process.

He shook his head in disbelief. When the slow-moving word about what had happened to Maxine finally made its way to him at his cabin on the outskirts of Marietta, Maxine had wrapped everything up and looked as if she'd hooked that good-looking kid Lucious Kimble along the way.

He took out his pipe and lit it. Inhaling deeply, he blew out a cloud of cherry-scented smoke into the air.

If there was one thing that could be said about Henry's daughters, they were smart cookies. But even smart cookies could crumble. From here on out, he was going to stay close at hand—just in case he needed to pick up any pieces.

Crazy woman, double lives, dead bodies—what next?

THE BAD PENNY

Shirley Hailstock

Chapter 1

"Start with the body" Taylor Chambers had heard that before. Her ex-cop, ex-husband often said it when he was working homicide. Taylor was no detective. She was a lawyer, a corporate attorney. She dealt with taxes, estates, and contracts. She knew nothing about surveillance, tracking down victims, or detective work. She hired detectives to work for her. Yet she couldn't pawn this case off on one of her firm's staff. Her father had trapped her. She was supposed to be on a plane back to her law practice in New Jersey following the reading of his will, but she'd been ambushed by his last request. She would start with the body, but she had no body. Susan Hilliard Frasier had vanished into thin air. She had not been seen by anyone who knew her in six years. If she was alive, she didn't want to be found.

Taylor pulled the car to a stop outside the Liberty Police Department. "Daddy, what are you doing?" she muttered to herself. Her voice caught, and she stemmed a fresh flow of tears. As she turned off the engine, she remembered her father bringing her here when he worked for the Liberty police. She used to love coming. He'd pretend she was his assistant, and he'd give her work to occupy her time. She was sure she'd been a major help to him then, filing papers and typing up letters on the word processor. He never let her read any of his cases, open or closed. "Confidentiality," he'd tell her.

The blue legal-size folder her father's lawyer had given her lay in her briefcase on the seat next to her. She'd read it more than a dozen times. Identical folders, in big white envelopes, had been passed to each of Henry Chambers's four offspring. Like being given grade-school exam folders, they had accepted their assignments. Each daughter, except Maxine, got a different case that Henry Chambers had not solved before he died. He wanted his daughters to solve them. This was her final exam, administered by her father, but Henry Chambers would not be there to see her succeed or fail.

Susan Hilliard Frasier: Missing Person. Taylor could see the typewritten tab sticking out of the corner of the case file. The fifty-three-year-old Savannah socialite had been missing for six years. In another year her family could declare her legally dead and finally start spending the fortune that had been in limbo since her disappearance. And a motley crew they were: vultures circling the almost-dead body. Taylor could already hear the sound of plastic ringing through cash registers. Everyone from Frasier's daughter to distant cousins was vying for a piece of her fortune.

Taylor stepped out of her rented, air-conditioned car at the twin oak trees that guarded the entrance to Liberty. Spanish moss clung to the branches, giving the whole place a look that said time had not touched this area of the earth. Everything here was as it had been from the moment she left it. The gauzy haze held time in place. Taylor loved the moss, though most people thought of it as a nuisance.

The heat surrounded her, sucking the cooled air away in one quick swoop. Her white suit clung to her skin, and quickly her comfort level was gone. She crossed the street and skipped up the stairs and into the building. The Liberty

Police Department's main building was a two-story structure that used to be the plantation home of Marcus and Kathleen Liberty. They'd given their name to the town and, after the emancipation, lost their family home to taxes. It had passed through several hands, but eventually became the police department.

The Missing Persons Department was on the second floor. Taylor walked up the wide, palatial staircase that spoke of an era that would never have imagined black boots stomping down the rungs next to the banister that had been carved in intricate detail by the slave-artists who called this house their home. She went through the glass service door and stood in front of a long, wooden counter that had more scratches and gouges than smooth surface. The room was brightly lit from huge windows that needed washing. An air conditioner had been placed in a hole cut in the wall. It chugged in an attempt to cool the room and its one occupant.

"May I help you?" A female sitting behind a metal desk typed on a computer. She neither looked up nor got up when Taylor walked in.

"Hello, Maize."

The woman glanced at Taylor, looking over the half-glasses that were attached to a cord around her neck. She pulled them off, and surprise replaced the perplexed look on her face.

"Oh, my God!" she shouted. "As I live and breathe. I never thought I'd set eyes on the likes of you again." Maize Brondell pushed her chair back and got up. She weighed twice as much as she had when Taylor had last seen her five years ago, yet she moved with agility. Coming to the battered counter, she took Taylor's hand in both of hers and squeezed it. "I was sorry to hear about your dad," she said, her face taking on a serious continence. "You know I always liked your daddy."

"Thank you." Taylor paused. She pulled her hand free. "How is your family?"

"They're all fine. Mother was in the hospital last year. Broken hip." She whispered the last as if she were saying her mother had syphilis or something equally dreadful. "My brother, James, moved to Memphis last spring. He's still starting one business after another. I don't know if that boy is ever gonna find something he likes. I pray he does." She rolled her eyes toward the ceiling, clearly telling Taylor she really felt the opposite. "And all my sisters are right here and fine. Now what can I do for you?"

"Actually, dad is the reason I'm here. He had several cases he was working on when he died, and I'm going to complete one of them. It involves a missing person."

"A missing person?" Maize frowned when she asked. "I don't know of any missing person your daddy was involved with."

"Susan Hilliard Frasier."

"Henry wasn't working on that." She dragged the last word out as if it had two syllables. Taylor had forgotten the slow twang that used to be incorporated in her own speech and how hard she'd worked to eradicate it. A word here and there came back now and then, especially when she was angry or when she was here in the surroundings of her childhood.

"It wasn't his last case. It was an open one, at least to him. You knew dad, so you know how he hated leaving things unsolved." Taylor gave her a tired smile.

"Let's see." Maize consulted the ceiling as she tapped her index finger against her cheek. "Susan Frasier must have gone missing seven, eight years ago."

"Six," Taylor corrected.

"She wasn't even from here. She's from up in Savannah."

"I know," Taylor told her. Savannah was actually twenty miles south of Liberty, but directions in the south were always up from wherever you were. Taylor found it ironic, since north was up and diehard confederates ranked the north and hell as two heads on the same coin. Maize, despite her ruptured smile, hung her flag with pride, but she was quick to say how she wasn't *really* prejudiced.

Maize stared at her. For a long, expectant moment, she looked as if she thought Taylor would leave. Then, with a tight smile, she said, "Let's see what we can find. Although it's been six years. That file is probably buried somewhere."

Taylor recognized a stall when she saw one. She had a masters' degree in stalling herself. She knew how to tie up people in one motion after another. If going to court was necessary, she knew how to ask for a continuance and get it. Maize wasn't quite as skilled as Taylor was, but Taylor knew that no matter where Maize looked, there would be no file on Susan Hilliard Frasier. Three minutes later, Maize confirmed her suspicions.

"Where do you think the files are stored?" Taylor asked.

"We send them to an archive in a mountain somewhere. I really don't know where it is."

"This is an open investigation, Maize. Susan Frasier has never been found. How could her files be sent away?"

Maize pulled her glasses off and let them hang around her neck. She leaned back in her chair. "Taylor, this is Liberty. We're not a big city, and we can't keep everything open forever. If Susan Frasier is still alive and wants to be found, all she has to do is pick up a phone. There's no crime associated with her. The woman is free—" Maize stopped. Taylor could have completed her sentence. She knew the woman was about to tell her that Susan Frasier was free, white, and over twenty-one. "She can go where she pleases," Maize finished weakly.

"You don't think it's a little strange that she left a teenage daughter without a word? And all that money?"

Maize shrugged. "Some people just have no sense of family."

"Did you ever meet Susan Frasier?"

Maize shook her head. "She came to the hospital fund-raiser one year. 'Course her husband Robert was on the committee then. That's the only time I was ever in the same room with her."

"Well, thank you, Maize." Taylor turned to leave. "Say hello to your mother for me."

"I will." Maize's voice sang the word.

Taylor had no doubt her mother would know she'd been asking questions. She turned back and glanced through the glass. Maize hadn't even waited for her to get out of eyesight before she was on the phone. No doubt by suppertime everyone in Liberty would know she'd opened the Susan Hilliard Frasier case.

Taylor shivered and remembered the old folks' saying when this happened on an apparently warm day. *Someone had just walked over her grave.*

Chapter 2

The heat outside was brutal. It pressed against her like sweaty hands. By mid-August the place would be one huge frying pan. Taylor pulled her sunglasses from her purse and slipped them on. She still had to squint. She felt like going back to her room and calling Kenneth. She would like to hear his voice. She regretted insisting that he return to New Jersey after the funeral. There was only the reading of the will to get through. Her father didn't have much to leave them. There was the house, which she didn't want. She earned enough to take care of herself and her daughter—more than enough. There was no need for him to stay when he had pressing responsibilities at home.

She'd expected to follow Kenneth back the next day, but that hadn't happened. He was there and she was still in Liberty and likely to be for the next couple of weeks. Yet she wanted to talk to him. Reaching for her cell phone, she started for the car. She got as far as the curb before hearing someone call her name. Turning around, she saw Sam Turner hurrying toward her.

"Sam," she smiled as he neared her. She dropped the phone back into her purse and reached her hands out. Sam took them both and pulled her into his arms for a bear hug. Taylor was instantly uncomfortable.

"I wanted to speak to you at the funeral," he said, stepping back. "There were so many people around you, and I was on duty. I had to leave before the burial."

"Thanks for coming." Taylor was tired of saying that to everyone she met. Each time she said it, it brought the loss of her father back and she had to swallow the rush of emotion that made her miss him terribly.

"I was just having some coffee," Sam said. "Why don't you join me?"

Taylor was headed for Savannah. She was hoping she'd have more luck at the Missing Persons Department there, but Sam Turner was Susan Frasier's nephew. He might be able to help her. Together they returned to the café next to the police station. When they were seated in a window booth and Taylor had a cup of rich, black coffee in front of her, she looked at Sam. He matched her in height, and he was one of the few men who wasn't intimidated by her six-foot, two-inch frame. His blond hair was already nearly white from the relentless Georgia sun. His face was too ruddy to tan. It was either lobster-red or wet-brick brown. Today he was well on his way to lobster-red. His eyes were dancing and happy, and the lines in his face came from the ready smile he was always willing to give.

Sam's mother and father moved to Liberty when Sam was six years old. He'd spent most of his life within fifty miles of here. He no longer wore a uniform, but he worked for the Liberty Police force.

"Are you staying long?" he asked. "I thought you'd be back at your practice by now." He paused to take a bite of his toast. "Your daddy was fond of telling us how proud he was of you and your sisters."

Taylor took a sip of coffee before answering him. "I don't know how long I'll be here. My dad left me a case he wanted me to solve. I'm staying until I fulfill his request."

"Anything I can do to help?" He looked over his coffee cup. His eyes were clear and inquiring. Taylor liked to read people's eyes. Some of her clients lied to her, and she'd become adept at routing out the truth. Sam didn't appear to have anything to hide.

"You might," she said. "He asked me to find your aunt."

"Aunt Susan?" Surprised, he dropped the cup back in its saucer.

She nodded. "I went to Missing Persons. Dead end. Maize said the file was in storage."

"I have one."

"What?"

He flashed her a smile. "I was, of course, very interested when Aunt Susan disappeared. I gathered everything I could find on her. I have computer files and newspaper clippings, copies of official reports."

"Sam, could I see them?"

"Of course. I'll send copies to the house."

Taylor looked down. She folded her hands and sat back. "I'm not at the house, Sam. I'm staying at the Fulbright Motel."

"That flea-bag. Why are you out there?"

"It's a long story. Maybe I'll tell it to you one day."

Sam didn't press her for an answer. He looked at his watch and said he had to leave. Taylor stayed and ordered breakfast. She hadn't had anything to eat, and after Sam's news she was ravenous. She ordered the full southern breakfast: ham and eggs with biscuits and lots of grits, swimming in tons of brown gravy. She would pay for it. She'd probably have to spend a month of nonstop running on her treadmill, but she ate everything on the plate and finished off two cups of coffee.

While she waited for the check, she looked through the window. She'd grown up here. Her father had lived here all his life. Taylor thought she should have known when something happened to him. She and her father had a connection.

They'd had it since she was a little girl. Of his four daughters, she was the one most like him. Everyone said so. She loved helping him. She wanted to be like him when she grew up. She was sure they could communicate with nothing more than thought waves. Yet those waves had failed to tell her that the signal between her and her father had ceased.

The day he died began the way most of her days did. She arrived at her office and turned on her computer. The mailbox popped up to alert her that she had unread mail. She smiled, knowing there would be a message from her father. On that day it had been there to greet her. She'd read it, smiled, answered him, and deleted his message. Before the day ended, she was an orphan. Message terminated.

Pushing her hair off her face, Taylor picked up the bill and read the amount. She left enough money on the table to more than cover it.

Taylor got in the hot car and turned on the ignition, but she didn't move to put the car in gear or to drive it away. Memory caught her, held her still, like the Spanish moss holding time in place at the entrance to Liberty. She was on a sliding board. It was cold, and she opened her arms as she flew down the incline and into her father's embrace. It was her first memory of him. She was three years old. She only knew that because of a photograph of her in the coat coming down the slide and her mother's handwriting on the back, *Taylor—age 3,* it said. Taylor had the framed copy that used to be on the mantel, next to her sisters', in the family room of the house where she grew up. It wasn't five miles from where she sat now.

Taylor wouldn't go there. A tear slipped from her eye. It rolled over her cheek. There was nothing for her at the house, she told herself. It was just a house and there was no one there anymore. Her sisters were probably on their way back to their homes, and her father was gone. It was just bricks and wood and windows. It held nothing for her.

Wiping her eyes with the tips of her fingers, she spied the

blue legal folder sticking out of her briefcase. Pulling it free, she looked inside. She could smell her father's scent on the pages. *Here's something to do,* it seemed to say. She read through it again. Taylor had seen many such folders, some thicker, some thinner. This one was about an inch thick. Her father's scrawl covered the typewritten pages with notes, questions, thoughts. Taylor felt he was talking to her. For some reason, he'd asked his four daughters to take up banners that had eluded him.

Hers was Susan Hilliard Frasier.

Savannah's Missing Persons Bureau didn't offer any fruit to Taylor's case, but at least she didn't have to fight for the file. The clerk in the office was alone when she got there, as Maize had been back in Liberty. It was during the lunch hour, and the rest of the office staff had gone to eat. Only a seventeen-year-old high school student on an intern program manned the department. When Susan Frasier disappeared six years ago the girl hadn't yet cut her twelve-year molars.

Taylor found nothing outstanding in the folder: a standard photograph of the victim, a statement from her daughter, who reported her missing, and rudimentary police reports, which led nowhere. But a reference to Liberty caught her eye.

"Thank you . . . Dorrie." Taylor read the girl's identification badge hanging around her neck. Dorrie took the dark green folder. "Do you think I could have a copy of the reports in here?"

Dorrie smiled. "Sure, ma'am. There's a copy machine right here." Dorrie pointed to a desktop machine that sat on an old typewriter table. She copied the entire file on the antiquated machine and placed the pages in a large white envelope. She passed it to Taylor. "There you go, Ms. Chambers."

"Thank you again. You've been extremely helpful." Taylor turned to leave, but Dorrie stopped her.

"You're from up north, aren't you?" Taylor heard that question often, but it was usually asked by someone in New Jersey about her being from the South. "I love the way you talk," Dorrie went on. "You're a lawyer." She stated it rather than asked.

"I practice in New Jersey," Taylor told her.

"I'm going to be a lawyer, too," Dorrie told her. "It's why I chose to work here instead of at Six Flags. All my friends wanted the amusement park: free rides and all, you know, the perfect tan by the end of June, but I wanted to learn something about the law."

"Have you done that so far?" Taylor looked around the cramped room. She liked Dorrie. She had paralegals and student interns in her office. She would have hired this energetic young lady, but she would have taught her not to freely give out department information to any stranger who walked through the door.

"Not much," she conceded. "Mostly, I just do filing and entering information in the computer. The files are in really bad shape for a city this size. I can type the files in any order I want. It's rather boring, so I skip around in the years, picking whatever sounds interesting."

Taylor could see this talkative young lady would keep her here all day if she didn't stop her. "I had better go now so you can get back to your work."

"For instance," she said as if she hadn't heard Taylor. "I just saw that your lady, that Mrs. Frasier, she disappeared the same night that the little Dalton girl was killed."

"Dalton girl?" Taylor stopped. "Mrs. Ava Dalton's daughter. From Liberty? Mrs. Dalton taught French at the high school." She'd actually taught at the white high school until they'd integrated it. Taylor had been caught in the court-ordered busing program when she was in grammar school. By the time she went to high school, the demonstrations and people chaining themselves to the school doors had ended.

"That's the one," Dorrie broke into her thoughts. "It was a

big story. I even remember it being in the newspapers and on television when I was a little girl. The Dalton child was raped and murdered. They found her poor little body all battered and bloody, with a bullet in her back, right out there in the woods between here and Liberty. I guess that's why we got a report on her. Both Liberty and Savannah claimed jurisdiction. Finally, Liberty took it. They never did find her killer."

"Dorrie, I don't have any reason to request it, except that Mrs. Dalton was a teacher of mine, but could you give me a copy of the Dalton child's file, too?"

Dorrie was very accommodating. Taylor left the police station with two files in the white envelope. She got back into her car and drove around for half an hour. Savannah was certainly a beautiful city and Taylor played the tourist. Savannah was cut up into squares that sectioned off different architectural styles, time periods and ethnic backgrounds. It had rules and idiosyncrasies like any large city, but here they were softer and more refined. She loved the old restored homes, with their huge windows and histories that went back before slavery. It wasn't all ante-bellum or Sherman on his march. It was fraternities and sororities and traditions that had lived through the decades.

She'd once thought of opening a practice here, buying one of the brick houses with the fancy ironworks and setting herself up within a stone's-throw of her family home, but she hadn't. She'd gone to law school in New Jersey and settled there.

Finally, she left the trees and plazas behind and started for Liberty. She was anxious to read the files Sam promised to send her. Then the Dalton child entered her thoughts. Who would want to kill a child? And did her death and Susan's disappearance have a connection?

Driving was a relaxing adventure for Taylor. She loved to take the car and go for long trips to nowhere. She could turn off the radio or CD player, roll the windows down, and let the fresh air blow through her hair—or roll them up and turn on the air conditioner. Either way, her mind would take in the beauty of the countryside. Often she'd find herself on her way to the shore, driving down the Garden State Parkway where the trees were green and lush and the road was clear of people. Or she'd end up in the mountains near eastern Pennsylvania. The hills sometimes were rolling and the landscape patch-worked; sometimes the elevation could make her ears pop. She'd think of things, solve a problem if she needed to, or just smile at the loveliness of being alive.

Here, where she'd spent her formative years, the land was flatter, but there were more trees—many more trees to keep her insulated from the great expanses of land on the other side of the straight, silvery road.

Taylor thought about people disappearing. Why would someone just leave and not come back? She'd done it. She'd been away from Liberty for five years; longer, if she didn't include the short visit at Christmas four years ago. She'd argued with everyone then and left in anger, but she hadn't disappeared. They all knew where she was. Susan Frasier had gone away and not told anyone she was leaving or communicated with anyone since.

What would make a person do that? Fear came to mind first. She was afraid of something. But what? She was a wealthy woman. She left everything behind. In limbo, according to the notes her father had written in the margin. She couldn't be declared dead for another year, so her money was intact. Her bank accounts hadn't been touched, and no one had heard from her. If it was fear, then she'd be afraid of someone finding out she'd withdrawn money from a bank.

To get away from a bad situation was another reason to leave. According to her father's report and the one Susan's daughter had filed, Susan had no pressing problems. Her bank statements and telephone records showed nothing out of the ordinary. No large withdrawals on a regular basis to indicate blackmail. No telephone calls to unknown numbers. No huge charges to her credit cards. And she maintained her appearances at the charities and organizations that women of her station and society dictated she attend. Then suddenly she was gone, vanished as if she'd been abducted by aliens.

She could be out to punish someone? Who could it be? She was widowed, and her daughter said they were on good terms. There was no indication that her mother would want to punish her.

And worst, she could have been involved in an accident where no one knew her. Her identification could have been lost. It was a long shot in this day and age, but it was a possibility and Taylor was taking all possibilities into consideration.

Of the reasons Taylor listed she discarded most of them. She could find no reason for Susan Hilliard Frasier to disappear except for something unknown, and the unknown was usually feared. That brought her back to fear. Susan was scared of something, or she was dead. Taylor's gut told her the woman was alive.

And her gut was usually right.

Chapter 3

Liberty only had six police cars, and three of them were outside Sam Turner's house on DeKalb Avenue. The decals on the doors read Liberty Police Department in blue and white block letters. The lights across the top rotated in rapid succession, throwing red and blue light against the white vinyl siding of his two-story colonial. Taylor Chambers slowed the rental car as she came close to the house. She wondered what was going on. It wasn't her usual route to turn down DeKalb Avenue, but she thought she'd take the chance that Sam was home and she could pick up the files he'd mentioned this morning.

Taylor parked on the street across from the commotion. Neighbors gathered, looking at each other, wondering the same thing she was. They didn't appear to know anything. Taylor got out of the car and closed the door. She hesitated, looking over the crowd. Then she crossed the street and passed through them as if she were a relative and often came to this house. There was no one at the front door, and she walked right in.

Inside the place was a mess. Tables and lamps had been upended, books lay over the floor, the doors to an entertainment center had been pulled off, and the television, which should have been inside, lay on the littered carpet. Sam's house had been deliberately trashed.

There were three men in the room other than Sam: Sheriff Bennett Carew, Bubba Wilson and Ward Dalrymple. They were all talking, asking questions, or milling around. Sam sat on a stool a foot away from the breakfast bar. The uniformed policemen stood around him.

"Sam," she called. The conversations that had been going on stopped. Four men turned to look at her: Sam, the sheriff, and two of his deputies.

"What are you doing here?" Sheriff Carew frowned as he stared at her. He'd scared Taylor as a child. She felt a trickle of sweat slide between her breasts, but Taylor was no longer ten years old. She stood in front of criminals and judges on her way to the white-collar work she did these days. An overweight, redneck sheriff from a backwater town would not get the better of her.

"The door was open," she said, the authority unmistakable in her voice. "I have an appointment with Sam. What happened?"

"It's gone, Taylor," Sam said.

"What's gone?"

"Everything. My computer, my printer, my scanner. My office was ransacked. They took everything, including my files."

"Susan's files?"

He nodded.

"What is your interest in this?" Bubba Wilson asked. He chewed a wad of gum as he'd done even in high school. Clarence Wilson had been called Bubba since he was born. Taylor thought he should have insisted they call him by his real name when he joined the police academy, but he hadn't, so instead of commanding respect he was still that sneaky kid from out by the swamp. He was one of Liberty's five deputies.

"My interest isn't police business."

"That's not what I heard," he contradicted her. "I hear you're looking into an open case."

"Open," she paused, "is relative. As of this morning, no one had worked that case in six years."

Taylor wasn't surprised Bubba knew the details of her visit to Missing Persons. She was sure both Sheriff Carew and Deputy Dalrymple had received a sentence-by-sentence reconstruction of her conversation with Maize Brondell.

"Nonactivity doesn't constitute closure."

Taylor smiled. "Big words, Bubba. I guess you've taken some law classes since I've been gone." She smiled. "It shows."

"Just why are you here?" This came from the sheriff. "I thought you'd be on your way back north." He said north as if it was on a planet populated by three-headed monsters.

"I'm here to find Susan Hilliard Frasier."

"She's dead."

"Is that a fact, sheriff? Death would certainly close the case of a missing person."

"She's as good as dead. No one has heard from her in years."

"Six years, sheriff. And in one more her family can legally petition the court to declare her dead and execute her will."

"If you know something, young lady," he took a step toward her, "you are bound by law to turn it over to me."

"If I know anything, I'm bound to turn it over to the Savannah Police Department, sheriff. Mrs. Frasier was a resident of that jurisdiction. She was reported missing in that jurisdiction. In fact, I wonder why there's an *open* file in the Liberty archives, wherever that might be."

The air turned thicker as they stared at each other. Taylor knew he was an enemy. She didn't know why. Carew had hated her father. He probably transferred that hate to her. Sam got up then and came to her.

"Sheriff, there isn't anything to know. Aunt Susan's been gone for six years, and the files that I had are now gone."

He hung his head, looking around at the debris of his life. Carew acted as if he hadn't heard Sam. He stared at Taylor. She stood her ground. Her father had taught her that, and it worked in most situations.

"Come on, boys, we're through here," the sheriff said. The uniforms filed out. Ward Dalrymple touched his hat as he passed her. Taylor stepped back out of the way.

She breathed a sigh of relief when they closed the front door.

"Can I help you clean up any of this?" Taylor turned all the way around. Everything had been pulled out or down.

"I can do it," Sam said. His voice had defeat in it, too.

"They really trashed this place."

"Yeah."

"I wonder why?"

"Theft."

"This doesn't look like theft," Taylor told him.

"If you saw my office, you'd know it was."

"Is it the same throughout the house?"

He nodded. "Every room."

"All of them?"

"Even the bathroom."

"Sam, they were looking for something."

"They must have found it. Everything I had was on that computer or in the file cabinet."

"Then why trash the whole house? Why didn't they take the television, the CD player, or the DVD? Why just break everything?"

"It reads more than a theft. Someone wanted to get at me."

Taylor stared at him. She didn't nod, although she wanted to. Whoever came into his house today wanted more than files and a computer hard drive. They wanted to push Sam's face in the mud. Taylor knew it had to do with her. She'd begun asking questions, and someone didn't want her to find the answers.

Taylor didn't like the feeling that lifted the hairs on her neck. She could feel there was something hidden here. She wished she was back in her law firm and away from the secrets and lies that swarmed about in the fragrant air around Liberty.

At her car, she breathed a sigh of relief. The envelope with the return address of the Savannah Police Department lay on the seat where she'd left it. The car doors were still locked. She hadn't consciously locked them, but as a female she was instinctively cautious.

She got into the oven heat and quickly switched on the air conditioner. Picking up the envelope, she peeked inside. The reports were still there: Susan Frasier's and the child's. She put them back and slipped on her seat belt. Then she put the car in gear and pulled away from the curb.

It had been a day filled with open questions, and it wasn't even dinnertime. Since she'd spoken to Dorrie and the Dalton child had been mentioned, she couldn't shake the feeling that there was something about the two that linked them together. But what?

Taylor turned the car around and headed out of town. She thought she could get Sam's reports and then go to her room. With everything laid out in front of her, maybe she could see a pattern, one her father had missed. He was a good detective and if there was anything to be found, he would have found it. But she'd run into a roadblock. Maize first, and then Sam's files. All she had was the file from Savannah, her father's, and a little girl's that might have nothing to do with the first two.

Taylor pulled into the driveway of the Fulbright Motel. She parked in front of her room and climbed out of the car, taking the papers with her. Her room was up a concrete flight of steps on the second floor of the two-story structure. When she opened the door, she froze. The room had been ransacked. Sam's house came to mind. Someone had been here. She stood paralyzed, looking at her clothes and jewelry strewn over the floor. The mattresses had been pulled from their frames and tossed aside. Drawers stood open, with various amounts of clothing hanging both in and out of them. The lamp on the desk had been knocked over, and the desk drawer lay on the floor. The space where she had set her laptop computer was empty. Taylor drew in a breath, then remembered she'd taken the machine with her. She held it in her hand.

Taylor couldn't go in. She closed the door and went down the stairs to the motel office.

"My room has been vandalized," she told the clerk.

"What?" The clerk looked at her as if he didn't understand.

"Call the police."

The man picked up the phone, but clearly looked as if he didn't know what was going on.

"You can look yourself, but in the meantime call the authorities."

He did as he was told. When he got off the phone he said, "They're coming."

"Do you have a safe?" she asked.

"We got one."

"Could you put these things in it?" She gave him the computer and the files she'd been holding. She watched as he opened the old-fashioned safe behind him and then closed it again. "I won't leave them long. As soon as the police leave, I'll be taking them. And I'll be checking out."

"Ma'am, I'm awful sorry. I've owned this motel for years, and we don't know trouble out here."

"Did you see or hear anything earlier? Was anyone lurking around my room?"

"I didn't see anyone, and the staff didn't mention anything unusual."

The police cars came blaring into the driveway. Both she and the manager went to join them. The same three policemen who had been at Sam's house a half-hour earlier were now in the room she rented.

"What is all this?" Sheriff Carew asked.

"Someone has broken in here and ravaged the place," Taylor relayed the obvious. She wondered how this man had ever gotten elected.

"Is anything missing?"

"I didn't go in, sheriff. I thought it would be best to have the law here when I crossed the threshold. But you can see someone has been inside and pulled out everything."

"Looks like they were looking for something. You got any idea what that might be?"

"No, sheriff. I haven't been here long enough to acquire any belongings."

"Been here long enough to go to Savannah."

Taylor eyed him as she would a crooked judge. "You know, sheriff, you fit the picture of the ol' country sheriff: bumbling, ignorant, uneducated, but it's all a lie. You have this town sewn up, don't you? Nothing passes by that you don't know about or have your hand in."

"I know I can't change how you think I look, but the rest of your description fits a good lawman. And I'm a good lawman."

"Then you should know why someone around here would be interested in my room."

The sheriff shook his head.

"Maybe it's all those questions you've been asking about Susan Frasier." Ward Dalrymple spoke for the first time.

"Why should that upset anyone? If Mrs. Frasier left of her own free will, then there is no reason for anyone to be nervous."

"It's just that it was a bad time, and no one wants you coming back here and digging up the dirt."

"Maybe we'd better stick to the current crime." Bubba

Wilson surprisingly defused the escalating tempers. "Why don't you take a look around and see if anything is missing." He looked at her.

"I don't suppose you'd want to fingerprint the place," Taylor stated.

"And find everybody that's been in this room in the last three months? Half of them the underage boys of this community. Take my word for it, it would be a waste of our time."

Taylor went inside and looked through everything. There was nothing missing. She hadn't brought much with her. She expected to leave quickly and had only brought the jewelry she was wearing and another set to wear to the funeral. In the room were only her clothes, some miscellaneous fruit, and several bottles of water. The fruit had been dumped in the trash and the bottles of water burst as if someone stepped on them until they exploded.

"There is nothing missing."

"Well, we can file a report if you want," the sheriff said. "I don't see a reason. Nothing is gone. All this looks like is you're a bad housekeeper."

"I'd like a report filed," Taylor said. She knew the legal system. It ran on paper. Without the proper filing, everything could be thrown out. If she made no complaint, they could accuse her of vandalizing the room. And she didn't put that past Bennett Carew.

"Why don't you two go on," Ward said. "I'll take the report."

Half an hour later, Taylor felt as if she'd ransacked her own room. Ward Dalrymple treated her like she was the criminal, but she made sure the motel owner stayed and told what he knew. When she signed the report, she handed the pen to the motel owner and pointed to a place where he should sign. Dalrymple said nothing, but Taylor could feel he wanted to pull the paper away from him.

"I'll need a copy of that, deputy," the owner said as he

handed it to him. "For my insurance records," he went on to explain. "You can't imagine how picky those people can be."

"I only got one copy."

"There is always a copy for the victim," Taylor explained the law to him. She knew it was unnecessary.

"We got a machine in the office. I can make as many copies as we need."

The three of them went to the office, and copies were doled out as needed. Ward Dalrymple got in his car with a face redder than the bulbs on the bar on top of it. Taylor had the pleasure of laughing as he pulled away. It was the most fun she'd had since returning to Liberty.

Chapter 4

There was nothing to compare to the Fulbright Motel in Liberty. Since Liberty had no cultural significance and no tourist business, except for the few people who traveled up from Savannah to tour the old ironworks factory, the area couldn't support another motel and therefore there were none. Taylor checked into the Savannah Sheraton and wondered why she hadn't done it in the first place. Her room was clean and bright and familiar. She had a safe in her room, but Sam's burglary and her own experience had made her additionally cautious. She'd gone to the local copy shop and had copies made of the documents. She made two sets of backup diskettes. She used FedEx to send one of them to her office and stored the other in the safe in her room.

By the time Taylor was settled, she was also hungry. She hadn't eaten since breakfast, and it was nearly seven o'clock. The temperature outside was still in the nineties. She had picked up the phone to call room service when she thought of Sam. She had records now. Maybe the two of them should go over them. She rejected the idea. She met Sam by chance and they discussed Susan Frasier. Less than three hours later

his house had been burglarized. Maybe she'd better see what
she had before involving anyone else.

When a waiter brought her dinner, Taylor had turned her
computer on and was busily making notes on the files she'd
created with all the information she had so far. He set up her
food, then she closed and locked the door behind him. The
steak was juicy, the way she liked it. Between bites she read.
The file from the Savannah Police had a little more in it.

Susan Hilliard Frasier was reported missing on the nine-
teenth of June. Her daughter, Ellen Frasier, signed the report. Susan had gone to a convention and was on her way
home. She'd called to say when she would arrive, but had
never gotten there. The police questioned Rene DePeres in
North Carolina, a friend Susan visited en route home.

According to him, she was planning to drive straight
home. She made no mention of additional friends to visit,
and she never called him after she left. The personal notes of
the police officer who visited Rene DePeres, Detective
Wayne Markham, stated he believed the man was telling the
truth. Taylor made a note to visit Detective Markham. She also
made a note to call her office. She needed some research information, and she didn't want anyone in Liberty knowing
she was requesting it.

She switched from the police file to her father's. Susan
had attended a car show. Taylor wondered what kind of car
show. It wasn't listed in the file. There was a list of people
her father had called from the show Susan attended. His
notes said he got nowhere with them. Those who remembered her didn't know where she was going when she left.
None of them recognized the name Rene DePeres.

Taylor looked at the list. None of the names meant anything to her. She attended a lot of car shows, and she knew
plenty of people with antique cars. Then she noticed *1957
Chevolet* written next to one of the names, Stuart Fry. She
grunted. The people she knew had cars much older than
1957.

She went on, trying to find something that would lead her somewhere, but there was nothing there. Susan Frasier had effectively wiped herself off the face of the earth and left nothing behind. Nothing except a lot of money. Her father's file had bank statements, telephone records, even household bills, yet there was nothing to help her. She picked up her glass of ice tea and drank the remains through the straw. There had to be something she and her father had both missed.

She picked up the last file, the one on the Dalton girl. She put it down, not in the mood to read about a child being killed.

Maybe Ellie would be able to help her with something tomorrow.

Ellie Fraiser Porter, called Ellie by everyone who knew her, lived in her mother's house on Palmer Square. The house was huge: red brick with large white pillars. The gates surrounding it were forged ironwork that came from the Liberty Forge in the twenties. They were fancy, ornate, and strong. Highly polished, they gleamed in the afternoon sunlight.

Taylor walked up the drive. Moss hung like hair from the huge oak trees. This was a different world. It had a quiet elegance, with a charm that was different from any she'd seen before. The trees could make you feel small, insignificant, and afraid, or provide the appropriate frame for strength, purpose, and a world of tradition. The house reminded Taylor of Liberty, not timeless so much as time suspended, waiting for something that would never be. She wondered if it was waiting for its rightful owner.

Taylor pulled the old-fashioned rope that rang a bell somewhere in the house. She heard nothing. The door opened almost immediately, as if someone had known she was there. It was a woman in a nurse's uniform.

"Hello," Taylor addressed her. "I'm Taylor Chambers."

She smiled. "Mrs. Porter is expecting you."

The nurse led her to a room along the back of the house, overlooking a garden in full color. Huge open windows looked out. Curtains billowed into the room, bringing the scent of magnolias with it. There were flowers everywhere and groupings of floral-patterned furniture. Ellen Frasier Porter sat on a sofa with a book in her hand.

She looked up as Taylor came in. "Taylor, is that you?"

She nodded. Ellie smiled. "I didn't think you'd remember me."

"Sit down." She indicated the chair across from her. "Pardon me if I don't get up. It's harder these days." She patted her stomach.

"I didn't know you were pregnant," Taylor told her.

"Seven months," Ellie frowned. "It has been complicated all the way."

"Is everything all right?"

"Oh, yes," she said. "All I have to do is wait. It's the waiting that's hard."

Taylor understood, but she hadn't come here to compare pregnancy stories. "Ellie, my father initially looked for your mother after she disappeared."

Ellie reached for a glass. She filled it with lemonade and handed it to Taylor. Then she poured one for herself.

"You did know I hired him?" She didn't wait for an answer. "I asked your father and he tried, but he couldn't find her."

"That bothered him," Taylor told her. "He left me her file and asked me to look into it."

"You're reopening her case?"

"I don't think I can do that. I'm not a cop. I am looking into a few things. I wondered if you'd review what you remember about her disappearance."

"I don't remember much. Everything was so normal. There was no reason for her to up and leave with no word."

"Anything could be important."

"I've told it all before to the police."

"I know, but I haven't been able to get all the police reports. Would you mind going through it again?"

"It was so long ago. I'm sure Billy is right."

"Billy?"

"My husband. I married Billy Porter." Taylor knew that. Billy Porter owned several upscale furniture stores in and around Savannah. He'd taken over his father's one store and in the last few years had turned it into a successful chain. Taylor remembered seeing newspaper clippings of him cutting the ribbon to open his new businesses in her father's files.

"Billy says if my mother was alive, she would call me."

Taylor heard the anguish in her voice. She understood the need for a parent.

"I think she is alive," Taylor said. She shouldn't have told her. She knew that. She had no proof, nothing to back it up other than her own intuition, but she believed Susan Frasier was alive.

"I do, too," Ellie said. "I can't tell you why I think so. Billy certainly doesn't." She frowned when she mentioned her husband's name. "He thinks she's . . ." she hesitated as if she couldn't say the word. "Our phone number is the same. She would have called me if she could. We don't talk about it anymore."

"Would you talk about her to me?"

Ellie stared clear-eyed at her for a moment, assessing her motives. After a moment she began. "The day she left started off a lot like this. It was beautiful, clear, and for a while the humidity wasn't wilting. Mother had gone to one of those car shows she liked so much. I never could understand it. It's just an old car."

Taylor couldn't explain this, either. She understood Susan Frasier's love for the cars. Growing up in this setting, in a house that predated the Civil War, with two-hundred-year-old trees and antique furniture, how could Ellie not share her mother's appreciation for the past?

"She called me to let me know she was coming home," Ellie went on. "She said she would probably be back that night. If she didn't get here, she had decided to stay the night at a motel and would be here in the morning. She never showed up."

"Where was she?"

"The show was in Virginia, but she'd stopped on her way home and spent a few days with one of her friends in Winston-Salem. She called me from there."

"The friend? That would be Rene DePeres?"

Ellie nodded. "Your father interviewed him, but he could provide nothing to help."

"Did she mention what motel she was planning to stay in?"

Ellie shook her head.

"Did she have a favorite place?" Ellie frowned. "A favorite type of place. Would she be more likely to stay at a roadside inn or find something like a Sheraton or a Holiday Inn?"

"Many people think Mother has a lot of airs. They probably expected her to stay at a three-star hotel, but she's really down-to-earth. As long as the place was clean and safe, she'd stay, but I don't think she did this time."

"Why is that?"

"It's the car."

"The car?"

"She was driving that old car. She didn't often drive it when she went to shows. Usually she'd have the garage jack it up on a flatbed and one of her drivers would take it to the show. She'd either follow in another car or ride in the truck."

"This time was different?"

Ellie shrugged. "I don't think so. She was excited before she left, but no more so than for any other show."

"What about the way she sounded on the phone."

"Normal. That's just it, Taylor." Ellie shifted in her chair trying to find a comfortable position. She finished adjusting her seat and ran her hand over her protruding stomach. "Nothing about anything that happened was abnormal."

Taylor thought this must have been what baffled her father. Usually something was out of the place, even if it was only a feeling. There should be something that was slightly off-center, but with Susan Frasier it appeared God was in his heaven and all was right with the world. Yet no one had seen or heard from her in six years.

"Except that old car." Ellie spoke almost to herself.

"What about the car?"

"Mother never made it home, but the car did."

"How?"

"That's just it. We don't know."

"What happened to the car?"

"It's in the garage. Every now and then Billy has a mechanic come and take it out. He says the engine needs to be kept in running condition."

"Why is that?"

"I don't know. He wanted to sell it, but it's in Mother's name and she's missing, not dead."

So he was caught, Taylor thought. Until Susan Frasier was declared legally dead, the car and everything else she owned was in limbo.

"Would you like to see the car?"

"Yes," Taylor said. She got up and, seeing Ellie struggling, she went and helped her. "Put your arm around my neck." Ellie did as she was told. She used Taylor as leverage to haul her bulk up from the sofa. Taylor remembered her doctor using that method to get her up when she was carrying her daughter, Julianne. She was amazed that after thirteen years she still remembered the procedure.

Ellie put her hands on her back and stretched. "It feels good to stand up."

She started walking toward the open French doors. Taylor followed her. They walked through the garden. The garage was on the side of the house. It was a separate building with enough space for four cars. All the doors were closed. Ellie stopped in front of the first door. She pressed a code into a keypad, and the door started a slow upward roll.

"Billy had the doors set up this way so we wouldn't have to get out of the cars to open them."

As the door curled into the space above their heads, the shadow rolled over the back of the car.

"Oh my God!" Taylor gasped. "I was expecting a '57 Chevy." She walked into the garage, eyeing the car as the thing of beauty it was. "This is a 1909 Pierce-Arrow. It came off the assembly line in Buffalo, New York. Only a handful of them were produced, and only a few remain in service."

"You know about cars?"

"I have one of these."

"You do?" Ellie's surprise was evident.

"A 1934." Now Taylor understood why her father had left this case for her. She and Susan Frasier shared antique cars as a passion. Taylor continued to circle the car. It was clean, well-maintained. The leather seats were polished and soft. The finish looked as if it had just come off the showroom floor. Taylor let her hand pass over the fender as she went by.

"It's a beautiful piece of workmanship," she said to no one in particular. She turned back to look at Ellie. She looked uncomfortable. Taylor didn't know if it was the car or her pregnancy that caused it. "I won't be much longer," Taylor explained. "You have no idea how the car got here?"

Ellie shook her head. "I waited for Mother to return. When she didn't I got worried and called Billy. We were only dating then." She gave Taylor a smile.

"What time was it then?"

"About midnight. I'd waited all day."

"I don't suppose she had a car phone?" Car phones hadn't been that popular six years ago, but rich people had them.

"No."

"Go on, tell me about the night."

"Billy said I was being silly, that my mother could take care of herself. He stayed with me until about three o'clock. When he started to leave, he discovered the car."

"It was here?"

"Yes . . . I mean no. It wasn't in this place. It was parked in the garage, but in the last bay." She pointed toward the end of the structure, which had two other cars parked in it. "Down there where Billy parks now." Billy's space was empty. "That's when we called the police. They came, but told us they couldn't do anything. She was an adult and had the right to come and go as she pleased, even if she didn't tell me where she was going. They said she probably came home and took another car, but no other car was gone. My car was in the shop and mother's regular car, a white Cadillac, she'd loaned to Sam."

"Sam Turner?"

"He loved driving that big old boat around Liberty. He said it helped him pick up girls." Ellie laughed.

"Ellie, your mother has a lot of money."

Ellie nodded.

"In a year." Taylor spoke slowly.

"What's going on here?"

Both of them jumped. Billy Porter stood in the doorway, the sun behind him. He was a big man, of solid muscle, and looked more like a bodybuilder than a furniture salesman.

"Billy, what are you doing here in the middle of the day?"

"I have a better question. What is she hauling up skeletons for?"

"So news has reached you."

"Billy, where are your manners?"

"I left them in the North," he returned. "Now, Ms. Chambers, I think this conversation is over. My wife is very fragile right now and she doesn't need you coming in here upsetting her."

"Billy—"

He cut Ellie off with a look.

"It wasn't my intention to upset anyone. You look more upset than Ellie."

"Would you like me to show you to your car?"

"I know where it is." Taylor walked past him and into the light outside the garage. She turned back to Ellie. "It was nice seeing you again, Ellie. Good luck with the baby."

Then she looked up at Billy. "Good luck to you too, Billy. For some reason, I think you're going to need it."

Chapter 5

Detective Wayne Markham was a red-faced man about five-foot, six. Taylor towered over him like a basketball player over Tiny Tim. He no longer worked for the police department but operated his own agency, which provided guided tours for people visiting Savannah. Taylor met him at his office on Mercer Street. The place was busy with people coming in and out and buses leaving, being serviced, and going out again.

"We can talk over here." Taylor followed him into an office that was quiet when he closed the door, but he didn't stop there. He opened another door that led into the back of the building. They crossed into the inside, which looked like a warehouse. "You said you were here about the disappearance of Susan Frasier."

"That's right. You interviewed one of the last people who saw her alive."

"Rene DePeres. I remember. I was assigned to investigate the disappearance of Susan Frasier. I found very little. I followed all the leads her daughter gave me, but I found nothing." They kept walking. They went through the warehouse and into a small building that looked like a house.

"Do you live here?"

"Not anymore. I did when I first started the business, but it supports me now and I live on Stone Court." Inside, it was still a house. There was a living room with a sofa and comfortable chairs. The dining table was clear of dust, and the kitchen had the smell of coffee. "I come here when I need a little quiet or to remember where I came from."

"So do you remember anything that could help me find Susan Frasier?"

"You think she's still alive?"

"I do," she told him.

"Why?"

"I don't know. My father had good instincts. He wouldn't have asked me to look into her disappearance if he thought she was dead."

"He might. Even if all you do is provide closure to Ellie and Billy Porter, they will have peace of mind and it will release all the assets Susan Frasier left behind."

"I think those assets have a lot to do with people wanting her dead."

"Well, I can't tell you anything more about Rene DePeres. I believed him when he told me Susan spent three days at his house and then headed home. After she left, he also left for an art show in San Francisco. I checked it out. He was definitely there when she disappeared. He could give me nothing more about Mrs. Frasier. Everything is in the report I filed."

"I'm having a few problems getting copies of reports. It seemed the Freedom of Information Act has been archived everywhere I turn and somehow the location of the archive has been wiped from all memory banks."

He laughed. It was a deep, resounding sound, and Taylor joined him. "Come with me." He walked into the den. Taking a key from a chain on his hip, he opened an old file cabinet. Reaching inside, he searched through several files before pulling one out. It was a small file, about a half-inch thick. "I thought you'd need this."

Taylor looked at the gray manilla folder. She couldn't believe her eyes, especially when he slipped an envelope from the folder that had Liberty County Police Department written on it.

"They were very lax at headquarters," Markham said. "I made copies of the files I was interested in. This was one of those that gave me nothing except the belief that there was something I was missing. I didn't like the feeling. When I left the force, I never forgot Susan Frasier. I somehow believed she'd show up one day with a good explanation."

Taylor accepted the folder. She opened it and started to read.

"Sit down," Markham said. "I'm going back to the office. Stay as long as you need to. If you want to take something with you, there's an old copy machine over there." He pointed behind Taylor. She turned around and looked at the old desktop machine.

"Thank you," Taylor whispered.

"No need to thank me," he told her. "I hope you do better than I did."

As he turned to leave, Taylor stopped him. "One more question."

"What's that?" He paused in the doorway.

"Do you think there's a connection between Susan Frasier and the Dalton girl?"

He waited a moment before answering. Taylor recognized the policeman in him. This was standard procedure. They taught it at police academies across the nation, and it was easy to see even when a man no longer wore a uniform, he was still a cop.

"I can't think of one." He looked at her for a moment. "But obviously you do."

"I haven't decided."

"Haven't you?"

*   *   *

There wasn't much in the Liberty file. Only one detail nagged at her—the time. Ellie had told her the Savannah police wouldn't declare her mother missing for three days, yet according to the Liberty file there were people out looking for Susan Frasier three hours after the Savannah police were called to her house. *Why was that*, Taylor wondered.

She made two copies of the file, one to put in the hotel safe and one to keep with her. She took the time to return to the Sheraton and store it. While there she called Sam and made an appointment to meet him. Then she called her office. Her secretary answered.

"How's it going down there?" Her voice was concerned. She knew Taylor went there for a funeral. "Are you relaxing and visiting some of the sights?"

"I wish I were. Did you get the e-mail I sent?"

"I got all the information you asked for. It's going out today."

"There's a change," Taylor told her. "I've moved to the Sheraton Savannah." Taylor fished through the desk drawer for an envelope with the hotel's address on it. She gave it to her secretary. "Send it to this address and make sure it doesn't go to the Fulbright. That's very important."

She didn't need to say that. The two of them had worked together since Taylor opened her agency.

"I'll make sure."

"Anything pressing I should know about?"

"We won the Rafter case. The judge awarded the three million dollars and added another five."

"That ought to pay a few bills."

Her secretary laughed. "What do you want me to do about your invitation to that dinner in Atlanta? You're so close, don't you want to go?"

Taylor had forgotten about the dinner. It was the annual car show dinner. Unlike Susan Frasier, Taylor rarely attended any of the shows, although she was invited every year through her membership in the Pierce-Arrow Society. Because of her company's large contribution, she was always invited to the dinner they held.

"It'll do you good, Taylor."

"All right, send in my acceptance."

Her secretary thought she was going to relax, and it might be a relaxing day, but Taylor had another reason: Susan Hilliard Frasier.

Twenty minutes after Taylor finished the call to her office and a shorter one to tell Kenneth she still loved him and that she was all right, Taylor was back on the road to Liberty. Sam met her at a roadside café north of the city limits. The place wasn't as nice as the restaurant where she'd had breakfast and the food had more grease and less taste, but there was no one there who knew her.

Sam got coffee from the counter and brought it to the table. Taylor spread out the files on the table, and Sam quickly read through them.

"That's about what I had," he said.

"Sam, why the time differences?"

Sam grinned at her. "You been up north too long. She was one of ours, Taylor. I know she lived in Savannah and that's a bigger place than Liberty, but we claimed her—least I did, and I was on the force. When Ellie called to ask if I'd seen her and I found out about the car and that the police in Savannah said she wasn't officially missing, I practically began the search myself."

"But why here? Susan wasn't supposed to be in Liberty."

"She came here often. And I had her car. She was driving that big thing she loved, and she'd loaned me her Caddy." He grinned again. She knew he was remembering the car and his use of it. Taylor had the same passions, and she owned several cars. Hers were beauties and they also brought back pleasant memories.

"But she hadn't called you. She said she was heading home."

Sam looked strange for a second. "I really don't know. I remember the sheriff giving us instructions. He backed me in the decision to try and find her. I was glad of that."

Taylor heard the resignation in his voice. Sheriff Carew probably didn't support him often. But he had supported him in the search for his aunt. Taylor couldn't help but wonder why.

"Something else was happening that night," Taylor said. "Mrs. Dalton's daughter was killed that night. Why wasn't Sheriff Carew out looking for her killer?"

"We didn't know about that at the time. The Dalton girl wasn't found until the next day."

"But her mother had reported her missing."

"By the time she came in, everyone was already out."

"Sam, it was three o'clock in the morning. Mrs. Dalton's report came in six hours earlier."

Sam sat, staring. "I don't know," he finally said. "I guess I forgot all about the Dalton child when Aunt Susan went missing. I know it sounds callous, I know—"

"It doesn't," Taylor interrupted. "I suppose if something like that happened to someone I loved, I'd forget about things that didn't touch me personally, too."

The child's murder still bothered Taylor. She pulled the folder aside. Melissa Dalton was six years old. She'd been playing in her yard on Fenwick Street. Taylor knew the neighborhood. She even knew the house where Ava Dalton lived. The backyard had a fence around it, and anyone looking at it would think it was safe for a child. But somehow Melissa Dalton had left that yard. Taylor wondered if the child had opened the fence gate, climbed over it, or if someone had taken her from the yard. Mrs. Dalton was divorced and her ex-husband lived in Louisiana. The report confirmed his alibi. So how had the child gotten out of the yard? And where did she go? She was only six years old. Liberty was small, but for a child it could be huge and everyone who knew Ava Dalton also knew her daughter. Yet her body had been found in the woods only a mile or so from where Taylor sat now.

She looked down at the report again. The signature was unreadable. She turned the page around and slipped it toward Sam.

"Who signed this?"

"Ward Dalrymple," he said, glancing at it.

"What about this one?" She pushed Susan's Liberty file across to him.

"That's the sheriff's chicken scratch. We often teased him about skipping the handwriting classes in school." Sam smiled, but Taylor concentrated on the two pieces of paper in front of her. Sam leaned back in his chair. "Why are you so concerned about the Dalton case? I thought you were only asked to look into Aunt Susan's disappearance."

Taylor scanned the pages, looking for something. "This is a small community. There isn't much crime here other than kids being kids and a few drunk and disorderlies, yet on the same night we have a possible kidnaping and murder and the disappearance of a prominent citizen. Their cases are never solved. For some reason I can't get it out of my head that the two of these events are connected to each other."

"How?"

Taylor shook her head. "I haven't a clue."

Neither of them saw the truck coming. Taylor heard the sound. It wouldn't have registered if she'd been crossing the street in the busy town of Princeton. Afternoon traffic was usually loud, but this quietness of the day and the absence of other traffic sounds alerted her senses. She turned.

A large black hulking pickup bore down on them. Taylor didn't have time to look into the cab. The gleaming chrome grill filled all the space in front of her like some big-screen television. Yet this was life. "Run!" she screamed. Sam had seen it, too. They took off, going toward the side, heading away from the oncoming vehicle.

Taylor didn't know if they had time. Her shoes dug into the graveled lot, making her footing precarious. She prayed she'd stay upright. Her heart pounded as she tried to run and hold onto the folders she'd carried into the restaurant. A stone slipped into her shoe. She stumbled. The files went flying. The truck engine revved higher. She stumbled again. She wasn't going to make it. The sound told her that. The truck was closer. She could feel the heat of it, see the bumper bearing closer to her with her peripheral vision.

A picture of Julianne flashed in her mind. She thought of Kenneth and what he would say when he discovered she'd been killed by a truck. She jogged faster, pulling her skirt up and extending her long legs.

Sam grabbed her arm. Using it like a rope, he whipped her around and forced her between two parked cars. Taylor slammed into one of them, the wind knocked from her. She slid to the ground. The truck smashed into the cars, momentum pushing them together, Taylor crouched on the gravel between. She covered her head, lying facedown on the sharp rocks. The edges cut into her arms and face. Sam lay a few feet away.

She heard the truck gears churn as the driver reversed. The few seconds gave them a measure of time. Neither said a word. Moving almost as synchronized athletes, she and Sam scrambled to their feet and jumped up on the back of a car. The truck started forward. Taylor glanced at it. The windows were dark. She could see no one. And there was no license tag. They ran across the trunks, cars bobbing like apples in a tin tub. The truck crashed into the cars.

It backed off and waited. Taylor and Sam stopped and looked, each waiting to see what move the other would make. The driver revved the engine, taunting them. It seemed they were suspended for hours: watching, waiting, playing the game. Taylor moved to the right. The truck started for her.

Quickly she reversed on her bouncing betty and went the other way. The truck wasn't as agile.

Three people rushed out of the restaurant, shouting and waving their arms in warning. The truck took off, spitting gravel and peeling rubber as the oversized tires made contact with the paved road. Taylor heard the gravel raining on metal bumpers as the truck careened away.

She closed her eyes. Her hands came to her chest to try and quiet her heart. Her knees gave out, and she slid down to the surface of the trunk. She dragged air into her lungs as if the atmosphere was about to be ripped from the planet.

Sam came up behind her. The people who'd come out of the restaurant were also there. Everyone was talking. Some were pointing toward their cars. Taylor saw their mouths moving, but heard nothing. Her heartbeat drowned out all other sounds.

She got down from the car. Sirens blared as she stood up and gingerly tested if she could remain upright. Two Liberty police cars pulled into the restaurant parking lot. A red-faced Bennett Carew got out of one.

"Just what are you playing at?" Carew asked her when they were back at the Liberty police department. Taylor's skirt was dirty, her blouse torn. She had scrapes on her arms, and she was sure her legs, too. Blood stained her sides from the cuts on her arms. No one asked her if she wanted to clean herself up. They had taken a report at the scene and bought them back here. Sheriff Carew had all the papers that were strewn over the ground after she dropped them.

"I was only having a meal with a friend." Taylor glanced over at Sam. He looked just as disheveled as she did.

"And what about these?" The sheriff picked up a couple of pieces of paper from her files and dropped them back on the desk. "This is confidential information. You shouldn't even have it."

"It's not confidential. It's a matter of public record under the Freedom of Information Act."

"Don't spout the law to me. This is Liberty. I am the law here." He paused. "And you don't live here. You're not on the force, and you have no P.I. license. Young lady, you're getting awful close to obstruction of justice."

Taylor knew she may as well talk to the wall, but she had to say it anyway. "Sheriff, at best all I've done is ask some questions about Susan Frasier and collect some public information. I don't need a license to ask questions."

Bennett Carew looked at her as if he wanted to squash her. She'd traded the law with him on a one-for-one basis, and it was obvious he didn't like it. He'd told her he was the law in Liberty, and she'd challenged that authority. "The best thing you can do is to forget Susan Frasier and take the next plane back to the lawyer office where you work."

Taylor stood up. She was getting nowhere, and she was angry. "I don't just work at that 'lawyer' office," she mimicked him. "I own that office. And I have a perfect right to be here." Taylor stopped before she brought up the fact that she owned property within the city limits. She wasn't taking possession of her father's house. There was no need to push Carew any further.

"Let me tell you something." He leaned on his desk, supporting his weight on hands. He glared at her. "I don't have the right to throw you out of town, but you'd better not so much as drive an eyelash over the speed limit. Any infraction of any rule in this town, and I'll have you thrown in jail and you'd wish you had left town."

Taylor smiled. She'd been threatened before and by better people than Sheriff Carew. "Sheriff, one would think you had something to do with Susan Frasier's disappearance." She paused, waiting for his face to go from normal red to the color of ripe beets. "Did you?"

"Get the hell out of my office," he shouted.

"Gladly." She turned and left.

On the street, Taylor felt better. She was sweaty and dirty, someone had tried to kill her, but saying her piece to Sheriff Carew was like exorcizing demons. There was nothing he could do to her, and if he tried anything she'd bring the full weight of her office down on him. If he wanted a fight, she'd give him one, but she didn't think he did. She'd asked him if he was involved with Susan Frasier only to play into his anger, but now she wondered who was involved with her. Someone in this town knew something about Susan. And if she had to go door to door, she was going to find out who it was.

Chapter 6

Atlanta, Georgia, was rapidly losing its distinction as a member of the South. So many northerners had migrated to the South, with job changes being as fluid as water, that the population of the south's mecca was its own melting pot. An advantage, Taylor thought, was the shopping. She'd found a dress that she loved for the society dinner.

She'd taken time to get to Atlanta a day early, spending it perusing the many shops in an upscale mall and buying souvenirs for Julianne and her secretary. Her daughter was past the T-shirt stage and too old for toys. She liked sports and reading. Taylor found a book on the history of the Atlanta Braves and a gold necklace with a pendant of the state of Georgia. A diamond stud sparkled from the place where Atlanta would be.

Taylor wore a tan-colored linen pantsuit and flat shoes for the car show. She thought of the ruined clothes from her encounter with the truck, but pushed it out of her mind. For today she would enjoy the classic roadsters from another time. She wouldn't think of Susan Frasier or anything associated with her, not even the 1909 Pierce-Arrow stored in her garage and apparently in driving condition.

The show was held in the convention center. Susan strolled past a 1921 Rolls-Royce Silver Ghost Cabriolet with carriage-like fenders, a 1932 Stutz that sported a goldish-tan exterior she'd yet to see on any other car, a 1928 Dodge Series 130 Victory Six Sport Roadster in two-tone green. There were hundreds of cars. It could take days to get through, and by the crowds milling about, some appreciating the workmanship, others gawking at the wonder of them, and children running about as if this was only another playground, Taylor was sure it would.

A few of the owners were with their cars, but mostly there were car managers or museum people overseeing the automobiles. Taylor smiled and stopped to speak with those she knew, most of them exclaiming surprise at her attendance.

"I was close," she told the owner of a 1934 Duesenberg Model J sport sedan with a padded top.

"I don't see how you can resist coming regularly," he said. "I love these classics. If I'm not in a couple of shows a year, I go through withdrawal."

Taylor was still smiling at his remark as she passed a Packard Model 1108, the 1940 sport sedan version. She didn't have a Packard in her collection, and she wanted one. Her mouth even dried as she looked at the beautiful lines of the car, the large white-wall tires, the fenders that reminded her of the graceful ascent of an airplane taking off. She took in the flat-top cabin, a trunk that looked like something you could pick up and carry onto a steamer bound for Europe, and the extra pull-down shelf for more luggage. It was an absolutely beautiful car.

"The car!" The thought hit her like a bolt of lightning. Susan Hilliard Frasier loved cars. Taylor looked up at the signs designed to help visitors find the restrooms and showrooms. She was looking for membership services. She worked her way back to registration.

"If someone wanted to join one of the societies, where would they go?" she asked a tall blonde about forty who smiled from one of the registration booths. The woman pointed her toward the membership hall. It was a cavernous room with booths set up for many of the societies. There were brochures and displays on the benefits of joining. It wasn't necessary to be a car owner to be a member, she heard a man at a Fox Society booth explain to a couple as she passed. She searched for the Pierce-Arrow Society. The red-and-green logo caught her eye, and she headed straight toward it.

"Hello," she said, stopping. Behind the booth was a woman with a name tag that read Leah Tudor. "I'm Taylor Chambers, and I'm already a member."

The woman glanced at Taylor's nametag. Immediately her eyes widened. Taylor knew her tag had a different color than the tags of the people who came to the show. She was a car owner, even if her car was not at the show. "You're one of our former board members."

Taylor smiled. She hadn't expected this woman to know that. She was about thirty, with short dark hair and a cut that meant she needed to do little with it except wash and go. Her eyes were an interesting color of hazel. They were compelling to watch, and Taylor had to remind herself not to stare at her.

"I wondered about the setup here. Is this system connected to the national office?"

The woman smiled. "It is. I've been after them for years to get this done. It cuts down on errors, and I can do everything here I can do in my office?"

"Great. I need some information about one of our members."

"That's confidential information," the woman stammered, the smile leaving her face.

"I know, but I'm—"

"Taylor—Taylor Chambers?"

She turned to see Matthew Connors. "Matt, how are

you?" Matt pulled her into his arms for a bear hug. Then he pushed her back, dropping his arms.

"Glad to see you here."

"Matt, can you help me? I need some information on one of our members." He didn't hesitate and she didn't wait, but rushed on. "I'm investigating a disappearance. I think the woman was a member of the society. I need to know if she still is."

He looked at Leah, who stood mutely behind the booth. "Give her what she wants. I've been on the board with her."

It was enough for Leah. She smiled and sat down at her machine.

"Thanks, Matt."

"You're welcome, but now you owe me." He smiled. "I'll expect dinner the next time I'm in Princeton. And it's on you."

"It's a deal," she said. He turned to speak to someone behind them, and Taylor looked at Leah.

"How can I help you?" she asked.

"I'm trying to find Susan Hilliard Frasier."

Leah typed. "Susan Hilliard Frasier's membership expired five years ago."

"What's her last address?"

"5574 Palmer Square, Savannah, Georgia."

Taylor bit her lip. *That's where her daughter lives now.*

"Can you access new memberships, people who joined after Susan's membership lapsed?"

"Sure." Her fingers flew over the keys. Taylor came around the booth and took a seat. She was careful not to invade Leah's space, but she wanted to see the screen. "It's all right," Leah said, as if she perceived her reason. "Come closer." Taylor pulled her chair up. The list appeared on the screen.

"See if there's a Hilliard?"

"No Hilliard."

Taylor knew it had to be there. Her gut told her this was the way. If she was going to find Susan, it had to be through the car. People gave up their identities, but they hung onto the things they loved. If Susan could no longer live in Savannah and have access to a daughter who loved her and was about to present her with a grandchild, she would have to keep her passion alive. And that meant the car.

"Give me some other names she could have used," Leah said, as if she really wanted to help Taylor.

"Her daughter's name is Ellen. Try that?"

"First . . . name . . . Ellen," Leah talked as she typed. "Three Ellens. Ellen Girard of Detroit, Michigan. Ellen D. West of Boston, Massachusetts. And Ellen Chandler of Buffalo, New York."

Taylor was shooting at stars. She wasn't really sure Susan Frasier was still alive, much less living somewhere under an assumed name. If so, would it be her daughter's? She needed to try and narrow her choices to an educated guess.

"Leah." Taylor thought of something. "Can you pull up birthdays with these names?

"Sure," Leah shrugged. "I can pull up everything we have on them." She began typing again.

"Wait," Taylor stopped her. "The original list of new members, get that and eliminate all years except 1948." Susan was fifty-six. She was born in 1948, and Taylor didn't think she would change a birthday even if she changed her name. Leah did as she was asked. The screen flickered and eight names showed. Taylor stared at the simple columns filling the small screen.

"Turner E. Payton," she read slowly, pronouncing the name distinctly as if she were standing before a jury and giving them a medical term they were unfamiliar with.

"Turner is generally a man's name," Leah said.

"So is Taylor," Taylor said.

Leah glanced at her and nodded. She scrolled across the screen. "Sex—female," she read.

"It's her," Taylor said.

"Are you sure?"

Taylor nodded. The two people Susan Frasier loved most in the world were her daughter, Ellen, and her nephew, Sam Turner. *She's calling herself Turner E. Payton.* Taylor would bet her office's receipts for next year that the *E* in the name stood for Ellen.

Taylor copied the St. Louis address and thanked Leah. She left the car show at a near run.

"Mrs. Susan Hilliard Frasier?" Taylor stared at the woman who opened the door. Susan Frasier was older, but still the same woman she had been six years ago. Her face twitched a little, and Taylor saw the color steal under her features.

"You must be mistaken," she said in a controlled voice.

"I don't think so," Taylor told her. She pulled the photograph from the folder in her hand. "We need to talk."

The woman hesitated. Color painted down her face like white paste. Taylor watched her hands shake and her upper lip quiver. Then she stepped back. "Come in."

The house was nothing like the mansion on Palmer Square, but her presence was here. Taylor felt comfortable. A few moments later, Susan sat across from her in a living room that had fully lighted windows with a glass of lemonade in her hand.

"I've been expecting you—or someone like you for years. How did you find me?"

"The Pierce-Arrow Society," she said. "I'm a member, too. We all have a passion for something. You had to be close to the car even if you can't drive it."

She smiled. "I loved that old car."

"I saw it." Susan's eyebrows went up. "I spoke to Ellie. She's married to Billy Porter. They're expecting their first child in two months."

Tears sprang to Susan's eyes.

"Why don't you tell me why you disappeared?"

"I can't go back there," she said instead of answering the question. "I have a life here now. A husband. He knows nothing about Susan Frasier, nothing about Savannah, nothing about . . . that night."

"What happened that night?"

Susan fidgeted. She looked at the glass in her hand for so long Taylor didn't think she was going to answer. Then she began to speak. "I was almost home." She set her glass down. "When I got to the turnoff for Liberty, I remembered my nephew, Sam, had one of my cars. I was driving the Arrow and I was tired. I took the turn, hoping he was home. I'd rest awhile, get something to eat and drive the last few miles back. About ten miles before I got there, a child ran out in the road. She was naked and afraid, wild-looking. There was blood all over her. I almost didn't recognize who she was. Right behind her came a man. He aimed and shot before he knew I was there. He turned, staring at the car. I knew he couldn't see me because of the dark and the lights in his face, but I saw him clearly."

"Was the child Melissa Dalton?"

Susan nodded. "He started to raise the gun. I reversed immediately and backed around the bend. He shot, but nothing hit me or the car. I kept backing up, too scared to take the time to stop and reverse direction. I knew he was behind me. I expected to see headlights reflecting off the upholstery at any second, but it didn't happen. Finally, I turned and drove as fast as the Arrow would go."

"Who shot the girl?"

Susan Hilliard Frasier swallowed. "Ward Dalrymple."

"Deputy Ward Dalrymple?" Taylor put her glass on the table to keep from dropping it.

"He was still wearing his uniform."

* * *

U.S. Marshal Mike Edsen met Taylor's plane when it landed in Atlanta. Susan Frasier, now Turner Payton, and her husband accompanied Taylor. They went directly to the marshal's offices on Peachtree Street, and Susan told her tale.

"I'm going to be frank with you, Mrs. Payton," he said. Taylor's heart sank. She'd found Susan, but justice would not prevail. "Your story could be perfectly true. And I believe it is," he rushed to tell her. "But all we have is your word against his. We can't use any of it. Without something hard to go on, you might as well return to St. Louis and forget this ever happened."

"Forget that a child is dead and a cop killed her?" Taylor was on her feet.

He spread his hands. "What do we have?" He looked at Susan. Her husband squeezed her hand. "Mrs. Payton looks like a good citizen, but she's been missing for six years. She returns with this story, and there is nothing that can be found. Any evidence that might have been in those woods six years ago is gone now."

"So we do nothing?"

"What do you suggest? I'm open." He threw the ball back to Taylor, and she didn't like it.

"I have some evidence," Susan said in a quiet voice.

Taylor and the marshal stopped staring at each other so they could look at Susan.

"Go on," the marshal said.

"They were beating the woods looking for me. That old car was a dead giveaway. Everyone knew I owned it or if they didn't it wouldn't be hard to figure out. It was the only one in Savannah." Susan stopped and her husband, who sat silently listening, took her hand in a supportive gesture. "Dalrymple called out to me by name. I had to shut the engine down to hide the noise. At first he tried to make a deal with me. Bring me into his conspiracy. I said nothing. My heart was beating so hard and I was too afraid to speak. Then he threatened me, saying he would find me and I'd be sorry. After a while he threatened Ellie. He said if I said anything—*ever*—he would make sure Ellie paid for it. I had no choice." She stopped. Tears clogged her throat and rolled down her face. Edsen handed her a box of tissues.

She wiped her face and took a calming breath. "Ellie was only sixteen. I couldn't let them hurt her. As long as I didn't say anything, she would be safe."

"So you disappeared?" Edsen asked.

She nodded. "For a few days. I hid at a friend's house who was out of town. No one knew I was there. I was so scared. I knew they would kill me or go after Ellie. I was sure they were watching the house and I was afraid to telephone. I hoped the car in the garage would let her know that I was all right."

"How did you get this evidence?" Marshal Edsen steered her back on track."

"After I left and the story about the Dalton girl was in the news, Carew and Dalrymple said they were playing cards, that they spent the entire night at Carew's house."

"Carew is in on this, too?" Taylor asked.

"I didn't see him on the road, but I knew he was lying, so he must have known about Dalrymple or been in on it. I knew I had to come back. If I were going to protect Ellie I had to find something that would implicate them."

"You have got a lot of nerve, lady."

"Don't pin any medals on me, Marshal. I was scared to death, but I have a daughter to protect."

"What did you do?"

"Carew's wife corroborated the story," Susan said. "She said he was home that night. She couldn't know that. *She* wasn't home that night. She worked at the Fulbright Motel. "I found out later she was filling in for one of the clerks who was pregnant. Carew said she didn't work that night."

"The report says she called in sick and stayed home."

"She didn't," Susan insisted. "I saw her there myself. I

saw Mrs. Carew going into the motel. She was wearing her uniform." Susan paused, taking a moment to collect her thoughts. "After I heard that news report I assumed I would need proof, some kind of insurance if I ever got caught. They were the police, and they had killed that girl. So I went to the motel and stole the videotape."

Marshal Edsen looked as if he wanted to ask a question, but he stayed silent.

"I stole it because Carew's wife was known for corroborating her husband's stories. And I was scared. I thought they'd find me before the sun came up. And like the Dalton child, I'd have a bullet in my back. The surveillance tape is dated and has his wife on it as she went about her duties in the motel."

"Do you know if the motel ever reported a stolen tape?" Marshal Edsen asked.

Taylor shook her head. "No one reports that kind of thing in a motel unless there is a theft of personal property." Taylor remembered her own trashed room. The tape machine mounted in the hallway outside her door had been no help then.

"There wouldn't be a report," Susan said. "I pulled off the label and put it on another tape. I figured they reused the tapes and who'd notice one missing if they all had labels?"

Susan continued her story. "After I got the tape, I felt a little more secure. I had something concrete in my hands, but Carew wasn't the man I'd seen in the road. Even with the tape, there was nothing to protect me from Ward Dalrymple. So I went to his house."

"You went to Dalrymple's house?" Taylor was surprised. "That was a gutsy thing to do. What did he say?"

"He didn't see me. Neither of them saw me."

"Neither?"

"First I went to Carew's. Dalrymple never made a move without Carew's approval. I didn't know why they killed that child, but I knew it was the two of them. I figured they were still out looking for me, so they wouldn't think I'd show up at their back door. They were both there."

"Carew and Dalrymple?" The marshal needed concreteness to the story.

Susan nodded. "I looked in the kitchen window. My heart was beating so hard I didn't think I could breathe. If I'd known they were going to be there, I never would have had the nerve."

"What were you looking for?"

"I didn't know—something, anything, that could keep me alive. They were arguing. I couldn't hear what they were saying, but Carew was reading the riot act to Dalrymple. I got scared that they'd find me. As I started to leave I saw something on the trash can. It was a smear, but it was dark. I had to get down to see that it was blood, dried, but definitely blood. I opened the can and found Carew's shirt. He'd thrown it out. It was torn in several places, as if he'd been in a fight. There was dirt mixed with the blood. I was so angry. They'd killed a child and they were going to get away with it. They were the police. Who was going to investigate them? So I took it."

"You still have it?" Edsen perked up.

She nodded. "The pocket has his name stitched into it. After that, I went to the second cop's house."

Taylor watched Edsen shake his head in disbelief.

"Dalrymple is unmarried. His back door was open, and I went in. His uniform lay on the table in his laundry room. It was neatly folded as if he planned to wear it again, but it was still smeared with the child's blood. I found another uniform in his closet. I put it in the laundry room and smeared it with catsup. I figured he'd never know the difference, especially after it dried."

"What did you do then?"

"I left."

"The uniforms were covered with the girl's blood. Why didn't you go to the police?"

"I thought of Ellie. It would take a while for the police to believe me, if they did at all. I didn't know the uniforms had the child's blood on them. It could be their own blood. They could say anything. I'd had a run-in with Carew before. I thought of this as insurance, so I left a note."

"A note?" Taylor repeated.

"I told them I had the videotape from the motel, but I said nothing about the clothes."

"Where are the clothes now?"

"I hid them. I wanted to see Ellie one more time. I took the chance of going home. I left the car in the garage and put the clothes in a trunk in the attic. Then I left on foot. No one would think to find me hitchhiking. I picked up a bus on the county route."

"And you never looked back?" Edsen asked.

"Not quite. I stayed on the bus until it got to Tennessee. I wasn't headed anywhere in particular, just as far from Liberty as I could get. Two days after getting to Tennessee I was involved in a traffic accident." She looked at her husband. "I was hit by a car."

"It was my car." He spoke for the first time since they'd entered the room.

"I didn't remember anything after that. I didn't know who I was or where I was going. Franklin took responsibility for me." She squeezed his hand and smiled at him. Her next comments were for the marshal, but she looked directly at her husband. "Two years ago I remembered everything. It wasn't like a bolt of lightning. I got up and made coffee and while it brewed I sat at the table in the kitchen and all the memories flowed back like opening a box and finding photographs that evoked points of time. I told no one."

"We're going to have to get those clothes and have them tested."

She nodded.

"Meanwhile, we'll put you in protective custody."

Susan looked at her husband. He nodded assurance.

"What about my daughter? She's going to have a baby."

"I'm sure we can get this done fast."

Proverbial Bad Penny. Sheriff Carew threw the newspaper down on the desk. The headline jumped out at him just as the grainy photo of Susan Hilliard Frasier had, squinting as she looked about. The story said she was at the Atlanta airport. A little older than he remembered, but it was definitely her.

"Dalrymple, come in here," he shouted through the door. The deputy came in. Carew threw the paper at him. "What does she know?"

"Nothing, sheriff," he said. "The paper only says she's obviously not dead. No one interviewed her."

"No one? She got in a car registered to the U.S. attorney's office. Someone sure, the hell, did interview her."

"What could she say? There is nothing she knows. It's her word against mine. She's been gone for six years. Who's going to believe her over me?"

"You better be right," he told him. "Or I'll fry you myself."

Taylor opened the FedEx envelope the Sheraton business office had held for her for several days. She started reading before she got to the elevator. She'd expected most of what was there. It was no surprise that most of Susan's family would benefit financially from her death or that Billy Porter needed money to finance the expansion of the furniture business. He'd overextended himself, projecting sales greater than they turned out to be. He was sitting on a wire when it came to money. Sam could use it, too. He owed quite a bit to credit cards, but he had no real vices.

What surprised her was Ward Dalrymple. He'd spent a few years out of Liberty. He'd been arrested in New Orleans on a charge related to pornography. The charge had been dropped, and he had returned here.

"Ms. Chambers?" Taylor turned around. The clerk from the business center stood behind her. "I almost forgot to give you this. It was delivered this morning."

Taylor took the second package. It weighed less than a pound and was addressed to her, but with no return address.

"Who brought this?"

"I don't know. It was on the desk when I came in."

Taylor eyed it strangely. "Thank you." She dismissed the clerk. She wasn't expecting anything and since Susan was back on Georgia soil and the word was out, she was overly cautious.

In her room, she called former detective Markham. "How can you tell if you have a letter bomb?" she asked.

"Do you think you have one?" His voice was serious.

"Yes."

"Where are you?"

"In my room at the Sheraton."

"Leave it where it is and get out of there. I'll be right over." He hung up before she could ask if he knew anything about bombs.

Taylor felt her character analysis of him had been correct. He would never stop being a cop. And he must have come to the hotel by some means other than a car. He arrived within minutes, without fanfare, but with three other people. None of them wore uniforms, but Taylor could see cop as surely as if it had been tattooed on their heads. She met them in the lobby. Without a word of exchange, they followed her to her room.

"Are you the bomb squad?" she asked when the door closed behind her.

"Yes, ma'am," one of them said. "Where is it?"

"On the desk." She pointed as she spoke.

"You should leave us alone." Another man was already pushing her toward the door.

"Wait—"

The door closed in her face. It opened a minute later. Everyone came out.

"What happened?"

"Nothing," Markham said. "They put it in the box." She looked at the box one of the men carried. "This hotel is much too crowded. We're taking it someplace safe and controlled."

Taylor didn't ask where. She went with them. She rode in a car with Markham while the others piled into a van.

"You found her," Markham said as he negotiated the traffic.

Taylor nodded.

"What was the story?"

"It's still unfolding, but I will tell you it's connected to the Dalton girl's murder."

The van turned several corners and then into the driveway of a large police department.

"What are they going to do?"

"Open it."

When they went inside, she and Markham followed. They put the box in a reinforced glass room. Everyone else remained on the outside. Using handles that extended from one side of the glass to the other, one of the men started a slow procedure of opening the package. It seemed to take years. Each time a flap of the brown paper came apart Taylor gritted her teeth or jumped. Each time nothing happened. When the final flap opened, the man used a mechanical claw to grapple the paper and pull it aside. Left on the desk was a black case that looked like a videotape container.

Dextrously, he manipulated the metal tools until it was open. Turning the case to face the window they found a tape, not a bomb.

Taylor exhaled.

Chapter 7

Kiddie porn. Taylor turned her face away from the television screen. She couldn't watch the things the children were doing. They weren't old enough to know what they were doing, and some of them were begging and screaming. She heard voices in the background telling them to be quiet. Everything from soothing to authoritative.

"I've seen enough," U.S. Marshal Edsen said. "Where did this come from?"

"I got it in the mail," she told him, then related the story. When she finished, he said nothing. "Is it enough?"

"The Dalton girl isn't on this."

"If you let it go to the end, you'll hear the voices discussing her and what to do with her. Then someone curses and says she's running. After that the film just rolls. I assume they ran out after Melissa, and that's when Susan Frasier saw her get shot."

The marshal started the tape again. Taylor left the room. She couldn't view it. She'd been forced to the ladies room and lost her lunch the last time. When he finished, he could call her. She waited, pacing the hall in front of his office. It seemed like hours passed, but it was only a few minutes. Finally, the door opened. She turned expectantly.

"It's enough," he said.

Cars converged on the converted plantation house from all directions. Sirens blared, disturbing the peace and calling all within hearing distance to the circus created by the noise. Men in black suits jumped out of cars, some with guns in hand, others with FBI written on shirts or jackets in large bold letters.

They ran up the steps of the white house and through the front doors. Taylor and Markham went with them. The marshals must have known where Carew's office was. They went straight for it.

"Sheriff Bennett Carew?" Edsen addressed him. Carew stood up slowly, his eyes shifting from one man to another, then another. He didn't answer. "You're under arrest for the kidnapping and murder of Melissa Dalton."

There were a host of other charges, Taylor knew, but this was good for a start. Carew didn't say a word. They handcuffed him and took him away. She saw Dalrymple come out of the other office, also handcuffed.

"Justice will finally be done," Markham said quietly. They stayed behind. Everyone else moved behind the procession as if they would hear something that would make tonight's dinner conversation more lively.

"Not for Ava Dalton," she said. "Susan Frasier gets her life back. Ellie gets her mother, but Mrs. Dalton gets nothing."

"No nothing. She gets to see her daughter's killers pay for their crime, and she'll know that no other mother has to suffer like she did under the hands of those psychos."

* * *

Flight 157 would leave the Savannah airport in three hours. Taylor was packed and ready to go. She'd called Julianne and talked to her for hours. She needed to contact her daughter, know she was safe and happy, after everything ended in Liberty two days ago. Julianne was still away with her father, but Taylor felt good listening to her talk about the English soccer games she'd seen while they were visiting. Her daughter had discovered she liked Agatha Christie and bought a ton of her books, she said. Taylor listened with tears in her throat until she finally hung up the phone and slept.

Susan Frasier and Ellie Porter had invited her to lunch after they found out about the arrest. She'd gone to Ellie's house, and Billy met her with an apology for his bad manners. She enjoyed the time with them, a reunited family. They seemed happy and genuinely glad to have Susan back. Susan was glowing as the grandmother-to-be, and her husband also seemed to fit right in.

All the loose ends seem to be tied up, Taylor thought as she looked around the room. There was nothing else to do except turn in the rental car and get on the plane. But Taylor felt one more area of unfinished business needed resolving. She got in the car and headed toward Liberty. She needed to go home.

The place looked empty when she pulled into the driveway. She got out of the car and looked at the house. The grass was cut, the gutters straight. Everything looked well-maintained. She pushed away from the car and started for the door.

"Excuse me," someone said. Taylor turned. The woman coming toward her was small, with gray hair. She was thin and her face was sunken, as if she'd been ill a long time.

"Mrs. Dalton," Taylor said, and went toward the woman. Taylor wasn't usually demonstrative, especially to people with whom she only had a nodding acquaintance, but she hugged Mrs. Dalton as if the two of them had been intimate friends for years.

"Thank you, Taylor," she said when they separated. "I can't explain what it means to me to have Melissa's killers found. And if it wasn't for you, I would never have known."

The story was all over town now, Taylor knew. It was a small community, as she'd said so many times. The story of the kiddie porn tapes and Deputy Dalrymple had been front-page news.

Tears rolled down Mrs. Dalton's cheeks. "Don't cry, Mrs. Dalton. It's over now."

"It is, Taylor. It's really over." She hugged her again. "Thank you. Thank you for Melissa, and thank you for giving me back my life."

Mrs. Dalton released her and walked away. She was still crying, but Taylor knew they were healing tears. She watched her until she turned the corner and moved out of sight.

Then Taylor walked up the driveway to the front door of the house where she grew up. Inside it was dark, with the shades down. She walked through the space. She smiled, looking at a photo on the mantel. She was on the slide with her arms outstretched. She was sliding into the loving arms of her father. She turned back. They had had a wonderful life in this house, she thought. Images of one of her sisters dressed in her prom gown came back. Her mother's tears when she told her she was getting married. They hadn't had everything they ever wanted, but they had all the love that was possible to receive.

She walked through the rooms, remembering things that made them laugh and cry: Christmas, picnics, school plays. Then she remembered their special place, she and her father's. They used to hide things there when she was a child and wanted to be first in his eyes. She understood parenting more now, but then she wanted to be an only child. It was in the attic, an old secretary that had many compartments.

Their place wasn't any of those. It was a secret place on the side, a hidden drawer that opened when you released a spring under the lid. She reached toward the spring.

He probably had a special place for each of his daughters. Henry Chambers was too loving to favor one daughter over another. He loved them all, but loved them differently.

She released the spring. The drawer popped open as if it were in continual use. Inside was a piece of paper. She knew it was from him. Often, unexpectedly, but when she most needed it, she'd find a note from her father, something he'd left to cheer her up. It could be a present or just *I love you* written on a sheet of notebook paper.

This time it was a note. It was dated three months before he died. She read it. *Always remember I love you.*

And she always would.

●◆●

Purvis read the headlines of the Liberty Sentinel: Heiress Susan Frasier Found Alive. Porn Ring Uncovered.

He snapped the paper closed. Worry lines were etched across his walnut brown forehead. Liberty was growing more sinister by the day, he thought. Or maybe it always was. Sure Henry hinted at things, he had his suspicions, some of which he shared with Purvis. But this.

Purvis spun his chair to face the window. He stretched out his long legs and braced his heels on the window ledge. He would have never pictured Ms. Corporate America Taylor Chambers as a sleuth. But she had Henry's blood running through those veins of hers. Truth be told, ninety percent of being a lawyer was sniffing out the facts. Taylor had accomplished that and then some. Henry would be proud.

Purvis folded his arms across his chest and sighed deeply. They say the best kept secrets can be found in small towns, he thought. Well, Liberty was becoming a perfect example. One by one the town's dirty little secrets were being unearthed and Henry's daughters had the shovels. Two down, two to go. He only hoped that they weren't digging themselves into holes they couldn't get out of.

Identity
Crisis

Bridget Anderson

*For Terry, who understands when writing
sometimes comes before eating,
but still asked, "Huh, will ya?"*

Chapter 1

At the reading of her father's will, Samantha Chambers shed her tears and hung her head in shame. Too busy with her own career, she hadn't visited him like she should have. Now it was time to do as her father had asked. Initially she'd refused, but later, she realized she owed him this much. She'd never been interested in a life of investigation or law enforcement of any type. And now, here she was, doing just what her father had wanted, if only for a little while. Parked alongside the street, she read over her father's notes for the third time.

The garage door flipped up, catching Samantha's attention. She put the notepad down and leaned over in her seat as a silver Lexus backed out of the driveway. On surveillance outside of Hugh Noble's house in her two-year-old Toyota Camry, she pretended to reach into her glove compartment as he passed in the Lexus.

Her father, Henry Chambers, discovered that Hugh Noble wasn't as wealthy as he pretended to be. Neither his expensive home in Alpharetta, Georgia, nor the new high-powered car he'd driven away in was registered in his name. Instead, they were registered to Mike Davis. Her father's investigation into the fiancé of little Miss Wendy Wilmington, Liberty, Georgia's, wealthiest daughter, had only begun before he died. It was up to her to put the pieces together and close the case. Hugh visited Liberty often, but lived in Atlanta.

She wasted no time starting her car and making a U-turn to follow him. She drove slowly and stayed far enough behind so she wouldn't be spotted. *Okay, Mr. Noble, what are you hiding?* She'd prepared to follow him wherever he took her.

Mrs. Wilmington hadn't heard of a financial advisor who didn't know much about the investment industry. That's why she'd hired Henry to do a background check on Hugh Noble. Although her daughter was in love with him, she hadn't been fooled so easily. She thought his eyes were on their money, and not their daughter.

Other than his secretary, Hugh worked alone. On Monday and Tuesday, Samantha had paid his office a visit, but it was closed. Today, at his house, she got lucky.

Hugh raced through the streets of Alpharetta before pulling into a Quick Trip convenience store.

Samantha drove past the store and into the McDonald's lot next door.

He stepped out of his car dressed in an expensive looking, light blue sports coat and slacks. He didn't seem to notice her as he strode inside. She reached for her notepad and wrote down the time and their location. Samantha remembered her father going over his notes, and it had surprised her how much he'd written on one small sheet of paper.

She jumped at the shrill sound of her cell phone. Snatching the phone from her purse, she answered in a short and quick tone. "Hello."

"Sam, it's Ed. Where are you?" he asked.

"I'm at McDonald's."

"McDonald's! What the hell are you doing there? You don't even eat red meat."

Not wanting to discuss the case with her boyfriend, she

hid the whole truth. "They sell more than hamburgers, you know. I'm grabbing a snack, what do you want?" She tried not to sound too annoyed.

"Are you going home after work tonight?"

Sam reached over to the passenger seat and popped open her daytimer. "I think so, let me check my appointment book." Every couple of seconds she glanced up to make sure Hugh hadn't left. He hadn't.

"I might be a little late. I've got a meeting at four o'clock. Then I'm meeting the manager of this new group, Exclusive, for happy hour. But I'll try to make it quick."

"Don't bother. We were invited out tonight, but I told them we couldn't make it. I knew you'd be too busy." He gave a frustrated sigh into the phone.

Sam looked up and caught Hugh as he left the store and headed to the bank of pay phones along the side. She tossed her pad onto the passenger's seat and kept her eyes on him. Ed kept talking, but she didn't hear a word he said. Sam thought about how she would complete the background check on Hugh without being a private investigator.

"You know, that's your problem. You don't have time for me, or anybody else. All you have time for is that damned job. You live for that freaking record company." The anger in his voice thundered through the phone.

"Eddie, look," Sam tried to concentrate on the conversation, and watch Hugh at the same time. Hugh hung up the phone and trudged back to his car. His lips moved as he talked to himself on the way. When he glanced in her direction, his lips turned up in a sneer and his brows creased into a frown. Not a pleasant phone call, she presumed. He started the car and whirled out of the lot.

Sam pulled out of McDonald's with the phone cradled between her ear and shoulder. "I've got to go. Can we talk about this tonight?" A horn blew at her when she jumped out into traffic not wanting to lose Hugh. Keeping her distance, she spotted him a couple of car lengths ahead.

"Don't bother, I won't be in tonight. I'm going out."

She blinked with surprise at the sudden dial tone before throwing the phone onto the passenger's seat. He never cut her any slack. However, she didn't have time to worry about him right now.

Hugh pulled into SunTrust Bank, exited the car, and stepped up to the ATM machine. Sam waited patiently as he made his transaction and returned to the car. This time he entered Interstate 75, and she floored the accelerator to keep up with him. After what seemed like a high-speed chase, he exited at Courtland Avenue. She continued to follow him until he pulled into the parking lot of a popular strip club, The Gentleman's Club. Sam parked across the street.

She wanted to put on a pair of dark shades, but they wouldn't do any good. If any of her industry peers saw her car parked outside this club, she'd have a hard time trying to explain herself. Working with the A&R Department—Artist & Repertoire—for Valentine Records, she'd bailed numerous artists out of jail after a night at the club. But she'd never entered the place herself, and she wasn't about to tonight. After about fifteen minutes, she decided to leave.

The next day Sam paid another visit to Noble and Associates, hoping to get some information. The small investment firm shared office space with several other businesses. She stopped in the restroom on the first floor to check herself out before proceeding to Hugh's office on the seventh floor. Looking in the mirror, she wanted to see how the wireframe glasses looked on her. The glasses, along with her expensive tailored suit, the pantyhose, and her borrowed diamond stud earrings, were all a disguise to her. She never dressed up like this. She'd taken over thirty minutes on her makeup job to pass for a prim and proper southern belle. Sam wanted Hugh to think she was wealthy, so she tried her best to look the part.

Once inside the cramped, dingy office with dusty fake plants, a woman came from a back room to greet her.

"Hello, may I help you?"

Sam smiled at the petite woman who approached her in her low-cut, form-fitting, orange-and-white minidress. She looked more prepared for a night at the club instead of a day at the office.

"Yes, my name is Vivian Banks and I'd like to see Mr. Noble." Sam had created her alias on the way up in the elevator.

The woman looked Sam over before tilting her head to the side. "Do you have an appointment?"

Sam stepped up to the desk that served as a divider between them. "No, I'm sorry I don't, but I hoped I'd be able to see him for just a minute. I really need some investment advice." Sam watched the woman as she walked up to the desk, dropped a folder, and flipped open a desk calendar. She used the eraser of her pencil to flip through the pages.

"May I ask who referred you?" She gave Sam a suspicious look.

"I'm sorry, I didn't get your name?" Sam extended her hand to the woman.

"I'm Porsche, Mr. Noble's secretary and assistant." She held her head high as she shook Sam's hand.

"Oh, that's cute. As in the car?"

"Yeah, that's right. Just like the car." She responded grinning.

"Well, Porsche." Sam smiled, stifling the urge to laugh. She then let out a sigh. "I was referred to Mr. Noble by a friend who told me he might be able to help me out."

Porsche ran her tongue along her front teeth, then pointed to the chair across from her desk. "Have a seat."

"Thank you." Sam took a seat.

Porsche looked up from her calendar "Mr. Noble is out of the country this week, he'll be back next week. How does Tuesday afternoon suit you?"

"He's been out of the country all week?" Sam asked, surprised.

"That's right." Porsche raised her chin and eyeballed Sam. "All week."

Then who was that I followed around yesterday? Or was she lying for him? But why?

"Tuesday of next week will be fine," she managed to respond.

Sam's curiosity grew stronger. Her father's notes provided her with a lead, but nothing more. She didn't have the tools of a P.I., but she had ways of getting the information she needed. If it worked in the record industry, it should work anywhere. She left Hugh's office ready to have this case wrapped up in a few weeks, maybe less if she played her cards right. After all, once she proved he wasn't rich, the case would be solved.

Chapter 2

Sam sat at her kitchen table drinking her morning cup of coffee, and studying her notes. What she needed was a plan, and some help. She had to find out what Noble and Associates was worth, and who the hell Mike Davis was. She glanced up and looked out the window into her back yard. How would her father handle this case? she asked herself.

Before her meeting with Hugh next week, she wanted to have as much information on his company as possible. She got up and went downstairs into her office. First stop, the Internet. If you could find anything on the Net, she should be able to find something on Noble and Associates.

She surfed the Net, from the White Pages to a few simple downloadable databases, with no luck. What she needed was access to the Information Broker, which she couldn't link into since she wasn't a P.I. After a couple of hours, she stopped and left for work.

Her secretary, Barbara, greeted her when she entered the office. "Hey, Sam. How you doing?"

Sam gave her a vague smile. "I'm okay I guess."

"I'm real sorry to hear about your father. I bet the service was beautiful."

"It was."

"He's resting peaceful now. And we're glad you're back, things are getting busy around here." She handed Sam a stack of mail. "All this came while you were out."

Sam leafed through the mail, only interested in anything that appeared urgent. Most of the mail was addressed to Ms. Samantha Chambers, but a few pieces were addressed to Valentine Records, Publicity Dept.

"Is this it?" she asked, walking into her office.

"That's everything. You also had a few callers who didn't want to go into voice mail. I left those notes on your desk."

"Thank you."

The dimmer switch moved up as the lightbulb finally turned on in Sam's head. *That's it!* She could check his mail. Mail tampering was against the law, and she knew it, but if she didn't get caught no one would ever know. *Was the mail going to the house addressed to Mike Davis or Hugh Noble?*

She settled in, returning a few phone calls and giving the mailman plenty of time to do his job. She left her office slightly nervous. Since she didn't have access to the databases her father used, she gave herself permission to do whatever to solve this case, even if that meant breaking the law a little.

Sam drove past Hugh's house slowly, scanning to see if she saw anyone. The neighborhood was quiet and deserted. His mailbox sat at the end of the driveway with the red flag up. *Good.* She stopped her car in front of his neighbor's house. Before getting out of the car, she saw a woman in a large brim hat next door bending over a flowerbed. She decided not to chance it. Instead, she crept down the street before circling around the block. She'd come this far; she wasn't going back until she had a peek inside that box. This time she saw the woman with a basket full of flowers walking toward the back of the house.

She stopped short of Hugh's house. Her heartbeat increased as she looked at the little black box that possibly held a clue. Butterflies danced in her stomach as she jumped out of the car, leaving the motor running and the car door open. Like a lioness going for her prey, she rushed up to the mailbox and pulled the door open. With trembling hands she grabbed the envelopes, then glanced over at his neighbor's house to make sure she hadn't returned.

Inside were a few utility bills addressed to Mike Davis, several advertisements for Resident, and a small newspaper. Paranoid, she peeked around again before opening the paper enough to see the heading. The *Liberty Sentinel*. It was addressed to Mr. Hugh Noble. *So this is how you keep up with what's happening in Liberty.* She closed the paper, then jumped when she heard a churning sound.

The garage door opened. She threw the mail back in the box and hurried back to her car. Her hands shook as she gripped the steering wheel. She didn't think anyone was at home. Shifting into drive, she pulled off faster than she wanted to.

"Keep it cool girl, slow down," she said aloud.

She couldn't leave without finding out who was coming out of Hugh's garage. In her rearview mirror she saw the car backing down the driveway. She whipped into a driveway and killed the engine. From this position she had a perfect view of the black BMW as it cleared the driveway and slowly moved down the street.

Sam grabbed her binoculars from the passenger's seat to get a closer look at the man inside. It definitely wasn't Hugh. His long braids and black sunglasses made him resemble a twenty-something reggae singer. He hadn't noticed her; his cell phone distracted him.

Sam twisted in her seat and kept the car in view as he

crept down the street. She read off the license plate number, then grabbed her pad to jot it down. *Got it.*

On the way back to her office, she wondered who that guy was. *Could he be Mike Davis?* He looked too young to own a business and a six-figure home. However, now she had his license plate number, so she could find out who he was. All she needed was someone to run the number through the DMV for her. She didn't have any DMV contacts, but she'd find a way to get the information she needed.

Over the next several days, Sam placed calls searching for someone she knew who had a DMV contact, but hadn't come up with anything. A few days later, she attended a goodbye party Valentine Records hosted for one of their executives who was leaving the business. She cruised the floor of Club Kaya to make sure everything was in place. The minute she saw Rich Jackson, she knew her problem was solved. An Atlanta policeman, Rich moonlighted as a security guard for Valentine Records.

Rich loved the perks of his extra job, like being surrounded with beautiful women from time to time. He'd never let them down and was excellent at his job. He stood in the foyer of the club talking to a guy from A&R.

"Hello, gentlemen, are you enjoying yourselves tonight?" Samantha asked as she joined them.

"Oh yeah, always. Anytime Valentine throws a party, it's always off the hook." Rich smiled at Sam.

The guy from A&R shook his head and smiled. "It's the bomb."

"I'm pleased. But Tommy, I noticed from across the room that you weren't dancing tonight." Sam swayed over to Tommy and gently linked her arm into his, moving him away from the foyer. "Now we've got more women than men in here tonight. Baby, you finish that drink and hit the dance floor."

One of their young recording artists stood close by. Sam grabbed her by the arm and introduced her to Tommy. "Okay, you two, no standing around holding up the walls. Get out there and shake your groove thing."

They stared at each other for a moment before the young woman took Tommy's drink, set it down, and pulled him onto the floor.

Sam walked back over to Rich. "Rich, I need a big favor from you." She stood almost toe-to-toe with Rich in her three-inch heels. He was as big as a bull and very muscular.

"Sure, what can I do for you?" He smiled, resting his hands behind his back.

"I've seen a guy following one of the girls, so I wrote down his license plate number."

"You need me to have this guy picked up?"

"No, nothing like that. He's probably harmless. I thought maybe you could run the number through the DMV for me, and let me know who he is." She reached down to scratch the back of her leg, and Rich's gaze followed her hand.

"Sure, you know I'll do anything for you. But, don't you want me to scare him a little? Who's he been following anyway?"

She leaned forward, holding Rich's arm, and stroked his chest with her other hand. "Rich, I know you sometimes shake up people for Valentine Records, but that's not what I'm asking for." Rich worked out and was proud of his body; she knew that, and used it to her advantage. She leaned in closer to almost whisper in his ear. "Baby, I don't want to hurt anybody. I'd appreciate all the information you could get me on this guy though." She squeezed his arm.

He grinned and looked down at her hand on his chest. "Sure. Keep stroking my chest like that, and we'll get you whatever you want."

She playfully pushed him and they started laughing. Everyone at Valentine was used to her hands-on approach. She couldn't help being a touchy type of person.

"Is it all right if I get that number to you tonight?"

"Yeah, I'll be here all night."

"Thank you, Rich. I owe you one."

"Yeah, well how about some concert tickets? I'd like to go see Sade when she comes next month."

Sam grinned at him. "And I thought you were doing it for me." She should have known better; nobody did anything for free anymore.

"For you, and concert tickets." He winked at her.

"I'll place a call and see what I can do."

"Thanks."

Sam's drive to Liberty for the Wilmington family picnic had paid off. She peered at Hugh through her binoculars as he walked through the grass like he was dodging land mines. He wasn't exactly the outdoors type she detected. He joined the Wilmingtons for their annual family picnic in Liberty Park. This was an event Sam knew he couldn't miss—not if he was courting little Miss Wendy Wilmington. All the aunts, uncles, grandparents, and cousins were in attendance. Whether Hugh knew it or not, today was a test. If he passed the family's inspection, he was in. Unless she could prove he'd lied to them all.

He greeted Wendy and her mother with a kiss, then appropriately shook the men's hands. From her vantage point in the parking lot that looked over the pavilion, she could see Wendy's face blush with happiness. She grinned and held onto Hugh's hand like a lovesick puppy. Mrs. Wilmington didn't seem so impressed; she eyed him skeptically as he moved about the pavilion.

Sam watched Wendy make a fuss over Hugh, feed him, and even wipe his mouth. He returned the affection with plenty of hugs and kisses in front of the entire family. They appeared to be in love and happy. Maybe Hugh's wealth didn't matter if he made Wendy this happy. Her Eddie never showed her that much affection, especially not in front of anyone.

Before she came to any more conclusions, she needed to talk to someone else in the family. The park was crowded with families having picnics. The Wilmingtons had spread out over most of the area, playing touch football, volleyball, and throwing Frisbees. She put down her binoculars and got out of the car. The volleyball net was far enough from the pavilion. She joined the park crowd, and made her way over to the Wilmingtons' volleyball game.

As she got closer she searched through the crowd, calling out her cousin's name. "Jonathan." She edged closer, pretending to be looking for someone. "Jonathan," she called again.

Maya Wilmington turned and waved at her once Sam stood almost directly behind her. "Samantha, is that you?"

"Hey, Maya, how you doing, girl?" Sam joined their little group and reached out to hug Maya.

"I'm fine. How are you? I heard about your father passing, and I'm real sorry. What a shock. You must be devastated."

Sam had found the right person, Maya, who could talk your head off. "I'm doing okay. I came down to spend a little time with my family. I see you guys are having your annual picnic." She looked around the crowd to make sure Wendy and Hugh were still at the pavilion.

"Where are you living now? Girl, I lost track of everybody once I left school."

"I'm in Atlanta." It was a fact Sam was sure Maya already knew.

Two small children ran up to Maya and grabbed her by the legs, gasping for breath. "Mama, can we go swimming, please Mama, can we?" They tugged at her skirt and looked up at her like two little angels.

"No, you may not. We don't know what's in that pool. You can swim when we get home." She smiled up at Sam. "They know I hate public pools. You can't tell about some people, and they let anybody in that pool."

She ran her hand over her children's heads affectionately and took their hands from her skirt. "Go find your father and ask him to buy you some ice cream."

"Okay." They ran off, focused on ice cream.

"You have beautiful children." Sam bet those were two of the most spoiled children in all of Liberty.

"Oh, thank you. They're spoiled rotten, but why not? My parents spoiled me, and I turned out fine." She smiled at herself and looked at Sam as if waiting for a confirmation.

Sam merely nodded and glanced around. There was no way she'd agree to that.

"Were you looking for someone?"

She'd almost forgotten. "Yes, my little cousin Jonathan. You didn't see a little boy in green shorts and a Braves T-shirt run by here, did you?"

"No, I don't think so. How old is he?"

"Ah, he's seven. A little small for his age, but he's seven." She glanced toward the pavilion again. The happy couple was still enjoying themselves. Wendy sat on his lap now, in the eighty-degree heat.

"Sickening, isn't it?"

Sam turned to Maya and saw her looking at the couple also. "Is that Wendy?"

"Her and her boyfriend. They act like two teenagers. Kissing and hugging in public like that. You'd never catch Roland and me slobbering all over each other in public. They should be ashamed of themselves."

"They look very happy. Is he from around here?"

"No, as a matter of fact, he's from Atlanta, too. Maybe you know him, Hugh Noble?"

Sam peered at him and shook her head. "No, I don't think so. What does he do?"

"I don't know. Something in investments, so he claims."

The sound of doubt caught Sam's attention. "You sound as if you don't believe him?" This is what she'd gotten out of the car for.

"Girl, he's a bullshit artist. I can see it, but Wendy can't."

"Why do you say that?"

Maya gave her a why-so-many-questions look, then shrugged.

"I mean, your parents seem to approve of him. Didn't I read in the paper about their engagement?"

"Unfortunately, yes, but that guy doesn't know the first thing about investments. Hugh suggested some stock to Roland, but when he looked into it he said it would have been a bad investment. I'm telling you, he doesn't know anything about stocks and investing."

"Where does he work? Maybe he's new."

"Huh, he says he's had his own business for over ten years. But giving out advice like that can't be profitable. He tried to tell Uncle Walter how risky the market is, then proceeded to lose ten thousand dollars for him."

"Another bad investment?"

"You got it. Speaking of bad investments, here comes the happy couple now."

Sam froze.

Chapter 3

She couldn't face him now. Not before she had the case solved. Once he saw her face, she'd never be able to follow him without being detected. She touched the back of her hair and glanced over her shoulder at the same time. The happy couple left the pavilion and walked their way. She had to get out of there.

Shielding her eyes from the sun, she peered through the crowd and saw her getaway. "Maya, I think I see my little cousin." She eased away, looking back at Maya. "Tell Wendy I said hello and I hope to see her before I leave town, but I've got to catch this little guy before he gets to the pool. You know how nasty that thing is."

Maya cringed. "Yes, get him before he jumps into all that bacteria. It was nice seeing you again."

"You too, bye." She called out to her imaginary cousin again, "Jonathan." She made a swift exit to the other side of the swing sets before returning to her car. She hoped to run into more people like Maya. If everyone sang like a bird, she'd quickly have this case all figured out. She checked the picnic area with her binoculars again. The happy couple was engaged in a game of croquet. She had what she needed from this picnic. Time to hit town and see who else entrusted Noble and Associates with their money.

Sam returned to Atlanta ready to prove Hugh Noble was a phony and his business was a front. For what, she didn't know yet. But she was determined to find out. She tried to ring Rich to see what he'd found out for her, but he was on duty.

The doorbell rang and she glanced up at the mirrored clock on the wall. It was time for Eddie to pick her up for lunch. When she opened the door he had on his usual college professor attire: black slacks, white shirt, and a silk blue vest. If he ever showed up in a pair of jeans and a T-shirt, she'd probably pass out.

"Hey you ready to eat?" He gave her an unaffectionate kiss on the cheek and walked past her into the living room.

She stood with the door open, staring at him. "What happened to, 'I miss you, did you have a good trip?' "

"Look . . . I'm surprised you even have time for lunch with me. I've told myself not to get stressed out over your job anymore. You're a busy woman, and I can respect that."

If he had wanted her presence at one of his stuffy dinners, he would have had a fit that she left town without him. Since he hadn't needed her, the trip went unnoticed. She closed the door and went to grab her purse.

"What did you go home for anyway? I thought you were working on something for your father here in Atlanta."

"The Wilmingtons had a family picnic, and I wanted to see if this guy showed up."

"What guy?"

She had called him days ago and told him about the case, but she'd only told him so much. "The guy I'm doing the background check on."

"You followed him to Liberty?" Eddie didn't like the idea of her working on the case because she wasn't qualified.

"I didn't follow him. I got there before he did. I only went down to see if he showed up."

"Did he?"

"Yes, and I found out some more information." She sat down on the couch next to Eddie. "Seems like he's making investments for people and losing their money. Supposedly he's been in business for over ten years, but he gave . . ."

"Why are you getting caught up in that mess? Just get the information on the business and turn it in. You don't need to be following that guy around and meddling into his business. Everybody makes a bad investment or two. That doesn't mean anything."

"Try four or five. I found a few more people who'd given him money to invest; none of them were singing his praises. Except for one woman who claims he made about three . . ."

"Damn, Samantha. End this right now." He jumped up from the couch. "It's bad enough that you work yourself to death. Now you're running around chasing some man that you don't know the first thing about."

She stood to challenge him, even though he was pissed at her; he only called her by her full name when he was upset. "I'm working this case for my father, and I won't stop until I've found out everything I need to know."

"Look, your father's gone, and solving this case won't bring him back," he retorted.

She reached out to slap him, but he caught her hand. "You insensitive bastard." The words dripped from her lips with spite. She tugged, trying to pull her hand free.

"Sam, I'm sorry. I didn't mean it like that. You know what I meant."

"Get out!"

He let go of her hand, taking a step back at the same time. "Come on, let's go to lunch and forget it."

"That's your solution to everything—forget about it. Well, I'm not going to forget about this one. Get out!"

She pointed toward the door, giving him a keep-your-mouth-shut look. All she wanted him to do was leave. She stormed past him and yanked the front door open. The minute he cleared the door, she slammed it behind him. The muscles twitched in her jaw as she stood there so upset she wanted to scream.

Tuesday morning rolled around, and Sam was more determined than ever to keep her appointment with Hugh Noble. She draped herself in the same diamond stud earrings, glasses, and pantyhose. The only change was her suit. She borrowed an expensive Couturier suit from Nordstroms that had the tags taped to the inside. She made sure not to wear any perfume because the suit was going back tomorrow.

Eddie had called and left several messages, but she wasn't speaking to him, no matter what he had meant to say. Rich still hadn't called.

She walked into the cramped office that looked a little better for wear today. Someone had dusted the fake plants and added a few live ones. A large crystal vase full of fresh flowers was on his secretary's desk. The office was empty again.

She walked over to the magazines on the table and picked one up. The address read Noble and Associates, with a post office box number. She needed that number. Opening her purse, she found a pen and reached for a scrap piece of paper.

"Hello, Mrs. Banks."

She looked up at an attractive white woman in her mid-thirties. *What had happened to Porsche?* "Hello."

"You are Mrs. Banks, right?" The woman moved from behind the desk, gliding toward Sam as graceful as a swan.

"Yes . . . That's Ms. Banks, and I'm here for a two o'clock appointment with Mr. Noble." For a brief moment she'd forgotten her new name.

"He's expecting you." She walked over and shook Sam's hand. "I'm Doris, his secretary. Can I get you anything? Coffee, tea, or a soft drink?"

"No, thank you, I'm fine."

She walked over to her desk and picked up a small clipboard with a pen attached. "I just need you to fill out this short form. Mr. Noble likes to have some general information before he conducts a consultation." She handed Sam the clipboard.

She scanned the form. He wanted her address, income, and investment information. "I'm not actually here for a consultation. I just wanted to speak to him for a minute."

"Well, in the event that your visit leads to a consultation, we'd need this form filled out. Why don't you have a seat. It'll only take a minute to fill out. I'll let Mr. Noble know you're here." She walked down the short hallway and entered an office.

Sam sit there biting at her lipstick and creating information to fill in the form, the same way she'd created her new name.

Doris returned and retrieved the clipboard. "Mr. Noble will see you now."

This is what Sam had expected the first time she visited his office. Signs of wealth. Instead, she may have gotten the real picture.

"Those flowers are beautiful," she commented as she passed Doris's desk.

"Thank you. Mr. Noble gave them to me for my birthday."

Stepping into Hugh's office was like entering another world. This was a far cry from the cramped reception area. Sunlight flooded the large space from the huge window behind his desk that overlooked the parking lot. Cream-colored overstuffed chairs circled his desk and two matching couches framed the walls. Large pieces of colorful art hung from the walls.

He hung up the phone as they entered the room and stepped from behind his desk, smoothing his tie to greet her. Doris handed him her form before leaving. For the first time Sam got a good look at him. Strikingly handsome with a strong athletic build, he flashed a pearly white smile at her and extended his hand.

"Mrs. Banks. It's a pleasure."

"That's Ms. Banks, but call me Vivian," she insisted, turning into her gracious, confident, wealthy alter ego. Shaking his hand, she noticed his watch. Sam knew her watches, and she knew a Wittnauer when she saw one. This two-toned case was set with diamonds. He'd paid a thousand or more easily for the watch.

"Okay, have a seat Vivian and tell me what I can do for you." He returned to his leather high-back seat. "My secretary tells me you didn't come for a consultation." He gave an inquiring look down at the form Sam had filled out. When she didn't respond, he glanced up and smiled.

Her heart fluttered in her chest as the knot constricting her throat grew larger. She tried to remain calm and swallow the knot. She couldn't believe she was doing this.

"I'm not quite ready to invest any money at the moment, but pretty soon I'll be coming into a rather large inheritance and I wanted to talk to someone about my options."

He gave Sam a long, searching look as he rested his elbows on the chair armrest and assumed a steeple position with his hands. "How much of an inheritance are we talking, if you don't mind me asking?"

"Half a million dollars." She hoped to catch a spark in his eyes, but didn't. He merely shook his head, and she continued talking. "So you see how come I need a little direction. I don't want to let that much money sit in the bank gaining nothing."

He seemed amused, but he didn't jump at the bait like she'd hoped. She stood up and walked over to look out the window. "I notice the art you have here. I thought about investing in something like rare art, or jewelry."

He swirled sideways to watch her at the window. "Good choices. How soon will you be getting this inheritance?"

"In a couple of weeks. My grandfather left it to me. It's not like I need the money, but I don't want to throw it away either." She turned to face him. "Do you know what I mean?" Her sudden spin caught him off guard. He had been looking her over. Rising from his seat, he walked over to stand by her at the window. "I know exactly what you mean, and I think I can help you."

She gave him a coy smile and held her hand against her chest. "Thank you, I knew I'd come to the right place." His eyes blinked as he looked at the ring on her finger. At least that caught his attention.

"That's an exquisite ring."

She held her hand down to examine her fingers. "Thank you. It was handed down from my mother. It's been in the family for years." She strolled around the office, examining the art closer.

"Are these originals?" she asked, wishing she knew more about art. She had no idea if they were worth anything or not.

"This one over here is." He pointed to a colorful array of musicians on the wall behind his desk. "The others are prints. Are you into art?"

"I'm learning to appreciate it. What is this one called?" She pointed to the original.

"That's *Jammin* by Charles Bibbs." He walked back to his seat and picked up her form.

"Very nice." So his office gave the appearance of a little money; that didn't mean he was wealthy.

"Let's see here. If you don't mind I'd like to make a few notes."

"No, go right ahead."

"You've got half a million dollars coming to you." He wrote that down at the bottom of the consultation form. "I wouldn't suggest putting your money into jewelry, or art, right now."

"Why not?"

"Because the stock market is so wide open. It's a buyer's market. I could recommend a few good investments for you. And, if you'd like, we can process the transactions right here in the office."

The fish was biting. "How would I know which stock to choose? I'm afraid I don't know much about things like that. My daddy used to say it's a man's place to take care of the finances, but that was yesterday. Today a girl's gotta be able to take care of her own finances." She perched on the edge of her seat. "Unless, of course, she has someone like you to help her." She smiled suggestively at him.

"That's what I'm here for, to make your investment choices easier." He grinned back at her, suddenly amused.

You mean, to take my investment money.

"I can work up something if you'd like." He opened his drawer and pulled out another form. "All we'll need is for you to fill out this form and sign it for us. By our next appointment I'll have a package all ready for you. You can feel assured you'll be making a wise investment choice." He slid the form across the table to her.

Sam gave the form a quick once-over. This time he wanted bank account numbers and all. Did he think she was a fool? Was the word *idiot* written on her forehead when she walked into the room? She tried to mask her shock and astonishment with an innocent smile.

"Well . . . I'd like to think about it for a few days. Is that all right with you?"

"Sure, take your time. But be careful if you go to anybody else. There are a lot of unscrupulous people out there. I wouldn't want one of them to take advantage of you."

A chill ran up her spine. *This man was dangerous.*

"Uh, would it be possible to get a list of references?" she asked, tilting her head to one side.

He leaned back in his seat. "I'm sorry, but we don't give out that type of information. It's an invasion of privacy, and I keep my clients' information in the strictest of confidence. You understand, don't you?" The suspicious look returned to his face.

"Of course I do." She struggled to control the quavering in her voice.

Chapter 4

"You see Ms. Banks . . ."

"Call me Vivian, remember?"

"Vivian, I can understand you wanting references, and in most cases I wouldn't do business without checking references either. However, the investment industry is a different ballgame. If we gave that kind of information out to anyone who asked for it, our clients' names would find their way onto every telemarketer's list in town."

Sam couldn't believe him. Every company gave out references. "You do have references, don't you?" she asked in the most innocent way.

"Oh, of course we do. But I only share that information under special circumstances. You can, however, feel free to call the Better Business Bureau." He stood, signaling her time was up.

She'd struck a nerve. She rose and extended her hand, giving him a big smile. "Mr. Noble, I want to thank you very much for taking time out of your very busy day to see me. I feel better about this money already."

He chuckled and shook her hand. "Good. Now you take

that form home and think it over. I hope you'll let us help you. I know we can protect your inheritance for you."

"I'm gonna do just that."

"In a couple of days give my secretary a call, and she'll set up your initial appointment."

"Oh, I forgot to ask one thing. How much are your services?"

"The initial visit is two hundred and fifty dollars. We take a look at your existing portfolio and see how we can improve it. In your case, we'd outline a good place to house your half a million dollars."

Sam let out a hearty sigh. "Well, you've answered all my questions. I'll leave you now to get on with your business."

He walked her to his office door. "I do hope we'll see you again soon."

"Oh, you shall. Thank you."

In the reception area Doris had her back to Sam, typing away. She stopped and looked up as Sam headed for the door.

"How did your meeting go, Ms. Banks?"

Hugh closed the door to his office, so Sam used this opportunity to get better acquainted with Doris. "It went well. Mr. Noble is a very nice man."

"He's a doll, isn't he?"

"Can I ask you something though?" Sam stepped even closer to the desk.

"Sure."

"He kept referring to 'we.' Does someone else work with him?"

Doris leaned toward Sam, speaking barely above a whisper. "That would be Mr. Davis, but you wouldn't want to work with him."

"Is that Mike Davis?" she asked, slightly excited. Someone knew him.

"Yes, it is. But, he's never here. I've been here for a little over three weeks, and I haven't seen him yet." She glanced back to make sure Hugh's door hadn't opened. "You're doing right by sticking with Mr. Noble."

"Thank you, Doris, uh . . . what's your last name?"

"McCall. Doris McCall."

"It's been a real pleasure meeting you, Doris." Sam shook her hand.

"Yes, and we hope to see you again soon."

Sam left the office not sure what to think. She wondered who had worked with Mike Davis. Was he the owner, and just away on business for the last three weeks? She needed to get her hands on a copy of that client list; then she could find out who was who.

Before going to work Sam stopped by her house to change clothes. She also checked her answering machine, but there was nothing from Rich. On the way to work she called him again on her cell phone. This time he answered.

"Rich, you're a hard man to catch. You got anything for me?"

"Hey, Sam. Sorry about that. We had a little trouble in Buckhead, so I've been pulling a lot of overtime. I did get you something, though."

"Great, what you got?"

"Sam, this guy is bad news. He's got a rap sheet yea-long. If he's following one of the girls, you need to report it."

"Rich, I can handle it. Just give me the information."

"Not over the phone. Can you meet me this afternoon?"

She didn't want to get Rich involved in the case, but she needed that information. Besides, she knew her father used his police contacts all the time.

"Okay, where do you want to meet?"

"How about Mick's in Lennox Mall at three o'clock? We can grab a bite to eat at the same time."

"Sure. I can't get into my planner right now but I don't think I have anything scheduled, so I'll see you then."

Sam had no idea why he'd chosen Mick's. The restaurant

was in the middle of the mall, right out in the open. She worked through the lunch hour right up to three o'clock, then had to run out telling Barbara she was taking a late lunch. Rich sat at a table flirting with the young waitress. He stopped as Sam approached.

"Well, here's my lunch date now," he announced as the waitress stepped back, letting Sam into the booth.

"Hey, Rich. We've got to make this fast. Sorry, but I've got a full afternoon."

Sam ordered her favorite fried chicken salad before looking at the folder Rich handed her.

"For starters, he's a thief," Rich began as she read. "I'm talking a little of everything from forgery to burglary. Looks like your boy has a thing for jewelry, too."

She read the name on the folder. "Lorenzo Lewis." Somewhere in the back of her mind she thought it might be Mike Davis. How was this Lorenzo connected to Hugh?

"So, you ready to tell me what's going on?" Rich gave Sam a sidelong glance.

Her eyes widened innocently. "It's probably nothing. I just saw this car outside of . . ."

"Sam, what are you involved in? After I got a name and address from the DMV, I ran this guy through the National Crime Information Center's database. That's where I got most of this information. He's not the type of guy who follows young rap acts around. Whatever he's involved in, you better bet it's big."

She smiled at him guardedly. She supposed she owed him an explanation.

"No, he's not following the girls. Actually, he's connected to this guy I'm doing a background check on. I'm not sure how he's connected, but I saw him coming from the guy's house a couple of days ago."

"Why are you doing a background check on somebody? Can't you hire somebody to do that?"

"It's a long story, but I'll make it brief." She proceeded to explain how this case landed in her lap and why she had to solve it. She also pointed out the fact that she could use his help. He wouldn't have the same emotional involvement in the case, but she hoped that wouldn't stop him from helping her.

"Wow, you've got your hands full." Rich grabbed the folder. "You know, I pulled everything with this guy Lorenzo's name on it. I think I saw that company's name in here, too." He flipped through the pages, scanning quickly. "Yeah, is this the same company?" He slid the folder around on the table where she could see.

Sam read the notes about a civil court case on Noble Investments, where Lorenzo was employed. The state attorney general's office in Virginia sued the company for ten thousand dollars, on behalf of one of his clients. She skimmed with interest at the proof she needed that Hugh was a con artist.

The waitress brought their food. Sam picked up the folder, but kept reading. She couldn't believe what Rich had provided her with.

"Yeah, this sounds like him." She shook her head. "He's just changed the name of his company. Looks like Lorenzo worked for him at the time. Maybe he still does."

"If they're working together I'd say they're running some type of scam here in Georgia now. If you've got any proof of that, I know some detectives who would be glad to look into it."

She shook her head. "No, just a suspicion. Is it possible you could run the same type of check on Hugh Noble?"

"You got another license plate number or a social security number?"

"The plates are registered to another guy, but if you can run them through that National Crime Registry thing too, I'd appreciate it." She reached inside her purse and pulled out a sheet of paper. "Here's the plate number."

"You're just turning into a little private dick, aren't you?"

"Rich, I've got to wrap this case up. I had no idea it was going to lead to something like this and take up so much time. Every time I find out something, it leads me to something else. This woman is getting way more than she bargained for."

"Okay, I'll run this through, and let you know what I come up with. It might take me a little while, but in the meantime, stay away from those guys. I'll help you all I can. Just let me know what you need."

"Thank you. I really appreciate this."

"No problem. Hey, any luck with those concert tickets?"

Sam laughed. "See, I knew there was a reason you were helping me. You're doing it for Sade."

"What can I say, I'm in love with her."

"Barbara has an envelope for you. Two tickets, row C, center stage."

"Sam. It's a pleasure doing business with you."

She made it to the Marriott in time for her meeting with the former organizer of Jack The Rapper, an industry conference. Valentine Records was planning to host their own industry-related conference next year, and she had to go over all the publicity related details.

Even while she was working, she couldn't stop thinking about the case. She wished she had the time to take off and do nothing but work this case until it closed, but things at work were too busy. She carried the details around in her head, trying to sort them out. *Were Hugh Noble and the young thief working together? And how did Mike Davis fit in there, if he did at all?* Questions, questions, that's all she had. What she needed right now were more answers. And she thought up a way to get a few.

"Doris, run all the usual checks on Ms. Banks and file this away." Hugh handed Doris the general information form Sam had filled out.

"Yes, sir. Do you think she'll come back?"

He turned his nose up. "I doubt it. Run the check anyway, but I don't think we'll see her again."

"You had a call a minute ago." She handed him a pink slip of paper.

Hugh read the note. He had a message from Lorenzo. "I've got a few phone calls to make. Could you take messages for me until you leave for lunch."

"Yes, sir."

He entered his office, swung the door closed, and marched over to the phone. Hitting hands-free, he dialed Lorenzo's number and paced around his chair.

"Lorenzo speaking. Talk to me, baby," he answered in a cheerful tone.

"What's up? I got your message." The thumping of the car stereo vibrated through the phone.

"I just wanted to let you know everything's set for that charity thing."

"Turn that music down so I can hear you. Did you get my ticket to the dance?"

"You know my boy hooked you up. This invitation looks just like the real thing. I can't even tell the difference."

Hugh snatched the receiver from the base. "But will the guy at the door be able to?"

"No way. Don't worry, everything's cool. You gettin' things all set up on your end?"

"I'm working on it. I need to make one more trip to Liberty this weekend. When I get back . . ."

"Hold up. You're still working that chick in Liberty? I thought that was a done deal?"

"It is. I've just run into a few complications."

"Man, you better just hit that and get out of there. Losing your touch or something?"

"Don't worry about me. This might be even bigger than I originally thought. I've got it under control."

"Cool. I talked to Maurice, and it'll take him about three weeks to unload the stuff this time. He's counting on you, too, man."

"You don't need to remind me." He glanced at his watch. "Gotta run, I need to meet my barber in twenty minutes."

"Man, you stay at the barber's. What you got, stock in that joint or something?" He laughed at Hugh.

"If you play the part, you have to look the part. You let me take care of my department, and you handle yours."

"My stuff is always tight. Well, go do what you're good at. Later, man."

Two mottos crossed Sam's mind as she got out of the car. *By any means necessary,* and *A girl's gotta do, what a girl's gotta do.* The first one came to mind while thinking about a picture her father had of Malcolm X. The latter was her own. She didn't climb all the way from intern to publicist by sitting back and waiting for things to happen.

She hurried through the revolving doors of the Equity building, carrying a bundle of papers. She sashayed up to the guard station, smiling. "Hi . . . you must be the night shift guard?" she asked, panting to catch her breath.

The overweight security guard sat behind his desk and eyeballed her over the rim of his glasses. "That's right. And who are you?" he asked in a tone that said she wasn't getting in no matter what.

She shuffled the bundle to one arm as her purse fell from her shoulder, sending the papers scattering all over the floor. "Oh, my goodness. And I've got to have these on my boss's desk when he gets in tomorrow morning." She bent down to pick up the papers.

The security guard waddled around the desk. "You need some help?"

Looking up at him with pleading eyes, she responded, "Please. I'd appreciate it."

He blew out a heavy sigh and bent down to assist her. "You need to sign in, you know?"

As they stood up he handed her the papers he'd picked up. She laid everything on his desk and pulled her purse back up on her shoulder. "Of course, I've also got a slight problem." She shuffled through the papers, pretending to put them back in order. "I lost my badge and I just came from Kinko's getting this presentation all straightened out. My boss needs it in the morning."

The guard had moved back to his desk and regarded her with interest. "What's your name? Where you work?" He grabbed a clipboard and flipped through the pages.

"Doris McCall. I work for Noble and Associates." She watched him scan the list for her name. She glanced at his nameplate. "You see, Harold, I've only been on the job a few weeks, and I think I've lost my badge already. You would be doing me a big favor if you could let me into the office, just this once." She pleaded with him.

"I don't know about that. I'm not supposed to leave my post unless . . ."

"Come on, Harold, help a sister out. I'd owe you one big-time," she continued to plead, leaning over the desk.

Harold's smile grew larger, but he shook his head no. "I can't do that, miss."

She straightened up. "Harold, who would know? I'll run in, get this presentation in order, and put it on his desk. I'd be back before you knew I was gone. Come on, baby, have a heart. I really need this job." She pouted when he looked up at her.

Harold shook his head as he reached for his keys. "Okay, just this one time. You make sure to get yourself a new badge."

Sam walked around the desk and grabbed his arm. "Thank you so much."

"And make sure you get after-hours access, too," he said like a grumpy old man.

She smiled at him and saluted like a soldier. "Yes, sir."

"Come on." He looked back at the front door. "We have to make it quick. I need to be on this door."

"Harold, I think we're going to become big buddies. Looks like I'll be working a lot of overtime on this job."

"Yeah, if you don't quit like all the others." He pushed the elevator button.

"What do you mean?"

"You're the fourth secretary that's been up there this year. I can't keep up with you guys. They ain't been in this building all that long."

"Do you know Mr. Noble?" The elevator door opened and she walked in behind him.

"I know of him, that's all. He comes in sometimes after hours."

"Have you met Mr. Davis?"

He shook his head and looked a little confused. "Mr. Davis? His name's not on the list downstairs." The elevator door opened on the seventh floor and they exited.

"Is everybody on your list?"

"If they work in this building they are."

"What if he doesn't need night access?"

"Doesn't matter, he should still be on my list." They reached the door of Noble and Associates and he ran his badge through the magnetic strip to activate the door. He turned to look at her. "Who is he?"

Sam shrugged. "I don't know. I've seen his name on a few documents and I thought he might be someone who works for Mr. Noble some of the time."

Harold held the door open for Sam as she squeezed by. "Harold, thank you so much for this. I'll make it as fast as I can."

"Yeah, well, I can't wait for you. I've got to get back downstairs in case somebody comes in." He pointed into the office. "Don't you want to turn a light on first?"

"Oh, yeah." Thank goodness the sunlight coming through

a small window helped her find the light switch. She put the papers on Doris's desk and set her purse down next to them.

Harold continued to eye her a little suspiciously. "Once you leave this room you know you can't get back in, so don't go to the bathroom unless you're ready to leave."

Sam shook her head and pointed at him. "You're right, Harold, and thank you. I won't walk out until I'm ready to leave." She sat down in Doris's chair.

"All right, I'm gone."

She thought he'd never leave. Once she heard the elevator door close, she went to work. First, she jumped up and hurried to Hugh's office. She tried the door, but it was locked. She went back to the reception area.

Where could that client list be? She went through all of Doris's desk files and found nothing. Then she tried the filing cabinet against the wall; it was locked. She banged her hand against the cabinet, then went back to Doris's desk. *The keys had to be here somewhere.* Under some papers, she found a set of keys. *No way. I couldn't get that lucky.* Easing over to the filing cabinet she put the key in; it turned.

"Doris, didn't anyone ever tell you to lock your desk once you put keys inside." She threw the keys on the desk and started going through the top drawer. After finding nothing, she decided to skip all the way to the bottom instead of working her way down. *Bingo.* Among the files labeled Important was one marked References. She pulled the folder out and sat at Doris's desk again to leaf through it.

Harold looked up at the clock on the wall. *What was that girl doing up there?* If anyone found out he'd let her into the building without authorization, that'd be his job. He flipped through the list again and read the names of the employees of Noble and Associates. Her name was there all right.

She sure was a pretty little thing with those big black eyes and those full hips. She had an exotic, sexy look to her. He hoped she did work a little overtime; he looked forward to seeing her again. He got up and decided to go see what was taking her so long.

Sam found one copy of a document with names, addresses, and phone numbers. No other information was listed. A Post-it attached read, *Copy only as needed.*

"Looks like I need a copy." Sam took the paper and walked over to the tabletop copier. She had to wait for the machine to warm up. Glancing at her watch, she wondered how long she'd taken. The copier finally came on. Sam made one copy, then re-filed the document.

Flipping through the files again, she found something else useful: insurance papers with Hugh's name and social security number jumped out at her. Quickly she grabbed the document and ran back to the copier.

Harold rode the elevator up to the seventh floor and got off. If management found out he'd let her up without proper authorization, he could get fired. He had to make this quick and pray no one came in to notice he'd left his post. The door to Noble and Associates was still closed. *What could that girl being doing in there?*

Finished snooping, Sam closed and locked the file cabinet. She picked up the bundle of papers she came in with and threw them in the garbage under Doris's desk. Glancing down, a folder labeled *V. Banks* caught her attention. She picked up the folder and found her general information form inside.

She sat down to read the handwritten notes attached. *No such address or zip code found. The phone number is to a restaurant in Norcross, Georgia. Invalid information.* Looks like she wouldn't be paying his office another visit. She put the folder down and stuffed her copies into her purse. Sam rushed over and turned off the light switch. The office went black.

Harold slid his badge through the magnetic strip and opened the door.

She groped for the knob and turned it as the door flew open and she was propelled through the door literally falling into the person on the other side. Her breath caught in her throat.

Chapter 5

"Hey, little lady." Harold held his hands out in an attempt to catch Sam. "What's wrong?" He reached over and flipped on the lights.

"Oh, boy!" Sam exhaled. She put a hand on her chest to steady her breathing. "You scared the hell out of me. I didn't expect anyone to be on the other side of the door."

"Sorry, but you were up here so long I came to see if everything was okay."

"I, ah—I got a few more things together. Did I take too long?"

He looked around the office and nodded his head in approval. "No, but we better get back downstairs. I've got to get back to my desk."

Sam walked out the door while he held it open. He turned out the lights. "Harold, buddy, I really want to thank you for letting me in. You don't know what this means to me."

"Ummhum. You're welcome. Just take care of that badge."

Sam thanked Harold again and sashayed out to her car. Her excitement was bubbling over, and she tried not to break into a full sprint. The moment she closed and locked the car door she pulled out her cell phone. With her heart pounding away in her chest, she dialed Rich's number. She got his voice mail.

"Rich, this is Sam. I've got another piece to the puzzle that I need your help with." She left Hugh's social security number on his voice mail.

The next day, Sam sat down with her secretary to go over several artist appearances that were coming up. Since the night before she was very proud of herself for finding a way to get her hands on that client list. By hook or by crook, she would solve this case. She hoped her father would have been proud of her, but she knew he would have called her stunt dangerous. She called it exciting and clever private-eye work.

"Sam, I've got the limos and the security taken care of. How about the promo pictures?" Barbara laid a folder on Sam's desk that had the day's activities sketched out inside.

"We've got plenty of photos for them to autograph. I just hope we've got enough posters. If we don't, you know those kids will lose their minds. See if you can round up enough of those T-shirts we used last time. Just in case we run out of posters, we have to give them something." Sam loved her job. Artist appearances were exciting and hair-raising at the same time.

"You think of everything. Valentine is so lucky to have you. Do they realize that?" Barbara sat back and crossed her arms.

"Not according to my paycheck." They laughed as Sam swirled around in her chair and got up. She walked over to her credenza and picked up a small stack of postcards featuring their artist.

"We can take some of these, too. I'll use them for table decoration."

"I bet your father was really proud of you, wasn't he?" Barbara admired her boss's work ethics.

Sam turned to look at her giving a slight shrug of her shoulders. "I'm sure he was, but he wasn't exactly a fan of the music industry. I believe he thought I was wasting my time." She put the postcards back and returned to her desk. "He wanted me to be a cop, or a private detective like him. But I didn't have the passion for that kind of work."

"A private detective—that sounds like an exciting job. Did you ever go out on any cases with him?"

Sam leaned back, smiling, and thought about several adventures she had had with her father. "Yeah, one time we followed this guy in a neck brace. He went straight to the pool, took off his brace, and went for a swim. My dad started taking pictures of him, then he saw us." She laughed at the pictures that ran through her mind. "You should have seen him getting out of that pool. He had no idea who my dad was, but he didn't like having his picture taken. From what I remember, he cursed all the way back to his car. It was a riot."

"That sounds like a dangerous job, too," Barbara commented.

"It can be. It depends on the type of cases you take." Her background check came to mind. "Then again, what looks like a simple case, can turn into something more complicated."

"Had anybody ever threatened his life before?"

Sam shook her head. "No, never. People in Liberty liked my dad." She experienced a slight tug at her heart. Every time she thought about her father, she wanted to punish herself for not being there with him. She should have visited more instead of running around Atlanta trying to prove herself. Family was more important. She wondered how her sisters were getting along with their cases.

At home in her comfortable slippers with a cup of coffee at her side, Sam picked up the phone and dialed the first number. She sat tapping her fingernail against the table waiting for someone to answer the phone. To calm her nerves, she'd put on a Prince CD and tuned the volume down low.

"Hello."

Swallowing the lump in her throat, she looked down at the client list to make sure she asked for the right person. "May I speak to Ms. English?"

"I'm sorry. You must have the wrong number."

Sam repeated the phone number for her, hoping she'd just dialed the wrong number.

"That's the number, but there's no one here by that name."

"Okay, thank you very much." She hung up the phone and drew a line through that name and number.

The next number had been disconnected. After another wrong number, she finally reached someone.

"Hello," came a rough, loud voice from the other end.

Sam knew she had a bit of a rough voice herself, so she threw in a little French accent. "Hello, I'm looking for Mrs. Bickerman."

"She's not in. This is her husband. Can I help you?" he asked in a rather annoyed tone.

Bingo, she finally hit a lucky number. "Mr. Bickerman, you don't know me but my name is Brigitte Girard, and I'd like to ask you a few questions."

"About what?"

"About a company named Noble and Associates. Your name was given to me as a reference for the company."

"What the hell for! I don't have anything to say about that place."

Sam grabbed her pen. "Sir, I'm considering investing with Mr. Noble and I want to find out what your investment experience was like?"

"Don't waste your money. He took thousands of dollars from my wife and me. He conned us into a risky investment. We lost everything in a couple of months."

"Did you work with Mr. Noble or Mr. Davis?"

"Mr. Noble. I don't remember no Mr. Davis. I'm surprised he gave you my name. We had some pretty heated words. I called those consumer reporters down at the TV station, but they never got back with me. We're still going to talk with our attorney."

"Do you mind if I ask how long ago this was?"

"Let's see—about three months ago. Yeah, we waited weeks for him to get back in town. His secretary kept saying he was out of the country."

"Thank you, Mr. Bickerman. I appreciate you taking the time to talk to me."

"Sure. Just make sure you don't give him any of your money. That guy's dishonest."

After hanging up, she wrote down everything he had said. Now all she needed was proof on paper that the company was a front for something. She doubted that he was wealthy at all. He was just good at putting up a front. But where was he getting his money?

Dressed in her favorite turquoise strapless dress that tied in the back and revealed the keyhole feature she loved so much, Sam met her friends at Club Kaya. Tonight she didn't want to think about work or the case. She needed a little time to herself to just enjoy life. No Eddie to be bothered with, just the girls. Because she knew the club owner, they received a table in the VIP section.

"Okay ladies, drinks are on me tonight. Let's get wild and let our hair down. We work hard, and we deserve to play hard." Sam slammed her palm on the table.

"Here, here." The women sang in unison.

When the waiter came around, Sam ordered a glass of white wine, while the others ordered mixed drinks. Sam hardly went out unless it was for business, so tonight she danced and socialized until she was worn out. The DJ played music that kept the dance floor crowded.

Taking a break, Sam left the dance floor and went down the hall to the ladies room. As she stood in the mirror touching up her face, a young woman walked up next to her. The blood-red lipstick was the first thing to catch her attention, then the bloodshot eyes. But, she recognized those eyes.

"Excuse me, isn't your name Porsche?" Sam asked as she applied her lipstick.

Porsche swayed back on one hip and eyed Sam from head to toe. "Yeah. And who are you?" she asked in a blurred speech.

"Vivian Banks, remember me? I came in to see Mr. Noble a few weeks ago." She tried not to look down at Porsche's deep-cut cleavage, but she was astonished at how deep it was. Her breasts were practically hanging out.

"Hey, I remember you." She turned from the mirror and pointed at Sam.

"How's the job?" Sam asked.

"I don't even work there anymore." Turning her attention back to the mirror, Porsche applied more lipstick.

"What happened?" Sam asked, sounding genuinely concerned.

"That was just a temporary gig. I don't think he needed a secretary no way."

"Why not?" *What am I doing!* Sam hadn't intended on working tonight, so why was she pumping this woman for answers?

"Ain't no work. I sat in that damned office all day with nothing to do. Some of his buddies come in and they sit around in his office like they're working, but I knew better. That man didn't do shit all day."

"But didn't his work take him out of the country sometimes?"

With a turned-up lip, she waved Sam off. "Girl, he just told me to tell people that. He got phone calls from some guy overseas all the time. But he probably spent most of his time hanging out at The Gentleman's Club. I seen him down there before."

They moved away from the mirror, as other women needed to freshen up.

"So you never typed up any investment paperwork?"

"Oh, one or two things, but not much. You wasn't about to give him no money were you?"

"I'd considered it, yes."

"Girl, don't do it. Most of the time I was there him and his buddy were hitting on me."

"Really?" Sam was shocked in more ways than one. Wendy and Porsche were miles apart.

"Yeah, and trying to get my girlfriend to get him a ticket to the . . ."

The bathroom door opened and music came rushing in covering the tail end of Porsche's conversation. She staggered toward the bathroom door.

"I'm sorry, you said he was trying to get tickets to what?" Sam stopped her.

"The mayor's ball. My girlfriend used to work for the mayor's office. Once she convinced him she couldn't get tickets, he suddenly lost interest. Just like a man, ain't it?" She laughed and leaned over on Sam.

The smell of liquor wafted past Sam's nose, confirming why Porsche was so loose-lipped.

"Hey, come on over and join me and my friends. You're cool." She inspected Sam again.

"Thanks, but I'm about to leave. And thanks again for the warning, too."

"No problem."

Sam let Porsche leave the ladies room first; she didn't want to risk bumping into a friend who might call her Sam.

The next night Sam worked at the kitchen table on her case while she waited for her dinner guest. The doorbell rang and she hurried to put away her papers. She couldn't tell Eddie about any of her latest escapades.

She opened the door. Eddie stood there smiling, with a bouquet of daisies. He had to be the last of the big spenders. For once she thought it would be nice to receive a dozen roses.

"Hey, baby. I thought you might like these." He walked in, kissing her on the cheek as he passed.

"Thank you, but you really shouldn't have," she stated sarcastically. She sniffed the fragrance before going into the kitchen to place them in a vase. Eddie followed, dressed in his usual vest and jacket.

He walked over to the stove and lifted the lid on a pot. "Umm, something smells good. What we havin' tonight?"

"Peppered steaks with shiitake sauce and brown rice and orzo pilaf. It should be ready in a minute. Why don't you get out of that jacket? Aren't you hot?" She hated when he came over straight from work.

"Yeah, it is a little warm." He shed his jacket as he walked into the living room. Something on the couch caught his attention. He reached over and picked up the file folder with the name Lorenzo written on the front. Leafing through the folder, he realized what he was looking at and stormed into the kitchen.

"Sam, what's this?" he asked, holding up the folder.

She was so busy hiding the client list that she forgot about the work on the couch. "That's something Rich got for me. It's part of the case I'm working on."

"You're still meddling in that man's business? You're going to fool around and get yourself hurt if you don't stop." He threw the folder on the kitchen table. "This guy's got a police record!" he barked, then sat down at the kitchen table and leafed through the folder again.

She had some explaining to do, so she pulled up a chair and recalled some of the details for him. However, she didn't get very far before he cut her off.

"That doesn't prove a thing. Maybe the guy's a silent partner. Or he started the company but now he's deceased. Did you check into anything like that?"

She gave him a frustrated look. He didn't know everything. "I'm not finished yet. I've got a few more things to check out." He always poked holes into her theories, no matter what the subject. She picked up the folder and shoved it into the drawer with her client list. Then she proceeded to set the kitchen table.

"I'll be glad when you're finished with that mess. Maybe then I can see you on a regular basis. I'm surprised you're not attending some opening or party tonight."

She ignored him and changed the subject for her own selfish reasons. "Eddie, is your company participating in the mayor's ball this year?"

"I believe so, but I won't be able to go—I'll be gone on business. Why? Did you want to go?" He walked over and got out glasses for the table.

"Yeah, I thought about it."

"What, you actually have time to go somewhere with me, and I'm going to be out of town," he said sarcastically.

"I'll admit I have an ulterior motive. I want to go so I can do some networking. You fuss about my job so much, I thought I'd start looking for something else a little less demanding."

Eddie stopped in his tracks. "You're kidding?"

"No, and that ball would be a perfect place to network."

"I can't believe you're considering that for *me.*"

"Do you think you can still get me a ticket?"

"And you go without me?"

"Yes, but don't look at it like that. I'd be going for us. You'd be doing this for us, not just me."

He shook his head and thought for a moment. "Let me see what I can do. I didn't request any tickets, but I can probably get hold of one."

She walked over and kissed him on the cheek. "Thank you, baby. I owe you one."

Chapter 6

A couple of evenings later, Eddie called.
"May I speak to Cinderella?"

"Eddie, what are you up to?"

"I'm looking for the lady who's trying to get to the ball."

"Don't tell me, you got me a ticket?"

"Yes, ma'am. I'll bring it over later tonight. You will be home, won't you?"

"Make it eight o'clock. I need to work late tonight." Working on the case was taking up a lot of her day and pushing more and more work into the evening hours.

"Eddie, thank you so much. I'm glad you got my ticket, but it's too bad you can't go with me," she lied. She couldn't watch Hugh with Eddie around. Exactly what she was watching for, she didn't know. However, according to Porsche this was a function he really wanted to attend. He had to have a good reason. Maybe it provided a good way for him to line up more suckers.

"Well, have some fun for me, too. I just hope your networking pays off."

After Eddie hung up, Sam pulled out the documents Rich provided on Lorenzo and read through the part on Noble

Investments again. Hugh invested money for his client, with disastrous results. This couple claimed to have given him their life savings, then were unable to reach him. When they finally heard from him, he informed them of the loss. A week later, his office closed and he was nowhere to be found. She saw the pattern and realized he was up to his old tricks again. His business was a front to steal money from unsuspecting citizens.

Maybe he planned to marry Wendy and get her family's trust first, then rip them off. According to Maya, he'd already started. There was just one thing Sam kept harping on. Who was Mike Davis? Could he be a silent partner like Eddie suggested? Or maybe he was the brains behind the scheme. After all, he owned the house and the car. If someone tried to sue Hugh again, they could get his business, but not the house he lived in or the car he drove.

It sounded like enough to fill out a report and turn it in to Mrs. Wilmington, but Sam wasn't satisfied. She still smelled a rat.

Sam hated to just sit around and wait on anything, so while Rich worked on the social security number she had given him, she decided to do a little more research. She picked up the phone and reached out to her big sister for help.

"Maxine, I need a favor."

"Really now, having a little trouble?"

"Not really. I've almost got this case wrapped up. I know you're keeping daddy's business going. Does that mean you have access to his database?

"Yes, I believe I do. Now, whether I can find anything or not remains to be seen, but I'll try."

"Great." Sam gave her the social security number she had found in Hugh's office. "I need a date of birth, an address, and whatever else you can find from the Information Broker."

Maxine took down the information. "I'll see what I can find out."

Sam had expected her sister to make an attempt at telling her what to do. Instead, she was cooperative and helpful. They spent a few minutes on the phone talking about their father and why he'd left them cases to solve in the first place.

"I have to admit," Sam confessed, "this is very exciting. Now I see why Daddy spent so much time away from home. I've been running around all over town checking things out, and it gets the adrenaline pumping. I never thought I'd enjoy it."

"And to think only a few weeks ago you were fighting it. We're here to help and support you, you know. We're family."

"I know . . . and I should have called you sooner. We need to stay in touch, Maxine. How's everybody else doing?"

"Okay. When this is all over we'll have to sit down and talk about it. I want to hear everybody's story."

"I'm just out here trying to remember some of Daddy's tricks. But, I think I've got this about wrapped up."

"Good. Then we'll be talking about it soon."

Sam knew she couldn't approach Hugh's neighbors and ask them to tell her all they knew about him. If she wanted to know what they knew, she'd have to befriend them, or at least one of them. She went to the local florist and picked out an arrangement she really liked, and went to pay Mr. Noble a visit. Again, she made sure he was at work.

Pulling up to his house, she shoved her notepad under her arm and a pencil behind her ear. Dressed in khakis and a white polo shirt, she walked up to the front door. She looked for one of two things to happen. Lorenzo would open the door, or she'd have to seek out a neighbor.

After ringing the doorbell for the third time and not getting an answer, she turned and looked around the neighborhood. While debating which neighbor to call upon, she heard the garage door open next door. She strolled around to the side of the house and saw the flower lady walking out with her basket in hand.

"Hello," she called out in a friendly manner, smiling.

The woman looked over at Hugh's house and stared at Sam.

"I'm looking for the owner." She held up her flowers. "I have a delivery for him." To make it easier for the woman, Sam walked across the yard and up the woman's driveway.

"Honey, I don't believe he's at home. He works most days."

"Wow." Sam gave a disappointed look. "I wonder if he'd mind if I left them on the front porch?"

"I wouldn't do that."

"Why somebody would send Mr. Noble flowers at his home when he works every day beats me. I get deliveries like this all the time." She shook her head and tried to look frustrated.

"You must have the wrong house. There's no Mr. Noble over there."

"Mr. Hugh Noble, doesn't he live there?" Sam pretended to read the card again.

"Well, unless he's that young man who goes over there all the time. Mr. Davis lives alone."

Sam glanced up quickly, trying not to look so surprised. That explained the mail, the house, and the car being in Mike Davis's name. Maybe Hugh was his alias.

"Would that be Mike Davis?" she asked to be sure.

"Yes." She shook her head and gave Sam a puzzled look.

"Do you know the other young man's name?"

"No, I don't. He's a wild one, though. When Mr. Davis isn't at home, he brings women into the house and plays that stereo so loud I've had to ask him to turn it down."

"That doesn't sound like the type of guy I'd be delivering flowers to," Sam chuckled, hoping to keep her talking.

His neighbor seemed to warm up to Sam. "And his women don't look like the type to send him flowers either, if you know what I mean."

Sam walked closer, shaking her head.

"I think they're prostitutes. They wear very revealing clothes and dress like some strippers I saw on television one time."

They laughed about it, and Sam decided to leave the flowers with her. "Since he's not at home, why don't you keep these."

"Oh, I couldn't."

"Don't worry, we'll redeliver his tomorrow."

After convincing the woman Sam wouldn't get into trouble for leaving the flowers with her, she walked back to her car pleased she'd left the flowers with someone who loved flowers so much.

Sam pulled off trying to get Rich on the phone. She wanted to let him know that Hugh Noble and Mike Davis were indeed one and the same.

Unable to reach Rich, Sam went back to work realizing that her simple background check might turn into a case for the police. Hugh Noble or Mike Davis was having an identity crisis. Who was he really?

Dressed in a monochromatic beaded dove-gray gown, Sam strutted through the ballroom of the Marriott Marquis Hotel where the mayor's ball was held. She really did feel like Cinderella with all the crystal chandeliers hanging from the ceiling, only she was hoping not to meet Prince Charming— just to spy on him.

Now that she was here, she questioned why she'd come. What did she hope to find out?

"Samantha Chambers, how are you?"

Sam turned to see a statuesque woman in three-inch heels

with blond hair piled on top of her head. One of Eddie's coworkers greeted her.

"Hello, Renee, I'm just fine. Man, I haven't seen you since the Christmas party."

"No, honey, it's been way too long. Where's Edward tonight?"

Renee leaned in and they air-kissed.

She was way too phony for Sam. "He couldn't make it; I'm flying solo tonight."

"You mean he left you alone in that dress. Darling, you look fabulous tonight. I love that color on you."

"Thank you. You look great, too." Sam didn't want to tell her she looked about seven feet tall in those heels, that long form-fitting dress, and her hair stacked yea-high. She even towered over most of the men in the room.

"I love these balls, don't you?" She didn't wait for Sam to respond. "It's a great time to see old friends and make new ones."

Sam didn't want to admit it was her first time attending the mayor's ball. "If nothing else, it's a great excuse to dress up." Renee may love these events, but Sam hated them. Everybody was kissing up and trying to get on the who's-who list of Atlanta socialites.

She saw a few people she knew mingling about, but no Mr. Noble, Davis, or whoever he was. The room was large and packed with people pretending to be more important than they really were.

A waiter strolled by, and Sam grabbed a glass of wine. She left Renee and found a perfect spot at the top of the stairs to view most of the room. She perched herself in that spot, scanning the room for Hugh.

Minutes later, a familiar face came up the stairs calling out her name. "Sam, I had no idea you were going to be here. What are you doing sitting way up here?" A good friend and fellow publicist sought her out and came to share her space.

"Pamela, hey girl where have you been? I haven't seen you in ages." They hugged and exchanged kisses on the cheeks. Sam was genuinely glad to see her.

"I was so burned out, I had to take some time off. You know how it is; I never have any time to myself."

"I know exactly what you mean. Who are you with tonight?"

"My new beau." She flashed a big smile, batting her eyelashes. "Girl, I needed time to spend with my new man. I hit the jackpot this time." She turned and pointed toward the bar.

Sam followed her direction. "Which one?"

"See the guy next to the serving station. He's holding up his drink right now."

"Yes, I see him." Sam watched him reach out his hand and greet Hugh. She froze. *There he was!* And he knew Pamela's boyfriend.

"Pamela, who's that guy he's talking to?" Sam asked quickly.

"That's Hugh Noble. He's in investments. I don't know much about him, but he's a fine young thing, isn't he?"

Sam shrugged. "He is good-looking. Who's he dating? Do you know?"

"Nooo, but are you interested?" Pamela nudged Sam and winked at her.

"You know I'm still seeing Eddie. I was thinking about a friend of mine."

"Well, I'm not sure how serious they are, but he's been seeing Loraine Nelson."

Sam knew the name. Loraine was the successful owner of two Atlanta businesses. Local magazines and newspapers had run profiles on her numerous times. She came from meager beginnings and against all odds was now a huge success, or so the article read.

"How long has that been going on?" Sam asked, not really surprised to learn he wasn't faithful to Wendy. For a moment she had thought maybe he was seriously in love, but she should have known better. He was a true con artist. Was he planning on stealing this woman's money as well?

"Several months now. I've seen them together a couple of times."

Sam hadn't taken her eyes off Hugh, until he looked in her direction. She took a sip of her drink and looked back over her shoulder. Her whole purpose of being here was to watch him, not confront him. When she looked back, Hugh and Pamela's boyfriend were making their way through the crowd, headed her way.

"Pamela, I see somebody I've been trying to reach for months. Give me a call when you get back in the office; we need to do lunch."

"I'll do that. Take care, and maybe I'll see you later tonight."

She couldn't go down the steps, so she went up. Making her way through the crowd on the top level, she found the stair rail on the other side of the room. Looking across the floor, she saw Pamela, her boyfriend, and Hugh engaged in a conversation. Letting out a heavy sigh, she touched her chest. *That was a close call. I've got to be careful.*

"Somebody's glass is empty," came a masculine voice from over her shoulder.

She turned and was surprised to see the CEO of Valentine Records. "Mr. Graham, how are you?"

"Fine. I had no idea you would be here."

"I didn't know myself until two days ago. My boyfriend couldn't make it, so he gave me his ticket."

He held out his hand to lead the way down the stairs. "Were you on your way down?"

Actually she wasn't, but she couldn't explain why she was hanging around the top of the stairs. "Yes, I guess I was." Holding onto the banister, she glanced across the room for Hugh before descending the stairs. There was no sign of him.

"Are you enjoying yourself tonight? You look wonderful."

"Thank you, Mr. Graham. I'm having a nice time."

"Were you here last year? I don't remember seeing you."

"No, this is my first ball. I feel like Cinderella coming alone." She laughed, a little uncomfortable with the big guy. At work he stayed in his office, and she rarely spoke with him except in company meetings.

"Well, if it's any consolation, you look better than Cinderella tonight. How's everything in the publicity department? I don't get to that end of the building much, but I do see the work you do and I'm very impressed."

"Thank you, you do know how to flatter a girl." She gave him a coy smile and pretended to primp her upswept hairstyle. "Everything is going just fine. We've got the ground-level plans all worked out for the workshop next year. Most of the speakers are confirmed, and all of the performers are confirmed."

"You know, picking this up from Jack the Rapper is going to be a hard act to follow. He's brought in some pretty heavy talent over the last couple of years. Year before last, they had Prince, The Artist Formerly Know As, or whatever he calls himself these days."

"I know. We're really hoping to bring that caliber of talent also. I've contacted Russell Simmon's people to see if I could confirm him as a speaker. Let's keep our fingers crossed."

"Yes, we'll do that."

Sam took advantage of this opportunity to get better acquainted with the big guy at Valentine. Maybe he would think of her next time a great opportunity came up. She couldn't believe she had him all to herself.

"Sir, are you here by yourself tonight?"

"Yes, my wife had to be out of town tonight. She was all prepared to come, but her sister took ill, so she's in Arizona."

"I'm sorry to hear that."

"Oh, she'll be fine. That's okay, though, because it gives me an opportunity to meet more people. I usually spend the night surrounded with my wife's friends."

"So, you can party tonight and show your true colors?" Sam wanted to put her foot in her mouth. That wasn't the type of thing to say to the big guy.

He laughed and shook his head, standing there looking so controlled. She wanted to be like him when she grew up. He was a picture of coolness.

"Yeah, I guess I can do that." He took his hand out of his pocket and greeted a woman walking up to him.

"Loraine, it's great to see you again." As she approached he kissed her on the cheek.

Sam slowly turned to her left and tried to step away, but Mr. Graham reached out and touched her arm.

"Samantha, do you know Loraine Nelson?"

Sam turned and smiled at Loraine. "No, I don't believe we've met."

Mr. Graham did the introductions and let Loraine introduce her date.

"Hugh, I'd like you to meet Russell Graham, he's the head of Valentine Records, and this is Samantha . . . I'm sorry I didn't get your last name?"

"Chambers." Petrified, Sam tried not to look up at Hugh.

"Yes, Samantha Chambers. She handles all the publicity for the company. You know we need to talk, I could use your services."

"Oh, no, you don't, she's all mine." Russell put his arm around Sam and he and Loraine chuckled.

Sam shook Hugh's hand and glanced up at him. Then she saw it—a faint hint of recognition. He gave her his million-dollar smile, then turned to Russell. She wanted to turn and run away. If he mentioned that she'd been in his office as Vivian Banks, she had no idea what she'd say.

Trapped, she stood there trying to come up with a quick getaway. Loraine's ruby necklace and matching earrings caught her attention. The way the diamonds sparkled and almost blinded her, she knew they were real. Now her fifty-dollar costume earrings, which she thought were too expensive, looked like chips.

"Maybe Samantha could tell you a little about that. Sam?"

She heard her name and looked up to see all three of them staring at her. "I'm sorry, what did you say?"

"Loraine said that she'd like to have an in-store at her boutique in the mall. Maybe we can work it into the next album release. I'm sure you guys could talk it over."

"Sure, we can work something out. You're over at Greenbriar Mall aren't you?"

"One of my stores, yes. That's the location I had in mind."

"That's a perfect location." Sam talked to Loraine, but she felt Hugh staring at her. She could see him trying to remember where he'd seen her before. She had to get out of here!

"Well, folks, it's been great chatting, but my man and I have to try and catch the mayor before he gets away. Ciao." Loraine leaned over to let Russell kiss her on the cheek before walking away holding Hugh's arm.

After they left, Sam exhaled. Her legs were weak and she wanted to scream. She couldn't believe he didn't say anything. She had to get out of there before he confronted her.

While planning her exit, she watched the couple walk across the room. They stopped to greet the mayor, and Loraine chatted on while Hugh glanced back over his shoulder. Sam locked eyes with him and felt her throat tighten as his eyes narrowed. She knew she was in trouble.

Chapter 7

He couldn't remember what she'd said her name was, but it wasn't Samantha; he would have remembered that.

"Honey, what's wrong?" Loraine looked back to see what he was looking at.

"I've seen that lady somewhere before. Do you know if she's got a sister or something?"

"I have no idea."

Loraine introduced Hugh to the mayor of Atlanta, several business owners, and some of her girlfriends. He took mental notes of everyone he met. He'd hit pay dirt this time. Loraine was a wonderful woman, and smart. That's what he needed—a smart woman.

He left her with her friends and went to get them drinks. Standing at the bar, he had the sensation someone was watching him. He quickly turned and looked over his left shoulder. He didn't see anybody. The bartender handed him two glasses of chardonnay. Taking the drinks, he made his way back through the crowd. Halfway across, he had that strange feeling again. He stopped and quickly scanned the area.

He caught her! Standing on the steps leading to the top level was the woman from the record company. He grinned at her as she turned and continued up the steps. Vivian, that was it. Ms. Vivian Banks. *Okay Ms. Banks, what the hell do you want with me?* He walked back over to Loraine and delivered her drink.

"Honey, excuse me a moment. I need to make a quick phone call." He kissed her on the cheek and excused himself from her and her friends.

Sam searched the room, eager to find the exit. It wasn't twelve o'clock, but it was time for Cinderella to leave the ball. The knowing grin he had given her when she was on the steps, made the hairs on the back of her neck stand up. He definitely remembered her now. Maybe he didn't know that she was investigating him, but he had to know she was up to something. She made her way over to the railing for one last peek. Loraine stood talking to several women, but there was no sign of Hugh.

Sam took the elevator to the first floor, fearful he would see her on the staircase. When the door opened, she peered out before stepping off. She looked back over her shoulder before making her way to the exit.

"Leaving so soon? The party just got started."

Sam smiled at the young man attending the exit. "Yes, I'm not feeling very well; maybe next year."

"Okay, take care of yourself. We'll see you next year."

She slipped out of the room and into the parking lot elevator. After the door closed, she breathed a sigh of relief. She'd seen enough and was desperate to get home. He was setting up his next victim. Loraine probably wasn't as wealthy as the Wilmingtons but if the jewels dripping from her neck were real, and Sam had no reason to believe they weren't, then she wasn't hurting for anything.

The elevator stopped on the third floor and the door slowly opened. No one got on. Sam hit the first-floor button again, fearful a hand would appear in the door, pulling it open, and Hugh would be standing there. She shook her head and laughed at herself. *What am I so scared of? He doesn't know anything about this case. He probably just thinks I'm some crazy woman."* The door closed, and she took a deep breath. She'd watched too many scary movies, she told herself.

When the door opened on the first floor, she stepped off the elevator. The area around the elevator was dimly lit. The lightbulb that had glowed brightly when she'd arrived now flickered, obviously on its last leg. What sounded like a trashcan being knocked over caught her attention. She turned around slowly walking backwards, but didn't see anything, or anybody. She imagined Hugh stepping out of the shadows with a gun in his hand.

A hand gripped her by the shoulder. She jumped pulling away from whomever and spun around.

"Hey lady, calm down."

A man dressed in a tuxedo held his hand out to Sam. "Are you okay? You almost backed into that car."

She looked up at a blue luxury car creeping by. The woman inside smiled and mouthed, "I'm sorry," to her.

Sam shook her head at the woman and tried to smile. She turned back to the gentleman. "I'm okay, you just scared me that's all."

"You sure? You look a little shaken up."

Embarrassed, she pulled herself together and assured him she was okay. She thanked him and hurried to her car. Her hands trembled as she pulled the keys from her purse. Once safely locked inside the car, she let out a sigh of relief. "This case is getting to me. I better call it quits and give Mrs. Wilmington what I have."

Hugh found a pay phone and called Lorenzo. "I think we've got trouble," he said, looking around to make sure no one overheard his conversation.

"What's up?"

"I need you to check somebody out."

"What you got?"

Hugh gave him Samantha's full name and asked him to find out everything about her. "I want to know where she lives, what she eats, even what brand of toothpaste she uses. And make it fast. I need it before I leave for Liberty this weekend."

"You got it."

Finding his way back to Loraine, Hugh figured it was time to split. She still held court with her girlfriends.

He whispered in her ear. "Baby, I've shared you with these people long enough. Come on, it's time for me to escort my baby home."

Loraine smiled and excused herself from her friends. "Hugh, we haven't been here that long; we can't go just yet."

He pretended to whisper to her again, but nibbled on her ear first. "I want to show you how much I missed you."

She made her goodbye speeches as they exited the room, telling everyone that she suffered jet lag and needed to go home and rest. Hugh pushed her along, smiling politely at everyone. It still took them over twenty minutes to reach the exit.

Sam hadn't slept a wink all night. She checked her alarm system three times before finally going to bed. Somewhere in the back of her mind she imagined Hugh following her home and breaking in to get her. She'd picked up the phone to call Eddie, but decided against it. If she called him over, she wouldn't be able to hide the fact that she was afraid.

All this was so silly, she told herself. What she needed to do was call Rich and Maxine to see what they'd found out. It might not be as bad as she thought.

Before she could call Maxine, she heard from her. "Sam,

I traced that social security number you gave me, and you're not going to like what I found out."

"Bad news or good news?"

"I'm not sure. You tell me? I can only find information that goes back three years. It's like this guy didn't exist before then. And, I don't see any financial wealth to speak of. Sam . . . this doesn't look right. Maybe this number's incorrect, or he changed his social security number for some reason."

"Why would anyone change their social security number, unless they were into something really shady," Sam said.

"And don't you try to find out what it is. Give the police a call and let them track it down. Sam, this is way over your head."

"There you go, Maxine, telling me what to do again. All my life you guys have tried . . ."

"Stop it, Sam." She cut her off. "You always think somebody's trying to control you. We were only trying to keep you from making some of the same mistakes we made."

"Well Max, you're only three years older than me."

"Then Taylor and Morgan. You know what I mean. Sam, you know we love you and we don't want you to get hurt. And I know Daddy wouldn't have given us any of these cases if he had thought they would lead to us getting hurt."

"I know that."

"So, finish up your report for Mrs. Wilmington, turn your findings over to the police, and get down here so we can all sit back and discuss the cases."

"Fax me what you have and I'll see. I need to make one more call before I wrap this up."

"She went to college here in Atlanta, then joined Valentine right out of school. She worked her way up to publicist. She's single, and dig this." Lorenzo walked over to Hugh's desk, throwing a piece of paper on his desk.

"She's from Liberty, Georgia. Born and raised."

Hugh's eyebrows shot up in surprise. "She is?" He glanced over the paper on his desk before getting up. "Chambers, Chambers, where do I know that name from?"

"Didn't I tell you to hit that town and get out? You just had to start romancing that girl and everything. I would have . . ."

"You would have what? Walked up to her and announced your intentions? Pulled out a gun and took what you wanted? Or maybe broken into the house and risked getting caught? Don't tell me what you would have done." Hugh raised his voice as he walked across the floor toward Lorenzo.

"I would have completed the job," he said, sitting back down on the couch.

"You would have gotten yourself thrown in jail again. Then you'd probably only have about ten thousand dollars to show for it. You have to nurture these jobs. We're not dealing with chump change." He paced around the front of his desk and lectured to Lorenzo.

"I'm not going back to jail. You can keep playing with those broads if you want to, but remember your job. Look man," he stood to leave, "I'd like to keep listening, but I've gotta run. You know I've got business to take care of. You need me to find out anything else on that lady from the record company?"

His pupil wasn't in the mood to listen. Hugh opened the door for him. "Don't bother. I think I know where I can find out what I need. So get out of here and get to work."

After Lorenzo left, Hugh propped his feet back up on his desk and read over Lorenzo's notes. He didn't doubt anything that Lorenzo had provided. His contacts reached far and wide. He could find out just about anything Hugh needed, or could get him copies of just about any type of document he needed.

So what was this woman from Liberty, Georgia, doing pretending to need his advice? He couldn't figure out what somebody in the record business would want with him. What did she and Wendy being from Liberty have in common? He thought of a way to get that answer.

He opened his phone book and called Wendy's sister. Maya knew everyone in Liberty and the next several counties over in any direction.

"Maya, how are you this evening?" He'd gotten the feeling he wasn't one of her favorite people, so he needed to treat her with kid gloves to get any information.

"Who is this?" she asked in a rather abrupt tone.

"It's Hugh. You mean you don't recognize my voice?" He chuckled, trying to add a little humor to the call.

"No, I didn't. What's wrong?"

"Nothing. I just need a little information, and I can't reach Wendy right now."

"What you need?"

"I'm looking to do a little advertising, and this woman from Liberty was suggested to me. Samantha Chambers—do you know her?"

"Yeah, I know her."

Okay, so the most talkative woman in Liberty didn't want to talk to him. How he managed to get on her bad side he didn't know. He'd always had a way with women—a good way.

"Can you tell me a little about her? I mean what's she like? Did she go to school with you guys?"

"She's nice. She was in Wendy's class. Her family lived on the outskirts of town so we didn't socialize much. I can't tell you about her work ethics, but she's nice enough."

"Does she happen to have a twin sister here in Atlanta?"

"No. She's got three older sisters, but they're definitely not twins. Her father ran Chambers Investigations. But he passed recently, and all the girls were in town for his funeral."

"What is that, a private investigator firm?"

"Yes. I'm surprised you didn't see her at the family picnic."

He slung his feet off from the desk and sat up in his seat. "She was at the picnic?"

"Yeah. Well she wasn't actually at *our* picnic; she was just in the park. She didn't get to say hello to Wendy because she was chasing her little nephew."

"Did you by any chance tell her who I was?"

"I told her you were from Atlanta, but she didn't know you. Too bad you guys didn't get to meet then, huh?"

"Yeah, that's too bad," he said, his words tinged with menace.

"Are you going to be working with her?"

"Uh . . . I think so, and possibly real soon. Thanks, I'll talk to you later." The muscles in his jaw twitched as he abruptly slammed the phone down.

His instincts were right. She'd been following him. Now he remembered; he'd read about Henry Chambers passing in the Liberty newspaper. Was she a private investigator like her father? Or was she working for the police? And how much did she know about him?

He immediately picked up the phone and dialed Lorenzo's cellular number.

"Lorenzo, speak to me."

"It's me. Get back over here. I've got a job for you."

Chapter 8

After another long day at work, Sam walked into the house around eight-thirty and turned on all the lights. She didn't want to admit to herself that she was afraid; she was just being cautious. She turned the alarm and the porch light on. Eddie would be by soon for dinner.

After changing into comfortable loungewear she went into the kitchen to prepare dinner. Cooking relaxed her and was one of her favorite pasttimes. In order to keep her mind off the case, she turned on a little jazz to help mellow things out. With all of her spices and sauces out, she hummed to the music and swayed around the kitchen. In here she felt completely safe and comfortable.

The phone rang.

She wiped her hand on a paper towel and reached for the phone that was hanging on the kitchen wall. "Hello," she answered in a cheerful voice.

"Can I speak to Samantha Chambers?"

She reached over to turn down the stereo. "This is her speaking."

After a moment of silence, the line went dead.

She tilted her head and gave a bewildered look at the

phone. Could that have been Eddie? She doubted it, but why not check. She dialed star-six-nine to get the number. Instead, she got a recording saying, "This number cannot be traced." She hung the phone up with a trembling hand. Slowly she went back to the counter and prepared her meal. She tried to resume her humming, but couldn't remember the tune.

The doorbell rang.

Her heart almost leaped from her chest. She snatched a paper towel and bent over to catch her breath. Glancing at the clock on the microwave, she realized it was time for Eddie to show up. Exhaling deeply, she went to let him in.

Eddie walked in with a bottle of wine this time. That's what Sam liked about him; he always contributed something to the evening. The wine, flowers, tickets to a ball—he'd even shown up with French bread one time. Prepared to spend the night, he also had a small duffel bag that he dropped inside the living room door.

They managed to sit down to a meal without either bringing up Sam's case. Eddie spent most of the evening talking about some new developments on his job. Lately, they hadn't spent much time together, so Sam enjoyed the relaxed moment between them.

After dinner, she got up from the table and took his plate. "How about dessert?"

Eddie leaned back in his seat, patting his stomach with both hands. "I guess I've got room. What are we having?"

"Chocolate cake with sour cream icing." In the kitchen Sam cut the cake and returned with two healthy pieces.

When she walked back into the room Eddie sat at the table, fidgeting with his hands nervously. When Sam set his cake before him, she noticed he slowly nodded his head, and knew something was on his mind. She waited for him to speak out.

They ate most of their cake in silence. Eddie finally spoke. "So, how was the ball? I hope you didn't have too much fun without me?"

"I sure didn't. I walked around all evening making small talk."

"Any luck networking?"

She'd completely forgotten that's what she had told him she would be doing. "Well, I didn't get to do much networking. Mr. Graham was there."

"You're kidding—Valentine's CEO?"

"The one and only."

"Yeah, I guess that shot some of your networking."

"I met a few people, but I don't know if anything will come of it."

He put his fork down. "Sam, now I need something from you."

"No problem. What you need?" She stopped eating to listen to him.

He sat up and pushed his empty plate aside. "I've got a very important business trip to take, and I need you with me. All the other men are taking their wives or girlfriends, so I need you to do this for me."

He looked so serious he had Sam's full attention. "Sure Eddie. Where are we going?"

"To Arizona, next week."

"Next week! Eddie, I can't."

"You can if you want to. See, that's what I mean. I'm telling you how important this is to me and the first thing you say is, I can't. You don't even know why."

"Eddie, next week is bad for me. I can't get away."

"You could if you wanted to. For me."

She couldn't believe he was laying this on her. He knew she was in the middle of this case and how important it was for her to finish it. Going away right now wasn't something she could do, but how could she get him to understand that?

"What is the trip for?"

"It's an academic conference, and I'm nominated for a scholar award."

"You didn't tell me that. Congratulations." She walked over and hugged him.

"I just found out today. I hadn't planned on going to the conference until I found out I was a finalist in the competition. That's why I need you with me. So, what do you say?" He held onto her hand before she pulled away.

She stood there shaking her head and biting her bottom lip. She hated being put on the spot like this. The conference wasn't important to him before. *Now that he's a finalist, he wants to run to Arizona in case he wins, and he wants to drag her along in case he doesn't.*

"Do it for me?" He pleaded, letting her sit back down.

Sam sat back and kicked her legs out under the table. "Eddie, any other time I'd love to, but you know I'm trying to wrap this case up."

"You can work on the case when you get back."

"But I'm close to finishing it now. All I need is a little more time, and I'll have it all wrapped up. How about you go ahead and I can fly out before the award ceremony?"

He shook his head. "I knew it. This award may be the most important event of my career so far, and that means nothing to you."

"Why can't I fly out later?"

He stood up. "Because I want you there with me. It's important to me for you to be willing to give something up for me. But you can't do that, so now I see how much I mean to you." He took his plate and glass into the kitchen.

"Eddie, you are so selfish. What I'm doing means nothing to you, even after I told you how important it was to me."

He returned. "Sam, that man's not going anywhere. You can follow him around some more when you get back."

"I'm not just following him around. I'm getting the proof I need to complete my case."

"You told me all you had to do was prove he's not wealthy. I'm sure that hasn't taken this long. You're enjoying yourself and not realizing how much damage you can do."

"I've done more than prove he's not wealthy. I've found out that he's a con artist who uses women."

"You don't think his business is legit. That has nothing to do with that woman in Liberty that he's dating."

"It's all connected. He's using her and he's working on another woman right now. I saw them at the ball. That's what he does—romance these women, then take everything from them."

"You saw him where?"

She realized what she'd just said. Her head began throbbing and she felt a small headache coming on. "He happened to be at the ball."

"The ball you asked me to get you a ticket to? Where you'd planned on doing a lot of networking? To help *us*, is what you said."

"I know, but Eddie I couldn't tell you why I wanted to go. I knew you would act like this."

"You used me! If you wanted a ticket to that dance, you didn't have to lie about it."

"I couldn't say, 'Eddie can you get me a ticket to the ball, I want to see if Hugh Noble shows up so I can see what he's up to.' "

"You're right." He stood and walked into the living room and picked up his bag. "If I knew I couldn't count on you to do anything for me, I never would have gotten you a ticket to spy around on some other guy."

"Where are you going?"

"Home."

"Come on, Eddie, stay. Let's talk about it." She walked over to stop him. Tonight wasn't a night that she wanted to be alone.

"What's there to talk about. I need a woman who has time for me and doesn't just want to use me."

"Eddie, I really don't want to be alone tonight."

"Then call Mr. Noble, I'm sure you've got his number." He opened the door and stormed out.

Sam watched him leave, then slammed the door. She wanted to put her foot in her mouth again. Why on earth did she let that slip out? Every time he got upset, he stormed off. He didn't know how to communicate and work through an argument. If it wasn't his way, it was no way.

She made sure the alarm was on, then went to clean up the kitchen. After the kitchen was spotless, she showered and got ready for bed. At the foot of her bed was a videotape she had planned on watching with Eddie. She put the tape in and settled back to watch the movie alone.

Thirty minutes into the movie, she heard something outside and hit the mute button. Her bedroom faced the front of the house and set directly over the front door. A small streak of light came through the blinds from the streetlight. After several seconds she didn't hear anything else, so she continued to watch the movie.

Her eyelids slowly closed, then opened as she tried to stay awake. She'd really wanted to watch this picture, but the fatigue of working hard all day, then cooking all evening, was taking its toll. Her eyelids grew heavy again, then she heard another loud sound.

Thump, thump. The sound unmistakably came from outside, and not the television. She immediately hit the mute button again and her eyes widened in alarm. This time she threw the covers back and walked over to peek out the window. She didn't see anything, but she was positive she had heard something. She put on her robe and slippers and went downstairs. Afraid to turn on the lights, she tiptoed down the stairs. Once in the living room, she grabbed a poker from the fireplace stand to use as a weapon.

In the dark, she peeked out the living room window, then the den. She didn't see anything outside, but was sure she had heard what sounded like somebody dropping something. Looking out her back door, she began to wonder if what she had heard hadn't been a plant falling over on her back porch. It wouldn't be the first time. Convinced that's what it was, she turned off the alarm and grabbed her flashlight from under the sink. Slowly, she cracked the back door open.

She shined her flashlight around the porch from one plant to another. Next to the back step, she saw what she was looking for. One small plant turned over onto its side. *I knew it.*

She stepped out onto the porch and bent over to pick the pot up.

A black shadow crossed her view. She screamed and pointed her flashlight with a shaky hand. Her heart fluttered in her chest. A small possum waddled down the walkway and off into the grass. Her trembling hand slowed. She turned and ran back inside. Leaning against the locked door, she let out a nervous chuckle. *What the hell am I doing!*

She turned the alarm back on and sprinted up the steps. Throwing the flashlight on her bed, she sat down and picked up her cordless phone. After paging Rich, she walked over to the window and looked out again. The street looked quiet and peaceful. The movie was still playing, but she'd lost all interest in watching it. She was so nervous she couldn't remember if she'd turned on the alarm or not, so with her cordless phone in hand, she went to double-check.

Settled back in bed, cradling the phone, she waited for Rich to answer her page. When he didn't reply after five minutes, she paged him again. Waiting for him, she had time to think about what had just happened. She'd been scared by a possum, and a baby possum at that. How ridiculous she felt.

The phone rang, and she caught it on the first ring. "Hello."

"Samantha, it's Rich, I got your page. Is everything okay?"

She felt so stupid. She didn't want to tell him about the possum. "Yeah, I just wanted to see if you were able to get me any information."

"Man, you're working late tonight, aren't you?"

She looked over at the bedside clock. It was eleven forty-five, and she called him for information. "I know it's late, but I've had a busy day. Never mind, I'll check back with you in the morning. I'm probably disturbing you right now."

"No, actually, this is a good time. I couldn't sleep anyway. Hold on; let me grab something."

She hoped he didn't think she was crazy. This case was absolutely driving her out of her mind.

"Sam, I'm waiting on one more piece of information. But what I did find isn't pretty."

He proceeded to tell her most of what Maxine had said and more. It looked to him as if Noble and Associates was laundering money.

"Large deposits are being recorded into the company account via wire transfer from overseas. Then, a smaller transfer is made into a local account that we'll have to trace later. So far, we can't find the owner of the account.

"I hope you don't mind, but I laid this out to a detective friend without mentioning any names, and he'd like to take a look at the case. I think you've got some criminal activity going on here and the police would be interested."

"Really? You mean it's more than just making bad investments?" She'd had a gut feeling all along that something bigger was going on.

"Oh, and I saved the best news for last."

"That is?"

"This social security number belongs to a baby who died a few years ago. Looks like your boy purchased his new identity."

"Then who is he?"

Chapter 9

Sam woke up the next morning drained and exhausted because it had taken her so long to fall asleep after hearing Rich's news. Now, she didn't know who this guy was. Maybe he was Hugh Noble, or maybe he was Mike Davis. Then again, was it her job to find that out? She reminded herself that she had already proved he wasn't wealthy. It was time to turn her report in and close the case.

She dressed for work before fixing herself a bowl of cereal. While eating breakfast she told herself—it's over. She didn't have to think about this case any longer. Besides, she'd gotten dangerously too close. After turning her findings over to Mrs. Wilmington, she'd also give the police what she had and let them pursue him further.

Before leaving for work, she walked out on the back porch to pick up her plant. Not much of the dirt had fallen out, so she scooped it back into the pot and repositioned it on the step. She laughed at herself, thinking about the baby possum that had sent her running back into the house. Grabbing a broom, she swept down the steps before going back inside.

When she walked out the front door she saw an envelope

stuck under the door knocker. She had a suspicion it was from Eddie. She closed the door and grabbed the note, opening it on her way to the car.

MIND YOUR OWN BUSINESS BITCH, OR YOU'LL END UP LIKE YOUR FATHER.

She stopped dead in her tracks and stared at the words on the page. It was a threat! This definitely wasn't from Eddie. The note was typed on a plain white piece of paper, and her name was typed on the envelope. The thought that he had come so close to her home scared the hell out of her. *Now he knows where I live!*

She looked up and down the street for something, for anything. Was somebody watching her? She continued out to the car, and stuffed the letter in her purse. When she turned the key, nothing happened. Trying not to panic, she waited a few seconds and turned the key again—still nothing.

She jumped out of the car and ran back inside. First, she called AAA, then she paged Rich. As she paced around her home office, her anger grew. How did he know about the case?

Minutes later, the AAA mechanic arrived and checked under her hood.

"You got some enemies?" he asked.

"Why?" Sam asked looking over his shoulder.

"Cause somebody cut your battery cable. This car is dead."

She stood slumped next to him when her cell phone rung. She yanked it from her purse.

"Rich." Sam didn't even say hello, she knew who it was.

"Yeah, I got your page."

"They tore up my car," she said on the verge of tears.

"Who? Where are you?"

She walked away from the car over to the curb. "I'm at home. Somebody left a note on my door saying I'm dead, and cut my battery cable." She struggled to control her quavering voice. Right now she didn't mind admitting she was scared to death.

"Sam, I'm coming to pick you up."

"Don't bother, Triple A's here. I'm going to rent a car; I've got to get to Liberty."

"Hold on, don't go anywhere just yet. Remember, I've got one more piece of information I need to get to you. I should have it in a few minutes. Go ahead and get the car, but call me before you leave."

"Rich, I've got a plan. If it works, Hugh won't be making it back to Liberty. I'm going to my office to make a few calls, so buzz me as soon as you get something. I need to get on the road early."

"Okay, and Sam be careful."

"I will." She hung up feeling slightly better. The AAA mechanic had her car all ready to be towed away.

After renting a Ford Escort, Sam went into her office and waited for Rich to call. She worked out a plan in her mind to ruin Hugh's business even if the police didn't arrest him. She picked up the phone to call an old friend.

"Monica Rice, may I help you?"

"Hello, Monica. It's Samantha Chambers." Monica worked for the *Atlanta Journal and Constitution*.

"Samantha, how are you?"

"I'm great, and yourself?"

"Doing fine. I haven't heard from you in a while. Is everything okay at Valentine?"

"Yeah, just fine. But, Monica, I need a huge favor."

"Sure, what you need?"

Sam broke down the story in a way sure to get any reporter's attention, especially the whistle-blower. She painted Hugh's investment firm as a front to rob unsuspecting senior citizens from their life savings. She gave her Mr. Bickerman's name to use as a source. If he knew Hugh was going to be exposed, Sam was sure he wouldn't mind being a part.

Monica promised to run the story if Sam faxed her everything she had. Sam promised to do so. After the police picked Hugh up, Monica would have much more to report on.

"Samantha, how did you get all this information?"

"You don't want to know, and trust me—this guy is hot. There's more to this story, believe me."

"Sounds interesting."

"It is. Here's one more contact." She gave her Rich's number also. She wanted to make sure this story blew his business wide open and landed his butt in jail.

"Do you have any contacts in Liberty, Georgia?" Sam asked, hoping she did.

"At the *Sentinel?* No, I don't."

"Well, you might want to look for one. Hugh Noble is engaged to Wendy Wilmington, the daughter of the richest black family in Liberty. I'm sure there's another story there, too."

"Thanks, Samantha. Send me what you have, and I'll get right on it. I'll try to run something as soon as I check it out."

Almost as soon as she hung up, the phone rang. She picked it up on the first ring.

"Hello."

"Sam, it took a while, but I got it."

"Great, Rich, who is he?"

"His name is Richard English. He's originally from St. Louis. Our boy spent some time in a juvenile home before coming up with all of his aliases. And Sam, he's got a couple. Mike Davis, Hugh Noble, and Richard Anderson are the latest. I'm sure he's buying his identities. I can't see that he's spent much time anywhere. After a couple of years, he pulls up and leaves town. Noble and Associates has been around close to three years; maybe he's about to make another move.

"One other thing. He's a suspected jewel thief. Several women have filed reports on him, but he always skips town and starts over somewhere. Each report is over fifty thousand dollars. He's never been caught with anything, but they think he's guilty. The cops keep losing track of him. Sam, I think he's guilty, too, and we're gonna have to pick him up."

"He's all yours. I just need to give my client her report."

"I'll turn this over to Detective Jones. We've got enough to pick him up right now."

"Great. Well, I'm on my way to Liberty."

"You know any cops there?"

"I used to, but I'm not so sure now."

"Then take down my buddy's number and go see him. He's a cop."

"If I need him, I'll call. But, I don't think I'll need him. Right now, Hugh, or Richard is here in Atlanta." She took the number down.

"Sam, take it anyway. You never know."

"Okay, and Rich?"

"Yeah."

"Thanks for looking out for me. I owe you more than concert tickets this time."

Sam hadn't wanted to turn the case in yet, but Hugh gave her no choice. She wasn't going to get killed over this. Before leaving the office, she called Mrs. Wilmington.

"Hello."

"Hello, Mrs. Wilmington. This is Samantha Chambers. I'm calling to let you know that I've completed your case and I'd like to bring you the report right now." Sam hoped and prayed it was going to be okay.

"Samantha, how are you?"

"I'm fine."

"I talked with your sister, and she informed me you were wrapping up the case. I think it's so wonderful that you girls have followed in your father's footsteps. So, you'll be coming by today?"

"Yes, ma'am. You know, this case turned out to be more than I originally thought it would be. I think we need to talk about it right away." She saw no reason to mention that she was really a publicist and not a P.I. What did it matter right now; she had done the job.

"My goodness, this sounds serious."

"It's very serious."

"Okay, you're scaring me now. My daughter is about to go away with this man for the weekend."

"Don't let her. I think she should hear what I have to say first."

"I'll try to get her here. Can you be here by six o'clock?"

"Yes ma'am, I'm on my way now." Sam hung up with her heartbeat racing. This was it.

This was an emotional moment for her. She thought about her father for a moment and how many of these calls he'd made. Now, she'd actually worked a case for her father and she'd enjoyed it. It wasn't boring as she had thought when she was younger. For the last couple of weeks, she'd been on a roller coaster ride. But now the ride was over, and she wanted to get off.

Her stomach was tied into one big knot, constricting her breathing. She took a deep breath, thinking about what would happen after this. He would definitely find out she'd talked to the Wilmingtons, then he'd want to kill her. She'd planned to stay in Liberty for a few days. Maybe long enough for the police to pick him up.

If Eddie knew what she was doing, he'd probably break up with her. She was a woman that he couldn't control, and she didn't know if he'd ever get over that. She would give him a call after this was over with.

*　*　*

Once she reached the Wilmingtons several hours later, Wendy wasn't there. She'd gone shopping in Savannah to prepare for a trip, and Mrs. Wilmington couldn't reach her on her cell phone.

"I knew something was wrong," Mrs. Wilmington said after reading Sam's report. "He just tries too hard, if you know what I mean."

Sam nodded, trying not to show her surprise. Mrs. Wilmington didn't seem shocked or alarmed as she read. She kept nodding her head as if agreeing with everything; poised and sophisticated, even upon hearing bad news.

Sitting in the formal living room with its heavy draperies and rich cherry furniture, Sam didn't feel comfortable. The room was too formal and stuffy. There was no place to relax after a hard day's work and put your feet up. However, Mrs. Wilmington looked right at home in her peach suit and high heels. Sam concluded Mrs. Wilmington never stood in her heels for more than a couple of hours. She probably dressed like that all the time, too, Sam thought.

"For someone in investments, he never wants to talk about his work. And my husband talks investments all the time. We weren't about to let Wendy throw her inheritance away investing with that young man. And there's no way she's leaving with him this weekend."

"You believe she'd still want to after she hears this?" Sam sat there, shocked at how naïve the wealthy were. She talked as if they'd forbid Wendy, but she might still want to go. Had this woman not understood the full magnitude of what she'd just read?

Mrs. Wilmington reached over to pick up her glass of lemonade. "You don't know my daughter, Samantha. Wendy is a very stubborn young lady. At twenty-nine she's discovered her independence, and her father and I can't tell her anything. She probably won't believe a word of this, unless that thief tells her himself. She's in love, and for the first time.

"So what do you plan to do with this information?" Mrs. Wilmington asked.

"I've turned it over to the police."

"Good. Maybe Wendy will pay attention if the police pay him a visit."

"I'm afraid they may do more than that. He'll be going away this weekend, but not with your daughter."

"You don't think they'll use my daughter's name in any of this do you?"

"I'm almost positive they'll use her name."

"Are you sure there's no way of keeping her name out of it? Is there someone you can talk to?"

"I can't promise you anything, but I'll see what I can do."

"Samantha, thank you for following up on this case so well for me. You may have saved my daughter's inheritance— and possibly her life. I'm going to call Sergeant Kimble right now and tell him about this young man." They stood and exchanged handshakes.

As Sam pulled out of the circular driveway, she saw Wendy pulling in. She'd let her mother break the news to her that her romantic weekend was off.

When Sam pulled up to her father's house, Maxine wasn't there so she let herself in. She went up to her old bedroom and fell across the bed. This house felt safe and comfortable, just like her kitchen at home. She only wished her father were here to protect her. She could use a big hug right about now.

After Mrs. Wilmington hit Wendy with the news, Sam wondered how she'd take it. It was obvious Wendy loved him. But he was a con artist. Sam felt proud to have stopped him from robbing her blind.

Now that the cat was out of the bag, that wouldn't be the end of the story. Unless the Atlanta police picked him up, she feared Hugh would try to carry out his threat. She lay there thinking about everything she could do to protect herself should she need to. Her body relaxed into her old bed and her eyelids began to flutter. Too tired to fight it, she closed her eyes and drifted off to sleep.

Chapter 10

"Sam, we missed him. He left town before we got there. Did you hear me?"

She stirred, for a moment disoriented. Where was she? Then she remembered she was in Liberty. "What?"

"Are you awake? Did you hear me?" he asked in an urgent tone, sure to alarm her.

She sat up. "I'm sorry, Rich, I fell asleep. What did you say?"

"He's gone, Sam!"

Now she was fully awake. She moved to sit on the edge of the bed. "Gone where? You guys didn't pick him up?"

"We tried, but by the time we sent a car to his office, he was gone. His secretary said he was headed to Liberty for the weekend."

A chill ran up Sam's spine as she jumped up from the bed. "He's here?" she shrieked.

"Sam, calm down. I called my friend and filled him in. He's looking out for his car, and he'll pick him up as soon as he hits Liberty."

"What if he doesn't catch him before he gets to me?"

"But he doesn't even know you're in town."

"He will! I gave my report to Mrs. Wilmington, and her daughter pulled up just as I left. I'm sure she's told her everything. If he calls her, she's definitely going to tell him I was there. And if he found my house in Atlanta, he'll be knocking on my daddy's door any minute now." She walked over and looked out the window. Her reflection stared back at her as the blackness of the night made its presence known. She'd slept longer than she thought.

"Don't worry, we've notified the Liberty Police Department. Trust me, they'll get him."

Still peering out the window ,she could see headlights coming down the road. "Hold on, Rich." She watched the car get closer. All she could see was the dirt kicking up from the gravel road; the car wasn't close enough yet.

"What's wrong Sam?"

She squinted to make out the car.

"Sam, what is it?"

As the car got closer, she could tell it was Maxine. Taking a deep breath, she walked back over and sat on the edge of the bed. "Nothing, it's just my sister coming up the road."

"Look, you've done all you can do. Now, let the police take care of everything else. Tomorrow all of this will be over."

"God, I hope so."

"Hey, I gotta run. Get in touch with my friend, and get some rest."

"Yeah, right."

She went downstairs to greet her sister. In the kitchen she put on a pot of water for coffee. When she walked back into the living room Maxine hadn't come in yet. Sam wondered if she needed help with some groceries or something. She walked over to the curtain and peeked out. That wasn't Maxine's car after all; it was a police car.

She hadn't asked Rich to send his friend over to protect her. From the back she saw his figure standing at the door. Then again, maybe he had some good news for her. She hoped they'd caught Hugh. Not thinking, she didn't even look out the door—she just pulled it open.

As he turned around to face her, a sickening wave of terror welled up in her stomach. Her eyes became saucers and the chill of the night air crept through her body and up her spine. She stood there in shock and speechless.

"Hi, Samantha—or should I call you Vivian?" Hugh dropped his cigarette on the porch, then smothered it with his shoe. The whole time she'd followed him, she'd never seen him smoke before.

"Come on, which one do you prefer?" he asked in a toying way.

Able to finally open her mouth, she asked, "What should I call you? Hugh, Mike, or Richard?" She heard her own voice quiver.

He laughed as he pulled a small revolver from his jacket pocket. "Let's go inside and discuss it, what do you say?" He stepped in as she backed away from the door. Closing the door behind him, he nodded as he looked around the room. "Nice, real nice."

"What do you want?" she asked, backing up into the living room and staring at the gun. Trying to hide her petrified state, she put her hands on her hips.

"Ah . . . you're the one playing private eye. You tell me what I want."

"My sister will be here any minute. Would you please tell me what you want, and leave."

"Which sister is that: Taylor, Maxine, or Morgan? You see I did a little investigative work myself. I hope you've had your fun, because the game is over." He motioned for Sam to sit on the couch as he backed her farther into the living room.

She had never come face to face with a man holding a gun before, especially one pointing it at her. But for some reason she didn't think he would kill her. He didn't appear to be a killer, and she hoped he wasn't about to take it up tonight.

"That's right, *your* game is over. You can't cheat anybody else out of their life savings, or con any more women out of everything they have."

He gave her an incriminating smile. "Oh, so she's done her homework, too, or a little anyway." He nodded and gave her a seductive wink. "Very impressive."

Fear forced her to continue. Maybe if she stalled him long enough, someone would come to her rescue. "What happened this time? You get lazy? Or was she harder to crack than usual?"

He walked over and looked at some family portraits on the bookcase. "Nice. Four little girls wanting to be just like Daddy. But you got more than you bargained for, didn't you?" He walked over to a chair across from the couch and leaned on the back.

Sam chose to ignore him and see what she could get him to admit to. "Maybe you fell in love with Wendy Wilmington, and it was Loraine's money you wanted?"

He laughed a hardy, gut-wrenching laugh. "Oh, baby." He walked around the chair, then sat down and crossed his legs, facing her. He still held the gun on her. "You really need to stick to promoting music. Something you know about, instead of something you don't."

Her fear was slowly leaving her, and anger was taking over. Who in the hell did he think he was to come into her father's house and hold a gun on her? Anger kept her talking and confronting him.

"Or maybe it was their jewelry you wanted."

That got his attention. He looked up at Sam as a grin like the Grinch's crept onto his face. With his elbow on the armrest, he stroked his chin. "Well, she's not quite as dumb as I suspected. I'll give you credit for that one. Looks like there's always more to it than meets the eye."

"So how's the market overseas for jewelry these days?"

This time he looked shocked, and not too happy with her discovery.

"You don't know what the hell you're talking about." He gave a nervous chuckle.

"Then maybe your friend Lorenzo can fill me in on the rest."

Now she had his undivided attention. He looked at her as if he was now aware that she knew what he was really up to. She only prayed he wouldn't shoot her on the spot.

"Let me ask you something. How did you found out my real name?"

"The police gave it to me." She noticed a flicker of panic in his eyes. Now she had him scared.

He leaned forward, resting his elbows on his knees and pointing the gun away from her. "You really don't know who you're messing with, do you?"

"I know now."

"No, you don't. Don't you know that I can kill you, then dump your body and be out of the country before the police even find me?" He stood up and walked back over to the bookshelf.

"All that meddling old bitch wanted was to know if I was wealthy or not. You should have stopped there. I probably would have let you live then." With his gun he swiftly knocked the pictures off the shelf. They fell, shattering the glass on the floor.

Sam jumped as she sensed things were taking a turn for the worse. Could he also be a killer? She didn't want to die like this in her father's house.

He turned and walked toward Sam. "But you had to keep digging, until you dug your own damned grave."

Standing in front of her, he pointed the gun at her again. "Get up."

Scared to move, she stared at him—seeing something different in his eyes. He wasn't attractive any longer. He was a ruthless con artist who would do whatever he had to do to stay out of jail. Now he was going to kill her.

"Get up!" he yelled.

Staring at the gun, she slowly rose holding her hands up. "Look, the police don't know you're in town, so if you . . ."

"Shut the hell up and move." He waved his gun at her.

"Where are we going?" she asked, taking small steps.

"Just move." He pushed her out of the living room and into the hallway.

"Whatever you're thinking about doing, don't do it. You're a thief, not a killer. You don't want to do this."

He pushed her harder toward the front door. "Shut up and get into the car."

Every self-defense program she'd ever seen flashed through her mind. *Do not get into the car with him; you're as good as dead.* No matter what, she wasn't going to get into that car. She looked around for something to use or do to stall him. Unfortunately, her father's house was half a mile from the neighbors. He could kill her right here and no one would know until Maxine came home.

"What are you going to do?" She stood at the top of the steps not wanting to move, until she felt the point of the gun in her back and changed her mind.

"Down the steps, now!" He raised his voice and shoved her with the gun.

She took two steps and heard him dial someone on his cell phone.

"Hey, we've got trouble. I'm in Liberty and I need you down here as fast as possible. Don't go to my place, the police might be there."

Sam took the steps one at a time, landing on each step with both feet. He was too preoccupied on the phone to notice how slowly she was moving. In the distance she saw headlights coming down the road. She prayed it wasn't Maxine. She didn't want her sister to get hurt.

"Yeah, it's the lady from the record company. She went to the police. First, call Maurice so he can take care of everything at the bank. It's about eleven A.M. overseas. Then get your ass down here fast. Call me once you're outside of town."

Sam reached the bottom step and walked toward the police car he'd come in.

"Not that car, yours." He pointed with his gun to her car.

Glancing to her right, she saw the other car getting closer, but didn't want him to see it.

"There's another car in the garage." She turned and walked toward the garage, putting his back to the road. "Why don't we take that . . ."

"Where the hell are you going? We're taking your car." He waved his gun at her again. "Get over there."

She tried to stall again, but the headlights of the approaching car were closer and he noticed them. He glanced back over his shoulder, seeing the car closing in. Sam used this opportunity to make her move. She ducked and took off running toward her car, praying like hell that he wouldn't shoot her in the back.

Hugh spun around and shot at her. She hit the ground. Then he ran and jumped into the police car he'd driven up in. He spun off, sending gravel flying behind him. The car coming down the road speeded up with the police sirens blaring. When the car reached the Chambers residence, it stopped. A young woman jumped out of the car and ran over to Sam, who was lying on the ground. The police car gave chase.

"Samantha, are you all right?" Wendy Wilmington ran over to Sam and helped her up.

Trembling and barely able to stand, Sam dusted herself off. "Yeah, I'm okay." She looked up, surprised to see Wendy.

"My God, he shot at you. I'm so sorry. I can't believe it!" With her hands over her mouth, Wendy started to cry.

Sam could still hear the ringing in her ear from the bullet that passed too close for comfort. Thank goodness Hugh hadn't added marksman to his list of talents, or she'd probably be dead right now. The realization that he'd tried to kill her was enough to make her weak at the knees. She had to sit down.

Wendy helped her over to the steps.

"I had no idea until Mother talked to me and told me what he'd done. We were planning to go away for the weekend. He was taking me to Las Vegas." She spoke between tears.

Sam stopped shaking long enough to speak. "I'm just glad you showed up. He could have taken me out into the woods and killed me. Who was that in the car with you?"

"Officer Mason, one of Sergeant Kimble's men. After Mama told me everything, Hugh called to say he was on his way. We were leaving tonight to get an early start. I was so upset; I couldn't help but ask him about it. I didn't want to believe it, but he got so mad at me, he started yelling and cursing. He wasn't acting himself, so I called Officer Mason.

"Once he arrived, Mother told him everything, and he suggested we come out here and talk to you. I had no idea Hugh was so close to town when he called, or we could have been by here sooner."

Another police car went barreling down the road, speeding past them. The women sat in silence for a few moments.

"Wendy, I'm sorry he didn't turn out to be who you wanted him to be."

"Samantha, I just want to thank you for taking the case as far as you did. I can't believe you put your life in danger for me."

Sam looked back at the swing on the front porch and envisioned her father sitting there with her. "Thanks, but I didn't do it for you. I did it for my father and my family."

Sitting in the front seat of Officer Mason's car, Samantha rode to the station. Officer Mason had benefited directly from her father's integration of the Liberty police force years ago. He was also Rich's friend.

Hugh sat in a jail cell while the police talked to Sam. She started at the beginning, explaining how a simple background check turned into a case for the police.

"Richard English is suspected of stealing probably millions of dollars worth of jewelry over the last ten years. He starts his investment business in order to meet some prominent people. Later, he either robs them of money or jewelry. By the time they suspect him, he's closed up shop and moved to a new town, with a new identity."

Officer Mason nodded. "We picked up his partner the minute he hit town. He doesn't want to go back to jail, so I think he'll talk. Rich sent me what he has on the case, so I think we've got these two."

Sam wanted to cry she was so relieved. "Thank you for coming out to the house. If you hadn't, I might not be sitting here right now."

"Samantha, what you did was incredible. Your father would have been proud of you." He reached across the table to shake her hand.

"Yeah, he taught me well. Whether I realized it or not." She gave him a knowing smile and shook his hand.

She left the office, wanting to go home and be with her family.

Two days later, the *Atlanta Journal-Constitution* and the *Liberty Sentinel* ran stories on Noble and Associates. Hugh Noble's business was destroyed, and Richard English's career as a criminal was over.

●◆●

Purvis Wayans chuckled to himself as he poured a cup of steaming black coffee into his favorite NFL mug. The con men had been conned by a little lady. Hugh Noble and Richard English would have a long time to think about what they'd done. The uncovering of the scandal was the talk of Liberty, thanks to Samantha Chambers. Truth be told, those Chambers sisters were the talk of the town ever since they'd come back. Seems like trouble had a way of finding them or as Henry would say they *found trouble.*

Little Samantha. He remembered the days when all she wanted to do was tag along behind her big sisters. She wasn't tagging along anymore. She was all grown up and could tangle with the best of them.

He took a sip of the steaming brew and stared at the envelope, addressed to him in Henry's familiar scrawl. "Purvis, don't open this until the last case is solved."

His curiosity was killing him. He'd held onto the envelope since the reading of Henry's will. He'd kept its existence a secret from the sisters. More than once he'd been tempted to break the seal, especially after what happened with Maxine and then Taylor.

Purvis tugged in a long breath. There was one more case to solve. But he sure couldn't figure out what it could have to do with Morgan. She'd hightailed it back to California right after the will was read. No, he couldn't see any connection.

He lifted the envelope from the desk. What last secret do you have for us Henry?

REDEMPTION

Shelby Lewis

Chapter 1

It was 7 P.M. Friday night in Temple City, a bedroom community ten miles north of San Jose, California—heart of the Silicon Valley, center of cutting-edge computer chip technology and electronic engineering in North America.

In the Valley, computer firms ran twenty-four/seven, as did most grocery stores, gas stations, gyms, and other places of convenience. Every ethnic food imaginable was served within a twenty-mile radius of Temple City, including Ethiopian, Greek, Chinese, Japanese, Hungarian, Mexican, and French.

There were three major shopping malls, six strip malls, four executive-style hotels, four movie theaters, four libraries, five bookstores, and bowling, skating, and golfing within the same twenty-mile radius.

In the Valley, the air was dirty from the thousands of cars that sped across freeways and expressways any time of the day or night. Mild temperatures kept flowers in bloom, from the camellias of winter to the azaleas of spring and the lilies of summer.

There were no clear seasons in the Valley, a climate which spawned the "California look" of shorts and sandals for most of the calendar year. There was seldom thunder or heavy rains. The weather rarely produced either extreme of steaming heat or bitter cold.

The mild weather and dense urban culture made the Valley a favorite stomping ground of major football, base-ball, basketball, and hockey teams. When there was no man-made action around, Mother Nature sometimes contributed with an earthquake. There was always excitement in Temple City. On this early summer night, there was no exception to this rule.

Morgan Chambers thrived on the twenty-four hour con-venience at her fingertips. Everything she wanted was easily within her reach, time-wise and in distance. In Temple City she had found her niche, a self-styled nook in a busy me-tropolis a long way from her hometown of Liberty, Georgia.

In Liberty, the pace was too slow for Morgan, its resi-dents of seventy thousand people more inclined to visit nearby Savannah for entertainment than they were to hang around town hoping for something exciting to happen.

As soon as she could, Morgan beat it out of Liberty to strike her own fortune in the world. It had taken twenty years, but in that time she had forged a life which kept her sat-isfied, in spirit and in health.

Finding her niche meant she had also found peace for herself, an inner calm that came from turning her dancing hobby into a promising full-time career. At Morgan's Miracles, a two-story building on Twenty-second Street, Morgan trained girls to dance as ballerinas. Her clients were young, black, and gifted.

Tonight, Morgan's inner calm lay shattered. In the wake of this ruined peace she realized her life would never be the same again; the illusion of personal safety was gone. In Temple City, a heinous crime had been committed: murder one, a capital homicide.

Beside the victim's body lay a mysterious note. The note

was the reason why she'd been summoned by local authorities to attend the crime scene.

The note was a 3" by 5" index card, white paper, blue lines. Morgan glared at the index card as if she stared down a sworn enemy. Her name was on that card. *Her name.* Safe inside a clear plastic evidence bag, the document was easy to hold by its edges without disturbing prints or other vital clues about the identity of the victim's killer. Morgan studied that card from every angle. Next, she studied the victim.

The victim had been murdered in the east parking lot at Lake Tyler, a public park and community center in Temple City. A student in a modern dance class, Tandra Emory was a twenty-six-year-old social worker at the Blythe Pavilion Center, a mental health facility at Temple City Regional Hospital, one mile northeast of Lake Tyler.

She had gone to dance class straight after work. There were ten other students in class at Lake Tyler's community center, yet not one student heard the attack against Tandra by her crafty killer.

Grief poured from the mouths of those ten remaining students. What happened to Tandra could easily have happened to one of them. Had the music been too loud? Was that the reason no one heard the dying dancer scream?

The lake grounds were peppered with transients. Had one of the homeless asked for money, only to kill Tandra after she refused to give it away? The victim was engaged to be married. Had her boyfriend, someone she trusted, come along and stolen her last breath? If so, why Lake Tyler? Why not terminate Tandra in a less conspicuous place?

If her boyfriend betrayed her, his presence would explain why Tandra hadn't screamed for help during her attack: she recognized the assailant. In the midst of the grieving going on, the defunct dancer's friends were pondering the same questions the police were probing in their quest to detect whodunit.

Morgan scrabbled together the sights and sounds of the crime scene into her mental database: the wails of the grieving women, the short sharp scream of the victim's fiancé upon his arrival, the cool feel of the night, the unnatural light of police cars shining bright onto the paved parking lot and into the darkness beyond the community center.

Fifty minutes ago, she'd been sitting in front of the television in her living room, on the verge of eating two hot apple turnovers on a chipped china plate as she savored buttered rum–flavored coffee in a solid blue mug while reading an oldie-but-goodie romance book by Monique Gilmore. Fifty minutes ago, she was at peace, and then she received the disturbing telephone call from local authorities.

Peace.

Morgan forced herself to relax. On two counts of ten, she drew a cleansing breath. With each breath, she supplied her lungs with air—slowly, evenly. On the count of the twenty-first breath, she said, "This can't be happening."

"Believe it," said a voice behind her. Homicide detective Joe Carter was recording notes into a handheld dictation system, its microcassette on a continuous spin as he cataloged the images confronting him. Spectators milled about, hoping to glimpse lurid details to later report to their family and friends.

Crime-scene technicians worked as if the spectators were not present, as if they were alone with the still-warm body of crucial evidence. The background sounds were those of a carnival sideshow: hushed voices punctuated with shocked exclamations "Ooh!" "Ah!" "Oh, my God!"

Morgan remained focused on the dead woman, a wit-robbing sight. The woman was Morgan's height and weight. Her muscles were taut and fit, also like Morgan's. On the victim's feet were worn-out ballerina slippers. It could be Morgan herself lying on the ground, slender neck bruised and broken, the magic of her dancing feet lost forever.

On the heels of her own father's recent death, Morgan

wasn't quite able to cope with the drama she now faced, and yet, she was forced to cope. The note in her hand made it impossible for her to do anything else.

Joe Carter tugged her gently by the elbow. He led her to his unmarked police car, a dark blue Ford Taurus sedan. Together, they sat on the hood. He was the first to speak. "Do you have any idea who wants to kill you?"

Morgan shoved her glasses up the bridge of her nose with the point of her right index finger. She and Joe had worked together for five years on Temple City's Special Crimes Task Unit.

The year before, she had retired from the unit as a police sketch artist. What she hadn't left behind was the sense of camaraderie she'd established with many of the people she worked with at the Temple City Police Department. She and Joe remained close.

Based on this friendship, Morgan's response to his question was equally to the point, equally candid. "Of course not." Her eyes, dark brown, highly intelligent, showed little agitation. Her cool countenance was a brilliant tour de force.

"Leroy wants you under guard twenty-four hours," he explained. His heavy voice, equally cool and equally controlled, reflected none of the anger jack-hammering his stomach and chest. This case was so close to home he felt battered to the bone. Morgan was the only woman on the planet he trusted with his life. A future without her in it was too grim a vision to face.

Oblivious to his intense distress, she never shifted her gaze off the crime scene. "Oh, yeah?"

Joe knew she was pissed, but he didn't care. Fifty minutes ago, watching her back became his number-one priority. "Leroy will take a shift and I'll take a shift. More guys from the station will keep tabs on you, too." Ever-vigilant, deeply schooled in the subtleties of her personality, he added, "But you don't want interference, do you?"

"No."

"Didn't think you would." He took her hand in his. His skin was rough and bore no jewelry. "What do you want to do?"

Her response was immediate. "Find the victim's killer. What else?"

Joe flexed his shoulders. They were broad, hard, fit from lifting weights three nights a week at the Gold's Gym near the Temple City Police Station. Like Morgan, he wasn't married, nor did he have children.

He preferred to remain unattached. Being unattached simplified his lifestyle. As a homicide detective, he kept odd hours. As a sketch artist for the Special Crimes Task Unit, so had Morgan, another reason why she understood him so well.

They were kindred spirits, their mutual friendship built on trust and faith versus sex and desire, the latter a glowing ember never allowed full flame for fear the very emotions binding them together might blaze, burn, then incinerate from twenty-four hour scrutiny. It was far better to detect and destroy crime, something entirely objective, even though it, too, occurred around the clock.

This shared way of thinking solidified the core bond of affection between Morgan and Joe. The result was a relationship honest and true, free of sexual content, yet rich because of their physical and emotional differences, much like Dana Scully and Fox Mulder in the *X-Files* television show.

Joe pitched his voice for her ears only. "Leroy won't let you work this case. You're a civilian now."

She considered the validity of his words. Leroy Whyte headed the Special Crimes Task Unit and had been her direct supervisor five years running. Medium height, gray-eyed, brown-skinned, and balding, Leroy was considered fair by his subordinates because he listened first, made decisions second.

He didn't dally with gray areas in life. For him, problems were either black or white, good or bad. Once he evaluated facts, sorted, then filed them in his mind, his decisions were generally iron-clad.

There was nothing rash about Leroy. In this way, he reminded Morgan of her father, Henry Chambers. Thinking of her father bolstered her spirit. Henry tackled problems head-on, confident that eventually the truth would be revealed and justice served.

Joe was right; Leroy wouldn't let her dig for clues in the dancer's death. Still, she had to try. "Speak of the devil," she said. "Here he comes now."

Leroy dispensed with salutations, preferring to deal with essentials only. He directed his words to Morgan. "Take a trip 'til this thing cools down."

"I'm not a runner."

"You're not invincible, either," he countered. "Whoever created this mess is hardballing. Obviously you had no threats or strange things happen, or you'd have said something by now."

"Correct."

Long furrows marred Leroy's brow. Even when he wasn't frowning, permanent lines creased his skin. "This is what worries me, Morgan. You're not a hell-raiser. You teach little girls to dance, for Christ's sake. I figure the big question is this: who'd want to link your name with murder?"

"Apparently," she said, "somebody who hates my guts."

Joe interjected. "You must know something without realizing it, Morgan. Has anything unusual happened in your life lately, anything at all?"

Baffled by her connection to the murder, she had thought of little else. "Just my father's death. At the reading of the will, he wanted me and each of my three sisters to solve a case from his detective agency. I refused."

Leroy was all ears. "What did your sisters do?"

"For sure, my sister Taylor accepted a case."

Leroy was silent only a moment before asking, "Did her case involve murder?"

Morgan swept her shoulder-length hair away from her left cheek with an agitated hand. She wished she had paid more attention to the particulars of her father's will. She had been so intent on retaining her own meticulously constructed lifestyle in California, she had ignored the fact she would never escape her Georgia roots.

Her father was born and raised in Liberty, Georgia. His legacy for his daughters lived on in Liberty, Georgia. By ignoring some of the facts of her father's will, she might have missed an important clue to this murder in Temple City. The idea was far-fetched but not impossible.

From her mother, Hazel, Morgan had learned that everything she experienced in life was connected in some physical, spiritual, or mental way. Considering this concept, she realized it was up to her to discover the connection, if one existed.

What did she remember, she mused, about those cold cases of her dad's? Not much. She sighed in disgust. "I think Taylor's case involved a missing person."

Leroy swept his gaze over Morgan's dark honey-colored skin, her dark brown eyes, and her petite body. He couldn't believe anyone would want to hurt her. She had been a sketch artist, not a beat cop or a homicide detective.

As a sketch artist, she hadn't been in the forefront of homicide investigations; she'd merely been a tool for use in the apprehension of suspects in the difficult cases Special Crimes investigated.

She made pencil sketches of possible suspects. To do this, she listened to descriptions from troubled witnesses, many of whom felt more relaxed relating one-on-one to a young, sympathetic woman, skilled at bringing the subtleties of a criminal's face into vivid detail.

Morgan used all of her senses to create a credible image for the witness to validate. When she heard fear in a victim's voice when describing a suspect's features, she built tension into the face of the drawing: a tightness of the flesh about the suspect's eyes, at the corners of the suspect's mouth, a breath of attitude from the suspect's personality.

The end result of her intuition and mechanical skill was often stunning. Morgan's sketches aided in the successful capture of seventy-six percent of all cases she had worked on in her twenty-year career in law enforcement.

Leroy couldn't think of a criminal who wanted payback against her. The puzzle she faced was exceptional, as there appeared to be no reason behind the madness. "What about your other two sisters?"

Morgan shoved her rear end off the hood of Joe's company car. She paced, then stopped to face both men. "I don't really remember, to tell you the truth. When I quit Special Crimes, I quit everything that had anything to do with the murder business. It's another reason why I tuned out a lot of that stuff about Dad's cold cases during the reading of his will."

Leroy angled his bald head to the side. "Why don't you want to solve one of your dad's cases? Cold cases are usually real thinkers, puzzlers. As a sketch artist, you dealt with puzzles all the time. I'm surprised you weren't interested."

At last, irritation broke through the intelligence in Morgan's eyes. She considered Leroy's questions an invasion of her privacy, but then, so was the mysterious note left by the killer at the crime scene. Explanations were required. "I didn't want to work with Dad while he was alive, and I sure don't see myself working his old cases now that he's gone."

Softly, she added, "I'm about moving forward, not backward. I wish I could bring my father back, but I can't. I don't see how solving one of Dad's cold cases is going to make a difference in my memory of him."

Leroy thought a minute. "Did any other sister refuse a case?"

Morgan's sigh was long and heated. "No. I believe all those hours Dad pulled at that detective agency of his brought on the heart attack that killed him. I don't want anything to do with his agency. I don't want anything to do with crime at all. It's why I quit the police force."

She paused, tethered her taxed emotions together. Thinking of her father's death within sight of Tandra Emory's body iced the blood in her veins. The last thing Morgan wanted to do was to shake with nerves in front of spectators.

"Look guys," she said. "I want to live my dreams now, not later. Dad's death was a wake-up call for me. What his business meant to my other sisters, I can't tell you. We all shared a love for Dad the man, not his career. That much I can tell you."

The head of Special Crimes piece-worked the crime scene in his mind. While scanning the cram of tightly pressed flesh for anything that didn't fit, he allowed Morgan's frustration to flow over and around him as he mapped his next step. There was much to consider.

Back history was important, but did little to shed light on the current problem she faced. He focused on the single idea that she couldn't escape. "Regardless of how you feel about your father or your own reasons to retire from the police force, you're involved in another murder case anyway. This case isn't cold, but it's definitely a puzzler. You're in the mix, whether any of us like it or not."

Her melancholy was as tangible as the evidence being tagged and spirited away by forensic experts. "Apparently so."

Joe joined the discussion. "Something else happened, Morgan. A year ago, you helped solve a particularly nasty murder. That could also be a connection."

Morgan's tolerance for sustained, high-energy drama short-circuited. She didn't want to think about that case, either. She wanted to focus on teaching ballet, nothing else, but that was out of the question. "That's all a blur."

Joe couldn't believe her bold-faced lie. "A woman was killed after her dance class. You helped find the man who strangled her. This homicide might be related."

"The other victim was blond and blue-eyed," Morgan countered.

"She was a dancer."

"Modern dance. I teach ballet. There is a difference."

Joe raked a hand over his face. "You're not being objective, Morgan. Dancing is a connection between the case last year and the case today. The fact that a year exactly has passed is another objective fact. What if the perp for that crime was only practicing?"

She was shaking her head in denial before he finished his sentence. "We caught the perp," she reminded him.

"Did we, Morgan? To this day, he claims he's innocent of murder."

"We found DNA."

"He was her boyfriend."

Morgan paced again. The trial for that case had been ugly. Until now, she'd been successful in relegating those events to the closed files in her mind. "There was enough evidence to convict."

"Circumstantial."

Frustrated, she dug into her shoulder bag for a fine point pen and a 4" x 6" pad of blank white paper. She sketched the crime scene. The act of drawing soothed her jagged nerves, a sensation akin to a nicotine hit in a chronic cigarette smoker. "Whatever. Look, assuming the guy I helped put in jail is really innocent, he might want me dead. We can start our investigation there."

Leroy pulled the pad from her fingers. "Stop. There is no 'we' on this case. It's too risky."

She looked at Joe for help. Dark-skinned, dark-eyed, his features beautifully sculpted, his body elegantly dressed despite his gruesome profession, Joe Carter inspired anger in Morgan instead of lust. He opened his hands, palms out, as if to say, "What can I do?"

She glared at him. "Traitor."

"No," he said, softly, dangerously. "I'm not a traitor. I'm

your friend. Leroy is right when he says it's too risky for you to stay directly involved."

She gave both men an I-don't-give-a-fuck-what-you-think look. "The name Morgan Chambers is on the note found on the victim's body. The victim is wearing ballet shoes with a hole in one toe. Look down, fellas."

Leroy ran a hand over his bald head. "Shit."

Joe slid off the hood of his car and onto his feet. "How did the killer know you have a hole in the right toe of your ballet shoe?"

"He's been in my closet."

A muscle flexed in Joe's jaw. His rage was dark. When he spoke, rage had hammered his voice into a hoarse facsimile of the real article. "Maybe he's seen you dance?"

"Impossible. I only wear these slippers when I'm puttering around my apartment because they feel soft and comfy. I don't wear them to the studio. The only way anybody would see my slippers is by coming to my house."

Joe had been to her house many times, but hadn't seen those slippers. His eyes ran from Morgan's head to her feet to her head again. "You're wearing them now. Why?"

"When I got your call, I shot straight from the apartment. I'm also wearing sweats with Clorox stains on them. Like I said, I was puttering around the house cleaning up and whatever. When you told me to get over here and make it quick, I did exactly that."

Leroy noticed something else. "You brought your sketch pad."

Her frown implied he wasn't too bright. "I always carry a pad in my purse. What are you getting at, Leroy?"

"Aside from the way you're dressed, you act as if you're here in an official capacity. The killer might have anticipated this reaction from you. The killer might be here, Morgan."

Joe took a step toward her, his movement involuntary. "I'm going home with you tonight. I'll sleep on the couch."

She was appalled. Too much of her privacy had been invaded this night. "No, you will not go home with me." Each word was equally weighted with the same watch-it-buddy attitude. "Besides, you can't sleep on my couch indefinitely. I might as well start off the way I'm gonna keep going."

Joe met her stare with enough force to shock a look of wonder behind the wire rims of her designer glasses. "Who said I can't stay forever?"

Morgan groaned. In all these years, he'd never trampled the formal boundaries of their truly excellent friendship. It made her angry that he wasn't listening to her back-off body language or her leave-me-alone words.

"Come on, Joe," she said. "This isn't the time or the place to screw around with our friendship. Get a grip on yourself before I say something I'm damned sure to regret."

Leroy eyed the younger woman with a paternal once-over. Tandra Emory's killer had destroyed everyone's comfort zone by redirecting the lines between friendship and business. Nothing about this crime was strictly business.

He said, "Under normal circumstances, I'd agree, but these aren't normal circumstances." His nod to Joe was presumptive and territorial. "Go home with her. I'll get one of the boys to drop your car off later."

Morgan stuffed her sketch pad into her purse. She was mortified to find herself in the position of victim, and against common logic, she fought this high-handed plan. She wasn't a child, and chivalry was dead. "No man sleeps at my place without an invitation."

She turned to Joe, then jammed a finger in his chest. "Follow me home if you like, check inside every closet and behind every door if you want to, but when I say hit the road, that's what you're gonna do."

He knew she wasn't blowing smoke. "It's a start."

Her face said otherwise. She felt adrift, betrayed, humbled, and frightened. She did what she did best—fight back. "It's a finish. I won't be babied."

"Don't be stupid, Morgan."

"I'm determined to live my dream, Joe. I turned down Dad's unsolved case so I could stick with teaching kids to dance. I'm not bowing to a killer. If this guy wants me dead, let him try it. Both my eyes are open. This poor woman here probably didn't know what hit her."

"She probably trusted him."

Morgan softened a fraction so small only Joe could tell the difference in her demeanor. "I don't trust too many people. Whoever is after me isn't a friend."

Leroy shook his head once in disgust. "You don't know that, another reason you shouldn't be on this case. You're ruling out people you know without giving yourself time to think about it."

The last of her composure snapped. She pointed her finger at her former boss's seen-everything face. "Hey, I'm the one who suggested we start with the guy in jail for the dance murder last year."

"Leroy's right, Morgan," Joe said. "Someone wanted to be sure you didn't think this woman's death was a fluke. There could be more than one Morgan Chambers, but there's probably only one Morgan Chambers who wears dark gray ballerina slippers with a hole in the big toe. My guess is that the killer knows you in real life or he feels he knows you in fantasy life. Either way spells trouble. You can't afford to turn down options when it comes to tracking down this guy."

"You're talking about my friends, Joe!"

"I am."

"You're my friend. Are you telling me you could be the killer?"

He crossed his arms over his chest, legs braced wide, face solemn. Everything about this night was blown out of any known context he'd ever experienced as a veteran cop. "I didn't know about the hole in your slipper."

"But you know where I keep the spare key to my house."

Leroy faced Joe. "And where is that?"

Joe stared into the distance. "On top of my refrigerator."

"See," Morgan said. "If I'm gonna put my friends on the suspect list, I'd have to start with him."

Leroy ran a hand over his head again. "Shit."

A muscle flexed in Joe's jaw. "Ditto."

Despite her bravado with Leroy and Joe, Morgan was thankful she had such fiercely loyal and dedicated people in her life. Striding away from the disgruntled men, she handed the killer's macabre message to a crime-scene tech. In bold block print, the note read: *Next time, Morgan Chambers, it could be you.*

Chapter 2

Cheated out of peace, haunted by death images of Tandra Emory, struck by guilt for denying her father's last wish, Morgan rammed the stick shift of her vintage sports car into gear. She'd bought the refurbished red classic straight after high school, preferring it over the high-tech cars in the Temple City landscape. Her private speed machine was the main keepsake she treasured from Liberty, Georgia—that, and her father's penchant for fighting crime.

Right now, she needed Henry's expert advice, his down-to-earth brand of common sense, a practical judgment ethic he'd instilled in her mind from day one of her childhood memory. His three-rule credo had become her own code of conduct once she left her Liberty roots to join the Temple City police force:

Number one: stay focused.

Number two: details make the difference.

Number three: justice always prevails.

Morgan sped through the restless city, her reason scored by the screams of Tandra Emory's disconsolate lover, Tandra Emory's horrified friends. In one hour, on one night, one savage event had shattered her perfect little world.

There was power in the number one.

One represented self. The self was human. To be human was to be frail. To be frail meant Morgan could die, any place, any time. She gunned the fine-tuned engine of her much-coveted car, skidded around a street corner, righted herself, then proceeded on a near suicidal course of perilous speed, cold skill, and shipwrecked emotion. The scream of the tiny car's wheels on asphalt catapulted her mind back to the crime scene, back to the 3" by 5" index card with her name inscribed on top.

Her name.

Damn.

She skidded around another street corner, smacked a curb with the rear passenger tire, righted herself, then continued down the potential path of destruction she'd set for herself. "Daddy," she said, "you should be here. If you were here, I wouldn't feel so alone."

Gear shift.

"I miss you, Daddy." This, a whisper.

Morgan released the tan convertible drop-top from its closed position. Immediately, wind from the careening car whipped strands of her hair against her face. Hair scratched and clawed at her skin, strands of it tangling in the arms of the glasses she couldn't see squat without. Wind raced against the curve of her dark honey-colored cheeks, dried the hot, bitter tears of her fear-induced frustration.

Beneath the outrage was the constant sorrow she felt about her father's death, a man whose work ethic kept him from the people who loved him best, his wife Hazel, their three other daughters: Samantha, Maxine, and Taylor. After Hazel died, giving birth to Sam, part of Henry had died along with her; that part was his soul.

Conscience alone had tethered him home to his children. Lack of soul kept him distant. His great folly had been to love his wife more than he loved his daughters, more than he loved himself. The framework of the Georgia judicial system had enabled him to rebuild life after Hazel's death—his life, not his daughters'. Morgan knew this. They all knew it.

Morgan resented it.

Justice and order were the sticks Henry used to measure past feats and future goals. But was it just, she wondered, for him to corner criminals by sacrificing his daughters' needs for fellowship, for paternal intimacy?

She didn't think so.

Henry's dedication to his job had ripped a hole in her life. His lackadaisical child rearing had forced her to head a tribe of sibling sisters; each, in her own way, angry with their workaholic father, their absent mother.

Their mother.

Gently, Morgan put her hand on the gear shift of her flying machine. She eased the gear down a notch, another notch, one more. She pulled the car to the nearest curb. At the curb, she returned her drop-top to its proper position. She got out of the car, her manner defiant. Let the killer see her. Let him come. Let them finish together what he started alone.

Hazel Chambers had taught Morgan to keep her cool. Keeping cool meant keeping an open mind. An open mind meant examining the sights, sounds, and emotional messages she experienced in her twin quests for truth and justice.

In life, Hazel's opinions had run alongside and complementary to her husband's physical stand about those themes; Henry had fought on the front lines, his wife on the sidelines. Their children had existed somewhere in between, each of them watching, each of them learning, each of them scored with indelible notions of right versus wrong.

There were three serious pressures growing up in the Chamberses' household: huge expectations to win, to perform, to succeed. The deep entrenchment of these values had served to push the sisters apart.

All Morgan ever wanted from her father was the chance to be a kid, unaware of his profound pain, his terminal loss of soul. That was then. As it was for Tandra Emory, for Morgan, the past was dead.

She was determined to figure out her connection to the dancer's death. She wanted the satisfaction of seeing justice served. The methodology required to achieve those goals centered her troubled mind. Step one was to get her man: Tandra Emory's killer.

She climbed the steps to the apartment she lived in alone above her business. She was committed to a cause, and the cause was survival.

Joe fell into stride beside her. "You've controlled your feelings."

"Yes."

"I won't let you get hurt."

She shrugged her shoulders. "If it's my time, it's my time."

"Fate."

"Whatever."

Joe patted the gun in the holster beneath the light suit jacket he wore. "I deal in the concrete," he said, "the here and now. Somebody comes after you, Morgan, it'll be the last thing he does. No questions asked."

"I'm not into vengeance," she countered.

At the door of her apartment, he took the keys from her fingers. "I am."

He shoved her behind his back. Together, they entered the apartment. She flipped on the light beside the front door. The white-on-white décor remained intact. Morgan's home was a sanctuary, and it showed in the minutiae. Soft sofas, fine prints, natural artifacts.

This was a home where jazz played on the stereo system during quiet time, where candles were lit when it rained, where a woman planned recitals for fledgling ballerinas, girls too young to break holes in their dancing slippers.

"Morgan," Joe said, "keep your entry light on from here out. If it's off before you come in, run."

Hate for her predicament clouded her mind in a red haze of anger. She shoved her glasses up the bridge of her nose with a finger. "I never run."

"That's why I'm here."

"You're here because I'm not an idiot. That woman's death was vicious and unnecessary. Stupidity on my part would only complicate matters."

"No doubt."

"I won't catch this guy if I get killed."

Joe stopped his search of the apartment to glare at her. "That won't happen." His tone was harsh.

"It could happen."

"Don't piss me off."

She laughed, the sound coarse, bitter. Tandra Emory was a prime example of the maxim, what will be, will be. When Tandra entered dance class with her friends this night, she planned to exit with her friends. How could she know death was only minutes away?

What will be, will be.

Satisfied the living room was secure, Joe paced the balance of the three-bedroom apartment. When he returned to the living room, he found Morgan exactly where he'd left her; the only difference between then and now was that she'd stopped laughing. She was crying, her eyes intent on the hole in the big toe of her dancing shoes.

He activated the safety mechanism on his gun. He stuffed the gun into the holster beneath his suit jacket. Eyes cold, face intense, he walked over to Morgan, lifted her chin with two fingers, and kissed her.

This was not the romantic kiss of a lover. This was a kiss because . . . because things were so fucked up. After Joe finished, after he expressed his feelings completely, he used his finger to dash the tears off her face. She was livid.

She jerked a thumb at the front door. "Beat it."

"That's my girl."

"I'm not your girl."

The expression on his face remained entirely unreadable. "No, you're my best friend. I don't want anything to happen to you, Morgan."

She held the door open for him. "I promise I'll be careful. Go home. Get some sleep."

"I'll go home in an hour. That's when one of the guys is dropping off my car and Leroy is swinging around to cover the first official shift."

"The first shift?"

"Yeah. I needed to see for myself you were safe for the night. I'm gonna check out the studio downstairs, the grounds, the windows, the lights."

"The usual."

"Right," he said. "The usual."

"Thank you."

"You're welcome."

Her expression said it all: affection in the form of faith, trust, and the subtle devotions derived from long, intimate relations between dear friends. Theirs wasn't a sexual relationship, although in lonely moments, after difficult cases, they had each been tempted.

Joe was Morgan's comrade, a man privy to her innermost secrets, her heartfelt desires. Yes, there was love between them, a love of shared work, shared space, shared memory, and mutual respect.

To this great friend in spirit and mind Morgan said, "I'll be all right."

The look on his face remained illegible. "Yeah."

The click of the door behind him signaled the end of one chapter, the beginning of a new one.

News of her father's death had reinforced Morgan's choice to chase her dreams instead of Henry's. She believed the pressures of owning a detective agency had caused his fatal heart attack. She wanted none of those pressures.

When the will was read, each sister presented a case to solve, via letter, in order to secure inheritance, Morgan rejected her case, determined to stick with her fresh start in life, her dream career.

And now, now she'd been pulled from retirement after all, not by the reading of her father's will, but by the note left on Tandra Emory's dead body, a woman with a hole in the toe of her ballerina slipper. The entire episode posed a conflict for Morgan.

For her, conflict stemmed from a love of art versus a sense of duty. Choosing art would jeopardize her life; choosing duty, her art. She had either to find Tandra Emory's killer or ignore the problem presented by her death. Duty won.

Morgan stuck her foot out, stared at it, analyzed it, was shaken by the hole in the slipper, the hole in her peaceful life. Nothing could ever be the same again. Not one thing. Mortified, she shot a glance at the front door.

She wanted to run. For a Chambers, running was never a viable option. Ever. It was fight or flight. Do or die.

Fight or flight.

She would fight.

Chapter 3

It was 7 A.M. Morgan answered her telephone the first time it rang. She'd been awake most of the night. "Hey, Leroy."

"How did you know it was me?"

Cordless phone in hand, she paced her apartment. The place felt silent, civilized, and pseudo-safe. "Joe is parked in front of my building."

"He's early."

Morgan smiled. "He never left."

Leroy paused a moment, as if choosing his words carefully. "Listen. I want you to focus on teaching those little girls of yours to dance. That's it."

"I am. Five days a week. Saturdays are reserved for the odd recital. I'm glad today isn't one of those days. My nerves are frazzled."

Leroy drove his point home. "Stick to dancing. Period. Joe and I will concentrate on breaking this case."

Morgan toughened her voice. She was serious about being involved in Tandra Emory's murder investigation. She was every bit as expert in crime fighting and detection as Leroy and Joe. She understood the system, she just didn't carry a gun. "Not without me you won't."

Leroy had legal and political clout. They both knew he could force her into compliance if he chose. In truth, her only edge was their past history together. He set the parameters. "You're a civilian. You're not a P.I. You're out."

"No way," she said, her voice decisive and crisp. If she didn't stand firm, if she waited for Leroy and Joe to come to her with the details of the homicide investigation, she'd wait in silence. Their first priority was her protection. Their second priority was the truth. Her only priority was the truth. She aimed to get it.

There wasn't time to wait for secondhand news of the dissected details regarding motive, opportunity, and the murderer's identity. Morgan wanted the facts firsthand. Getting the facts firsthand meant staying as active in the case as she could.

Leroy emitted a sound that was part grunt, part snort, part bark of derisive laughter. For him, this sound was an expression of emotion. For him, things weren't black and white when it came to Morgan.

During this crisis, his emotions weakened his position. In the end, he gave ground, softened his voice. In his own way, he adored her; not as a man cares for his lover, but as a father for his daughter. "I figured you'd say that."

She laughed. His capitulation was a vital victory. She knew it cost him a chunk of pride to keep her on the case, even though her involvement was nothing official. She also knew that if Tandra Emory's killer managed to kill her, too, Leroy would hold himself personally accountable. One thing Leroy didn't do was half-step. Neither did she.

"What's the plan?" she asked.

"Establish the victim's pattern of habits, check the transients for possible eyewitnesses to the murder. I've got a team in place already."

"What about the boyfriend?"

Leroy's sigh held a hundred degrees of disappointment. "I badgered him half the night. Don't think he did it."

Morgan said softly, "Too easy." The case would be simpler to solve if the boyfriend had been the killer. The twenty-four-hour surveillance could be canceled. Her life wouldn't be in jeopardy. Order would be restored and justice served—in a perfect world.

"It is, and it isn't."

She sat down on the edge of the sofa, picked her sketch pad up from the coffee table, and studied the image she'd created the night before. Nothing of significance caught her eye. "What do you mean?" She tossed the pad onto the table and watched it slide off the top to hit the floor.

"If you'd had a chance to talk to him, you'd understand," Leroy said. "Bottom line is this: I tried my best to make a connection and haven't found any connections that fit. I believe the best way to solve this case is to work from your end back to Tandra Emory. The hole-in-the-toe thing is too unique a clue not to get after right away."

"That's what I think."

"Then you'll also agree that if this guy really wants to kill you, he'll find a way."

"I never said it wasn't possible." Eventually the twenty-four-hour surveillance would be called off. Eventually, she would let her guard down. They all would. Eventually, the killer would strike and win. Eventually just didn't have to be today.

Leroy didn't sugarcoat his anger. "Don't get smart with me, Morgan. There's too much at stake here."

Tired of being bossed around, she snorted in disgust. It was her life that was in jeopardy, not his and not Joe Carter's. "No kidding."

"If you focus on dancing, you'll be easier to monitor and protect."

"Monitor me all you want. I'll protect myself."

"Okay, Dirty Harriet."

She laughed. "I don't mean to be such a hard ass—"

"Could have fooled me."

"—but I refuse to give in to the fear."

"So you admit you're scared." He sounded relieved.

"Of course I'm scared, Leroy. More than that, I finally understand what drove my father to keep going even when he was tired or scared or whatever."

"What?"

"Personal satisfaction."

"Oh, yeah?"

"Yeah. I mean, Dad's ambition wasn't based on money or recognition, it was based on his own satisfaction. I guess I feel it's ironic that after his death, I have the urge to solve one more case. Dad said that a lot to Mom. 'Baby,' he'd say, 'I'm gonna do it just one more time.' "

"She wanted him to quit?"

"She wanted to move out of Liberty, but Dad loved it there. When she died, she took part of him with her. He became a total workaholic."

"But now you understand why?"

"Yeah."

His voice was gruff when he spoke. "I'm giving you the chance to back down, Morgan."

"I know."

"But you won't."

"How can I, Leroy? For some bizarre reason, I think Tandra Emory was murdered because of me. In good conscience, I can't pretend last night's kill was a bad dream. Until the perp is found, no dancer in Temple City is safe from harm. Too many dancers are gonna be looking over their shoulders as it is. In some crazy way, I'm responsible for that paranoia."

Someone leaned on the doorbell to her apartment.

She said, "That's Joe."

"I hear him. I'll hang up after you let him in."

"You don't want to talk to him?"

"He knows what he's gotta do."

"So do I."

She opened the door to a disheveled, grumpy looking Joe.

He strode past her, shut and locked the door behind him, then headed straight for the kitchen. "I'm starving."

For all her courageous pretense, she was glad to see him. "You make the coffee. I'll scramble the eggs." To Leroy she said, "What time do you wanna meet tonight for briefing?"

"Six o'clock. Your place."

"I teach a class at six."

"I know. I want to check out the parents of your students."

"No."

"Yes, Morgan. If you're going to be involved, you've got to think straight. Everybody you come into contact with, who has opportunity to get into your closet, has to be checked. Thoroughly."

She groaned at the loss of privacy, for herself, for her clientele. "You're right. I know. I just don't like it."

"You won't like being strangled either."

Her voice dropped a notch. "Low blow."

"It's the truth. Keep the rose-colored glasses off your face, Morgan Girl. You know as well as I do that when it comes to murder, most victims know their killer. It's why we have to concentrate on your inner circle of family and friends. While their daughters are being coached in the fine art of ballet, the parents are idle. One of the parents could easily have used your distraction during class to study your apartment."

Joe read the mixed emotions on her face. He saw rage, sorrow, disgust come and go. He added his two cents to the telephone conversation. "Whatever he's telling you, Morgan, I'm with him a hundred percent."

She ignored him and spoke to Leroy. "I know what all has to be done. I just don't like it. I mean, everybody in my life in Temple City is a suspect. From now until this case is solved, I'll be looking over my shoulder. I'll be looking for double meanings behind every spoken word, every gesture. Okay? See you at six."

After she hung up, she kicked the sofa. "This sucks."

Joe strode over to her. He grabbed her by the shoulders, lifted her onto her toes, leaned nose to nose, and said, "Believe in me."

"I want to."

"Do it."

"Aye, aye, Captain." She pulled out of his arms.

He backed off. When her temper was riled up, Morgan turned into a prickly pear. He said, "Feed me and I'll go."

"Deal. The quicker we crack this case, the better. I've got a feeling the killing has only just begun."

Chapter 4

Day three.
Victim Two.

Morgan's inner calm wasn't just damaged, it was demolished. For certain, life would never be the same as it was before Tandra Emory's murder. Never again would she believe in personal safety as something concrete. Nobody was safe.

In Temple City, a multiple murderer was on the loose—someone, presumably male, with a chip on his shoulder and a nasty agenda to do more harm than good in as short a time as possible. It was obvious to those directly involved that each crime was connected; the mode and method for each kill were too close to ignore the obvious.

Morgan assembled her thoughts by assessing the felonies with a philistine eye. Hostile to her predicament, she cut away her fear from the hard details of the crime scene and the nearby rabble of rubberneckers. This was no simple task, not when her heart hammered and her adrenaline demanded action.

Victim Two was not into modern dance. Valerie Prescott was into classical ballet. Murdered in the parking lot in front of her condo, she could easily pass for Morgan's sister. Like

Tandra Emory, it appeared Valerie Prescott died of manual strangulation.

Beside the victim's body was a note, nothing mysterious about it. On the white 3" by 5" index card were the words, *Show time, Morgan.* The writing, the card, and the positioning of the card were the same as the Emory killing.

Morgan knew there wouldn't be any fingerprints for the Temple City forensic staff to find; the note on Tandra Emory's body had been clean. There was no reason to think the new note would contain incriminating DNA evidence on it, either.

She handed the note to Joe, who kept pace beside her. He said nothing. The murders, so close together, had captured the attention of the entire city. Temple City residents wanted results, fast.

Like her, Joe understood more lives might be at stake if the case of the murdered dancers wasn't solved soon. He had her back and for this, Morgan was thankful. The last thing she wanted to be right now was alone.

She waited until they were inside his car, the windows raised, the doors locked. "Why doesn't the son of a bitch just kill me?"

In silence, Joe drove to where Leroy stood, beside the coroner's wagon. The Special Crimes Unit leader accepted the 3" by 5" card, promptly turned it over to a waiting crime-scene tech, nodded his head once to Joe, then resumed his conversation with the chief medical examiner, Marley Witherspoon, a blond-haired, blue-eyed dynamo, a woman as dedicated to her job as Kay Scarpetta in Patricia Cornwell's books of crime fiction. Only this was no fantasy felony; the malice and mayhem were for real.

Joe drove straight to the safe house Leroy had designated for Morgan's safety. It was a three-bedroom A-frame on the western outskirts of Temple City. The neighborhood was established in the late 1960s, was well-developed and nondescript. It was a great hideaway.

Inside the safe house, Morgan spoke the unthinkable. "The bastard jammed my own raggedy slippers on the victim's feet. Mine."

Joe used his foot to shove a couple of chairs away from the two-person dinette table in the kitchenette. He tossed a tablet onto the Formica veneer table top. He said, "Number one, this isn't a spree killer we're dealing with. This isn't some guy whose gonna kill someone every day or two for a week or two and then stop."

"No," she agreed, "this is a signature killer."

"We know we're dealing with a man. He's strong, between six-three and six-five."

"Is Timothy Skruggs all right?" Morgan asked, referring to the cop who'd been guarding her apartment and dance studio. The perp got past him to enter her apartment. Inside her apartment, the culprit stole the slippers later found on Valerie Prescott's foot. Morgan had been in her dance studio at the time.

Joe rested his back against the gray vinyl chair. "Skruggs has a huge knot on his head, but mostly he's embarrassed."

Morgan shivered in true trepidation. "He's lucky to be alive."

"So are you."

She couldn't allow fear to make her falter in her quest for justice. "Tell me what happened."

Joe flipped through the pages of his note pad. "He saw a light in your apartment. Skruggs investigated the light source without backup or even calling for backup. That's why he's embarrassed."

Thinking hard, Morgan chewed her bottom lip. After three beats, she said, "That doesn't tell us why Skruggs and I are alive or why Valerie Prescott is dead."

"Hence the safe house."

"I'll need to call the parents of my dance students, tell them classes are closed indefinitely."

"Leroy has Special Crimes already on the job."

She was truly thankful. Dealing with perturbed parents wasn't an issue she wanted to handle at the moment. Her life dangled on total disaster. She couldn't afford any Skruggs-styled slips in judgment. "The man thinks of everything. I guess that's why he's the boss."

Joe rotated his massive shoulders, flexed his arms, cracked his knuckles, and resisted the urge to hug the hell out of her. She couldn't afford to deal with her terror and his, too. "Let's brainstorm."

"Shit."

Briefly, Joe's deep admiration for Morgan's strength and resilience glowed in his eyes. She had nerves of steel, even if she was scared spitless. "The perp is meticulous. He positioned the bodies precisely. There is nothing about his actions to suggest he's out of control, Morgan."

"No."

Joe took a deep breath. "That's why you're my top assignment."

"Damn."

"I need a list of every single person you know."

"Impossible."

"Leroy has the Unit compiling a list of every case you've worked on, every sketch you've drawn."

She spoke with conviction. "This isn't somebody I know, Joe. This is somebody who knows me."

"I think you're right."

She was clearly relieved. "That saves time."

"We have no time, Morgan. It's logical you'll be the next victim."

"Tell me why you think I'm right."

"The guy made a mistake."

She jammed her glasses up the bridge of her nose with a stiff finger. "Say what?"

Joe tapped the tip of his fine point pen on the note pad as he tried to master his rage over the danger Morgan faced. He worried he wouldn't be there to protect her.

Tap.

Tap.

Tap.

Joe laid the pen down, locked eyes with his former partner, and seriously considered carrying her straight off to Mexico. She'd never do it. "The spare key you gave me in case you lost your own was blue."

"So?"

"I have another blue key on my chain. Yours matched perfectly, which is why I put your spare key on top of my refrigerator. I was too lazy to mark either key and since I use mine all the time, I kept that key on my chain instead of yours."

Morgan frowned. "So?"

"The killer isn't breaking into your house, Morgan. He's using the spare key you gave me. The one I had on top of my fridge."

She was surprised. "Now that's a twist."

"After I heard about Skruggs's attack and that the killer walked in and out of your apartment so easy, I followed a hunch. I checked to see if my key was where I put it. It wasn't."

"Someone's been clocking me a long time." She angled her head to the left. "Watching you, too."

"That's a fact."

Someone knocked on the safe house door. Leroy entered. He knocked as a courtesy only. There were armed men on guard outside, two. He tossed a red file folder in Joe's direction, then joined him at the table, its vacant chair still warm from Morgan's body. She was prowling the room.

He said, "The media made the connection between the two dead women number one in the news. The fact they are both dancers is of key interest."

Morgan squelched the urge to scream. The assailant had access to every space of her life, except for her mind: in her mind, she was free. He couldn't possibly know what she was thinking. She wished he did. She wanted him to know, to understand she had every intention of catching him. The killing had to stop.

She pressed a hip against the kitchen counter. "This has to have something to do with Liberty."

Leroy rolled a pencil between the thumb and index finger of his right hand. "I've wondered the same thing since you were adamant about not having enemies in Temple City. When asked about anything unusual in your life recently, you mentioned your father's death. It was your first thought. Given your level of professional expertise, I'd say we should run with that angle."

Joe rotated his shoulders twice, his neck once. He was long on questions, short on sleep. He swiped a hand over his handsome but haggard face. "We're a big jump away from Liberty. Your dad died a year ago." He frowned, then said slowly, "A year ago exactly, right?"

Morgan stilled. "Yeah."

"To use one of your favorite words, shit." Some crimes were motivated by season or anniversary. Joe suspected Henry's death was the catalyst for the Temple City kills.

Morgan's laugh was a heinous concoction of raked-up hell and scraped-over horror. "You can say that again."

Leroy rifled through the paper and photo contents of the manila folder. "We don't have time for a deep study of this thing. Like I said, the media has its teeth in this mess. Temple City is gonna peak and explode if we don't get this guy soon."

Morgan took the set of colored photos Leroy extracted from the file folder. At first, she stared at the yellow Crime Scene—Do Not Cross tape that separated Victim Two from the bystanders who studied the dead woman with jaded eyes.

Even in death, victims One and Two were beautiful women. Neither woman was married. Both women danced for pleasure, as a hobby. Until recently, Morgan had danced for pleasure, too. Now she danced to earn a profit, as an instructor.

Could that transition be enough to spark a set of terrible murders? No. The people she most passionately connected to were in the safe house with her. Beyond the two men in the safe house, she was passionately connected to her family. "Maybe I should call my sisters."

Joe nodded. "One of them might remember something significant about the funeral proceedings. Maybe some after-funeral gossip circulated around town and they've heard about it."

Morgan spoke half to herself. "I'll ask them. Right now, I'm wondering how this guy slips in and out of private homes without notice. He kills without notice. He must be incredibly ordinary to look at."

"Initially we thought it might be a vagrant," Leroy said. "They tend to operate on the edge of society, visible to the public eye, but not closely monitored."

"You've got a point," Morgan said. "The crime scenes are public places. They're too specific to be random and too in-your-face to be considered frenzied or rushed. This guy takes his time, even when he doesn't have much time to spare. It's as if he starts off with a plan. Once he executes, he vanishes."

Joe studied the photos. "There is no mutilation, no sexual assault, but something is driving this guy to keep killing. What we're seeing isn't so much brutal as it is calculating. The coldness of it worries me."

Leroy said, "That's what bugs me the most. The coldness of the attacks warrants attention. This guy acts as if he's emotionally detached from the victims."

"Whatever," Morgan said. "Bottom line is this. Every perp leaves a clue, some kind of thread that connects him to the crime scene and to the victim. For one, we know this guy is unhappy. We know he's got a mental screw loose. We also know that to kill once for some people is more than enough. To kill twice in the same way confirms we've got a controlled perp. He won't be easy to catch."

Leroy pulled out the photographs of the 3" by 5" index cards. "You're referring to the missing fingerprints."

Morgan said, "Yeah, his calling cards."

"His best signature," Joe clarified.

"Joe's right," Leroy said. "According to Unit procedure, we always look for the unusual aspects of a case, then analyze them."

"The fact they're both dancers is unusual," Morgan said.

"True," Leroy agreed, "but that could be coincidental. What makes the killing of the dancers unusual is the ballet slippers with the holes in the big toes. Under no circumstances would that be considered normal or coincidental, especially coupled with the notes."

"He's right," Joe said. "The name Morgan is common. A Morgan who dances professionally and who has a hole in her dance slippers is significant. The slippers differentiate the uncommon Morgan from a field of other Morgans."

She spoke up. "Okay. We've got some specifics to work with. We also have something unusual, the anniversary of my father's death, which coincides with the onset of my new business as a dance instructor." She snapped her fingers. "Instructor. Those women were students of dance."

Leroy wrinkled his brow. "The distinction could be important, especially if a third woman is killed and she happens to be a student. It might be a comment on your mental capabilities."

Morgan said. "I'm worried about the kids I teach."

"He's targeting women," Joe said. "He'd have to know every one of those kids would be supervised and scrutinized after the killings went public, as they are now. Besides, he could have popped off the kids easily at home, on their way to or from school, at play."

"Don't forget the slippers," Leroy said. "The slippers aren't made for a young girl. They are made for a woman, either young or old, but not a child. The girls you teach look like children. I've seen them."

Morgan visibly relaxed. "You're right. Focusing on the girls would sidetrack us. So," she drew in a deep breath, released it, "the shoes are critical."

"Critical enough to break into Joe's house for a key, knock out a patrol cop, and rob a former member of the Temple City Police—you. See the connection?"

"Cops," Joe said.

"Right," agreed Leroy. "Your dad was a cop."

"And this is the first anniversary of his death," Morgan repeated.

"Yeah," said Joe. "We're all in agreement this guy is smart. Maybe it's someone who was either a law student or a prisoner who studied law behind bars."

Morgan said, "What are you talking about?"

"Maybe the killer seems so smooth because he studied the basics of crime-scene forensics from a textbook. Prison libraries have ample study material. Police academies have study material," Joe explained. "Get my drift?"

"He's right," said Leroy. "We could be dealing with a detective wannabe or a savvy ex-prisoner. We could also be dealing with someone who studied you personally, Morgan, and wants to get even with you for some infraction you never realized occurred."

She said, "Humph, it's the note isn't it?"

"Yeah," Joe said. "The note was precisely written on paper that is uniform and totally clean of fingerprints. This guy isn't just going for the kill, he also wants to rattle you."

Frustrated, mystified by her connection to the dancers' murders, Morgan slammed her fist against a wall. She was forced out of retirement, back into police action. This time she was at the forefront of the investigating team, not behind the scenes as a sketch artist.

From now on, what she said and did, the way she conducted her private and professional lives, could mean the difference between living or dying for some other woman.

Morgan didn't want a third homicide victim on her conscience. When she spoke, her voice was a sinister hiss, "I can't wait to nail this guy."

Joe fingered the gun in his holster, "Me either."

Chapter 5

Morgan tossed aside the *Better Homes and Gardens* magazine she'd been thumbing with rapid, no-time-to-really-look-at-anything-in-detail speed. In her present state of mind, she couldn't tell the difference between English décor or French country. Her stamina and psyche were stripped to vital elements. "I'm hungry."

Joe switched off the thirteen-inch, convenience-only television set. He'd been watching reruns of the *I Love Lucy* show, the episode where Lucy and Ethel were shoving chocolates into their mouths as the treats came off a factory conveyor belt. He suspected the image of food reminded Morgan she hadn't eaten since the day before. Neither had he.

He stretched an arm toward the telephone, a cream-colored cordless the same make and model as the telephone Morgan had at home. The telephone served as an unwelcome reminder her life was a vortex of paranoia—so much so, she might never stop glancing over her shoulder again.

She'd never been this edgy, this spiritually withdrawn, her sensibilities arranged into a system of confusion; her days and nights orchestrated by a madman who remained face-less, nameless, and driven to kill.

Joe couldn't stand it: the sitting, the waiting, the disinte-grating nerves, the heartburn. The mind-freezing fear. He forced a light note into his voice. "I'll have one of the guys swing something by. What do you want? Chinese? French? Greasy American burger and matching fries?"

She tossed the magazine down on the gray-and-gold striped loveseat, shoved her glasses up her nose, and snatched her purse off the scuffed hardwood floor. She wanted high-octane fuel. Serious calories. "Ice cream on a sugar cone. Banana nut. You drive."

His smile was crooked, his voice as rough along the edges as the dark eyes that studied her every move. If his nerves were frayed, hers were fried. It was the no-see way she'd misused the magazine that inspired him to break the police-enforced monotony they shared.

He was too much a veteran cop not to know it was dan-gerous to change venues, but then, they weren't unsuspect-ing women walking alone in the dark, either. He carried a gun, one he wasn't afraid to use.

They'd been in the safe house eighteen hours straight, and should've stayed in the safe house until Leroy and his Special Crimes Unit had a workable bead on the double homi-cide. They should, but they wouldn't. Couldn't. The walls had closed in on them.

Soon, some other dancer might lose her life to the killer Temple City police had yet to capture. Soon—and all they did was flip through magazines and watch reruns in black and white. Waiting was a slow death in itself. Too slow.

Her brow wrinkled in deep lines of concentration, Morgan said, "I know you'll think this is weird, but . . ."

He waited three seconds. "Spit it out."

"I feel like a sitting duck."

He shoved her toward the front door. "Come on. Let's get

some Baskin-Robbins." It was her favorite brand of ice cream.

It was Tuesday, the 6 P.M. traffic crush was nearly over, even though several thousand cars remained on the road anyway. Morgan felt free, even if the illusion of freedom was false and felt only briefly. She had never been one to stay inside the house for long.

She'd been on the verge of picking and sniping at Joe, all because he was an easy target. She couldn't afford to get on his bad side. His presence could mean the difference between her living or dying.

He drove swiftly, his grip on the steering wheel confident. He could taste the Chinese food they planned to pick up for dinner that night, after they stopped for ice cream—lemon chicken, honeydew melon soup, and egg rolls. His favorites.

In ten minutes they would reach their destination, a popular strip mall known for its multicultural foods, its candy and coffee shops. He could hardly wait. Neither, he knew, could Morgan. As he drove, she gazed into her right side mirror. Four miles away from the strip mall, she noticed a Volvo station wagon coming up fast. She jabbed Joe in the shoulder. Hard.

In response, he rammed his size twelve, double E leather boot on the gas and ordered, "Take my gun."

"No."

"Morgan." In one word, he conveyed a meaningful mix of anger and disgust: he couldn't steer the sedan and shoot, too.

"Just drive, Joe." She'd never used a gun in her life, and there were too many people on the road for her to start using one now. She was an artist, for God's sake. A dancer. A teacher. A . . . victim.

The sedan continued its forward leap into the congestion of cars and suddenly skittish drivers. The Volvo was left in the dust.

Once it was clear the other car wasn't after them, Morgan

laughed, the sound flustered and jittery in the sudden still-ness of Joe's sedan. "I guess we're pretty wired. That car had a lady in it with kids. You must have alarmed the mother when you hit the gas so hard."

He'd alarmed a lot of people. Many of them were cussing and pointing dirty fingers in their direction. Two were on cell phones, perhaps calling police with the license and make of Joe's company car.

"Good," he said, ticked off a little over what had turned out to be a minor drama. His adrenaline was still running hard, his breathing heavy. "She ought to pay more attention to her driving."

Morgan tried to defuse his adrenaline high. He was like a bull confined to a pen too small for him to move his body. He wanted to buck the walls down. "Spoken by a man with no kids."

His laugh was reluctant, brittle, and brief. His eyes con-tinued to roam, the hairs on his neck refusing to lie down, and yet he humored her, his best friend. "Amen to that."

A loud popping sound, followed by a punch in the dri-ver's-side door, shocked them both. A champagne brown Isuzu Trooper slammed into them. Nearby cars scattered, their drivers anxious to get beyond the road-rage range.

His reflexes razor-edged, Joe maneuvered between cars, sometimes riding on the shoulder, mostly staying out of the way of the fender-benders he and the assailant were creating during this cat-and-mouse chase over the expressway. The sport utility kept right behind him, gaining.

This time, Morgan used his police radio to call for backup. She and Joe had made the same mistake as Skruggs: they'd been cocky, overconfident in their joint abilities, cer-tain good would triumph over evil.

Joe wound up in the commuter lane, scraped the center di-vider, over-corrected and nearly lost control of the sedan. The driver of the sport utility fired off another bullet. The sedan's rear window burst from the impact of the shot. The

Ford twirled on the road, its front fender facing oncoming traffic.

Chaos ruled.

The Volvo had flipped onto its roof, one hubcap spinning across the black top, over the shoulder of the expressway, and out of sight.

The stench of burned tire rubber overpowered the air.

The silence was deep. As yet, there were no sirens. There was no movement from the overturned car. The Isuzu had disappeared with the ease of the spinning hubcap—over the expressway and gone.

Together, Joe and Morgan raced to the Volvo, a late-model station wagon the color of red, blood red. The woman at the wheel hung suspended in the air, unconscious. Her children, two girls, were crying but otherwise were all right. In this instance, safety belts were in place, air bags deployed, lives saved.

The children, ages seven and eight, were students in Morgan's Tuesday-Thursday beginning dance class. She knew it was impossible to reopen Morgan's Miracles now: no sane parent would entrust a child with her—a woman marked for murder—any time soon.

Her grief was nearly inconsolable, and it was all she could do to resist the crazy urge to scream. This whole thing just wasn't fair, it wasn't; but like her mother always said, life was never fair.

After rescue workers cared for the accident victims, which included several minor, car chase-related incidents, Leroy took statements from Joe and Morgan. Afterwards, he refrained from reaming them on leaving the safe house without some kind of escort. They'd been fools and they knew it. No sense rubbing in the obvious.

"This is one big mess," he said. "The expressway will be closed for hours, north- and southbound lanes." He scraped a hand over the top of his bald head, where a vein pulsed thick in heavy agitation. "Morgan. I want you out of Temple

City. Pronto. There's a red-eye leaving tonight for Georgia. I got you booked. Also, I've got a friend on the Savannah force who'll make sure you get to Liberty in one piece."

Morgan knew she was lucky, damned lucky. "I'll be on that flight. Too many people are getting hurt." Not even her students were safe.

Joe spoke to her without taking his eyes off the ruined Ford. "I guess you were right—about us being sitting ducks. That guy must have followed us from the safe house. I didn't see him coming. I didn't get his description or the number on his license plate. I got nothing. Nothing."

Leroy glared at him.

Joe was glad the older man kept his mouth shut. Almost to himself he added, "Now, I know how vics feel when we ask for stuff like that, only they don't remember anything. Besides feeling stupid, they feel helpless, too."

Morgan grimaced. "Vics don't remember anything because they're scared shitless. We were scared shitless." Her eyes drifted off to the point where the sport utility had made its exit. "Makes me wonder why I'm still alive."

Joe finally looked at her and she wished he hadn't: His face was cold and hard and cruel; a lawful man stripped to kill-or-be-killed mode. "Me, too."

She was the first to break their glance. She was afraid—of the enemy, of Leroy's suppressed rage, of Joe's lawlessness. These were her friends, her dear, loyal friends, and they were disintegrating into criminals right in front of her eyes.

At that moment, Morgan didn't trust either man to turn in her adversary without killing or wounding him first. As if the men were her father and brother, she shuddered over their varying degrees of scarcely suppressed violence.

This whole business had become way too personal, way too treacherous for her to trust anything other than her own instincts, and they were screaming bloody murder. "The answers we need must be in Liberty," she said.

Leroy took two rapid strides in the direction of the first

officer on the scene, stopped, pivoted, and said, "Morgan Girl, you've got one hell of an enemy out there. When you get back to Liberty, remember this: Everybody in that town is a suspect. Everybody."

His parting shot brought Joe one territorial step closer to his ex-partner's side. He wanted to hold her tight, protect her, but theirs wasn't that kind of friendship and never would be. He didn't doubt that she'd slap his face if he tried to hug her anyway. With his fists jammed tight into his pants pockets, Joe was a human explosive, the killer in possession of his detonator switch.

Morgan shifted her attention from time-bomb-ticking Joe to Leroy, the magnificent man who reminded her so much of her dead father, and knew this killer had to be found before vigilanteism reared its nasty head. These men were her self-appointed heroes, and very, very soon, they would stop at nothing to keep her safe.

Her power diminished because it lacked direction, Morgan stalked off, her equanimity vanquished, her sense of self disconnected from everyone she loved, everything she knew. A uniformed officer awaited her with a pair of ready-to-rumble motorcycle cops as escorts. She had to pack her bags and head to the airport. Now.

She said, to no one in particular, "I don't believe this shit."

Chapter 6

Packing for the red-eye flight to Georgia, Morgan called Taylor. She told her sister everything, beginning with Tandra Emory's murder, ending with the wrecked Volvo.

"I agree with Leroy," Taylor said, after a moment's thought. "You should get out of Temple City. It's way too dangerous for you there."

Morgan stuffed underwear in a small suitcase. She only planned to take essentials and a briefcase-styled handbag. She didn't plan on being in Liberty long. She planned on getting her life back together. "I hate being manipulated."

Taylor snorted. "As if anybody doesn't mind. Still, I think it's best you go home. Kick some skeletons loose from the closet."

Morgan closed her eyes, an image of her sister coming to the forefront of her mind. Over six feet tall, Taylor easily intimidated men and women. A lawyer and mother of one, she was probably the most like Henry Chambers of all the sisters.

Like Henry, Taylor enjoyed solving puzzles. Like Morgan, she enjoyed classic cars. Taylor liked to collect them, Morgan to drive them—fast.

At the moment, Morgan wanted to trade her packing duties for one quick spin in her convertible, top down. Only, she couldn't. Somewhere outside her windows was a killer, a man who knew intimate details about not only her private life, but the lives of her closest friends. This killer didn't just present puzzles, he created them.

To create meant to bring into existence. As creator, the killer designed a universe composed of motive, method, and opportunity: beginning, middle, and end. It was a murderous cycle set on repeat and rewind. Somehow, Morgan needed to find a path out of the circle, devise an escape from under the cat's paw.

If she could only survive long enough to understand the reason for the game. "Hey, Taylor," she said.

"Yeah?"

"What's the common factor in the four cases Dad left behind?"

Taylor's response was prompt. "They were cold. Puzzles really."

"And what do puzzles cause?"

"Bewilderment. Confusion. Frustration. Challenge."

"Right," Morgan said. "The puzzle pieces must be snapped together to form a picture, the picture that only the killer, the creator knows."

"You're constructing a profile." Not a question, a statement.

"Precisely."

Taylor laughed. "Lead the way, big sister."

"A puzzle creator is clever, but the puzzle solver is also clever."

"Equals."

"Only in the sense that they both are interested in puzzles," Morgan said.

"Your point?"

Morgan's gaze flicked around the room, as if gathering strength from its familiarity. "The puzzle creator is always one-up on the puzzle solver because he knows the answer to the riddle. He's also one-up because he must keep the puzzle solver mystified from the first playing piece of the game to the last."

"As in interested."

"Right."

"I disagree," Taylor said. "Your mutual interest is in the puzzle itself, not its resolution. Once the puzzle is resolved, both parties lose interest in the game. The puzzle creator, the killer, is using the game to challenge you in a duel of minds, kind of like pitting yourself against a computer in an electronic card game."

"Say what?"

Taylor spoke with care. "Playing against the computer is fine as long as the wins and losses are superficial. Example, the game is superficial if there is no money involved. Involve money, the game becomes important, perhaps critical, depending on the size of the winning pot and the rules of the game."

"In this game," Morgan said, "The stakes are life and death. Not just mine, either. Having lives other than my own in the mix forces me to play the game, to solve the puzzle designed by the killer just for me."

Taylor exhaled slowly. "So," she said, "we're back to the beginning."

Morgan snapped her suitcase shut. "Liberty."

"It's where I first learned of the case Dad left me, a case involving a missing socialite, one Susan Hilliard Frasier. But, hey, enough about me. Bottom line is that I love you. I wish I could be with you right now, but it would only complicate the puzzle. I think your hunch to go home is the right thing to do."

Morgan stuffed a fresh sketch pad into her purse, along with extra fine point pens. "Probably. I can't do much of anything around Temple City anyway. Leroy won't let me clean my nose without explaining my actions first."

Taylor sounded surprised. "Leroy won't let you investigate?"

"No."

"Wise."

"It's another reason why I called you," Morgan said. "I had to talk turkey and I couldn't do it with Leroy or Joe."

"What's on your mind?" Taylor asked.

"I'm thinking the killer made the crimes personal by placing my name at the scene of the first crime and my shoes at the scene of the second crime. Since the puzzle being worked is composed of real people and real things, I understand how very important what I do means."

"Everything you say and do is critical."

"This is scary, Taylor."

"I'm with you, Big Sis. Let's get back to your killer profile. You've decided he's clever."

"Controlling," Morgan said.

"Observant," Taylor added.

"Determined," Morgan said.

"Precise."

"Precise is the overriding factor," Morgan pointed out. "He knew where I kept the old shoes and where Joe kept the spare key. He knew the exact moment to make his kills."

Taylor added color to their mental sketch. "He also knew the shoe on the second victim would ensure your involvement with the case, despite Leroy's insistence you stay low. If the killer knew you and Joe, he must also know Leroy. It's almost like you're being pushed to Liberty. Not even the safe house was safe."

Morgan's voice dropped in pitch. "Who would have so much interest in me?"

"Someone who's known you a long time. As kids, we grew up in the same house our entire lives. In my experience, the oldest grudges are the deepest grudges."

"Which brings us back to Liberty," Morgan said. "Again."

"And to Dad."

"Yeah."

After a pause, Taylor said, "Question?"

"Shoot."

"All us sisters were in agreement that Dad's business could be sold, but not the family home, why?"

Morgan answered instantly. "Because of Mama."

"And you say this even though she's been dead half our lives."

"Of course."

"If you look at this thing sideways, Morgan, it's possible this murder business is about you and your relationship with Dad or Mom, or about their relationship together."

"Taylor, I called you for moral support and a reality check. This isn't an X-File we're dealing with here."

"I don't know, Morgan. What if there's some unfinished business that didn't die with Mom and Dad?"

"Your lawyer's mind is picking at every possibility, even if it does sound ridiculous. Even though that's why I called, I'm so rattled right now, I'm not thinking straight. My circuits are overloaded, Taylor."

"Listen. You're the only sister left to solve a case of Dad's. Maybe you have to solve the one he left you whether you want to solve it or not."

Morgan slung her purse over her shoulder. She was as ready as she'd ever be to hit the road. "I'm starting to think so."

"Maybe Dad wanted us to get some kind of peace after his death. Let's face it, after Mom died, he wasn't the premier dad he once was. Maybe he's trying to tell us all something from the grave."

"You're giving me the creeps."

"People are dying, Morgan."

"Yeah, and I'm probably next."

Chapter 7

The Chambers family home was exactly as Morgan remembered it, a well-built structure with white siding, only now, the home had a recently updated roof and a fresh coat of paint on the trim that bordered the eaves.

While it was true that the Chambers sisters chose not to live in the patriarchal house, the women made certain the building and its property were kept in excellent condition by hired help they trusted.

This home represented their father's secondary legacy, a physical connection to a shared past, the beginning of all their dreams, the source of their ambitions, the one place where their mother had ruled and her imprint remained.

The windows in front of the family home were dressed in beige-colored blinds that were open, the edges of rose-patterned lace visible at the borders of the windows. It was a wonderful old southern home, one built with quality material, enhanced with laid-back charm. The home could have easily dressed the cover of *Southern Living* magazine.

The moisture-rich lawn was immaculate. The sidewalk, cracked from time and lined with weeds, was the only flaw in the home's immediate landscape. The air, heavy with the

scent of sprawling green-and-white honeysuckle vines, reminded Morgan of early childhood, of her mother.

The well-kept house seemed to beckon Morgan, to welcome her. The sight of it boosted her spirits, as did the
memory of Hazel Chambers, the home's amateur landscape architect and dedicated homemaker. In this place, a
family once lived—her family, and yes, it felt good to be
here.

Morgan left her rented economy car on the tranquil resi-
dential street, made her way over the red brick walk, with its
familiar herringbone pattern, to the wide front steps of the
house that held so many memories, not all of them good, not
all of them bad.

Today, haunted by the Temple City murders and an old
Liberty crime case, Morgan was forced to reconsider Henry
Chambers, the man, versus Henry Chambers, the father. In
Liberty, the past collided with the present: His past. Her pre-
sent.

In Liberty, she feared that tarnished secrets simmered beneath smiling, familiar faces. From Trinity Haskell, checker
at the local supermarket, where she'd purchased supplies for
the next few days, to Bill Griffin, owner of the neighborhood
gas station, and Mrs. Joanna Lowell, the retired school-
teacher who lived across the street from the Chamberses'
house.

Thanks to Leroy's warning to trust no one, Morgan felt as
if every person in town knew something, had heard something, suspected . . . something.

Taking her limited luggage inside, she unpacked in one of
the guest bedrooms, removed the jacket of her cream-toned
pantsuit, and kicked off her traveling shoes. In the cool comfort of the modest-sized kitchen, she stuffed the basic food
and dairy items she'd purchased into the almond painted refrigerator. She had the same colored fridge in her own home,
that place where she no longer felt safe, the reason why she'd
returned to Liberty.

Worn out, Morgan decided it was past time to catch her breath, to relax, to rethink the good things in her life. Her first step was to indulge in the simplest of pleasures—her immediate surroundings: light, air, and water. She removed a tall clear glass from one of the cupboards, then filled it with cool and filtered water from the kitchen sink.

Once she regrouped, she'd find her mother's favorite glass pitcher, the one etched in roses, and fill it with the kind of sweet southern iced tea that was as symbolic to Morgan of Georgia as the honeysuckle vine winding its way throughout her mother's gardens.

She carried the water to the back porch, the space screened and glassed against insects. The porch room, decorated in floral patterns and willow-work furniture, was the heart of the house, not the kitchen.

Sitting in her mother's rocking chair, Morgan reviewed her plan of action: involve authority figures with her plight, beginning with Purvis Wayan, her father's old friend and confidante. Leroy had already briefed the local police.

She'd worked too hard to let an unknown adversary destroy her future. The parts of the killer's puzzle were on the table in her mind, all the outer edges in place. It was time to work the middle, time to end this ugly thing, and get on with the rest of her life.

Rocking gently, water glass in hand, Morgan breathed the scent of blue, yellow, and pink cabbage roses planted twenty years ago by her mother. On this porch, in Hazel's chair, she embraced the Chamberses' legacy, the Chamberses' strength—and knew she'd been right to come home again.

Let Leroy and Joe turn over every stone in California. In a town as small as Liberty, the word *California* would ignite bits of fire in the minds of long-time locals, which in turn would keep their tongues from wagging.

People from California were foreigners. People like that didn't know how to take things slow, how to stretch a glass of sweet iced tea from one hour to the next. Those melting-pot people didn't know how to sit still in a porch room as the tail end of dusk mellowed into a long, honeysuckle- and rose-scented evening.

It had been years since Morgan had indulged in such old-time southern graces, but she still remembered how to go with the flow, how to watch fireflies light the night. Nobody would talk to Joe or Leroy or anyone else from California investigating the two unsolved homicides. But, people would talk to Morgan, a hometown girl, out of curiosity if nothing else.

People would talk, and she would listen. She would sketch. She would plot, then scheme. If there was a slim connection between Liberty and Temple City, she'd find that incriminating nexus.

Murder.

Family.

Dad.

Was she dealing with the rage of betrayed love, of betrayed trust? Hadn't she felt betrayed when her father preferred work over raising his daughters? Hadn't she felt rage when she assumed her mother's role, that of rearing and guiding her younger sisters? Unfortunately, the answer to every question was a painful, heartbroken, yes.

But Morgan, too, had betrayed. She'd betrayed her father by not honoring his final wish, his last command, and maybe, just maybe, that's why she'd rejected him. He'd commanded. Not in person, but via his lawyer, after his death.

In the end, it had taken two murders to bring her back to Liberty. Who was really calling the shots, she wondered: the killer, or Henry Chambers? What was the connection to Liberty and to Temple City? How much time did she have to solve the killer's riddles before another woman died?

Two strangers: murdered.

Two cities: both diverse.

Two puzzling cases: one old, one new.
Connections.
Family.
Betrayal.

Morgan leaned her head against the top rung of the rocking chair, its hundred-year-old frame built with cypress, its surface protected each year with a water-resistant clear stain. An heirloom in Hazel's family long before her birth, the rocker had been gifted from mother to daughter, one generation after another, to be used, not tucked away for safekeeping.

The wooden chair was one more reason why the Chamberses' home had never been sold: Which daughter had the right to receive it? The oldest child, because of seniority? Or the youngest daughter, because her memories were the least strong inside the closed circle of four sibling girls?

Memories came from living, living from experience. Morgan thought of her beautiful, memory-sacred mother, sitting in this same rocking chair, and felt solace for the first time since attending the site of Tandra Emory's murder at Tyler Lake in Temple City.

In Liberty, Morgan was free from Leroy and Joe's claustrophobic protection, unconfined by the rules of fair play that bound and led the Temple City Special Crimes personnel. She was no longer hiding out in a safe house that had never been safe.

She was in Liberty, and Liberty was home in the primeval sense. In her mother's home, she didn't have to wear a civilized face to cover her crude feelings. Here, she was completely herself, more so than ever before, and she knew why.

She knew it was because this home, this shrine to Hazel Chambers, was a resting place, a thinking place. It was white honeysuckle, old cabbage roses, and a porch room adorned with handmade furniture, its quality durable enough to withstand a century of time. In this treasured place, her courage was resurrected, her pride restored.

Morgan navigated her nimble mind through the double homicides. With her artist's attention to details, she mentally reviewed the photographs taken, closeups of the victims. She reviewed the cataloguing of the crime scenes before and after removal of the bodies, after measurements were taken, evidence collected, notes written and recorded.

She'd watched and she'd listened. She'd reviewed the accumulated data regarding both murders. But what clue had she noticed that was so small a clue she hadn't considered it important?

What connected Liberty with Temple City, other than herself? Could the clue be the fact she'd shunned her heritage, which was, when she really thought about it, her father's passion for crime detection, an infatuation that resulted in his own detective agency and her ultimate rejection of it?

To stop the endless chain of potentially unanswerable questions, Morgan concentrated on her father's three rule credo:

Number one: stay focused.

Number two: details make the difference.

Number three: justice always prevails.

The integrity of the evidence taken at the crime scenes and the resulting lab reports were kept legal and safe; Leroy had made sure of that, from the initial transport of the collected samples, to the processing, to the reporting.

She couldn't find fault with the facts, only with their interpretation. In this regard, she'd rely on instinct to guide her. Relying on instinct, on subconscious profiling of established clues, she'd find the focal piece of the killer's puzzle.

Since coming to Liberty, Morgan had only one misgiving, that she'd discover something about her parents, or her past, she'd regret finding out. Still, she had to dig, had to stop another killing, had to open her father's old file, the tattered blue one entitled: *The Case of the Missing Child.*

Where, Morgan wondered, could that little girl be?

Chapter 8

The ringing doorbell broke Morgan's reverie. Intrigued, she answered the summons. At the front entrance stood Carlotta Biggs, a former Miss Black Cotillion, former Miss Black Liberty, and perennial Miss-Know-It-All. She was also one of Liberty, Georgia's resident troublemakers. Morgan hadn't seen the woman in years.

Suddenly edgy, the retired sketch artist skimmed her eyes over the unexpected visitor through the glass storm door that separated them from each other. Reluctantly, she reached for the latch on the door. Obstinately, she didn't release the lock on the latch, didn't open the glass door. A natural caution stayed her right hand.

Glass: a hard, brittle, and transparent substance, easily broken. *Door:* a moving barrier for opening and closing an entrance. What should she do? Morgan wondered. Should she open the glass door? Or should she close its solid wood counterpart, thus denying Carlotta Biggs the free access she desired?

Morgan touched her fingers to the lock, and Carlotta waited. In this single defining moment, this surreal instance between friend and foe, Morgan remembered her dad's mantra: *justice always prevails*. Her personal credo—number three.

She opened the door.

As usual, when it came to Carlotta's grand entrances to any room, there were no social preliminaries, such as a welcome-home-it's-so-good-to-see-you-again smile. As the woman stalked smugly over the wooden threshold onto the braided floor rug, Morgan could tell nothing had changed about her visitor in the many years that had separated them until now—not the woman's bad attitude, not the woman's sharp-witted eyes, nothing. Also, as usual, Carlotta Biggs was dressed in black.

She wore a black hat over black hair, black eyes in a black face, blackberry colored lipstick on distinctively shaped lips, lips that were as naturally dark and lush as her individuality, a persona perfectly framed in a Barbie doll body.

She was draped in a lightweight black dress that left her shoulders, arms, and lower thighs bare. On her feet were ridiculously slim sandals, heels three inches tall. Her fingernails, toenails, and handbag matched the paint on her sneering, sensuous lips.

Carlotta Biggs was stunning, and she knew it. "So?" she said as she shouldered her way into the house, "you had the nerve to come back."

Morgan continued to study the tall woman with the precision of the professionally trained artist. No detail went unnoticed, not one flicker of eyelash, not one shade of the ebony Barbie's overt cynicism. For all Carlotta's nearly overwhelming chic, Morgan remembered her as a vindictive, stop-at-nothing-to-get-what-she-wants pain in the ass.

But, Morgan mused, could this aging glamour girl have slipped from simple narcissism into the treacherous terrain of a psychopath, a signature killer? Morgan didn't want to believe it, but something was seriously out of order; she could feel it, only what? And why? She opted for an in-your-face approach. "What I do is none of your business, Carlotta. Never was. Never will be."

"Always so damned quick with the answers." Carlotta flung a glance beyond the foyer. The house, cool and quiet, meticulously maintained by hired help, smelled of lemon oil. The setting was elegant and stylish, the perfect background for the oh-so-casually-calm Morgan Chambers.

Carlotta couldn't quite restrain the sense of inferiority that came close to disarming her, and, for an instant, her nerves of steel rattled one against the other. This wouldn't do, not now, not ever. She shifted tactics. "I remember you like coffee," she said somewhat graciously; "so do I."

Morgan almost smiled at the calculated request for hospitality, almost. Carlotta wasn't an innocent child whose rude behavior might be excused as ignorance; rather, she was a grown woman skilled in setting Morgan's teeth on edge. Carlotta Biggs had always been trouble, and Morgan wasn't in the mood to play nice.

She said, "It's seven-thirty in the morning, Carlotta. Even though I'm already dressed, you weren't invited and I don't want you here. Not now, anyway. Leave your number, and I'll get back to you."

Carlotta's upper lip curled into a tattletale sign of anger. "Even as a kid you were a sanctimonious little bitch."

"I guess it takes one to know one." Morgan put her hand in the middle of Carlotta's chest. She shoved the well-dressed woman across the welcome mat and then slammed the wood door in her face. She didn't have time for this shit.

Both women knew Carlotta wouldn't make a formal scene, not in this well-established, bound-to-be-somebody-home neighborhood. Southern belles of Carlotta's caliber didn't make public displays worthy of over-the-fence gossip—they just got even.

Thoughtful, Morgan went to her father's study, a room dominated by burgundy leather. Seated in the chair at her father's desk, she placed a fresh sheet of paper on the old and familiar desk blotter. At the head of the paper, she wrote: *SUSPECT:* Carlotta Biggs

Morgan dialed her sister, Taylor, who answered her phone immediately. "Hey," Taylor said, "you all right?"

"How'd you know it was me?"

"Caller I.D."

Morgan cut straight to the point. "Carlotta was here."

"And before noon, too. I'd forgotten about her."

"To tell you the truth, Taylor, Carlotta and I have been enemies for so long she's like an old shoe, the kind that gets shoved to the back of the closet and forgotten."

"I'm thinking old shoe with a hole in the toe."

For Morgan, this was an ugly thought. "The Temple City killer couldn't be Carlotta Biggs."

"Never say never," Taylor warned. "I think you should tap into Dad's resources and get a rundown on her. His lawyer will help."

Morgan suppressed a tremble of fear. It was one thing to look for an anonymous enemy in Temple City—quite a different, far more personal and unsettling matter to look for an enemy among the people she'd known in Liberty, her hometown, her birthplace.

Carlotta had always been tantalizingly beautiful, had always been fundamentally mean, and, until now, Morgan hadn't given much thought to why. She'd simply ignored the problem in her typical *whatever* fashion.

In Liberty, her value systems had been introduced by her mother and nurtured by her father, systems that supported the maxim: thou shalt not kill. She'd always thought Carlotta was crazy, but only in a figurative way.

Could the Barbie doll cutie be seeking some cruel sort of revenge, some childhood-related fantasy to seek and destroy? To show up unannounced on someone's doorstep, fully antagonistic, was unreal. And how, Morgan wondered, had Carlotta known she was in town in the first place?

It could have been the Liberty grapevine, but what if Carlotta's arrival was much more sinister than a simple case of being too nosey for her own good? "God, I'm tired, Taylor."

"As you should be. But I don't see how you're gonna get much rest with people like Carlotta showing up out of the blue, especially after catching a red-eye when you weren't planning on taking a trip."

Morgan rubbed the bridge of her nose. "Tell me about it. Anyway, at nine this morning I've got a meeting with Purvis Wayan. He's anxious to talk to me."

"Good."

"Taylor, I'm in over my head." For a proud woman, this was a difficult confession for Morgan to make. If the killer was watching, she wanted to appear fearless. In her mind, being fearless meant being strong, despite adversity.

Her father had been fearless, brave when confronted with doubt, courageous when confronted with danger. She recalled the example he presented in life and stiffened her spine. He'd simply stood for the truth.

The search for truth was the reason she had returned to Liberty "I'm scared," she said, "but hungry for the truth."

"Being scared right now is a good thing," Taylor said.

"You sound like Joe. He'd say something like that to me." Morgan missed him already. A sound thinker, he made an excellent companion and confidante. She took him for granted, something she hadn't realized until he wasn't there.

Having Taylor involved in the murder crisis, even though her input was strictly minimal and conducted by telephone, her presence and concern spanned the gap between Temple City and Liberty.

Like Joe, Taylor was someone Morgan trusted with her life. It was important to know everyone in her past wasn't an enemy. Considering Carlotta Biggs a suspect was alarming enough.

"I always liked Joe," Taylor admitted.

"You only met him and Leroy once, when you came to California on a business trip, but you act like you've known them forever."

"It's true we haven't been particularly close over the years, Big Sis, but when we talk, we talk. I feel like I know these guys as well as I know my officemates at work."

"I'm actually lucky," Morgan said.

"Why?"

"I don't have to worry about whether or not the California cases are being handled properly because I know they are, thanks to Leroy and Joe and the rest of my cop friends in Temple City. Being in Liberty helps me feel useful. Let's face it, without a P.I. license and some sort of co-operation with the police, I wasn't going to get too much digging done in California. Leroy wanted me out of the picture, and I guess I am."

"Listen up, Morgan," Taylor said. "You might want to arrange for some type of bodyguard."

"I won't be a victim."

"This is a commonsense issue."

"This is a small town," Morgan argued. "If Carlotta can show up at seven-thirty, then the rest of the busybodies in town are up, too, especially the ones right on this block. Whoever said homeowners make the best police was right. This neighborhood is owned largely by the original players. I don't need someone to guard the house or me personally."

"I hear you. Still, Carlotta Biggs. Huh. I remember she always hated living in the sticks."

Morgan recalled the image of Carlotta in black on black, a color the woman had favored even as a child. "She always called me a spoiled princess, only she was the one going out to Miss Black Beauty this and Miss Black Beauty that. I never did."

"You did want to dance," Taylor said. "Now you create little dancers. Little black princesses in tutus and ballerina slippers. I'd say you succeeded in life in a way she never has or probably will."

Morgan snorted, disgusted with the entire scenario. "It's not my fault she didn't marry well or finish college or win Miss USA or whatever the hell it is she wanted to do after high school."

Taylor's tone was thoughtful. "She thinks it's your fault she didn't get the lead part in *Snow White* when you guys were kids. I'm younger than you, but I remember the local gossip about it."

Morgan came back to earth. She couldn't grab at straws just to satisfy a quick itch to return to Temple City, to Morgan's Miracles, to the life she'd carefully crafted only to have a killer deliberately destroy. The loss of control made her want to scream in frustration. "It's too easy to build a case around Carlotta."

"So who says this has to be difficult?" Taylor said. "Why does it have to be some unknown and crazed individual out there for all the drama to make sense to you? Carlotta is a very viable candidate. At least temperament-wise. She's just not a man, and we think the killer is male. She's in Liberty, and that separates her physically from the crimes that were committed."

Morgan sighed hard enough to blow the hair at her temples. If Carlotta was calling the shots for the Temple City murders, it meant she had an accomplice. "Let's just say it would be easier if there was some crazed individual in Temple City. Much easier to get on with my life after the killer is caught."

"Maybe I'd buy that, Dorothy, if it wasn't for the slippers."

"Yeah," Morgan said. "The bastard took them right out of my closet, which irks me to no end. I mean, I was absolutely clueless that somebody was coming in and out of my house. I hate knowing my home was violated like that. My privacy is shot all to hell and so is my temper. I want this business over with as quickly as possible, but I don't want to grab at the first weird thing in Liberty just to solve this case in a hurry. Nobody wins during a rush job. When the killer of those two women is caught, I want justice to be served, hard."

"Death penalty."

"Yep. As much as I can't stand Carlotta, I find it difficult to believe she's suddenly a murderer. She had years to kill me when we were growing up. Scratch that name."

"So," Taylor said, "you really had put her on your suspect list."

"Of course. All that animosity after so many years isn't right. I never understood it in the first place. Knowing she's still tripping over God knows what is way too weird."

"More like neurotic. Still, she's not a man," Taylor reasoned. "You think the killer is male."

"I do."

"Carlotta could've hired a hit man," Taylor suggested.

Disgruntled, Morgan massaged her closed eyes. She was running off adrenaline and very little sleep. "This whole thing is a nightmare."

"You'd better get digging. Make sure you keep that appointment on time with Dad's attorney. Take care, Big Sis, and keep me posted."

"I will."

"And Morgan?"

"Uh huh?"

"I love you."

In that instant, Morgan felt strong. She was not alone. "I love you, too. It's good to know I've got you on my side."

"What other side could there be?"

"Well, we haven't been close over the last few years. We've been even more distant since Dad's death."

"Blood is blood. I'm here for you and so are Max and Sam. We're sisters. When you hurt, we hurt, too."

"Don't make me cry."

"Chin up, Morgan. I'll update Max and Sam. You keep doing what you're doing."

"I'll call you tonight."

"I'll be here."

Morgan hung up the phone. Some part of her psyche was afraid to discover the truth about the killer's identity. The very search for truth had power, the power of change; she was talking to Taylor who was talking to Max and Sam, thus reinforcing the common bond of blood that linked the sisters together, despite their disagreements over the years and the deaths of their parents.

As the oldest Chambers daughter, at times Morgan bullied and badgered and bossed each sister, had nurtured, honored, and adored them, had run all the way to California to not only find a niche for herself but to get away from the burden of being a surrogate mother.

There had been such resentment over the years between the young women that it was a relief to find comfort in Taylor's love, even though they spoke only over the telephone, and now, in a state of acute crisis.

Their words had been brief, their underlying feelings expressed in the emotional shorthand natural to siblings. There were some things only siblings shared with each other, never with a parent or a lover or a friend, kind of like the language derived by twins or other multiple siblings.

Maybe that's what the cold cases were all about, Morgan mused—getting the sisters together again, forging a new bond together, finding strength in their shared history instead of animosity. It was too late to find out what her father's last days were like, much too late, and for this, Morgan was sorry.

She headed toward the guest bedroom to collect her jacket, shoes, purse, and rental car keys. As she glanced in the foyer mirror on her way out the door, she wondered what Carlotta was doing.

Carlotta swung her vintage-red roadster into her driveway with enough fury to get scratch on the asphalt when she applied the brakes.

She lived in a small A-frame house that needed new paint, new sod, and a new mailbox because the one she had was leaning to the right, a victim of Mr. Armstrong's left rear bumper on his 1985 Chevy Suburban. Carlotta hated her life.

She hated her life because she'd spent most of it trying to be number one in a world full of number ones. She'd discovered that a beauty queen's beauty was easy to come by and easy to lose.

Becoming Miss Georgia hadn't happened, Miss Teen USA hadn't happened, Miss America hadn't happened, and Carlotta doubted that at this point in her life it ever would. At forty, she was a beauty, but she was no longer a beauty queen. She was a hair stylist in a Liberty beauty salon.

She'd tried to get out of Liberty, tried and failed. Morgan didn't just get out of Liberty, she'd managed to land herself a cushy job, loyal friends, a big-city life. Carlotta hated Morgan Chambers even more than she hated Liberty, Georgia.

Morgan was born into the lap of opportunity, something Carlotta felt she took for granted. Carlotta hated what Morgan stood for: truth, justice, and the American way— Henry Chambers's way.

Henry had given Morgan the opportunity to do something unusual, to finish the last unsolved case in his files, and she had refused. Refused. The nerve of her.

Since finding out, all Carlotta had wanted to do was out-smart the ever-wonderful, ever-successful Morgan Chambers. Morgan with the three beautiful sisters. Morgan with the thriving dance business. The great case she hadn't wanted to solve. The great life.

If only, Carlotta mused, she could have been . . . Morgan.

Chapter 9

The lawyer's offices were the same as Morgan remembered. Purvis Wayan still had the creaking leather chair she remembered as a young girl, soft now with time and wear. The lawyer's office smelled warm and familiar, the cherry-flavored tobacco he used as much an integral part of his establishment as the desk, chair, file cabinets, and books that adorned the air-conditioned room in the federal-style building.

Morgan looked at the elderly man and felt a hot wave of nostalgia, a homesickness for her father and for good times past. Purvis and Henry had been so close over the years, they were often mistaken for brothers; or, at the very least, first cousins.

When Henry needed advice, it had been to Purvis he'd gone. After Hazel's death, the men had grown closer, and like Henry, it was to Purvis Morgan had turned to in her own time of need and distress.

"Purvis," she said, "I'm in trouble."

"I know." He puffed on his pipe. "Tell me what's not public knowledge."

Morgan broke things down for him, beginning with the

Temple City murders, ending with Carlotta's grand entrance. "And here I am."

"You say you don't have any true enemies, but I think you were right to put Carlotta on your list of suspects. Her behavior was odd this morning, even though what she did to you was completely in her character. Your father also had enemies, something that went with the job, and you're not going to know them all. When Henry left those sealed envelopes to each of you girls after his death, I wasn't privy to what the envelopes contained. Let's deal with your own envelope. What did it say?"

"Dad had received a tip about a woman murdered some forty years ago. She was a cleaning woman. The murder was never solved. At the time of the murder, the victim was young, unmarried, and had born a child, a girl. Dad didn't know what happened to the baby girl. The note didn't leave a clue about where to look for her, although it did give a bit of history about the murder victim.

"Dad felt that because the woman was young, black, and poor, her case was never given proper attention by the local authorities, who figured it was a black-on-black crime, perhaps by one of the woman's reputed many lovers. Dad had a feeling the case was important, but he never properly pursued it.

"After forty years, the cleaning woman's murder was definitely cold. I read the case file on the victim: Stephanie Blevins. She'd been manually strangled, like the women in Temple City actually. No sexual molestation was noted. There were no defensive wounds recorded by the coroner."

"I'm glad you read your father's file," Purvis said. He nodded his head once in approval. "He always kept a detailed one."

"Dad's feeling was that Stephanie Blevins's death had been written off as a crime of passion. From what I figure from his case file, there wasn't a very involved investigation into her death. The woman's employer was wealthy, white, and prominent, the reason the murder was quietly investigated, quickly labeled, and eventually swept under the rug."

"Until somebody sent Henry the anonymous letter, which asked him to reopen the case," Purvis said. "Henry wanted you to do something about solving that crime, Morgan. Why didn't you? As you know, there's no statute of limitations on murder."

Morgan paced with agitated steps. She didn't want to deal with the murder of Stephanie Blevins. She didn't want to be in Liberty. She wanted to be in Temple City, at peace, the way she'd been before the theft of her ballerina slippers with the hole in the big toe.

A bit testy, she said, "I just wanted to keep moving forward with my life, Purvis. I just didn't see how the resolution of that crime was gonna make a difference in my life or in the life of that baby girl."

"That baby girl is a woman now."

"Yes. Whoever she is, she's gone on with her life. I know I have. What point would it make for me to dig up old wounds?"

"Murder is a capital crime. Stephanie Blevins deserves justice. Obviously, your dad thought this case was important enough for you to bring it to resolution."

"I'm retired from the police force."

"You're a Chambers," Purvis said, his tone accusing. "Is it really in you to let an unsolved murder remain unsolved if you have the power to bring a killer to justice?"

"I want to teach girls to dance, Purvis. If I hadn't been so hung up on pleasing Dad in the first place, maybe I could have been a professional dancer instead of making my living as a sketch artist for the police department. Maybe I could have had a different life."

"Henry didn't stop you."

"He didn't push me to achieve my own goals, either. Even now, after he's buried, after all the funeral food and condolences are gone, he had the nerve to leave me one more case." Morgan didn't try to hide her anger.

With bodies piling up, there was no time to be overly polite and social. Although she couldn't see herself being as rude as Carlotta, Morgan recognized that she was definitely on the defensive.

Purvis blew a long stream of cherry-scented smoke into the cool air of his office. He didn't mind the fireworks display of Morgan's temper. She was rarely riled. He wanted her to be off balance.

If she was off balance, he figured she would be more wary and conscious of everyone she met on the street. Carlotta might have knocked on the front door of the Chamberses' house, but half of the rest of Liberty was just as aware of Morgan's arrival as Carlotta was, as he was aware, as probably the Temple City killer was aware. He said, "Henry did the same for your sisters."

Morgan stopped pacing long enough to glare at Purvis, who met her stare with the finesse of a seasoned lion. She enjoyed a good argument, something she missed doing with her dad. "And they didn't like it any more than I did."

"But they accepted the cases he left for them. Maybe you won't find happiness, young lady, true happiness until you close the circle your dad wanted closed. You know that destiny business has some merit."

She flopped into one of the pair of leather chairs that matched the executive chair behind the massive wood desk that stood between herself and Purvis. "I'm grown. I do what I wanna do."

He laid down his pipe. Gone was the friendly-eyed elderly family lawyer and friend. In its place was the talon-sharp intellect of a man skilled at manipulating the law, masterful at extracting truth from liars, in dealing with belligerent people, in deciphering the truth. He, too, believed in honesty. "Why are you here, Morgan? In Liberty? In my office?" His voice was subdued, raspy, intense.

She wasn't easily intimidated. She pushed her shoulders against the leather seat. She forced the air through her nose, evenly, calmly. She was not a child. She was not about to be bullied by a man old enough to be her father. "I'm here to get a killer off my back." Her voice was equally flat, equally intense.

Purvis faced off with the young woman he admired. She was tough, but he'd been practicing law ten years before she was born. If she got up and stormed out of the office, never to return again, she'd leave with the truth spoken between them. It was the least he could do for Henry.

"You're here because you feel guilty," he said. "You should have solved that case, and now you think those two dead women in Temple City are your fault, your responsibility."

"What if I do feel that way?" she said. There was no bravado now, only cool logic, the calm of careful reasoning. Purvis was right. She'd been wrong to deny her father's death wish. If Henry had wanted her to solve a case, knowing the negative way she felt about his business, he must have had an incredibly good reason.

"Do you think I'm guilty?" she asked.

He picked up his pipe. Fondled it. Put his lips to it. Sucked on it. Blew out the smoke. Put it down again. "I think you'll never forgive yourself if another woman dies either here or in Temple City and you didn't do everything in your power to solve the original murder. I think you want to make sure that if anybody else dies, you've crossed all your T's and dotted all your I's."

Morgan's stare drilled into him. "But do you think I'm guilty?"

The old lawyer tossed aside his professionalism. In its place was the ragged edge of wisdom. "It's not what I think

that matters here, Morgan. It's what you think about yourself. I don't have to live with the rights or wrongs of not
solving your dad's case. You do.

"I don't have mysterious notes at even more mysterious
crime scenes with my name written on them. My career isn't
on the line. Yours is. My dream isn't on the line. Yours is. My
father didn't leave me any legacy at all, but yours did. So like
I said, Morgan, it's not what I think that matters, it's what
you think about yourself."

Her chuckle was a low, rusty sound in the genteel legal
office. "You sound like my dad. Thanks for the kick in the
pants."

"You're welcome."

Morgan recalled the intensity of Carlotta's anger, the suddenness and the solidity of it. It was the only lead she had in
a case that still baffled her. "Carlotta Biggs is the only person on my list of suspects."

Purvis studied the bowl of his pipe as if it was a rare find.
"But you want to believe she's innocent of murder."

Morgan threw her hands in the air. "After all these years
of being my enemy, what's the point in trying to kill me
now?"

"Perhaps that's the idea, Morgan," the lawyer reasoned.
"Everything has its time, especially murder."

She eyeballed him as if for the first time, and maybe it
was the first time, because on this day, she saw him through
the eyes of a grown woman, not the eyes of a loved and favored child. This man had known her father for longer than
she'd been alive.

He had to know more than he let on—about the cleaning
woman who died forty years ago, about the dead woman's
bastard infant, about Henry's unsolved cases. Morgan
cocked her head to one side. "You've known Carlotta as long
as I have."

Purvis almost smiled. At last, Morgan had accepted the

responsibility of the task her father had left for her. Not on the mental level of a professional woman, not on the instinctive level of survival, but on the spiritual level: this case and all the murders, past and present, were the medium in which she reconnected with her dead father.

She also reconnected with her soul, lost, until now, in the bittersweet sanctuary of the Chamberses' elegant, lemon oil–scented home. Why else had she returned to the homestead, when a hotel with computer, fax, and other electronic amenities was better suited for her crime detection needs?

The Chamberses' home wasn't equipped with security guards or security cameras, but it was definitely equipped to feed Morgan's beleaguered soul. Henry had known this about his household, the reason why he'd never left Liberty. And now, his troubled child had come home, back to her roots, back to her destiny.

"I knew Carlotta's adoptive parents only in passing," Purvis said. "I don't know if she is the child of the murdered cleaning woman or not. It's possible, but then, most anything is possible if you keep your mind open."

"Adoptive?"

Purvis rested his back against his chair, crossed his legs, and said with disbelief, "You didn't know?"

"No."

For the first time, the old man was truly worried. "Whatever you do in the next few days, Morgan, just keep it simple."

She stood up. "Purvis, I'm gonna get answers if it's the last thing I do. Twenty-four hours is my goal."

"That's crazy."

She kissed his cheek. "You can say that again. This whole mess is crazy."

After waving goodbye and exiting the building, she walked straight into her number-one suspect. Morgan wasn't in the mood to play games. "What exactly is your problem with me, Carlotta," she demanded.

"You're breathing."

Morgan was appalled and didn't care if it showed. "That's extreme, Carlotta. I don't understand."

"You will."

"Is that a threat?"

"It's a promise."

Morgan grabbed the other woman's upper arm. "Obviously you have mental problems because I've never done anything to hurt you. I don't even know you."

"You will."

"That," Morgan snapped, "is definitely a threat."

Carlotta snatched her arm away. It was hot, humid, and she looked as pulled together as she had at seven-thirty that morning. "I almost don't care what you think."

"Almost?"

"You think you're so smart, you and your city talk and your city clothes and your city airs."

"We're too old for this cloak-and-dagger shit, Carlotta. Be straight with me."

The Barbie doll beauty looked as if she might spit in Morgan's face. "I hate the way you take over everything you touch."

Morgan angled her head sideways and scrunched her nose in true puzzlement. Carlotta looked physically ill. "Are you on drugs?"

Carlotta's glare was corrosive. "What? You think nobody in this world can hate your guts?"

"Not without good cause."

"I've got plenty of cause."

"What has this got to do with my dad?"

Fire flashed in Carlotta's eyes. The slant of her blackberry colored lips was cruel. Her teeth were hard and unnaturally white. "Everything."

"My dad died a year ago. Is his death triggering some kind of freaky personal problem with you or something?"

"Or something."

Morgan figured she had nothing to lose except her life. "Did you have those women killed in Temple City?"

"What women?"

Morgan wanted to trust the innocent look on the other woman's face, but she didn't know how she could, not when Purvis had just warned her to be careful, not when the presence of evil hovered in the too-close air. "Anybody who follows me as tight as you do must know the reason I'm in town. I don't understand what's going on, Carlotta, but I will before long."

The ex-beauty queen's brow hiked up a notch. "Who's threatening who now?"

Morgan shoved past her and headed toward her rental car. " 'This isn't a threat, it's a promise.' "

Chapter 10

Morgan returned to the family home. At every turn, she felt threatened. Danger destroyed her security in Temple City and it had probably walked through the front door that very morning, right here in Liberty, that place where nothing exciting was supposed to happen.

All her natural curiosity, all her insight, her very need to serve and protect not just her own interests, but the interests of the many—in this case, the Temple City population of female dancers—was undermined by uncertainty. It was tricky to trust anyone, damned tricky.

She reminded herself she was too savvy to allow her growing anxiety to stop her from thinking clearly. The reality of Carlotta Biggs's open animosity was too vital a clue to dismiss with skepticism. In her long-term affiliation with law enforcement, and as a private investigator's eldest child, Morgan had learned to consider the impossible as possible.

Mothers killed their children and vice versa. Children killed their siblings. In-laws became outlaws. Rules of social conduct were sometimes blurred and when they were, the unthinkable became possible: immoral acts eased from the dark into the light, and for her, the light lived in Liberty.

Liberty: freedom from control or subjection—from restraint. *Liberty:* independence, emancipation—self-government.

Morgan directed herself to take control of herself. Only an amateur lived in panic mode. Pushing her composure into compliance, she entered her father's study. Professional persona in place, she sat at Henry's much loved and used battered desk, the Temple City murder file and the Liberty cold case file on the ink-smudged blotter in front of her.

Reaching for the telephone, she dialed Joe. In her mind, she pictured him on his cell phone, sitting in Temple City traffic, which is precisely what he was doing when she reached him after three rings. He said, "Talk to me."

She didn't bother to identify herself. He recognized her voice as well as a husband did the sound of his wife speaking to him from across the room, or on the telephone from the opposite side of the country. "I've got a weird lead."

"So do I." There was relief in his voice, relief to know she was safe, still angling for clues into the double murder mysteries they struggled to solve together. Despite the physical distance between them, the enigma they faced only strengthened their bonds of extreme friendship.

"You're kidding?" She bet he'd scarcely slept since she'd hopped the red-eye to Georgia. Excellent friendships were tough to come by, and their relationship stood in jeopardy every minute the Temple City killer operated with impunity.

"No, I'm not kidding." The pleasure in his voice was unmistakable. An end was in sight. Despite Morgan's cool, despite her professional tone, he knew her heart was beating far too fast to be normal, that excitement was flashing in her eyes, that her artist's fingers were itching to sketch the killer they both sought.

In turn, Morgan felt thankful not to be alone with her suspicions. To be understood, to have an expert sounding board to explore ideas and examine facts, helped her devise solutions to the problem she faced. On the other cross-country phone connection, her lifeline was the best friend she'd ever had.

He was the best, because everything they'd learned about each other was based on the experiences of adults, not the never-can-forgive-and-forget background she shared with Taylor, Max, and Sam.

Where the sacredness of blood could stifle from the weight of responsibility, the objectivity of outside relationships was a liberating experience for Morgan. These friendships were based on herself as an individual and not a member of a collective—the Chambers family unit.

She laughed. "You show me yours and I'll show you mine."

"We found a set of fingerprints in your apartment that matches the prints of a woman living in Liberty, Georgia."

Morgan forced herself to breathe. "Carlotta Biggs?"

He sounded surprised. "Yes."

"That's the same lead I have." This was said very softly. Everything was happening so quickly: the loss of Morgan's father, the loss of her privacy, the loss of her business, the lack of sleep, the fear, the isolation, and the subsequent paranoia. It took all of her inner reserves to stay committed to upholding truth and justice, regardless of how it affected the way she felt about her past, about how she might feel about her future.

"Is she a dancer?" he asked.

Morgan considered the aggressive way Carlotta moved. She didn't flow lithely, the way a cat walked. Instead, she promenaded, much like a formal march—decisive, and perhaps, territorial. "No."

"An instructor?"

After a moment, she said, "I have no idea, really, what Carlotta does for a living. I hadn't thought about her until she showed up on my doorstep this morning, and later today after I left the attorney's office."

"What did she do to arouse your suspicions?"

After Morgan updated him on her encounters with Carlotta, he said, "I still think your father's anniversary is the trigger for the kills."

"Seems like it. There's never been anything vague about Carlotta, never anything done halfway. I've always known her to be stubborn and a fighter, but never careless. If her fingerprints were found in my apartment, it could only mean that she wanted them found or didn't care if they were found."

"I agree," Joe said. "She's part of the past in Liberty, part of the present in Temple City. Tell me about the case your father left you in his will. You never did."

"I didn't go into it before, because I didn't think it mattered to anybody but me whether I took that case or not."

"It must matter. The fingerprints we found belong to a woman with a record of small acts of violence within the beauty pageant circuit, mostly in Georgia."

Morgan drew a circle around the only name on her suspect list. "Where exactly did you find Carlotta's fingerprints?"

"The closet shelves. The shoe boxes in the closet. The door itself. Morgan, she rummaged through your things."

It was alarming to Morgan to realize someone had ransacked her apartment so carefully that she hadn't noticed the trespass. "Why would she leave fingerprints in the closet, but not on the index cards left at the crime scenes?"

"Two different perps. I still think a man killed both women," Joe explained.

"Someone Carlotta hired. Is that what you're thinking?"

"That's exactly what I'm thinking."

Morgan's mind went flying, the mental images dark as crows, omnivorous, oppressive. To still her sailing thoughts, to focus, she extracted a blank sheet of paper from the top left drawer in her father's desk.

On the cream vellum sheet, Morgan sketched her number-one suspect as she'd appeared on the doorstep before being thrown out, on the doorstep after being thrown out, outside Purvis Wayan's law office. Then she sketched Carlotta, the child.

The dominant feature on each face was anger. But then, the more Morgan stared, the more she became aware of the inevitable—the Chambers nose. All the girls shared their father's nose and it was possible that Carlotta even inherited Henry's chin, the way he held his neck when he was . . . angry.

Could it be that Carlotta was the dead cleaning woman's child? That Henry Chambers was her father? That the missing link in Carlotta's life was the Chambers name?

Morgan threw the pencil she was using to the carpeted floor. No. Henry Chambers was an honorable man, a fine man. Honorable men stood up for their children, respected the women who bore their blood kin, and offered them both, mother and child, the protection of his name. Obviously, he hadn't done this for Carlotta. Not doing so was out of character.

Even if she hadn't always agreed with her father, Morgan had never doubted his integrity. She wouldn't doubt it now. She needed another piece to the puzzle of Carlotta. "Okay, Joe. It makes sense that two people are involved. At least two."

There was anger in Joe's voice, a fury rooted in fear for Morgan's life. "If the killer and Carlotta had access to your apartment, they also had opportunity to kill you. For some reason, you're supposed to be alive."

Morgan sifted through the drawings on her desk. This, too, was evidence, decisive data required to form a viable judgment. "But for what reason? Why not kill me flat out and get it over with? What connection do those Temple City women have to me?"

"All I can figure is that if you were killed in the beginning, your murder might have remained unexplained. The two dancers who were killed might simply have been lures to draw you into the game. If they were lures, it worked because you feel committed to the resolution of the murders even though Leroy made it plain you were to stay off the case."

"Okay," Morgan said, "let's go with what we've got. Carlotta wasn't shocked about the murders when I mentioned them. Since she left fingerprints in my apartment, knowing they were obviously on file within law enforcement, then she must have wanted me to come to Liberty. She was the first person to greet me after I got home."

Joe said, "Making her the first person in Liberty to show some aggression. We have concrete evidence in the form of fingerprints and reasonable evidence in the form of her behavior."

Morgan traced the childhood sketch of Carlotta with a fingernail. "She could have killed me in front of Purvis Wayan's law office. She wants me to figure something out."

"I'm convinced that the common piece in this whole thing is your father," Joe said. "He was the original reason you were in Liberty as a child. When he died, you were summoned back to Liberty. Even though he must have known how you felt about his business, he left you a case to solve. What you wouldn't do willingly, you are now doing out of obligation to the dead dancers in Temple City."

She said, "I agree. You work on a connection between Carlotta and the two dead women. I'll work on a connection between Carlotta and me. She's always been rude to me, now I need to know why."

"You can't guess?"

"No," she said, even though she suspected the truth.

"I find that strange."

"That I can have an enemy of the killing kind? Or that I never bothered to find out why Carlotta has hated my guts since we were kids?"

"All of it."

"I suppose it is strange," Morgan admitted. "I guess I've always considered her a pest. Nothing more."

"Old grudges die hard. Sounds like she's got a serious chip on her shoulder."

"My sister said something along the same lines. About grudges, that is. To tell you the truth, Joe, I've never cared about Carlotta one way or another. There are people I don't like and can't tell you exactly why I don't like them. I just don't. If Carlotta didn't like me as a kid, so what? I had plenty of friends and I had my sisters."

"Maybe this is all about family."

"Give me a break."

"I'm serious. If Carlotta, an old childhood enemy, could leave her fingerprints in the closet where you kept your funky old ballet slippers, then anything is possible. Having Carlotta be your enemy hits close to home. Home is fundamental. Death is fundamental. Murder means somebody was mad enough to take a life."

Morgan sighed with frustration. "Destroyed my life's work, too. It'll take a miracle to get parents to bring their kids back to my dance studio. I'm screwed, Joe."

"What if Carlotta feels that somehow her dreams were screwed because of you?"

Morgan snorted in disgust. "That's bull."

"No, it isn't," Joe argued. "Even after the circumstantial evidence against Carlotta was presented, you're still not gung ho about her as a suspect."

"She's the only person on my list."

"But you don't think for a minute she's a murderer, not really."

He knew her so well. "The perp had to be a male," she stated.

"The perp is probably a hired hand. A professional would keep fingerprints away from the crime scene. Check into the whereabouts of your suspect, Morgan. You've got everything to lose."

She hung up the phone. She sat down. She got busy. If Carlotta was the killer, she was definitely an amateur. Joe was right; only an amateur would leave fingerprints in her apartment. Even if Carlotta left them on purpose, it was a stupid thing to do.

In Morgan's experience with the Temple City Special Task Force Unit, there were three kinds of amateur killers: criminally insane, temporarily insane, and the kind who killed for reasons of passion, profit, mercy, or just for the thrill.

In the course of her career, she'd also discovered that a common quirk among amateur killers was a lack of a standard modus operandi. The fingerprints were the only physical clue that connected Carlotta to Temple City.

Connecting her to Temple City loosely connected her to the crimes. Had her fingerprints been found on the outer door of Morgan's home, the connotation would be much different. But Carlotta's fingerprints were found in the closet where the shoes were kept. That was specific.

The shoes were not simply linked to the crime scene, they were one of the props left by the murderer for Morgan to find. The fingerprints were part of the puzzle. The shoes were part of the puzzle.

The significant benefit of dealing with amateur killers was that they were often sloppy about clues and coverup. It was sloppy to leave traceable fingerprints. It was sloppy to confront Morgan at her home. It was stupid to confront her on a public street with witnesses. It was reckless to admit the anniversary of Henry Chambers's death was important.

Carlotta behaved as if she had nothing to lose, typical behavior of killers. Once the ultimate crime was committed and there was no turning back, then the killer understood the penalty for being caught was high, and usually permanent.

If the killer was Carlotta, what was she keeping Morgan alive to find out?

Within moments, she had Purvis on the line. "I've just been talking to one of the California investigators. He found Carlotta's fingerprints at my Temple City apartment."

If Purvis was shocked he didn't let it show in his voice. "Now you've got a suspect and can prove opportunity."

"Yes. Now all I need is motive."

"I'll look into Carlotta's background. Touch base with me in an hour. I'll have the police send a patrol car around your block between now and then."

"Do that."

"Be careful."

"I'm always careful."

Morgan put the phone down. She needed to think. Her favorite thinking place was still the porch, in the rocking chair that was a comfort and reminder of her mother. She left her father's study, the case files and pencil sketches of Carlotta on the blotter.

She didn't need a sketch of Carlotta. The other woman, still dressed in black on black in the wet Georgia heat, was sitting in Hazel's rocking chair, gun in hand. She said, "Have a seat, little sister."

Morgan sat. "Why do it this way, Carlotta. Why?"

"Because I was here first. Not you." Carlotta said, emphasis on the word *I*.

Morgan was appalled. "But murder?"

"The case of the dead cleaning woman you refused to solve? That was my mother. She and Henry were once lovers. I'm the oldest living Chambers daughter, not you. Henry's detective agency should have gone to me."

Morgan looked more closely. Were the accusing eyes staring back at her the eyes of her secret sister? Morgan had sketched too many faces not to recognize the tiniest details, the tilt of the nose, the size of the chin. Why hadn't she made the connections before it was too late?

Trust.

Betrayal.

Family.

She said, "Obviously you believe you're telling the truth. I just don't understand why you waited so long to get around to standing up for what you believed you had a right to have. You're gonna have to bring me up to speed."

Carlotta's gun never wavered. It was dark, and lethal, like the woman who held it with expert hands. "My birth was concealed. My mother and your father were lovers but he never really cared about her, just about Hazel. In fact, he didn't even know I was his child, at least, not at first."

Morgan had no reason to doubt her father's integrity until now. If it wasn't for the details of Carlotta's face, subtle but distinctive now that she was aware of them in person—had, in fact, already sketched them—she would have continued in her blind faith about her father.

In truth, he was a man first, her father second. Above all, Henry Chambers had been human. If Carlotta Biggs was truly his daughter, then so be it. "When did he find out about you and your mom?"

"Shortly before he died, he became suspicious."

"How did you find out we're sisters?"

"I found my mother's diary. I sent a copy of the diary to your father. Anonymously. He was looking into it and I followed him."

"He had to have known you were following him at some point."

"I'm sure he did. Neither one of us cared. He had the means to get the information we both needed."

"And did he succeed?"

"Yes."

"What about the dead dancers?"

"In my mother's diary, she said she always wanted to be a dancer. She said that if I hadn't been born, she would have danced."

"She became a cleaning woman instead."

"Yes."

"Who murdered your mother, Carlotta?"

"A dance instructor."

"A woman?"

"A man. He said he would teach my mother to dance but he lied to her. I guess you could say he wanted a private dancer." Carlotta recrossed her legs; she held the gun in place. For once, there was peace on her picture-perfect face. It was hot, but she looked fresh and focused. This was Carlotta's big moment. This was what all the killing had been about: confession and revenge.

Morgan threw her head back and sighed with relief. One way or another, the end was imminent. Either Carlotta would kill her before Purvis called within an hour only to find her phone unanswered, thus triggering police pursuit, or he would not. Morgan returned her gaze to that of her opponent's. "You don't need a weapon."

Carlotta shrugged. "Maybe not."

"All right, then. Tell me the rest."

"After my mother was killed, I was adopted. The funny thing about your dad is that I always wished he was my dad. He was kind and good and he worked so hard for his family. You never seemed to appreciate what you had. I used to want to be you, Morgan."

In spite of everything evil between them, the former sketch artist felt a catch in her throat. "Did Dad leave you something, a letter when he died?"

Once again, Carlotta's face was a terrible mask of anger. This was the woman that Morgan remembered. The former beauty queen pointed to the letter on the table. "Damn straight, he did."

"Who killed your mother?"

"Henry's best friend at the time, C. K. Bannikan."

Morgan frowned. "Where is C.K. now?"

"Probably holed up somewhere thinking of a way to get rid of me without incriminating himself. He killed the dancers for me in Temple City."

"Why him?"

"He owed me."

"You wanted him to bring me to you." It was a statement.

Carlotta's smile was crooked. After all, this was the sister she'd always wanted, the friend she'd coveted and never had. "Even though I've always hated your guts, Morgan, I always admired your smarts."

"Why didn't you go after my other sisters?"

"They weren't the oldest," Carlotta explained. "You were considered the oldest child, but in fact, I'm that child."

"Dad didn't know."

"When he found out the truth, it killed him."

"So now you're gonna kill me." *What will be, will be.*

"No," Carlotta said, "I'm gonna kill myself."

Morgan was appalled. "Why?"

"Someone . . . like you would never understand."

"Try me."

Carlotta's eyes touched every part of her sister's face, but her own expression gave no clue to what she felt inside, now that her goal of conflict and resolution was achieved. "I was raised as an only child. I failed at everything I tried to do. My birth mother was killed by her boyfriend, who happened to be the best friend of my birth father. She was killed because she refused to leave Liberty—and Henry. My father, your dad, didn't even know I was alive. Like I said, I believe the shock of the truth is what killed him. You know how much he prided himself on doing the right thing, and here he had a daughter older than you."

But Morgan knew in her soul that her father was a good man. "He would have left you something in that envelope. What is it, Carlotta?"

Carlotta shuddered, but the gun didn't waver. "His name."

Dear Carlotta:

I wish I had known. You have my own mother's eyes. My eyes. I'm probably as shocked as you are to discover we are related by blood. So much time has been wasted, so much time is left to be gained. I have investigated your mother's death and believe C.K. Bannikan is her killer. I've spent much time accumulating evidence against him, a difficult task since the murder was committed more than forty years ago.

In one year, I want you to show this letter to Purvis Wayan. I didn't think the house would mean anything to you, or the business I established, but I thought there was one thing I could give to you, and that is my name.

I only ask that you bear with me, for one year. After one year, I ask that you show this letter to Morgan as well—if she hasn't discovered you in that time, that is. She's been raised as my oldest child. In my absence, I'd like her to find out about you in degrees, as I found out about you in degrees, so that there will be no mistaking that I knew nothing of your life before now.

Perhaps it was cowardly of me to do it this way, but I am an old man. It was difficult to discover that my family name, Chambers, was somehow tarnished. I never would have allowed you to be without my name or my financial and moral support, and neither, I am proud to say, would Hazel.

Talk to Morgan. Your sister. If you two can work out your differences, so will the rest of the family. She's strong and her heart is in the right place. It shocked me to find out that your mother wanted to be a dancer, something Morgan has always wanted to be. I stood in the way of that career choice also. I thought it was frivolous. I was wrong.

I pushed Morgan into law enforcement and she still chose a way to use her creativity by sketching criminals instead of chasing them. She ran all the way to California to find happiness. She started work on Morgan's Miracles. She didn't tell me about it, but her

*sister, Sam did at Christmas. I figure that if anybody
can straighten this business out, Morgan can. Trust
her.*

> *Your father,*
> *Henry Chambers*

Morgan put the letter down. The entire letter was written in her father's own distinctive script. She spoke to her half-sister without looking up. "You started killing people before reading this letter didn't you?"

"Yes. I blackmailed C.K. into helping me. That was more useful than turning him in to police. By coincidence, C.K. lived in San Francisco, not all that far from you. I took that coincidence as a good sign. I didn't know my birth mother. Maybe if I had known her, I might not have felt the need to avenge her death."

"But you knew me."

"Right," Carlotta said. "I knew you and I hated you. Using C.K. to get even with you and Henry was a perfect method of revenge. Henry gave you the life I wanted, the life I deserved."

"Why did C.K. kill your mother?"

"Heat of the moment kind of thing. Henry didn't know my mother was pregnant when he broke things off with her. Later, my mother tried to pass me off as C.K.'s baby. C.K. killed her during an argument. He wanted to tell Henry about me. My mother didn't want Henry to know. She loved him you see, but Henry loved Hazel. So really, this is all Henry's fault. If he hadn't strayed from his wife, none of this would have happened."

"You said you found your mother's diary."

"My birth mother and the woman who raised me were distant relatives. Henry was a powerful man and my adoptive family feared him. They kept my dead mother's secret. They kept her diary."

"I find it hard to believe anyone would fear my father."

"C.K. Bannikan was Henry's best friend at one time. How did my adoptive family know that C.K. didn't kill Stephanie Blevins for Henry? Henry is dead, but C.K. is still alive. He was still a threat."

Morgan's face clouded with sorrow. One man's brief marital transgression had set the stage for murder. That Henry Chambers had spent his adult life fighting crime was an irony that destroyed the heat between Morgan and Carlotta. The truth had been revealed, but justice had yet to be served.

The gun shifted from Morgan's face to Carlotta's.

Morgan's heart leapt to her throat. All her emotions were in turmoil. They were women who had loved to hate each other, women who shared the same father, the same bitter legacy. "Don't kill yourself, Carlotta. We'll get through this somehow. Purvis will help us. All our sisters will."

Tears of shame spilled from the corners of Carlotta's eyes, Henry's eyes. Anger no longer held her together. "Now that I've done what I set out to do, what else do I have to live for?"

"Our father."

Carlotta flicked her eyes at Morgan. She cut them down to the gun. She flung them up to . . . her sister. "Sweet God," she said. "He picked the right person to figure out this mess after all."

Morgan took the gun from Carlotta's hand. She laid the weapon on the table, Hazel's table. "Yeah. I guess he did."

Hours later, after Carlotta was jailed, after Temple City police and her sisters were informed of the news, Morgan returned to her father's office, deep in thought. As a young woman, she left the family home vowing to build a life for herself independent of her father and her sisters. In the end, she was reminded that true happiness stemmed not from running from the past but by embracing it.

A rebel her entire life, hers was a story of redemption,

the paying off of familial debts, the recovery of a heritage lost and a heritage found, the compensation for sins committed, and the consequences of them.

At last, Morgan was free, free to dance—for herself, and for her dad, the man who taught her to live her dreams, despite adversity, ugly secrets, and terrible truths. Above all, Henry Chambers had taught her the true meaning of love, which she did freely, with all her heart, with all her mind, with all her soul.

Purvis pulled up in front of the Chamberses' home. The battered muffler of the 1958 Caddy sputtered, coughed and spewed a plume of gray smoke into the air. He knew Taylor would scold him until she was blue in the face if she saw the shape "Ethel" was in. The entire town had been after him to get rid of the heap—said it was an environmental hazard. But he and Ethel had been together for years and they'd hang together until the end.

He shut off the engine and took his briefcase from the passenger seat. The instant he stepped outside a backhand of heat slapped him square in the face. He pulled a handkerchief from his shirt pocket, mopped his face and walked to the front door. Before he had a chance to knock the door was pulled open and all four sisters stood in the threshold.

"It's about time," Maxine said in that no nonsense way of hers.

Taylor shook her head in annoyance and eased Maxine out of the way. "Don't mind her."

"What's this all about anyway?" Samantha asked before sashaying back inside.

"Give Mr. Wayans a minute to catch his breath for heaven sake," Morgan ordered. "Where are everyone's manners?"

Purvis patted her arm as he walked inside the cool interior of the house. "It's okay, Morgan. I know ya'll are itching with as much curiosity as I am."

The sisters looked at each other with puzzled expressions on their faces.

Maxine put her hand on her hip. "You mean you don't know why we're here either," she stated more than asked.

The sisters grumbled beneath their breaths.

Purvis reached for one of the glasses of iced tea that were set on the coffee table and sat down in what was once Henry's favorite chair by the window. He took a long, cool sip then set the glass down. He removed an envelope from his briefcase.

"This is from your father," he said quietly, holding up the envelope.

One by one the sisters found seats and fell silent, all eyes on Purvis. Much too slowly he peeled open the envelope and extracted a single sheet of typewritten paper. He cleared his throat.

My darling daughters,

If you are listening to or reading this letter, then each of you has completed the assignment I set out for you and I can rest in peace. You may think that everything you ve done and everything you ve gone through was to make an old man happy or maybe to ease your conscience. But what it really did was bring you all home, back together again as a family the way you once were.

I know you all have gone off and made your lives outside of Liberty. You thought this was a dull, nothing-ever-happens-here town. But you ve discovered otherwise.

My final wish is that you girls will keep the house. Keep it as your home. Visit it often. Bring your families. It is the last thing I have to leave each of you your inheritance, your history. And hopefully, one day, you will sit right where you re sitting now and tell your own sons and daughters not only what you ve learned about Liberty but what you ve learned about yourselves.

Just remember that no matter which road you choose, you will never be alone. You have each other, and me and your mother will always keep an eye on you. I only pray that the road you choose will always lead you home.

Always,
Dad

*   *   *

Purvis refolded the letter and placed it on the table. He looked across the short space at the quartet. They were no longer the tough, city-slick crime fighters, but simply four, loving sisters, crying and hugging each other who'd finally found each other and their way home.

He eased up from the chair and tiptoed out so as not to disturb them.

"Well, Henry," he said as the old Caddy chugged down the road toward home. "You solved your toughest case yet: a way to get your girls back together again." He shook his head and laughed. "And got your cases solved, too." He turned onto Main Street. "Still running things—all the way from up there."

Epilogue

Six months later

Chambers Investigation is in full swing with Lucious Kimble at the head and Maxine by his side. I think she just may be ready to change her last name. Taylor decided to relocate and opened her law practice right down the street from her dad's old office. From what I hear, she has more business than she can handle. Samantha is still doing her thing in Atlanta but she visits at least once a month. The last time I saw Morgan she was seriously thinking of coming back home to stay. She said Liberty could use a decent dance studio and Sherlock Kimble could use a good sketch artist every now and then.

As a matter of fact, I'm heading over to the Chamberses' house right now. All the girls are there and they said they need my help. Trouble is afoot in Liberty and they intend to find out just what it is and who's behind it. Those Chambers girls are about to turn Liberty on its ear again, and I can't wait!

Check Out These Other
Dafina Novels

Look For These Other
Dafina Novels

Grab These Other
Dafina Novels
(mass market editions)